LIFE ON PLANET EARTH

ANDY GORMAN

For those who seek adventure and dream of better days.

For anyone who still loves a good book in the age of streaming.

For the young and young at heart.

For all the citizens of Earth.

For the loved ones we've lost, the ones we have, and the ones we've yet to find.

Andy Gorman's biography is a work in progress. The best way to learn more about him is to visit his website:
www.AuthorAndyGorman.com

"If you want to go fast, go alone; but if you want to go far, go together."

African Proverb

1

EARTH

Liam Stone had been narrowly avoiding death every day for months—one hundred and seventeen days to be exact—and he didn't intend to ruin that streak now. Alone and nearly out of breath, he ran through the wreckage of the city, dodging parked cars and debris by instinct. His focus stayed on the skeletal remnants of the city's tallest building, which marked the designated extraction point.

The pack screeched behind him. Mad. Feral. Hungry. The wet slaps of their bare feet on the asphalt pattered like a violent storm. A flock of birds scattered from their rusty beam perches, fleeing from the discord of bodies colliding with cars and feet tripping over shredded tires below.

A flash of motion caught Liam's attention, a break in the gloomy stillness ahead. Humanoids. Not naked and deformed like the ones chasing him, but clothed in black battle gear like his. They stood together in the middle of the street, hunched over, catching their breath.

"Keep going!" Liam yelled.

Though he couldn't see their faces, the icons generated by his Halo identified them as the surviving members of his unit. Each had a personalized tag below their name: Zara (Shrimp-Legs), Tai (Man-Child), Raelyn (Red), and Wiki (The-Brain). Apparently, they had found a shorter path through the dark alleys and abandoned streets. How else would they have gotten this far ahead of him? Liam was the most agile candidate in the program—faster and stronger than the others by every metric. That was why his tag read Prime.

"Go!" Liam's throat itched from yelling. He hated when the comms went down. "What are you waiting for?"

This time they heard him. Filtered only by the luminescent Halos circling their heads at eye level, their pale, sweaty faces grew paler. After a moment of hesitation, they ran down the street toward the extraction point. As always, Zara lagged a little. Within thirty seconds, Liam caught up to her.

"Faster, Z!"

Zara's legs made an effort to speed up, but she looked fatigued. Once Liam passed, she fired a single shot into the pack. "Got one!" she said between breaths. "Two, actually."

That won't make a difference if you don't hurry, Liam thought. He jogged among Zara and the others for a moment before zooming past. By his estimate, the pack was now twenty meters behind.

"This way," Liam said, indicating an alley up ahead and to the right.

"Why detour?" Wiki panted. "We've got a straight shot."

"Trust me."

"Not a chance," Tai said, his voice booming. "Could be a dead end. I'm running for it."

"I'm with him," Raelyn said.

Big surprise, Liam thought. "Not my funeral," he said.

He veered away from the group and ducked into the alley, knowing that at least Wiki would follow. Zara, Tai, Raelyn—they never listened to him. If they wanted to die, that was on them. Safely inside the alley, Liam crouched behind a rusted dumpster.

"You wanna hide?" Wiki asked. "Here? We're almost out of—"

Liam shushed him. "Do you have a gun? I dropped mine back on Fifth Street."

Wiki raised an eyebrow.

"I know," Liam said. "Newbie mistake."

"You're a better shot, anyway."

Liam laughed. "That wasn't up for debate."

Out of the holster on his lower back, Wiki drew a sidearm, which looked too big for his hands. At sixteen years old, Wiki still had the height and build of his fourteen-year-old self. His stick-thin frame lacked any semblance of muscle tone. At least he was smart enough to hide in the alley, though. Liam could always count on Wiki to make the right choice—given enough data. By the sound of the screams coming from the street, the others hadn't made the right choice.

Liam took the gun. "That's our cue."

Soon the screams subsided, replaced by a ripping, chewing racket—the song of too many predators and not enough prey. Liam crept toward the street, glanced around the corner both ways.

"Wait," Wiki whispered, still catching his breath.

"For what? Backup?" Liam checked his Halo. "We're the last two on the ground."

"Isn't there another way we can go? A safer way?"

"Sure," Liam said, "let me summon a private car to take us there. I'll make sure it has air conditioning, too."

"You know what I meant," Wiki said, unamused.

"You saw the map," Liam said, tilting his head toward the street. "There's only one way, and we have to do this while they're distracted."

Liam exited the alley, and after a long sigh, Wiki followed. The two of them snuck through a forest of debris—garbage and broken bricks and things ruined by time. On the sidewalk, they found a mess of flailing subhumans huddled around the remains of the other candidates, limbs licking the air like wildfire. A flash of disgust crossed Wiki's face, but Liam remained stoic. He had seen worse. Much worse.

Focused on the feeding frenzy, the subs paid no attention to Liam or Wiki. They just squatted there, tearing through flesh using overgrown fingernails and teeth caked with grime. Long hair hung from their heads, filthy and matted against their naked bodies. Their knees scraped at the asphalt as they feasted, leaving marks of dark blood and tattered skin.

Liam's aural implant pinged a five-minute warning. Five minutes and the transport would leave them behind. Five minutes and it would be over. He readied himself to sneak past the pack, rolling his weight forward onto the balls of his feet. Then he took two silent steps, and breathed in slowly.

Two more steps.

The subs remained preoccupied, lost in a hungry daze, until one of the beefier male subs uncoiled its hunched spine and sniffed the air, its blood-soaked face like some grotesque mask hiding its predatory intelligence.

Liam stilled.

Most subs were blind, but this only improved their other senses. If you stripped away their deformities, they looked mostly human— but eerily different. Devolved. Animalistic. More monster than man. The one sniffing the air had a crooked scar scrawled across his face from eye to lip, a smashed nose.

Ugly.

Only when Ugly returned to his meal—a generous helping of Tai's left thigh—did Liam continue walking. He shrugged off the loss because he had to. Someone always had to die so others could live. That's how these things went. It was Darwinian, the survival of the fittest.

Breathing slowly, Liam chanced a few more steps forward. A dozen more paces and he would pass the pack. Wiki shadowed, walking a bit too loudly but planting his feet only where Liam did.

Nine more paces.

A scrawny female and a young male played tug-of-war with a length of intestine, while another three subs devoured a meager pile of what could only be Raelyn, judging by the mess of red hair. Liam looked past the violence. Yes, he had seen worse, but that didn't mean he enjoyed watching friends die again and again—and he and Rae had history. Ancient history now.

Sorry, Red.

Ugly's mess of a nose rose from the carnage and inhaled. Ahead, the birdless skeleton of the skyscraper beckoned, the transport vehicle hovering in a vacancy between floors. More subs would arrive soon, drawn in by the rumble of engines.

Five more paces.

Liam held his breath and quickly took the next steps, wanting nothing more than to make it to safety, to live another day. When he passed the riot of bodies, he turned and walked backward to keep an eye on the threat, feeling each step out before putting his full weight into it. He put a finger to his lips.

Wiki nodded.

They crept forward, nearly victorious, until Wiki made one of the worst mistakes possible. He only took his gaze off the ground for a second, but that was enough. He tripped on a crack in the asphalt. One of his feet shot forward in time for him to catch himself, but it landed on a triangle of glass, which burst into shards that jingled across the blacktop.

Ugly stiffened, tongue clacking as his body pivoted to face Wiki's back. He began to hobble forward. His jaw dropped open, revealing blood-stained teeth and a sinister hunger, despite the fresh meal bulging in his belly.

Liam halted, fingers tightening around Wiki's gun. His instinct was to raise and fire it, but a falling corpse would draw the attention of the pack. He thought about handing the gun back to Wiki, giving him a fighting chance since there was no way his friend could outrun Ugly.

Instead, Liam mouthed the word "run" then dashed toward the extraction point. Wiki followed, and Ugly scampered into a sprint as he tracked the trail of sound. Feet light on the pavement, Liam advanced gracefully through every obstacle he encountered—leaping over potholes, sidestepping debris, and ducking under broken light poles. He heard a thud behind him and stole a glance backward.

Wiki had tripped over a tire and face-planted into a puddle of motor oil. He didn't bother trying to stand, probably knowing it was too late for him.

"Damn it," Liam said, looking back at his friend.

Ugly continued his jerky sprint, snarling and gnashing his teeth, gore dripping from his face as he made his way to Wiki's prone body. His gnarled foot landed on Wiki's arm, but he continued forward. Perhaps he realized that Liam would make a much better second course than the scrawny kid covered in oil? Faster than any blind thing should be, Ugly homed in on Liam's scent. The distance between them shrank by the second.

Liam ran until invisible daggers stabbed his ribs.

Then he ran some more.

He leaped onto the roof of a sedan to get past a multi-car pileup blocking his path. When his feet hit the asphalt on the other side, his ankle rolled, sending waves of pain up his leg.

Cringing, he limped onward.

Behind him, safety glass shattered beneath Ugly's bare feet—too close.

Liam's body could take no more, so he stopped, turned to face his pursuer.

Seven or eight meters away, Ugly came around the front of a crashed bus. Liam raised the gun, which heated his palm as it charged. He could have made the shot from that distance, but he wanted to witness the evaporation of Ugly's face up close. These things were always more satisfying in high definition.

"Hey!" Liam shouted. "You with the messed-up face."

Ugly straightened his course and sped up.

Five meters.

Four meters.

Liam aimed between the monster's flayed nostrils. Excited, energetic matter churned inside his weapon, itching for release.

Three meters.

Two meters.

Close enough.

Liam smirked and squeezed the trigger, but it didn't budge. He tried again with no success. Then his implant pinged, and the world froze around him. Silence reigned as the transport's propellor blades stopped whirring. Birds hung in the air. The fires smoldering in dilapidated buildings, the cloud-rippled sky, the spit flying from Ugly's mouth—everything paused before slowly fading to black.

The simulation was over.

Liam sighed, more from relief than fatigue, and shut his eyes, which ached from not blinking for so long. Hands guided by muscle memory, he lifted his Halo then reached down to unbuckle his gravity straps. His body lightened. He exited the Earth Sim and hesitantly entered the bleakness of reality.

When Liam opened his eyes, he was no longer surrounded by an uninhabitable wasteland, but by a transparent dome overlooking an expansive lunar basin. Most of his unit had already unstrapped and gone to work, but he took his time. From his vantage point on the Tread Deck, he could see the one place he cared about going. The only place to go. There it stood, resting above the gray, cratered horizon, spinning slowly—a blue and green sphere enveloped by swirling white. Earth, the planet Liam's ancestors had come from long ago, where humankind had evolved—from tiny, single-celled organisms to complex creatures, from ocean to land, reptile to mammal. Earth, the place where *Homo sapiens* rose to the top of the food chain and became the dominant species, where they had once ruled everything. And where a single disease decimated the human population, causing civilization to crumble until all that remained was a city of three thousand people on a gray rock, stuck in orbit around a constant reminder of their failure. The founders called the city Omega—the last hope of humankind.

A synthetic female voice spoke into his implant. *"Ensign Stone, please report to the Farm Module for your work assignment. Tardiness is a punishable offense."*

Liam mocked the notification, mouthing every word of it. He heard it often enough. Even after the other candidates left, he lingered on the Tread Deck, peering through the dome at the shimmering hull of the Earth Transit Shuttle Resurgence, a towering spacecraft and multi-generational project that even his great-grandparents had worked on. The ship symbolized humanity's only chance to reclaim their lost planet—and Liam's only hope of leaving the cramped halls of Omega behind. Even if Earth still had monsters, anything would be better than the monotonous routine of life in the last human settlement.

2

OMEGA

When the doors into the Farm Module slid open, a wall of odor hit Liam—a dank, fishy mustiness barely concealed by cleaning chemicals.

"Did you forget to shower again?"

"Did you forget to set an alarm?" Smythii said, his gruff voice more disheartened than disappointed. "You're late. Again."

A balding man in his mid-forties, Smythii stood with heavy arms folded. His face resembled the moon's surface, cratered and gray, and his stance always seemed one notch too wide.

"Time is meaningless, Smythii, and—"

"Save it, kid. You've got a lot on your plate today." Smythii's dark eyes scanned his Halo's display. "Just give me a minute."

While Smythii worked, Liam looked around the Farm Module, a place he hoped to never see—or smell—again. Sunlight came through the ceiling, filtered by panels of fused silica glass. Row upon row of steaming nutrient vats filled the elongated warehouse. Androids manned most of the vats, testing levels and using specialized paraphernalia to add chemicals.

After a few minutes, Smythii tapped the side of his Halo twice to transmit a work assignment to Liam, who pulled down his own Halo, scanned the list, and groaned.

- *10 barrels of algae powder.*
- *17 barrels of shrimp pellets.*
- *20 barrels of dehydrated potatoes.*

A huge order, it would take all day to fulfill.

"Where's it going?" Liam asked, already bored.

Smythii always forgot a detail or two.

"ETS Resurgence loading dock. Just make sure you double-check the weight of the barrels. I've done it three times myself, but we can't make any mistakes. The engineers need a final weight before launch—to calibrate the instruments or something."

Stretching his triceps, Liam inclined his head toward one of the androids. "Aren't *they* programmed for jobs just like this? Why can't they do it?"

Smythii let out a chuckle. "Because androids show up to work on time."

Because they have no choice, Liam thought. "So, this is punishment?"

"No," Smythii said. "It's your job. You should be happy that I never report your tardiness. I bet plenty of seventeen-year-olds would gladly take this gig off your hands."

"I bet you're wrong."

"I could have you reassigned to something worse, you know."

"Worse than this?"

Smythii raised one eyebrow.

"Come on," Liam said, "I know you hate it here, too. Why don't we take the day off, maybe watch a movie in your office?"

"I might not be happy here," Smythii said, "but I'm reliable. I've worked every dirty job there is. Solar array maintenance, scrubbing the hab domes, all types of work in the mines. Should I go on? Your life's not that bad, kid."

Liam sighed. His life *was* that bad. Everyone's was. The entire population of Omega—the final survivors of humankind—all lived repetitive existences with little meaning. Yet somehow, no one could see it. Liam wished he could open their eyes. If everyone wanted to get to Earth, if everyone worked as hard as he did, they would all be there by now.

"Fine." Liam turned away from Smythii. "I just thought we could take it easy on my last day."

Liam bounced lightly on his toes down the central row, grateful for the lunar gravity because his muscles still burned from the morning's simulation—from the hard work that would bring him to Earth.

"You quitting?" Smythii raised his voice. "I didn't get any notice, kid."

"I'm getting reassigned."

•|•

With the most important day of his life approaching, Liam found it challenging to focus on work. He spent all morning collecting the appropriate barrels from the storeroom's organized chaos and strapping them onto robotic dollies. The work was repetitive but not difficult. Lunar gravity made the barrels light enough to carry easily, even though they were large enough to fit two people— if those people hated themselves enough to face the permanent shrimp stench that lived inside most of the barrels.

He yawned every few minutes, exhausted from waking up early for months to train in the Earth Sim. Lately, he had been getting an average of five hours of sleep per night—two hours fewer than Omegans were allotted—and the fatigue weighed heavily on his body.

Soon his efforts would all be worth it, though. Just one more night of sleep and the chosen candidates would be announced. He wondered if Admiral Reagan had already risen from stasis to prepare for the ceremony.

Once Liam had ten dollies daisy-chained together, he led them through the Farm Module, his final load before lunchtime. Androids buzzed and zoomed out of the way to make space for the haul.

Like most things in Omega, the halls outside the Farm Module were monochromatic and dull. Simulations and screens held color, and so did Armstrong Garden, but almost everything else resembled the barren, gray desert surrounding the last human settlement.

Liam never understood why the builders had bothered installing portholes in the hallways. Except for glimpses of Earth visible from some vantage points, everything outside looked the same. Some portholes just faced other portholes. It was pointless.

He stopped where two hallways met. From this corner, he could see the entirety of the ETS Resurgence. Enveloped by a framework of scaffolding at its base and a tower parallel to it, the shuttle stood mighty on a massive launchpad. Access roads led to it from all directions, a few of them currently in use judging by the clouds of moon dust and swells of regolith rising above them. The ship's nose climbed so high into the sky that it looked like it could float away. Its shadow fell to the gray dirt like the hand of some gargantuan clock, ticking down the days to its departure—six weeks and one day away.

Liam's first memory of seeing the ship scratched at his mind. It looked almost the same as it had when he was a young boy, when he clung to his father's hand and especially his words: *"We're building this for you, son. This is your ride home."*

The ETS Resurgence shimmered in the unfiltered sunlight, beckoning Liam toward his future.

Ten minutes late and starving, Liam bounced into the mess hall, which smelled only slightly better than the shrimp vats. Long stainless steel tables filled most of the space, and hungry citizens filled most of the tables, talking idly as they devoured bland nutrients washed down with bags of reclaimed water.

A teacher once told Liam that every drop of water in Omega had been in someone's urine, a fact he often wished he could forget.

He got in line at the food dispenser. When his turn came, he scanned his wrist, stepped onto the scale, and held a bag beneath the chute. By gripping the edges and pulling down, he made himself a bit heavier to trick the machine. He burned more calories than most citizens, so he felt entitled to a little extra. When his bag filled, the woman in line behind him moved forward mechanically, her eyes down. Liam smiled—no one ever caught him—and went to meet Wiki at their usual spot.

At the table, Wiki tore his attention away from whatever he was reading on his ocular implant, a silver lens that covered his right iris. "I can't believe you were going to let me die today," he said. "Actually. I take that back."

Liam took a seat. "Not just you. I knew the pack would catch up to the others."

"Wow. I'm not surprised, but wow." Wiki shook his head. "When are you going to learn that the Earth Sim is a team sport?"

"About the same time you learn that you don't have a chance with my sister."

Wiki's pale cheeks flushed to pink. "I don't know what you're—"

"Make room, boys."

The sound of Glo's voice deepened Wiki's pink hue. She stood behind him, hand-in-hand with Kal, one of the orphans she took care of in the Nursery Module. Platinum hair framed her face, pulled back into a tight braid that hung to her lower back. She wore a semi-permanent smile on her glossy lips, a pair of purple-tinged, crystalline earrings, and a gray shirt stained by baby spittle.

Wiki turned and stared.

"Are you going to scoot," Glo said, "or are we not welcome here?"

"Of course." Wiki scooted over and made too much room for her on the bench. "You know your presence is always welcome."

Yeah, that'll make her like you, Liam thought.

"Why are you so red?" Glo sat down beside Wiki. "And sweaty. Are you getting sick?"

Liam chuckled through a mouthful of nutrient pellets.

"Maybe," Wiki said. He took a big bite of his food. "Yeah, I haven't been feeling well."

"You should go to the infirmary," she said, and Wiki just nodded.

The five-year-old escaped Glo's grasp and scuttled under the table to sit by Liam, who ruffled the boy's wispy, brown hair.

"Hey, Kal."

"How do I be big like you?" Kal asked.

"It takes time. You just have to play a lot and eat a lot."

He handed his food bag to Kal, who sighed and said, "But I hate pellets."

Liam chuckled. "Everyone does, but they made me strong. They'll make you strong, too. They'll help you grow big and tall."

"But—"

"Eat those first, and I'll give you something special."

"A treat?"

"Something you've never had before." Liam reached into his front pocket and pulled out a small bag of freeze-dried berries.

Kal grinned and started shoving the pellets into his mouth.

Glo eyed the berries. "Where did you get those?"

"Work," Liam said.

Glo leaned in closer, and her voice dropped to a whisper. "You stole them?"

"Borrowed," Liam said. "I'll return them once I'm done digesting them."

"Gross," Glo said.

"Everything comes full circle," Liam said.

"Not the point."

"Relax. I only took a handful," Liam held out the bag. "Want some?"

"No. Liam, you could have—"

"All done," Kal said, his hand outstretched to claim his treat.

Liam gave him a few. "It's fine, Glo," he said. "More for us. Right, guys?"

Kal nodded, but Wiki's attention remained on his ocular implant. While Liam and Kal munched on the berries, Wiki's gaze occasionally wandered to his left, where Glo sat.

After a while, she asked, "What are you reading?"

"I found this article in the Archives. It's a list of famous stowaways. Well, the ones who survived. A lot of them died in transit because they ran out of food or water or air."

"Interesting," Glo said. "But what about the ones who didn't die?"

"Those stories are more fun." Wiki grinned. "One stowaway made it from Ireland to the United States by getting rolled onto a boat in a molasses barrel. His descendants claimed that this gave their family a sweet temperament."

Glo giggled at that, but Liam didn't get it. "Tell me more," Glo said.

Wiki's eyes lit up, as they always did when someone showed interest in his scholarly pursuits. "Did you know there was a stowaway that made it to Omega? It was on the LTS 98, one of the last Lunar Transit Shuttles launched from Earth."

"Did he survive?" Glo asked.

"Not for long," Wiki said. "Fleet Admiral Arlo airlocked the guy as soon as security caught him. Some say you can still see a mound of regolith where his corpse is."

"Really? That's crazy."

The conversation went on for a while. Liam was too busy chewing to participate. Still, he listened. The subject matter seemed mildly amusing this time, a lot better than the time Wiki spent their entire lunch hour talking about bioluminescent sea creatures.

"So." Glo slapped both hands on the table. "Are you two excited for tomorrow? I heard we get half the day off for the big announcement."

Liam yawned. "I can't wait to sleep in."

Glo let out a breath. "You have to take Mom to the infirmary. Did you forget?"

Liam's yawn turned into a sigh. "Can you do it?"

"It's your turn. I was going to—"

"I haven't had enough sleep in months, Glo. Please. I'll do it the next two times."

Her lips bunched to one side, then slowly softened into a smile. "Fine," she said. "But you better save me a spot at the ceremony."

"So I can see you cry when they pick me?"

Glo shot him a look. "So I can see your face when your wildest dream comes true."

"Wilder things have happened," Liam said. "I thought you didn't want me to go."

"That doesn't mean you don't deserve it. Whatever happens, I know you've worked hard for this. Dad would be proud."

3

STARSHINE

The next morning, Glo pushed her mother's wheelchair from their tiny apartment in Sector One, through the crowded halls, to the elevator bank. After waiting in line to hail an elevator, she wheeled her mom inside one and said, "Sector Seven."

The aluminum doors squealed shut, slicing through the sunlight that came from skylights on the surface, and the elevator lurched downward.

As soon as the light left, Glo missed it. She loved her home in Sector One, the only sector with natural sunlight because the rest were underground. The days that lasted two weeks, the long, long nights, the cycles of dim earthshine that illuminated the lunar landscape—none of it bothered her. In fact, she found the place beautiful. Sector One had more character than the other sectors. It was a historical district, a patchwork of old technology where the dismantled hulls of a hundred ancient spaceships formed the bones of the city.

When the elevator stopped, Glo pushed the wheelchair into Sector Seven and immediately shivered. The lower sectors had no charm, just frigid sterility inspired by sensibility and sensibility alone.

"I should have brought you a blanket, Mom."

"These old bones know the cold all too well. I'm okay, starshine."

Her mom always said that. No matter how bad things got, she stayed tough and resilient. Even on the day Doctor Jensen told her she had cancer, she smiled through it, and she had kept smiling every day since. Perhaps her mom thought if she said, "I'm okay" enough, it would become true.

"How's your brother?" Her voice sounded extra raspy this morning. "I haven't seen that boy in four days."

"Really?"

"He leaves before I wake up and comes home after I fall asleep."

Glo turned them into the pristine hallway that led to the infirmary. Not a single trace of timeworn graffiti decorated these walls.

"He's been training extra hard lately. You know how Liam gets when he wants something."

Her mom groaned. "He's just like his father. Dissatisfied with everything. I mean, I'm proud of him for working hard, I just"—she inhaled sharply, and her tone of voice became dismal—"Oh, never mind."

"You wish he would carve out some time for his sick mother?"

"His dying mother."

"Mom, you're not—"

"I am, starshine. I know it's coming. I can feel it. But I'm okay."

Glo couldn't imagine life without her mother. She would gladly die instead if it meant the universe would spare her life. Knowing the impossibility of that trade, she entered the infirmary with tears beginning to burn her eyes.

Doctor Jensen instructed Glo to stay in the expansive waiting room, which was mostly unoccupied, save for a few patients and family members scattered throughout. Most of them wore tattered hand-me-downs, but some sported pristine suits fresh from the factory. The elite, the dregs—they all got sick, just at different rates.

With her eyes closed, Glo rested beneath a blanket of sound—the murmur of a conversation, the soft crying of a baby, heavy breathing and coughing. Even with all this noise, the room was more peaceful than the Nursery Module where she worked. Tantrums spread like contagion there. Taking the opportunity to enjoy the relative calm, she slowed her breathing and began to meditate, trying not to worry about—

"Well, what do we have here?"

Glo blinked her eyes open. An older man, at least her mom's age, sat in a chair across from her. He had slick, dark hair on his head, which faded in color as it approached his gray beard. He smiled despite the brace around his neck.

"Are you all right, young lady?"

"Yeah," Glo said, "I'm just—"

"It looked like you were about to cry." The man's voice sounded strange, and Glo wondered if he came from a part of the city that she didn't have access to. He didn't have the booming drawl of the mineworkers, nor the perfect pronunciation typical in Sector Eight, where the government officials worked. When she didn't respond, he smiled again.

"What's your name?" he said.

"I'm Gloria," she said. "Gloria Stone."

No one but her mother called her Gloria, but the man's demeanor seemed to call for a more official introduction. She wasn't sure why.

"Well, you're very beautiful, Miss Stone. Even when you're sad." The man's grin doubled, and his eyes narrowed. He reached across the space between them with his right hand. "I'm Arthur."

His hand squeezed hers harder and lingered longer than necessary. As soon as he released his grip, Glo folded her arms and leaned back in her chair.

"How old are you?" Arthur asked.

"Eighteen."

Arthur grinned. He had a youthful smile. "Any relation to Elara Stone?"

"How do you know that name?"

My grandma's name, she thought.

"Elara and I, we were friends. It was a long time ago."

"Oh," was all Glo could say. She avoided eye contact, but she could feel Arthur's stare.

He sighed. "When did she kick the bucket?"

"What?"

"When did she die?"

A strange way to ask that, Glo thought. "Ten years ago."

"A shame. She always had the best stories, and the cookies she made—incredible."

"The best," Glo said. She could still remember the smell, though she couldn't recall the last time she had anything sweet.

"How did she die?" Arthur asked.

"The same way everyone in Sector One dies," Glo said. But that wasn't entirely true. Her father died in the mines before he could get cancer from the radiation. Yes, she loved her home, but living closer to the sunlight had consequences when there was no atmosphere to protect you from it.

Arthur nodded slightly, the motion restricted by his neck brace. "How are things up there?"

"What do you mean?"

"The Earth Transit Shuttle. How does it look?"

An odd question, Glo thought. Her lips bunched to one side. "Just how it always looks?" She paused for a breath. "Have you not been up top lately?"

"It's been…several years."

People assigned to the lower sectors spent most of their time underground, but even the most reclusive still came up for sunlight and air in Armstrong Garden every so often. To most people, a bit of daylight now and then was well worth the risk.

"Well," Glo said, "today's the day to go up. They're announcing the final candidates."

Arthur chuckled. "Oh, are they?"

"In the garden," she said. "Everyone's going."

"Is that so?" Arthur asked. "I guess I better go save myself a seat, then."

Arthur was behaving respectfully enough, but the way he looked at Glo when he stood to leave reminded her of the boys in school, the boys who claimed to be her friends until she grew breasts—the boys who seemed sweet but only ended up hurting her.

"Bye," Glo said, but he continued to stare.

"I'm sorry, you just"—Arthur leaned forward and gripped Glo's shoulder, which made her flinch—"You look so much like Elara. It's unbelievable."

With that, he left, but even after the doors closed behind him, Glo could still feel the heat where his fingers had made their uninvited advance. The same way sunlight came with radiation, beauty came with consequences.

4

ΛRMSTRONG GΛRDEN

"This should've started by now," Liam said.

Distracted, Wiki ignored him.

They sat on a patch of grass overlooking the amphitheater in Armstrong Garden, where hundreds of Citizens had gathered. It was the only space in Omega capable of holding a crowd that large. Actual trees lined the perimeter of the sunken, oblong amphitheater, where families and loners alike sat on lunarcrete steps, their excited voices mixing into a torrent of sound. Vines crept up trellises built into the domed ceiling like arms outstretched to greet the sun. Fresh, humid air carried the aroma of roses and grass—a tease of what Earth might have once smelled like. What it might smell like still.

Liam loved Armstrong Garden. Before he started spending all his free time in the Earth Sim, he went there often. He would lie in the grass, staring at Earth through the fused silica dome, sometimes with Raelyn or Wiki, but more often alone.

He checked his Halo for the third time. "Really, what's taking so long?"

It took Wiki a second to tear his attention away from his ocular implant. "I heard that the Admiral had a rough re-animation."

"And how did you hear that?"

"Information is available to those who seek it, my friend. Apparently, he's suffering from cryo-cough."

Liam stared at the platform in the center of the amphitheater, his toes tapping the grass. "Never heard of it."

"Tissue tends to degenerate with each cycle of freezing and thawing, particularly lung tissue." Wiki's eyes darted from side to side, scanning the stream of information available to him at all times. "According to the Archives, Admiral Reagan hasn't been re-animated in over fifty years, and this is his tenth re-animation. His lungs have seen better days."

"As long as he picks us for the mission, I don't care how degenerated he is."

Wiki nodded, lost in the stream, and their conversation lulled. As more people crowded into the amphitheater, Liam struggled to save a seat for his sister. A few rows down, he saw Tai, his bulky biceps strung over Raelyn's shoulder, barely grazed by her shoulder-length red hair. She was running her bionic fingers up and down his arm, caressing the skin with mechanical precision.

"You're staring," Wiki said. "I thought you were over her."

"I am," Liam said.

"Good, because she's clearly over you."

Liam lay back in the grass, taking up as much space as possible. His mind wandered to memories of Raelyn lying there beside him, talking about Earth and their future there. He didn't miss her, really. They only dated for a couple of months, and Liam had spent most of that time working or training. He just didn't understand what Tai had that he didn't. Not so deep down, he hoped that only one of them would get chosen for the Resurgence Mission. If it were Raelyn, Liam would never have to watch Tai flex in front of a mirror again. Spitefully, he summoned up memories of Tai getting eaten in the Earth Sim.

Minutes later, Glo's voice dropped into Liam's implant. Though he was accustomed to the constant intrusions, he still jumped every time someone spoke directly into his ear.

"Has it started yet?" she asked.

"Nope."

"Good. I'm leaving the infirmary now."

Liam yawned. "How's Mom?"

"Doctor Jensen wants to keep her overnight, run some tests. She'll be okay."

Their mother had been sick for as long as Liam could remember, but lately, she couldn't even get out of bed without help. Overnight tests couldn't mean anything good.

"I'm saving you a spot on the lawn," Liam said. "Hurry, though. It's packed."

Liam ended the call, his heart rate accelerating as the most critical moment of his life drew nearer.

•|•

When the crowd began to hush, Glo arrived, whispering apologies as she snaked her way toward Liam.

Commander Killion, the acting leader of Omega, stood in the center of the amphitheater. He wore the same militaristic buzz cut as many of Omega's authority figures. Liam only recognized him from this distance because of his age. In his early thirties, he stuck out among the other council members like Earth above a gray horizon.

Killion had a bigger build than most citizens, probably due to the extra rations the higher authorities got. Liam had delivered a barrel of spinach—the only viable spinach harvest from that quarter—to government headquarters down in Sector Eight just a week earlier. When Killion spoke, his voice boomed through hidden speakers.

"The day has finally come," he said. "Everyone in this room—and everyone watching and listening throughout Omega—you have waited for this your entire lives." He paused for effect. "Last year, four hundred and twenty of Omega's citizens applied for this mission, brave people willing to risk everything to accomplish the most important feat in human history, an undertaking over a hundred years in the making."

The crowd roared, and Killion glided to a different corner of the platform.

"We wish all of the candidates could fit aboard the ETS Resurgence, but today we must narrow the list down to just eighty crew members. The decisions weren't easy to make, but we're ready to announce the candidates chosen to become crew. And who better to make this great announcement than the man behind the Resurgence Project himself? It's my pleasure to introduce our sworn leader and protector, a man gracing the halls of Omega for the first time in half a century, Admiral Arthur Reagan."

"Arthur," Glo said to herself, her eyebrows falling.

"You know him?" Liam asked.

"We just met."

Wiki perked up. "You met the Admiral?"

"I think so. In the infirmary."

"Incredible," Wiki said. "You know he's Earthborn, right?"

Admiral Reagan rose from a seat in the front row, silencing the crowd. He crept up the steps and traded places with Commander Killion. When he turned around, Liam saw a glimmer of light reflecting off the center of his neck, directly below his gray beard.

"What is that thing?" he whispered.

Wiki squinted. "Looks like a mechanical lung vent. Didn't you learn about them in bionic anatomy? I swear you were there that day."

Liam shrugged. "Like I was paying attention."

Reagan drew a loud, choppy breath through his lung vent, a sound grotesquely magnified by the speakers. "Thank you for the introduction, Nikolai," he said.

His voice had a strange inflection to it, a jarring difference in how he pronounced his vowels.

"Six hundred and ninety years ago," Reagan said, "humankind fell victim to the most devastating pandemic in history, a threat that no one saw coming. You've heard the stories and seen the footage. Many of you have fought the products of the Terminal Plague in the Earth Sim. This disease baffled Earth's best virologists. It created monsters born of men, violent mutations in our DNA that got worse with each iteration. It crippled the first generation of victims and obliterated the next. Insanity bred more insanity, a flood no force on Earth could dam."

Liam didn't need another history lesson, but he kept his attention on Reagan's words, eager for him to get on with the rest of the ceremony.

"Within twenty years of the first outbreak, the Plague decimated Earth's population. Empires built up over centuries crumbled overnight, and civilization's order dissolved into chaos. This forced us to learn—contrary to what most of humanity thought—that our survival was far from guaranteed. Today, that fact is more pertinent than ever. You know how hard you all work to keep Omega running, the sacrifices you've made to help us cling to our fragile existence. It hasn't been easy, I know. With each generation, new challenges arise. I've lived my life in blips, watching you and your ancestors solve every problem thrown your way, and I know you will continue the hard work. Thank you."

A satisfied murmur swept through the crowd. Reagan moved from one side of the platform to the other.

"When Admiral Arlo led the exodus from Earth, the Endurance Initiative's primary objective was simple: to ensure the survival of humanity. This city was forged from the ashes of a world set aflame, and we've extended humankind's lifespan far past what seemed our inevitable end. No doubt, the Initiative's goal has come to fruition. We've put off our expiration date by half a dozen centuries. We've avoided the end. But still, our continued existence is not guaranteed. We cannot take our good fortune for granted."

A palpable silence—broken only by babbling children—filled the dome of Armstrong Garden as everyone in the crowd listened to Reagan's speech.

"In desperation, the Initiative fought for one goal only: survival. It was only natural for the founders of this city to have such a narrow focus. No doubt, watching the world end influenced their philosophy. Such thinking has gotten us this far, but I've never been able to accept that humanity will draw its last breath inside pressurized tubes, hiding from the monsters under the bed. Survival alone cannot be our end goal. No, I see a brighter future for your progeny. If the Endurance Initiative marked the end of human life on Earth, the Resurgence Mission marks a new beginning. It's a chance at not only survival, but the restoration of the human race and the reclamation of our home planet."

The silence thickened, and Liam's skin tingled, equally from excitement and anticipation. He couldn't wait to leave the pressurized tubes behind and breathe real air, to set foot on Earth as his father intended.

"Helmed by virologist and geneticist, Doctor Viola Collins,

centuries of work have been completed to crack the Terminal Plague virus. Her team has accomplished what no scientists on Earth were able to. They've developed an antiviral drug capable of inhibiting the virus's spread from generation to generation. Doctor Collins will be joining the Resurgence crew as Chief Science Officer."

Reagan gestured toward one of the seats behind him, and Collins stood. Liam hadn't noticed her before that moment. Her graying hair was cropped short like the councilmen surrounding her, making her blend in with them. When the crowd stopped cheering, she settled back into her seat.

"The objectives of the mission are simple—to establish a beachhead on the Pacific Coast of the former United States, to raise a generation of human beings immune to the virus, then—like the early homo sapiens who migrated out of Africa—to expand. Much like the challenges our city has overcome, the threats we will face on Earth will be far from easy. The planet may be more dangerous now than when we left it."

I don't care, Liam thought. I'm ready.

"Our telescopes and instruments can only tell us so much," Reagan continued. "We know none of the quarantine zones held. Radio signals stopped coming from Earth long before any of you were born. We don't know whether the plague has died off or evolved into something worse. The atmosphere looks healthier than it did when Arlo launched a hundred ships all those years ago, but we don't know what creatures are now breathing that air."

My air, Liam thought.

"One thing, however, is certain." Reagan paused and seemed to look directly at Liam. "We're in for the adventure of a lifetime. And rest assured, whatever challenges may come, I believe the eighty chosen candidates possess the skills, knowledge, and courage necessary for this mission to succeed. So, without further ado, I present the final list of citizens called to plant the seed of a better future in the earth of our past."

Thunderous applause echoed through the dome. Reagan cleared his throat and began reading from a tablet somebody passed to him. Old tech, but effective.

"From Sector One," he said, "Abbot, Richard."

Liam cheered, and Glo pulled Wiki into a side hug.

"Due to your extraordinary scholastic achievement and devotion to the study of history, you have been chosen to update the Earth Archives. Congratulations, Richard. You will forever be remembered as the new world's first historian."

"Congrats, Wiki," Glo said, beaming.

"Yes," Liam said, "fantastic work, *Richard*."

Wiki offered a humble nod and a closed-mouth grin. "Thank you."

The position was exactly what Wiki had always wanted. Liam felt happy for his friend, proud even, but the celebration didn't last long. He quickly returned his attention to Reagan, who continued to read the list in alphabetical order. Most names came from different sectors, but a few came from his own. When Raelyn's name was called, she squeezed Tai's arm with her bionic hand so hard that he yelped. Reagan continued through the list, indifferent to the celebratory sounds that erupted from different corners of the crowd. As Tai's moment of truth approached, his limbs grew increasingly restless. Liam smiled, fully prepared to celebrate the forced separation of his ex-girlfriend and her new boyfriend, but then—

"Sector One," Reagan said. "Beryl, Tai. For your excellent performance in the Earth Sim and peak physical fitness, you have been chosen as an armed officer."

Liam scoffed. Tai's performance could hardly be called "excellent," but the decision only bolstered his own confidence. Raelyn and Tai celebrated by fusing their faces together, and Liam looked away from the vomit-inducing sight.

Glo reached around Wiki to put a hand on Liam's shoulder. "You nervous?"

"Hell no."

Liam counted the chosen candidates as they were announced. The seconds between names felt like minutes, continuously slowing as Reagan read through the list letter by letter. When Reagan reached the last names beginning with S, Liam held his breath. His heart rate skyrocketed. His skin flushed.

"Next up," Reagan said, "Sector One."

Liam put his hands behind his head, stretched his spine.

"Stone," Reagan said, the word falling slowly off his tongue like a moonwalker stepping out of the airlock. Liam prepared to roar his excitement. He felt spring-loaded, pressurized, his body a volcano of anticipation. Then Reagan cleared his throat, smiled, and said, "Stone, Gloria."

Liam turned to his sister, who looked as shocked as he felt. Her eyebrows furrowed, and her jaw fell open. Glo wasn't even a candidate. Maybe it was a mistake? A mix-up in the system? A glitch?

"For your expertise in childcare, you have been chosen for one of the most important positions of all—overseeing the nurture of the next generation as we reestablish a minimum viable population on Earth."

"I," Glo said, but the rest of the sentence died in her throat.

Liam homed in on Reagan's face. For the moment, he ignored the strangeness of his sister getting chosen for the mission. It had to be some fluke. Even if she had applied without telling him, his name had to come next. It just had to. Sweating, he swallowed hard and focused once again on the speech.

"Sector One," Reagan said, and Liam breathed out a sigh of relief. Stone, Liam, his mind projected. Stone, Liam.

"Tomlin, Zara," Reagan said.

Liam froze. There's no way this is happening, he thought. Why did I get skipped? Did I get skipped?

"No," he whispered.

Armstrong Garden no longer felt like some blissful paradise—more like a bad dream, a simulation gone sour. Liam became vaguely aware of Reagan saying something about Zara's new position, but the words distorted in his mind, drowned out by disbelief. Wiki and Glo remained speechless.

"Are you telling me Shrimp-Legs got chosen, and I didn't?" Liam's voice rose, his breath now entering and exiting his body in a chaotic rhythm. "That Tai and Raelyn get to go to Earth, but I don't?"

"Liam, it's okay," Glo said.

Liam was standing now, though he didn't remember rising from the grass. Tai and Raelyn had turned, and many others stared as well.

"Sit down," Wiki said. "We'll figure it out."

"No," Liam said, tears beginning to gather in his ducts. "This is wrong. It has to be a mistake, I—"

"We'll talk to the Admiral after," Glo said. "I'm sure he didn't mean to pick me. I didn't even apply, Liam. You know that. I'm sure it's just a mistake."

"But—"

The word hung on his lips as reality hit Liam like a comet. It took every ounce of restraint he had to sit back down, to endure the torture of hearing the names and merits of every candidate chosen to live his dream—accomplishments that paled in comparison to his own. He took mindful breaths, an attempt to calm the panic brewing inside him. He wanted to scream, to break something, anything to release his rage, but he resisted those urges, clinging to the only sliver of hope he had left: that someone made a clerical error. After an uncomfortable amount of time passed, Reagan finished reading the list and began his closing remarks.

"Congratulations to all the courageous crew members of the ETS Resurgence. Commander Killion and I are excited to work with you. In fact, we've decided to accelerate the timeline of the mission. Why wait six weeks when we can reclaim our planet now? The new launch window commences in approximately forty-eight hours."

A mutual gasp swept through the crowd.

"Crew, your current work responsibilities will be reassigned to other citizens. Enjoy a couple of days of rest as you get your affairs in order, say goodbye to your loved ones, and prepare to make history. Orientation details will be transmitted to your Halos. Good day to all."

•|•

Followed closely by Wiki and Glo, Liam caught up to Admiral Reagan in the hallway outside Armstrong Garden. A pair of guards armed with plasma pistols and lightweight body armor walked idly by his side, but no one halted Liam as he came closer to the Admiral.

"Sir," Liam said to Reagan's back, but the man continued forward. "Sir?"

"What is it?"

Reagan stopped, turned around, and the guards perked up. Up close, Reagan looked younger than Liam had thought, the skin on his face taut despite his gray-speckled hair and hazel eyes that seemed to hold some ancient wisdom. He studied Liam and Wiki like he was unsure of who had approached him.

Liam stepped forward. "It's just— I wasn't chosen for the mission, and I should have been."

Reagan's mouth released an odd sound, something between a sigh and a laugh. "And why do you think that?"

Liam swallowed. "I have the highest Earth Sim score in my sector. You chose my sister, who didn't even apply for the mission. There must have been some mistake in the—"

"I don't make mistakes," Reagan said. His eyes found and lingered on Glo. "I assume you're the other Stone kid."

"Liam."

"Right," Reagan said. He yawned. "I read your file, Liam. I wasn't impressed."

What an asshole, Liam thought. Reagan turned away and continued walking, leaving Liam confused and distraught, but unwilling to falter.

"What?" Liam asked, matching Reagan's stride. "How is that possible?"

"Earth Sim scores weren't the only factor at play."

"I logged more hours than anyone. My biometrics are off the—"

"Pristine physical health is important, but not essential to the mission. We looked for candidates who possessed not only physical abilities, but also certain innate emotional characteristics. You missed the mark, son."

Liam made a long, exasperated sound. "But, sir. I worked so hard for this. I did everything in my power to earn my spot. I've been training every day since I applied. Harder than anyone. I—"

"I, I, I. This isn't about you, Liam." Reagan looked over his shoulder but didn't stop walking. "This is about the future of the human race."

5

ENSIGN STONE

Liam pulled down his Halo and entered the Earth Sim, the place he always went to blow off steam.

"Solo survival mode," he said. "Level nine. Rooftop."

After a brief buffer, the streetscape loaded. Liam's feet fell to the sidewalk beside a vacant apartment building with boarded-up windows. A herd of subs snarled in the distance. Knowing they would arrive in precisely five minutes, Liam used most of that time to attach explosive charges to the perimeter of the building, then he climbed up to the second floor on a fire escape ladder. Usually, he would have barricaded the front doors and sniped subs from the rooftop, but he wanted to try something new. His hands craved violence. He broke a window and entered a dark living room.

"Lights," he said, and his Halo lit up the room.

Liam raided the apartment for the supplies he knew would be there. He grabbed a baseball bat from one of the bedrooms, a shotgun from the closet in the hall. Outside the apartment, he heard glass breaking downstairs. He hurried to the stairwell.

"What is the record for simultaneous kills?" he asked.

Liam's Halo responded as soon as he finished his query. *"In this simulation, the record is—"*

"Not in this simulation," Liam said, ascending the stairs. "In all simulations."

"The record for simultaneous subhuman kills across all simulations is seventy-nine. It was set by Ari Glynt in the year—"

"Quiet," Liam said.

He needed eighty kills to beat the record. Eighty. Thinking about this number boiled Liam's rage, which had been simmering since the ceremony. In less than two days, eighty people—his best friend, his sister, and seventy-eight others—would leave Omega, and Liam would be stuck forever.

He opened the door to the rooftop, where he had to shield his eyes against the simulated sunlight. A ping sounded in his ear—probably another message from Wiki or Glo—and he ignored it.

"Fire charge one," he said.

An explosive went off far below him and blasted open the front doors. Liam crept to the edge of the building and looked over. He didn't know how many subs had already entered, so he started counting from one. They rushed through the doors in pairs and trios. Since he'd come through the second level, they wouldn't find his scent trail right away, but he still kept one ear trained on the stairwell.

His implant chimed. *"Ensign Stone. It is past curfew. Please return to your residence immediately. This is your first warning."*

"Good thing I have three." Liam's attention returned to the subs below. "Seventy-eight. Seventy-nine. Eighty." A ruckus came from the stairwell. "Just in time."

Liam brandished his bat and rushed to the stairwell door. A chorus of footsteps and grunts echoed up from the concrete chamber. After a few seconds, a single sub appeared at the bottom of the final flight. It climbed the stairs on all fours until it exited onto the rooftop. He pictured Admiral Reagan's face as he wound up for a hit.

Smack!

Bones cracked under the force of Liam's bat. The sub hobbled forward, its newly broken arm swinging wildly. He imagined Reagan's face again.

Smack!

Liam broke the sub's other arm then kicked it in the chest. It fell backward, tripped over the short, brick parapet, and splatted to the asphalt a second later.

It always surprised Liam how loud a body hitting the ground

could be. He wondered if it sounded the same in real life.

He returned to the stairwell just in time to knock a pair of subs out with his bat. More followed, stumbling over the bodies littering the final flight, so Liam switched weapons. Six shotgun blasts later, the doorway was blocked by a wall of corpses. Hands reached through gaps, hopelessly groping, and more would follow.

"Ensign Stone. It is past curfew. Please return to your residence immediately. This is your second warning."

"Almost done," he said to no one.

Liam fired his shotgun into the stairwell one last time, then dropped both weapons onto the rooftop. He climbed down the fire escape as quickly as possible. From the street, he could see movement behind almost every dirty window of the apartment building. The place was packed.

"Prepare to detonate all charges."

"Countdowns synchronized. Awaiting your command."

Liam jogged down the street to get a better view. He turned around to face the building, which filled his field of vision, then glanced at the kill counter displayed on the periphery of his Halo. Liam only remembered killing six or seven subs in the stairwell, but the counter read ten. Those kills wouldn't count toward the simultaneous kill record, but that didn't matter. There had to more than eighty subs left in the building—and the building would soon be rubble.

Easy, Liam thought. Why haven't I tried this before?

His lips wore a smile for the first time since before the ceremony. "Detonate," he said.

Nothing happened.

"I said, detonate."

The clouds stopped blowing in the artificial wind. Gangly silhouettes froze in the apartment building's windows.

"Ensign Stone."

"Damn it!" Liam yelled.

"It is past curfew."

He threw off his Halo.

•|•

When daytime approached, and Liam's early alarm chimed, he silenced it for good. He never wanted to enter the Earth Sim again. What point was there pretending to inhabit a world he would never see in person? If good news came back from the Resurgence Mission, Omega would build more Earth Transit Shuttles. Still, such an event likely wouldn't occur in his lifetime, not unless he went into cryostasis like Admiral Reagan to wait out the long years between missions. With this thought on his mind, he fell asleep again—until the sound of an incoming alert pinged obnoxiously in his ear. The sound made him twitch so violently that his head hit the ceiling of his sleeping pod.

"Ensign Stone, please report to the Farm Module for your work assignment. Tardiness is a punishable offense."

Liam groaned and rolled over, then closed his eyes again. Once his heart rate and breathing slowed, ten minutes passed in a single blink.

"Ensign Stone, please report to the Farm Module for your work assignment. Tardiness is a punishable offense."

Whispering curses, Liam considered using a sick day. He only had one per quarter, and they didn't roll over. Spending all day in his sleeping pod sounded nice. He couldn't remember the last time he took two days off in a row. At least a year, he thought.

He lay there for a while, utterly indecisive. It was the perfect day to avoid his responsibilities, yet he couldn't get himself to do it. Despite the sadness and fatigue shrouding his mental clarity, he had to do something to improve his situation. He couldn't just give up.

"Open," he said, and his bed slid out of its slot in the wall.

Quickly, purposefully, he got dressed, donned his Halo, and exited his family's apartment. A day earlier, he thought he'd never step foot in the Farm Module again. Even though it was the last place he wanted to go, he headed there anyway—but only because he needed to talk to Smythii.

•|•

Liam jogged through the hallway, touching down lightly on the textured aluminum with each stride. The lack of resistance made running through Omega nothing like running in the Earth Sim. He preferred the struggle, the weight, the sweat—the way he felt superhuman every time he exited the simulation.

In his speech, Admiral Reagan had mentioned the challenges the people had faced over the years, but to Liam, life in Omega seemed far from challenging. Showing up to work at the same time—or roughly the same time—every day? No problem. Growing algae from spores and breeding shrimp over and over again? Even the androids without upgraded AI could handle that. The real challenges awaited on Earth.

Liam's plan for the future never included the possibility that he would remain trapped on the moon. What would he do now? What kind of life could he possibly live? Would he grow old and complacent like Smythii, like everyone else who simply accepted the way things were? No, he decided, he would rather airlock himself than spend the rest of his life working in the Farm Module, waiting for the radiation to slowly kill him. But someone once told him only the weak airlocked themselves, and Liam didn't consider himself weak. He already had a new plan in motion.

Glo's voice entered his ear. *"Liam."*

He kept jogging, dodging people and androids alike.

"I know you're still mad, but I have to tell you something."

A bitter laugh escaped Liam's mouth. "Mad? That's an understatement."

"This isn't my fault."

Liam knew he had no right to hate his sister, but he couldn't stanch the jealousy seeping into him, couldn't ignore the fact that she was chosen for the mission instead of him.

"Are you at work?" he asked. "I don't hear any crying."

"I'm at— Well, I'm not supposed to disclose my location, but I'm at orientation." When he didn't respond, she said, *"I just wanted to tell you that I talked to Arthur—to Admiral Reagan, I mean. I told him I didn't want to go, that I never wanted to go. I asked him to give my spot to you instead, but—"*

The sound of sniffling replaced her voice. So much for no crying.

"But what?" Liam asked.

"I don't think I have a choice. Reagan says it's my duty. Liam, they—

They're putting me on that ship whether I want to go or not."

The news only worsened Liam's mood. Apparently, having a desire to make sacrifices for the mission counted for nothing. He and many others would have gone voluntarily. Why would the government force unwilling people to go to Earth when such a large pool of willing candidates existed? It made no sense. If Liam were in charge, anyone who wanted to go to Earth could earn passage.

"Liam, I—"

"I have to go."

"Wait," she said, and he waited, though he felt like surgically removing his implant to get away from the conversation. *"I'm going down to the infirmary first thing in the morning to say goodbye to Mom. I'd like to see you, too. Reagan's keeping us here overnight to scan our biometrics or something, so tomorrow morning will be my last chance to—"*

"Fine," Liam said. He entered the doors that led to the Farm Module. "I'll see you then."

•|•

Liam approached Smythii, who stood in the same spot he stood every morning, wearing the same clothes and the same disappointed scowl. Was the man disappointed in Liam? In himself?

"Well, look who decided to show up," Smythii said, eyes scanning his Halo. "You're late—"

"Again," Liam said. "I know. I just— My alarm didn't go off for some reason. I swear I set it last night."

"And the moon is made of cheese, kid."

Liam took a calming breath. "I know I'm not always on time, sir."

"Sir?" Smythii's booming laugh shook his sizable belly. "Since when do you call me sir?"

"I know I'm not always on time, but I always get the work done."

One of Smythii's eyebrows inched closer to his receding hairline. "What's this about, kid?"

"I'm"—Liam gulped, and an android zoomed past him—"I'm sorry I'm late sometimes, Smythii."

"Always. You're always late."

"Okay," Liam said. "I'm sorry I'm *always* late."

"Fine. Apology accepted. Now, we have a lot of—"

"And I was wondering if you could put in a request for my transfer?"

Smythii gave Liam a quizzical look. "I'm actually looking at a transfer myself. I heard radio operations is a pretty sweet gig, and there's an opening now that what's-his-face scored a spot on the ETS. What were you looking at?"

"I want to work in a deeper sector."

"I mean, the mines are always looking for able-bodied people, but like I said the other day, you have it pretty—"

"Not the mines," Liam said, steeling himself. "I want to work in Sector Eight."

Smythii chuckled. "You and everyone else. Government. Now that's a really sweet gig."

"I'm serious. I want to start a career there."

Liam's new plan was to rise through the government ranks over time, eventually becoming Commander Stone—no, Admiral Stone. As a key crew member, he would definitely get a spot on the next ETS, and possibly even lead the mission. He would have to travel through space and time to get there, but it could happen. He wondered what it would be like to step foot on Earth fifty or a hundred years later, how strange it would be to join a thriving human colony, to read Wiki's additions to the Earth Archives, to meet Glo's grandchildren.

"Really?" Smythii said.

"Can you help me?"

Smythii sighed. "I might know somebody, but you'll have to start in the trenches."

"That's fine," Liam said. If anyone had the determination to climb the ranks, it was him.

"I'm going to need you to prove that you're worthy of the recommendation."

"Of course," Liam said. "I'll do whatever it takes."

Smythii yawned. "Well, you can start by working a double today. Everyone happened to get sick the day after the holiday. Go figure."

Liam doubted he could even manage a single shift after the sleepless night he had, but he said, "I'll do it."

"Good," Smythii said. He tapped the side of his Halo to transmit the work assignment. "The ETS loading dock is swamped today, so you'll have to make the last delivery around midnight. You can go home after that. In the meantime, the vats in row seven need scrubbing and the…"

As Smythii listed everything that needed to be done, Liam had an intrusive thought, a question that probably wouldn't serve him well on his new path, but one he couldn't shake: Why can't the androids do it?

At lunch, Liam shoveled a meager meal of mashed roots and rehydrated vegetable paste down his throat. He didn't bother to put the food in the heater first. After he finished, he took a nap on the stainless steel table, using his forearms as a pillow. He dreamed about a hundred boats crossing some alien ocean, filled with explorers and pilgrims and refugees, where the elite enjoyed panoramic views from the upper deck while stowaways hid in dark cargo holds. As the people approached their destination, the sea became the sky and the boats transformed into rockets.

A crash jolted Liam awake. Wiki stood on the opposite side of the table, a big grin on his face. A tray full of food—actual food, not nutrient rations—sat on the table between them. The tray held crystalline sugar cubes in various colors, lab-grown meat wrapped in plastic, tree nuts from Armstrong Garden, and a hand-sized bottle of caramel-colored ethanol—all the delicacies of Omega.

"Moonfire? How did you—"

"I spent the rest of my rocks at the commissary," Wiki said.

"You still had rocks left after buying your ocular implant?" Liam yawned. "Wait, what are you doing here? Glo said—"

"They're only keeping the girls overnight. I'm free until morning."

"Weird. Do you know why?"

Wiki gestured toward the feast between them, and Liam popped a sugar cube into his mouth. The rare sweetness instantly overwhelmed his tastebuds.

Wiki said, "I assume they need their birth control implants removed."

Liam had nothing to say to that, so he continued to feast. He didn't like the taste of the meat that much, but the roasted saltiness of the nuts agreed with him, though it made him thirsty.

He eyed the bottle of moonfire.

Wiki said, "I'm saving it for tonight."

"I'm working a night shift."

"Since when?"

Liam shrugged. "I can't just keel over and die because I'm disappointed. I have a new plan, one that involves getting on Smythii's good side, so I'm working a night shift."

Wiki nodded. "Always plotting."

"You know me," Liam said.

"Come over after? I'll wait for you."

"It'll be pretty late."

"I don't think I'll be getting any sleep tonight, anyway."

Liam didn't harbor the same resentment toward Wiki as he did toward Glo, perhaps because he always expected that Wiki would make it to Earth. But at that moment, the proximity of his friend's departure hit him like a meteor—he saw it coming, but he couldn't prepare for it. Despite the sweet taste in his mouth, the thought of saying a permanent goodbye soured his mood. No, he forced himself to think, it won't be permanent. He would get to Earth someday.

"Are you okay?" Wiki asked. "I mean, your body language suggests that you're not okay, but—"

"You know people think it's weird when you comment on their body language, right?" Liam forced a smile. "I'm fine. Really."

"It just doesn't feel right, you know? Leaving without you."

"I'll be right behind you," Liam said, and Wiki gave him a confused look. "In fifty to a hundred years."

"Oh, I see," Wiki said, nodding. "Now that we've done it once, we should be able to build the next shuttle faster, you know?"

"Even better." Liam stood to leave, knowing that his implant would remind him to go soon enough. "See you tonight."

•|•

Smythii went home after the dinner break, leaving Liam with only the androids for company. As the hours crept by, he began to doubt his ability to maintain a show of good citizenship. Day one of his new path, and he already felt the weight of his future bearing down on him.

How easy the androids had it, he thought, unable to recognize the monotony of their daily activity. They didn't eat, didn't sleep, and only stopped working to recharge their batteries. He envied their lack of awareness, wishing he could turn off his own. If he could just put his body on auto-pilot, fast-forward through everything that needed to be done—the drudgery, the feigned respect, the responsibilities that would be thrust upon him over the years—then he might make it to the next mission with his sanity intact.

As midnight approached, Liam waited on top of an empty barrel in the storeroom. His plan to suck up his pride—to get to Earth someday by becoming an Admiral instead of obeying one—felt a lot like giving up. But what choice did he have? The Earth Transit Shuttle would leave without him in the morning. It had space for dead shrimp, brainless algae, and plastic barrels, but not for him. It would bring eighty humans to Earth, whether they liked it or not. With quiet acceptance, Liam prepared to rise from his seat, to make the last delivery of the night so he could go to sleep. Tomorrow, he would wake and do the same thing again. He would live out his robotic existence as long as it took.

As he stood, his heels tapped against the barrel beneath him, a barrel identical to all the others he had just strapped together to bring to the loading dock. He kicked his heels against it again, harder this time. A deep, hollow sound resounded through the storeroom. Slowly, a smile spread across his face, and his new plan was replaced by a newer one.

6

LAUNCH DAY

Glo sat on a chair beside the infirmary bed, waiting for her mother to wake. As the anesthesia wore off, an ember of pain smoldered in the center of Glo's biceps. The procedure had been minimally invasive, but the tiny incision still had profound consequences. Soon she would have the ability to produce children, an ability that many women envied but that Glo had not thought much about, even though she would be expected to have multiple children when the time came.

Her mother's eyes flicked open, and Glo placed a hand on her thin arm.

"Morning," she said.

When her mother smiled, the wrinkles beneath her eyes told a tale, a history written in peaks and valleys of radiation-damaged skin. Though her hair had thinned and silvered quickly over the recent months, and her face had sunken dramatically, she still looked beautiful to Glo. There was beauty in the eyes that had seen so much, the ears that never ceased to listen, the lips that still spoke wisdom.

"Good morning, starshine."

"How are you feeling?"

"Neither here nor there," she said, her voice just above a whisper. "More importantly, how are you?"

Glo sighed, unsure of how to answer.

Footsteps, conversations, and the clanking of medical equipment leaked into the room, dulled by the metal door.

"I feel strange." Glo's gaze found the wall for a moment, then fell on her mother's soft eyes. "Like none of this is really happening."

Her mother nodded, head sinking deeper into the pillow. "But it is. And you're ready for it, whether you know that or not."

Glo checked the time on her Halo, frowned, and shook her head. "I have to be at the launch facility in less than an hour. I didn't get to say goodbye to anyone at work, I don't know where—"

"Gloria." A hand touched Glo's cheek, hindering the incoming panic attack. "If you have less than an hour, do you want to spend it worrying about things you can't control, or do you want to enjoy our last moments together?"

The tears came then, hot and flowing. "How can I enjoy this? I have to say goodbye to everything I've ever known, and it's all happening so fast. I need to be here, with you and Liam, to take care of you."

"Breathe, Gloria." She glanced at the bandage covering Glo's incision. "Liam and I don't need you as much as humankind needs you."

Glo covered the bandage with her hand. "I—"

A harsh cough came from her mother's mouth, then another.

"Mom, are you okay?"

The coughing fit continued. It sounded terrible, painful, almost like she was choking.

"Doctor Jensen!" Glo yelled, helping her mother to sit up. "Nurse!"

Seconds later, the door flew open. A nurse hurried to the bedside and adjusted the slope of the bed. The coughing slowed, then stopped, and the room became silent.

"Something for the pain?" the nurse asked.

"I'm fine."

Glo sighed, relieved to hear her mother's voice again. "You don't sound fine."

"You'll make a wonderful mother someday, starshine. The way you care for others." She closed her eyes, and her lips curved into a smile. "Be fruitful, and multiply, and replenish the earth."

The poetry of the phrase struck Glo. "What is that?" she asked.

"Just some words from an old book."

They held hands for a while, an embrace that never ceased to comfort and calm Glo. She checked the time again.

"Liam was supposed to be here. I haven't seen him since the ceremony, and we've barely spoken." She frowned. "I think he hates me."

"Your brother will come around, Gloria. He always does." Her mouth released a breathy laugh. "Do you remember what he wanted to be when he was five, maybe six years old?"

"A miner," Glo said. She recalled how Liam would wear their father's mining helmet every chance he got, even though it came down over his eyes.

"He practically dug a bush out of Armstrong Garden with a spoon."

Glo chuckled. "He was just practicing."

"And when your dad told him that he couldn't be a miner, that it was too dangerous?"

"He followed dad to work because he wanted to see the danger for himself." Glo smiled despite the tears ruining her homemade makeup. She liked to remember her brother like that—young and cute, long before he got so serious. "He was always so stubborn. I don't think he'll get over this, Mom. It was his dream to go to Earth."

"It was your father's dream."

"Is there a difference?"

"Dreams come and go. Liam used to dream about being a miner. Then a scientist, then a janitor. That was the cleanest our apartment has ever been, by the way." They both laughed at that. "My point is—it will take time, but Liam will find something else to be passionate about, someone else he can choose to become. He won't stay mad forever. He can't. I'm sure he's already moving on to something else."

Glo frowned. "What if I don't see him before I leave? What if—"

"You don't need to say goodbye." She touched Glo's earrings, a pair of purple crystals that her father had found in the mines and fashioned into crude yet beautiful jewelry. "The people we love never really leave us."

Looking down, Glo wondered how many days her mother had left, how long the weakened muscles in her face would continue to lift that wrinkled smile, how many more insightful words she would get to speak. The people we love never really leave us, Glo repeated in her mind. She hoped that was true.

•|•

A murmur of nervous chatter filled the launch facility, a small module already packed with the other chosen candidates by the time Glo arrived. She scanned her wrist at the entry then searched the room for familiar faces, squeezing herself between arms and shoulders that hindered her visibility. She hated everything about walking through crowds: the collective heat, the inability to escape, especially the accidental contact with strangers.

She stepped through a gap in the crowd and found a pair of heterochromatic eyes level with her own. Her body softened at the sight of someone she knew.

"Hey," Wiki said, shuffling from side to side.

"Have you seen Liam?"

Wiki shook his head. "I was going to ask you the same thing. He said he would come over last night after work, but he never showed up. Didn't even call."

The concern Glo had about Liam's grudge against her dissipated. Instead, she began to worry about his safety. "When's the last time you saw him?"

"Wasn't he at home this morning?"

"No. When did you see him?"

"Yesterday. At lunch."

"He always wakes up before me. I figured he went to the Earth Sim. I didn't think anything of it this morning, and now— Oh, this is terrible."

Wiki grabbed his chin, stroked a beard that only existed in his imagination. "There has to be an explanation."

"I don't know," Glo said, holding back tears. Why didn't anyone know where her brother was? "Either he hates us or something bad happened to him. I'm really worried, Wiki, I—"

"Attention crew," Admiral Reagan yelled. His voice sounded

more robust than it had before, but it still had a rasp to it, as if he spoke through ribbons of metal. "Who's ready to get off this damn rock?"

Roars of excitement obliterated the silence. Arms pumped into the air, creating a wave of testosterone-fueled energy, an invisible charge that seemed to heat the air around Glo. She took a breath, wanted to say, "No, I am not ready to get off this damn rock," but remained silent.

"Your pressure suits are waiting on the bridge," Reagan said, his toothy grin shining white in the sterile fluorescent light. "Let's get ready to make history!"

A pair of sliding doors opened at one end of the module, and the crowd began to flow through them, an inescapable current that pulled Glo away from her old life and into a new one—a life without her family.

As the ship's engine rumbled to life, it occurred to Glo how the most life-altering moments either passed quickly or slowly with no in-between, how fear could stretch or compress time—or even stop it—and how a few minutes of trauma could leave scars that never healed.

One moment, Glo's body rested in the light lunar gravity, then everything became heavy. For a few seconds, she could focus on nothing but the weight, the pressure pushing the air out of her lungs. Then, mercifully, her head rose without help from her neck as gravity went away. Her arms floated out in front of her. She felt equally relieved and nauseous.

The launch passed quickly, a blip in her timeline that she didn't want to remember but knew she would never forget—like the day a few years earlier that changed her perspective on everything. The sequence of the launch—the feeling of being trapped, the unbearable pressure, then the sudden stillness—brought Glo back to the worst few minutes of her life. Only this time, it wasn't her boyfriend deciding what her body would do and where it would go—it was the society in which she lived doing so. And she couldn't fight back. She could only hide.

Glo stared at the inside of her visor, automatically burying the pain and anger associated with the memory under layers of distraction. It wasn't that she tried to forget what she had been through. Her mind simply resisted the memories, built up walls, a hiding place, until a careless touch or a lecherous glance invaded those walls, shook her back to that one life-altering moment—the day she learned that beauty had consequences and that men would do anything to get what they wanted.

"Attention crew," Commander Killion said through the ship's intercom. "*Atmosphere is standard. You may open your visors, unstrap your harnesses, and move freely about the cabin. Remember to keep to your own deck only. I repeat—your own deck only. You need to stay close to your assigned ejector pods at all times. Over.*"

When Glo lifted her visor, a dry chill attacked her face, and her breath became visible. Omega was never a warm place, but it had never been this cold. The clatter of buckles coming undone filled Deck Eight, the lowest deck, where Glo, Wiki, and ten other candidates had been assigned. Everyone else on the ETS Resurgence sat above on floors that narrowed as they reached the nose of the ship, the Command Deck.

With the launch vehicle detached, the only thing beneath Deck Eight was the Cargo Lander—an autonomous craft that would separate from the shuttle after atmospheric entry. The Cargo Lander held food and supplies, but most importantly, the biorepository—a remote cryogenic lab filled with thousands of fertilized human embryos collected over centuries. More than enough to reboot homo sapiens on Earth.

Glo pushed out of her seat, and the movement sent a jolt of nausea through her core. She floated over to Wiki, who was still strapped to the floor, typing furiously on a pair of keypads projected onto his thighs from the wearables on his wrists. He was focused on something that Glo couldn't see.

"What are you working on?" she asked.

At the sound of her voice, Wiki's fingers stopped moving. "I'm writing about the launch," he said.

"Getting started on the Archives already?"

"No," he said, looking at her now instead of the text on his lens. When he spoke to Glo, his eyes never strayed from hers, and she liked that. "This one is just for me. I keep a journal."

She nodded. "Well, I don't want to interrupt."

"Don't worry about it," Wiki said. He turned off his peripheral tech with a shake of his wrist. "I'm pretty much done. I just wanted to record some notes while the experience was fresh in my mind."

Glo found a porthole and floated toward it until it framed her face. Neither her old home nor her new home was visible, just a blanket of starry sky, a liminal space between her past and future.

"I can't believe we're here," she said. "After all of this. All of the effort that went into it."

"It's pretty incredible," Wiki said.

Glo nodded, still staring outside. "I wasn't supposed to be here. Why me?"

"You can thank the silkworms."

Glo turned away from the porthole. "What?"

"The parachutes on the ejector pods. They're made of silk—a lot of it—and it took decades to harvest enough. The mission would have launched years ago if Omega had the materials to mass-produce nylon. It would have been our parents here instead of us."

"What about the cure?"

"Old news. Viola Collins developed the antivirus before either of us was born. In fact, we've already been injected with it."

Glo glanced at the incision on her arm. What else didn't she know?

"The mission wasn't bottlenecked by her research," Wiki said. "She actually just came out of stasis with Reagan. So, you're here because of the silkworms."

"I guess I meant—why am I here instead of Liam?"

Wiki shrugged. "That, I can't answer. I'm baffled myself."

That meant a lot, because things hardly ever baffled Richard "Wiki" Abbot. He was socially awkward and overly analytical, but he always admitted when he didn't know something—unlike most young men, and older men for that matter.

"It just doesn't make any sense."

"None whatsoever," Wiki said.

Glo shivered, wishing she could forget everything she left behind, that her mind could build walls that high. She needed a distraction.

"Tell me more," she said, "about the ship."

"What do you want to know?"

"Tell me everything." She yawned. "And start from the beginning."

Glo settled into a comfortable position, her head resting gently on Wiki's shoulder. She knew he liked her—he always had—but also knew he wouldn't try to take advantage of the situation. She just hoped he wouldn't read too much into it.

"Lay some knowledge on me, my friend."

"Where should I begin?" Wiki said.

Glo closed her eyes while Wiki told the long-winded history of the ETS Resurgence, the multitudinous disciplines that had to come together to make the mission possible—from reverse-engineering ancient rocketry to mapping viral genetics. Asking no questions, she simply let his words wash over her, a comforting diversion from her thoughts, until she fell asleep.

•|•

Glo woke to the sound of voices coming from the opposite side of the deck—loud, tense, arguing, definitely male.

"We have to tell the Admiral," one said, his voice tight as if he spoke through clenched teeth.

"I don't think—"

"Can it, Wiki. This is treason, and you know it."

Still groggy, Glo circumnavigated the central column until the two boys came into view. With his back to the ceiling, Wiki floated between the hatch that led to the upper decks and a classmate of Liam's whom she recognized but didn't know personally. Raelyn— Liam's ex-girlfriend—had her hand around the boy's arm, holding him back from the fight.

"Actually, Tai," Wiki said, "it's not technically treason. According to section one of the—"

"You know what I mean." Tai lurched forward. "Now get out of my way."

"The Commander said not to leave our deck." Raelyn pulled Tai away from the hatch. "I don't want you to get in trouble, babe."

"Trouble?" Tai scoffed. "Why would I get in trouble for enforcing the law? I'm an armed officer now. It's my job to report insurrections."

"You're not an armed officer yet," Wiki said. "You have to be *armed* to be an armed officer."

Tai ignored Wiki and returned his attention to Raelyn. "You think I'll get in trouble? That's the reason you don't want me to go? Not because you two used to—"

"What's going on?" Glo asked. "What's this about?"

A half dozen faces turned to her, each in a different state of expression—heads shaking, eyebrows creased. One of them was a younger blonde girl Glo also recognized. She worked in a separate Nursery Module, but their paths had crossed a few times. She knew her name started with a Q, but she couldn't remember it. The rest were strangers.

"Somebody tell me what's going on."

Raelyn pointed to the far side of the room, extending a single bionic finger to indicate the cause of all the commotion. Glo turned and saw three people in black pressure suits, two with their visors drawn holding back the arms of the third—a prisoner not bothering to struggle against his or her restraints.

"If we weren't in Zero-G," Wiki said, "I'd tell you to sit down for this."

One of the captors pressed a button on the prisoner's helmet, revealing a male jawline, a mouth bent into a smirk, and a pair of eyes that Glo would recognize no matter her position in space.

"Hey, Glo," the prisoner said. "Can you help me out here?"

Speechless, Glo nearly lost consciousness at the sight of her little brother.

1

NOT TECHNICALLY TREASON

"What's that smell?" Glo retched and released Liam from her too-tight embrace. "It's disgusting."

When the breath returned to Liam's lungs, he laughed. "That's the smell of fourteen hours in a used shrimp barrel."

Glo gave him some space. "You stowed away? How is this even possible?"

"It was actually a lot easier than I expected." Liam side-eyed the two boys beside him. "I assigned an android to deliver the barrels, then I channeled my inner shrimp and—"

"You could have died, Liam! What were you thinking? You could've run out of oxygen down there, the acceleration could have killed you!"

"I was careful." Liam glanced downward. "Plus, I'm wearing a pressure suit."

"A pressure suit you stole," one of the boys said. "Look, the name tag says Tristan."

Liam smiled. "How do you know my name's not Tristan?"

"Because I know him," someone else said.

"I didn't steal it." Liam spread his hands out in front of him. "I just borrowed it. Listen, I'll even wash it before I give it back."

A chorus of angry shouts reverberated through Deck Eight, making Liam wish he had stayed in the Cargo Lander. He just hoped no one on the other decks could hear the commotion, that the hatches were soundproof.

"Enough." Tai kicked off the wall and glided over until he floated between Liam and Glo. "Family reunion's over. Do I need to drag you up to Deck One, or will you go willingly?"

Liam wanted to punch Tai—he often wanted to—but the majority of the room seemed to be under Tai's sway. Liam forced his arms to relax, gave slack to the springs to prevent an automatic recoil. Though it did sound fun, a zero-gravity fistfight would get him nowhere.

"Let me explain," Liam said. "If you still want to turn me in after that, then fine."

"Not a chance." Tai clenched his knuckles around the front of Liam's stolen pressure suit. "There's no way you're getting away with this."

Glo pushed Tai, which only sent her flying backward.

"Don't touch her," Liam said.

"She pushed me."

Liam glowered. "I don't care."

"I'm fine, Liam." Glo turned to Tai. "Will you just let him talk?"

"Why should I? He's a—"

"I want to hear what he has to say," she said. "I'm mad at him, too."

A few others muttered their agreement.

Tai shook his head and released his grip on Liam's suit. "Two minutes." He leaned in closer until Liam could smell the algae paste on his breath. "Man, you really didn't think this through, did you?"

Liam looked around the room, caught the fiery sprawl of Raelyn's red hair suspended in midair, the crease of worry between Glo's eyes, the vacant stare of a blonde girl who looked much too young for an interplanetary mission. "Looks like there's plenty of space here for me."

Tai scoffed. "I can't believe this. If you went to orientation, you would know how bad you've messed up. But why didn't you go to orientation?" Tai pretended to think, the best he could do with what rested between his ears. "Oh yeah, because you weren't chosen for the mission. We were."

Liam had to take a deep, shrimp-scented breath to prevent

himself from breaking Tai's nose. In his mind, he dared Tai to touch him again just so he would have an excuse to hurt him.

"Fair enough, but Zara," Liam said, scanning the room to make sure she wasn't there. "She's the slowest person I've ever met. You've seen her in the Earth Sim. Why was she chosen for the mission? And Glo— She wasn't even a candidate."

"It's true," Glo said. "I didn't want to come. They made me."

"It happened to me too," the younger girl said. She was pretty, pale, maybe fourteen or fifteen years old. Her blue eyes twinkled brightly in the dim light, glistening refractions of recent tears. The name tag on her pressure suit read Quinn.

"See?" Liam said. "Don't you all think it's a little sketchy that they were all chosen, and I wasn't?"

The room went silent for a breath.

"Sure," Tai said, "but no matter the reason behind it, they're supposed to be here. You're here illegally. And even if you were allowed to be here, that still wouldn't solve your problem."

"My problem?" Liam sighed. "What are you talking about?"

"Take a lap around the deck. Go ahead. Count the ejector pods."

Liam didn't need to take a lap. He could see half the deck from where he floated, so he doubled the number. "Six."

"Spot on," Tai said. "And how many seats do you see in each one?"

He glanced at one. "Looks like two."

"Right." Tai wore an egotistical smile, a feature he seemed to have been born with. At that moment, his face looked even more punchable than usual. "Now count how many people there are."

"What's this about?"

"Do it."

Reluctantly, Liam did so. "Twelve. Thirteen, including me."

Tai released a single breath of quiet laughter. "Do you see what I'm getting at?"

Liam nodded slowly, said, "I didn't know you could do math."

The smirk vanished from Tai's face. "You've always been such a funny guy."

"Rae thought so, too." Liam glanced at Raelyn and almost winked.

Someone in the room giggled, which made Tai's face redden. "You won't be joking around once we enter Earth's atmosphere, and you have no way to reach the ground."

Though Liam wouldn't admit it out loud, Tai was probably right. He hadn't thought everything through.

"I could go back down to the Cargo Lander."

Wiki chimed in. "Not a good idea."

"Why not?"

"Because it's going to pull some serious Gs when the retrorockets fire. Without the right harness, you could get seriously injured—or worse."

"How much worse?" Liam said.

"I'd say there's about a one percent chance you live."

"So," Tai said, his whole upper body flexing now, "how do you want to die, Liam? Outside the airlock once I report you, or do you want to try your luck in the Cargo Lander?"

Liam gulped down nothing, his mouth dry from dehydration. The Admiral wouldn't airlock him, would he? But of course, he would. At that moment, Liam realized how many holes his plan had—like a spacesuit missing the seals.

"Well?" Tai asked.

Liam opened his mouth to respond, to say he would take the one percent chance of survival, but Wiki beat him to it.

"Actually," Wiki said, "there's another way. The ejector pods were originally designed to hold three people. The third seat is just filled with supplies. The canisters are strapped into the original harnesses."

"How does he know that?" someone muttered.

"The ship's schematics have been open source for decades. Anyway, the supply canisters can be unstrapped. We can just remove one and—"

"Then the three of us can share a pod," Glo said, nodding along to Wiki's plan.

"Exactly," Wiki said. "Should be easy."

Tai sighed dramatically and addressed the group. "You're all so dense. What happens when Admiral Reagan finds out? That we all knew about this and didn't tell him? Do you all want to go down for Liam's crime? You really want to harbor a criminal?"

A riot of noes sounded through the deck, destroying Liam's newfound hope. He dug deep, grasping for anything that might save him.

After a tense moment, he said, "Admiral Reagan never has to know."

Tai grabbed Liam's arm and started pulling him toward the hatch.

"As soon as we land, I'll disappear," Liam said. "None of you will ever have to see me again. You can pretend I was never here."

"Tai," Wiki said. "I know you hate him. Believe me, he gets on my nerves sometimes, too, but think about it. Do you really want to sentence him to death?"

"I'll probably die down there, anyway," Liam said. "At least let me see Earth first. That's all I want."

Tai let go of Liam. His muscles relaxed a few notches. "I don't know. It feels wrong."

"I say we vote," Quinn said.

A long, cold silence filled the space between Liam and the arbitrators of his future. Tai tried to stare him down, to enforce his dominance, but Liam wouldn't look away. Who made Tai the leader of Deck Eight, anyway?

After a tense minute, Tai said, "Fine, but she"—he tilted his head toward Glo—"doesn't get to vote. On account of bias."

"Not to mention even numbers," Wiki added.

"Fine," Liam said. "That seems fair."

"All right, then." Tai punched his right fist against his left palm. "Let's get this over with. Will we turn Liam in or let him stay? I think you all know my choice."

The group arranged themselves into a rough half-circle surrounding Liam, their backs to the hatch.

"I vote we let him stay," Wiki said.

"Of course you do," Tai whispered.

"So do I," Quinn said.

The two boys who had held Liam back earlier voted to turn him in, swinging the vote out of his favor. Then, one at a time, the rest of the group cast their votes. Liam kept count on his hands until each of them had five fingers pointing outward. The decision would come down to a single vote.

"It's settled, then," Tai said. "Let's bring him up to the—"

"Wait," Liam said. "Raelyn hasn't voted yet." He watched her crack the knuckles of her organic hand with her bionic one. She avoided eye contact with both Liam and Tai, as if she didn't want the sight of either to influence her decision.

"Her vote is obvious," Tai said. Two months dating, and he still didn't understand that Raelyn made her own choices. "You really think she would vote for you? Tell me, why would she keep you around after—"

"Don't speak for me." Raelyn moved forward, her hair an inferno around her face. Liam had trained himself to hate her, but he still recognized her strength and courage, a couple of things he missed about spending time with her. "But you do have a point, Tai. Why should I vote to let you stay, Liam? Give me one good reason."

Liam had no answer for her. His mind searched for something to say that would appeal to her emotions, but then a strange hissing sound entered the room, distracting him from the task. Had the ship sprung a leak? If so, they'd all be dead, and they weren't. No one else seemed to notice the sound.

"Well," Raelyn said, "why should I do it? Why should I save you?"

"You shouldn't," a voice said from behind the group, deep, scratchy, and accented by centuries.

Beyond the crescent of people surrounding Liam, Admiral Reagan's torso emerged from the hatch above. Squinting through an open visor, he leered at the minuscule rebellion before him and shook his head firmly.

Air hissed into his mechanical lung.

8

EJECTORS

Liam didn't know what he expected Reagan to do next—whether he would yell or lecture or escort Liam straight to the airlock—but he definitely didn't expect the deep chuckle and wide smile that came to the Admiral's face.

"Well, look what we have here," Reagan said. "A bunch of kids acting like they run shit."

The redness drained from Tai's face. "I was going to turn him in, Admiral, even if the vote—"

"Shut up, son." Reagan spat toward the floor—or what would have been the floor if they were still on the moon—sending droplets of saliva floating through the air. "Adults are talking."

Apparently, leaving Omega had amplified Reagan's asshole-ness. Tai opened his mouth to speak again, but then snapped it shut. The group made room for Reagan as he inched forward. He stared at Liam the whole time.

"You just don't take no for an answer, do you, son?" Reagan stopped himself once he got a meter away from Liam. "I should airlock you right now, end this shit. But I'm curious, you know. How did you muster up the testicular fortitude to defy my orders?"

Liam shrank from each verbal blow. "I just wanted to be here, sir. To help with the mission."

"*You* wanted," Reagan said, then he leaned in closer, lowered his voice a few decibels. "Don't you remember what I told you, you little shit?"

Reagan took in a long, slow sip of air, which gave Liam time to recall their prior conversation.

"You said this isn't about me," Liam said, monotone. "That it's about the future of the human race."

"Bingo." Reagan was so close that Liam could see each individual hair of his gray beard, the shallow wrinkles in his timeworn flesh. "Yet somehow you had the nerve to endanger all of us, and you still expect no consequences. Do you know what happens if I let you off easy?"

Liam's shoulders rose and fell. "I would be very grateful."

"No shit," Reagan said. "But if you get to break the rules, others might start thinking that's okay. And it's not. You see? Phase one of Earth's repopulation will take decades, and undertakings of this magnitude require discipline. We can't afford disobedience, not now. Disobedience is death, not only for those who defy orders but for the entire human race. Is that clear?"

"I can obey," Liam said. "I'll follow the rules from now on, I swear."

"Your track record says otherwise, son." Reagan spat again, and this time a few droplets hit Liam's neck. "You've disrupted our future, and I don't appreciate disruptions. Do you know how much time and effort it took to get us here?"

And you were asleep for most of it, Liam thought, though he wished he could say it out loud.

"A lot," he said.

"People died for this, Liam, your father included."

"I—"

"You've dishonored his sacrifice."

By then, everyone but Wiki and Glo had scattered, as if their sudden disappearance from the conflict would prevent incrimination by association. Despite the frigid chill of outer space seeping through the walls, Liam felt spheres of sweat accumulating on his temples.

"Now," Reagan said, his rage frightfully and suddenly gone. "Come with me. The airlock is up on Deck Five. We're going to teach the rest of the crew a lesson they won't soon forget." He grabbed Liam's wrist, turned toward the hatch. "Like the ore your father mined to help us build this ship, consider this your contribution to the cause."

"Wait," Glo said, her hand on Reagan's forearm. "Please."

Reagan glared at her, and Liam thought he might slap her, but he only looked confused.

"If you do this," Glo said, "I won't help you. I won't obey your orders. I won't do my job."

Wiki floated closer, his hands shaking. "Neither will I," he said.

"Same for me," Quinn said, her voice steady despite her small size.

Liam hadn't paid her much attention until she spoke, but her willingness to save a stranger impressed him. The girl had guts. Her words eradicated the slight, condescending smile that Reagan had worn since coming through the hatch.

"Kids," Reagan spat, "acting like they run shit. Get your hands off me, Gloria."

Glo kept a hold on his arm. "You can't accomplish what you've set out to accomplish without people. How can you lead without followers?"

"Maybe I should airlock all of you, then. How does that sound?"

"And destroy the people you need?" Glo said. "Two of the three childcare specialists on board?" She glanced at Quinn. "One of the most knowledgeable humans left in the universe?" She inclined her head toward Wiki. "And the strongest, most fearless young man Omega has ever seen?" She stood tall, her eyes ablaze with an unstoppable protectiveness. "You told me that my grandmother was a friend of yours. How would she feel about you killing her only grandchildren?"

Reagan's expression slowly shifted from pure malice to a more muted rage. He dropped a hand to his belt. Only then did Liam notice the plasma pistol strapped there. Reagan wouldn't fire it, depressurize the deck, kill them all. Or would he?

"Oh, the power of the fairer sex." Reagan released his grip on Liam. "Good work, Gloria. I guess the four of you get to live." His hand gripped the pistol. "For now. Just don't forget who has the guns. Disobey me again, and no amount of pandering will keep me from making an example of you all. Is that understood?"

They all said, "Yes sir," even Liam, who couldn't believe the turn of events.

Reagan smacked Liam on the back. "Looks like you're getting your way, after all, son. You'll make it to Earth."

"Thank you, sir, I—"

"Before we get there, though, make sure you remove any preconceived notions of what your future might hold from that bratty little mind of yours." Reagan laughed bitterly. "You won't be working as a runner or a soldier or anything that requires your unmatched bravery and physical prowess. No, son. When we get to Earth, you'll be the same thing you've always been." He leaned in uncomfortably close. "A farmer. Good for one thing and one thing only...feeding those of us doing the real work. Understood?"

Liam gulped, silently celebrating his victory. He could tolerate Reagan's condescension for now—if it meant getting to Earth.

"Yes," he said.

"Yes, who?"

"Yes. Sir."

"That's better, son."

I'm not your son, Liam wanted to yell. You're not my father.

"And Gloria?" Reagan hovered below the hatch, one hand resting on a handhold, the other on the handle of his gun. "Why don't you come up to my cabin?"

Glo's bottom lip trembled. Her arms tightened around her body as if she could hide within herself.

"Did you already forget that you just agreed to obey my orders?"

"But—"

"Do you know how we survived all these centuries, Gloria? Leaders led, and citizens obeyed. Those who disobeyed were punished, as you all should be for this insurrection. Or"—Reagan pushed himself forward—"you can simply come with me."

"You promise you won't hurt anyone?"

"Of course," Reagan said. "Now, come. My cabin's more comfortable than this place. And it's a hell of a lot better than the wrong side of the airlock, don't you think?"

Liam clenched his fists, moved toward Reagan. "You're not taking her anywhere, you son of a—"

Reagan leveled his plasma pistol at Liam's forehead. "Did you already forget who has the guns?"

"Stop!" Glo yelled. "Don't shoot!"

"Back up, son." Reagan's aim held steady. Terrified, Liam had no choice but to obey. "That's your second strike. What'll it be, then, Gloria?"

Glo swallowed hard. "I'll come with you," she said, monotone.

Liam shook his head. "Glo, you don't have to—"

"It's fine, Liam." Glo took a breath then silently moved toward the hatch. "I'll be okay."

"I'll take good care of her," Reagan said, his gaze moving up and down her body. When she arrived by his side, he squeezed her between the shoulder and neck, fingers grazing her collarbone. He looked at Quinn, then Raelyn, then the other girls, then back at Quinn. The way he eyed the girl made Liam's stomach feel like it dropped out of orbit. "And you," Reagan said. "Commander Killion could use some company as well."

"What?" Quinn whispered.

Liam wasn't sure if she fully understood what was going on.

"Come on," Reagan said, inclining his head toward the hatch. "Everything's more fun in Zero-G." He smirked. "And I do mean everything."

As she went, Liam wanted to speak up again, to protest against Reagan's lewd and violent behavior, but he couldn't think of anything to say that wouldn't get him killed—and he had no weapons of his own. He never thought that someone else would have to pay the price for his crime, especially Glo. He looked at her, but she wasn't there—not entirely. The fierce protector from moments earlier had retreated into herself. And Quinn. Fresh tears blossomed in her eyes, orbs collecting but never falling. Maybe the girl did understand, and that made it worse. When the three of them exited Deck Eight, regret flooded into every crevice of Liam's mind.

What have I done?

•|•

Liam hadn't slept much in the shrimp barrel due to discomfort, and though he tried, he couldn't sleep now for entirely different reasons. Except for Wiki, no one spoke to him after Reagan left, and hardly anyone looked at him. Those who did offered no kindness, only indifference. He could feel their hatred for him, a palpable tension that made him hate himself more than he already did.

Strapped to the wall beside Wiki, Liam shivered; his pressure suit did little to shield him from the cold that crept through the metal. Or was the cold coming from within him? He wrapped his arms around his chest, fingers grasping shoulders.

Everyone else had a sleeping bag issued to them before leaving Omega, but Liam couldn't locate Glo's. He suspected that Tai had hidden it, but he didn't have the energy to fight. Only a few centimeters of titanium and fabric separated him from the vacuum of space, and less than ten hours of travel separated him from Earth.

In the meantime, he chose to suffer, figuring he deserved it. He could last ten hours in the cold, especially with the promise of a new world beckoning. As he watched the digital readout on the wall ticking down to zero, he planned for the future and silently plotted his revenge.

Sure, he would play farmer, but only so he could stock up on resources and gain an understanding of the planet. Eventually, he would leave the group for good, maybe convince a few others to go with him—Wiki, Glo, Quinn, anyone else who saw Reagan for what he was. They could explore the new world together, make their own rules, fight the monsters that didn't know they were monsters. Or he could kill Reagan, slowly and painfully, take command by force instead of patience. Kept warm by the rage bubbling inside him, Liam fell into a fitful sleep.

"Enter your ejector pods and strap in for atmospheric entry."
Commander Killion's alert jolted Liam into a semi-lucid state. Thoughts of open fields and desolate cities waiting to be claimed spun in his mind. He groaned and stretched, his body now feeling the abuse of squeezing into a plastic barrel for so long. When he

fully woke up, he saw Wiki's face, illuminated only by scattered sunlight that came through several portholes.

"How long?" Liam asked.

Wiki kept reading, the flow of words across his pupil only slightly interrupted by Liam's question. "Not long at all."

"Are they back yet?"

"Their pod was reassigned." Wiki nodded at a trio of crew members crowding into an adjacent pod, a canister of removed supplies at their feet. They didn't look pleased. "Apparently, those supplies are the least important."

"Still looks like a tight squeeze," Liam said. "I just hope Glo is"—Liam wanted to say "all right," but somehow, he knew that Glo and Quinn were far from all right—"I can't believe they went up there."

"They didn't really have a choice," Wiki said, his voice growing turbulent. "You took that choice away from them the second you—"

"You're really going to blame me for Reagan being a perv?"

Wiki looked away from his ocular implant. "Well, you could have stopped it."

"And get us all airlocked? What was I supposed to do? Punch Reagan in the face? He had a gun, Wiki. You didn't do much, either."

Wiki's head sank into his hand, and he began to massage his temples. "I wish I had." His tone grew quiet, defeated. "Your sister— She deserves a lot better than she gets. She's always so busy protecting everyone else: the kids in the nursery, your mom, you, now all of us. Someone needs to protect her."

Liam paused, thought about Wiki's words, and put a hand on his friend's thin shoulder.

"We will," he said. "Once we get to Earth, we'll never let Reagan near her again. He'll suffer for this."

Wiki stared into the distance, nodded. "I've been thinking."

"You always are."

"Reagan took Glo and Quinn with him, the two girls on our deck that weren't candidates. It's almost like he—"

"Like he handpicked them?"

"I don't know. Technically, he handpicked all of us. Well, everyone but you."

Liam doubted Reagan would ever forget, or forgive, him for stowing away. The crime would hang over his head forever.

"It was you who gave me the idea to stow away," Liam said. "I didn't think it would cause all this. I have enemies now."

Wiki clenched and released his fists. "We both do."

•|•

The ejector pod didn't have a true porthole, just a slit of heat-shielded silica that provided the tiniest glimpse of empty space. Liam and Wiki sat across from each other, knees against chests, bodies strapped tightly into shock-resistant harnesses. Foam braces surrounded their necks, snug against the bases of their helmets. Liam couldn't see how three people could fit in such a tight space, but somehow the reassigned crew members had done it.

The signal of their entry into Earth's atmosphere came first as a subtle glow through the slit, a plasma trail of hot ionized gas that grew brighter and brighter before beginning to strobe. It turned orange and pink, then the color of Raelyn's hair, a burst of energy hot enough to melt stainless steel. As Wiki had explained, the blunt-body design of the ship kept most of the heat away with a shock wave. Still, Liam felt an increase in temperature. His pressure suit became uncomfortably humid as he flexed his muscles against the deceleration.

The plasma trail soon dissipated, revealing a strip of green and blue and white through the slit. Jets fired, spinning and tilting the shuttle, aiming it toward their destination—the coast of a place once known as California.

"The ETS Resurgence is subsonic."

The ejector pods were almost entirely soundproof, but Liam could imagine everyone on board cheering. His muscles relaxed. The most dangerous part of the mission had passed.

"Deploying drogue chutes."

The Resurgence jolted as the forward cover detached, exposing several parachutes to slow the ship down further.

"Deploying main chutes."

Liam braced himself for another jolt, but none came. He made eye contact with Wiki, who had explained the entire landing procedure to him before entering the ejector pod. They were two steps away from making it safely to Earth, and something was wrong. The ship was supposed to slow enough for the ejector pods to fire. Then they would drift down to the beach under silk parachutes while the hull splashed down and the Cargo Lander made its controlled descent. But the main chutes hadn't fired, and by the colors Liam could see through the slit—they were quickly approaching impact.

"Initiating backup protocol."

A retrorocket fired, opposing their downward motion. Alarms blared, and the shuttle shook. It sounded like a hundred people were trying to get inside with hammers. Commander Killion spoke robotically, efficiently, almost too fast for Liam to comprehend.

"Ejector pods will fire in sequence by deck number. Firing One and Two."

Shadows broke through the blue-green light, almost too quickly to see, and Liam realized those were pods being jettisoned from Deck One.

"Firing Three and Four."

More shadows and a flash of white. Maybe clouds?

"Firing Five and Six."

Liam sensed the motion two decks above, or perhaps below, as the ejector pods deployed, pushed from the hull by small explosive charges.

"Firing Seven and Command."

Command? With the cockpit now gone, the announcement for the ejection of Deck Eight never came. For a split second, Liam wondered if Reagan had decided to let them die, to allow gravity to kill the budding rebellion on Deck Eight so he wouldn't have to. Then new colors came through the slit—mountain gray and stone black that signaled an immediate end rather than a new beginning. Liam took one last look at his best friend, drew in what he knew would be his final breath.

Then the ejectors fired.

9

SILKWORMS

Glo's ejector pod fell like a meteorite through Earth's atmosphere, and she had never felt a terror so intense. With her eyes sealed shut, she awaited impact, helpless to do anything else.

Images flashed through her mind, shimmers of memory that disappeared as quickly as they came: her mother smiling on her deathbed, Liam blowing spit bubbles as a baby, her father wearing the same helmet he wore every day—the one that could protect him from falling rocks but not from the mine collapse that killed him.

Everyone she had ever known paid a visit, all those who shaped her. She saw teachers and mentors, friends and co-workers, and every orphan she had ever watched. She saw the people she loved, the people who loved her—and the boy who pretended to love her but only loved what he could take from her. Then she saw Reagan's face hovering in front of her own, felt his rough hands, smelled his acrid breath—the clearest memory of all because of its recency, a nightmare brought to life the night before.

A violent tug shook her back into the present. She was still falling, but not in a weightless, terrifying way. As the downward motion slowed, she felt heavier. A lot heavier. The pod drifted from side to side, spiraling down to the ground beneath a parachute.

"Silkworms," Glo said.

She started laughing, and she didn't know why. There was nothing funny about nearly dying, but somehow the danger made her feel more alive than ever. Their exhilarating descent sent surges of excitement from her core into her extremities, numbing all the pain she carried.

"We're alive," she said, smiling against her will. "We're actually alive."

Quinn, who sat across from her, didn't seem to be having the same experience. Beneath her visor, her face looked the color of baby drool. Their helmet comm systems weren't paired, so Glo couldn't talk to her directly.

"Are you okay?" she mouthed.

When Quinn opened her pale lips to speak, the downward motion of the pod stopped abruptly. It swung violently then crashed.

•|•

Though Glo's experiences in the Earth Sim were limited to the required exercise hours, this much she knew: Earth's real gravity felt different from artificial gravity. It pulled her entire body down, each and every molecule, not just the places where the gravity straps touched. Her arms rested on her lap, fingers glued to the legs of her pressure suit. Her head fell heavy into the brace supporting her neck. With tremendous effort, she lifted her visor. Quinn did the same.

"You okay?" Glo asked.

Quinn groaned and unstrapped herself from the harness. The way the buckles fell so quickly to her lap looked unnatural.

"How do we get out of this thing?" Quinn asked.

The procedure had been mentioned briefly during orientation, but Glo struggled to recall it in her current state. She glanced around the pod, a nearly seamless sphere of metal sliced in half by one thin strip of silica.

"Above you," Glo said. "I think you're supposed to pull that strap."

Quinn yanked on the loop of fabric above her head. Glo's ears popped as air hissed into the pod. She found a handle on the adjacent wall and began to twist it.

"Wait," Quinn said. "What if the air is toxic?"

"It's not," Glo said, still turning the handle. "Don't worry."

"But what if there are subs out there? And other creatures?"

"If we see anything dangerous, we'll shut the door."

Quinn started hyperventilating. "Can't we just wait for someone to come get us? Can't we just—"

A small thud made the girl shriek.

"What was that?"

A repetitive tapping sounded through the pod.

"There's something out there," Quinn whispered, her hands now on her cheeks.

The tapping continued, and Glo wondered if someone had come for them. But no one could have made it here this fast, she thought. The air in the pod grew hotter, and she felt as if the interior was shrinking.

"It's probably just an animal," she said, though she didn't know if she believed it herself. "We just have to get out and find the others."

"Can't we wait for them to come to us?"

The pod continued to stifle Glo. "If anyone is hurt, they'll need help."

Quinn whimpered, her face wet with tears. "I'm scared."

"So am I," Glo said. "We're just going to take a peek first. No harm in that."

Glo started twisting the handle again but stopped before the hatch could open. She turned to the supply canister strapped to the opposite wall. When she pried it open, two small backpacks fell out and landed on her floor. She unzipped one of them and dug through its contents: packaged rations, a canteen filled with water, a blanket, and a sheathed knife. The knife's handle was a little too big for her hand, but holding it made her feel safer.

"Ready?"

"I guess," Quinn said.

When Glo cracked open the hatch, the tapping sound stopped, and a flurry of motion crossed the threshold. Wings and feathers?

"It was just a bird, I think."

When Glo opened the hatch completely, the light that poured into the pod temporarily blinded her, and she immediately noticed a strong smell—not unpleasant, but entirely foreign. It smelled like a hundred Armstrong Gardens. The fresh, earthy scent ignited something primal within her, and she took in deep breaths of the new air. When her eyes adjusted to the light, she saw a wave of motion, an undulating green mass. A soft crackle of sound coincided with the wave, and Glo realized that a canopy of moving leaves surrounded them. The breeze cooled her face, delivering another hit of the intoxicating air. She wanted to see more.

Quinn popped her head through the threshold and looked down. "Um, Glo?"

"Yeah?" Glo said, still mesmerized by the sights in front of her.

"I think we might be in a tree?"

Glo stuck her head out to confirm Quinn's assessment. About five meters down, she could see brown earth littered with fallen branches and dead leaves. Glo considered her options. A five-meter fall in Omega was harmless, but Earth's gravity made jumping a gamble she didn't want to take. The tree trunk didn't stand far from the pod, but it looked too thick to climb down. When she returned to the backpack, an idea came to her. She started cutting long strips of fabric from one of the blankets.

"What are you doing?" Quinn asked.

"You'll see," Glo said. She tied the strips together until she had three pieces about five meters long. "Do you know how to braid?"

Quinn flipped her hair. "Obviously."

They braided the three pieces together until they had a makeshift rope. Glo tied one end to the hatch's handle, then pulled as hard as she could to test the rope's strength.

"Ready?"

"Only if you go first."

Glo dropped the backpacks to the ground, took a deep breath, and dangled her feet outside the pod. The weight of her legs made her nervous—as if they could pull the rest of her over the edge. She took a moment to steel herself, then she gripped the rope with both hands and began to climb down, hand over hand. Her biceps protested immediately, setting fire to her upper arms.

The tree towered above her—a gnarled, ancient, oppressive organism, bigger by far than any living thing Glo had ever seen.

And yet it lived. It breathed. Her lungs bore witness to that life. It was incredible.

Halfway through the descent, Glo's protesting muscles started to riot. Her body shook for a moment before her grip gave out completely. When she slipped, her hands burned from the friction. She landed hard on top of the backpacks, which knocked the air out of her lungs.

"Glo!" Quinn yelled.

Glo gasped, still unable to speak. When she caught her breath, she sat up and took in the alien landscape—a forest that seemed to stretch on forever and ever. The reality of the situation set in, overwhelming her senses.

For all she knew, she was the first human to set foot on Earth in almost seven hundred years.

10

SOMEWHERE ON EARTH

Liam stood beside the ejector pod, his mouth agape. Never before had he witnessed such beauty: blue sky framed by great monoliths of natural stone, a field of long grass and wildflowers, ancient trees reaching for the sky. The place had no ceiling, no walls, just space waiting to be filled. He had seen vast expanses of emptiness before—lunar basins that stretched on and on—but the magnitude of the current landscape granted him a new perspective. A comfortable breeze caressed his face. He heard water moving somewhere beyond the tree line and started walking toward it.

"Wait." Wiki handed Liam a backpack. "Let's figure out where we are first."

"Somewhere on Earth, Wiki."

"I meant specifically." Wiki's gaze swept across the valley. Smoke rose in the distance, the only scar on the pristine landscape. "We're definitely not near the coast. The landscape suggests a higher elevation, maybe the Sierra Nevada mountain range. No, that doesn't sound right." He shook his head. "We're not supposed to be here."

While Wiki mused, Liam dug through his bag, found a bottle of water, and began chugging it. He couldn't remember the last time he ate or drank anything.

"Slow down," Wiki said. "We need to conserve as much as we can."

"There's more in the forest. I can hear it."

"And it probably has Giardia in it."

Liam raised an eyebrow.

"It's a parasite," Wiki said. "Unless you want violent diarrhea, I wouldn't drink it."

Liam smirked. "So, I should make sure Tai drinks it?"

Wiki ignored him as he observed the environment, analyzing it more than appreciating it. He pointed toward the sun sitting above a mountain peak, away from the smoke.

"I think we should head that way."

"Are you sure?"

"No," Wiki said. "I can't tell if the sun is rising or setting. Is there a compass in that bag?"

"A what?"

"Never mind." Wiki searched his own pack but came up empty-handed. Then he focused on his ocular implant. "I don't have a signal from the shuttle."

Liam peered into the forest. "Everything will be fine. Why don't we go for a walk?"

"A walk? I can hardly stand in this gravity. We should get our bearings first." Wiki drew in a quick breath. "We flew in from the west, and we were the last deck to eject, meaning the others should be west of us."

"What about the smoke?"

"Probably what's left of the shuttle, which should be to the east of us—so I guess I don't need that compass."

"Where do you think they are?"

"Hard to tell," Wiki said. "There's a chance some of our parachutes caught more wind than others. We could be scattered all over this valley. Some of the pods might have even landed in the mountains. Then again, I could be wrong about all of this."

"Say that again."

"There's a chance that some of our parachutes—"

"No, the part about you being wrong."

Unamused, Wiki shook his head. "This is bad, Liam. The Cargo Lander was supposed to jettison. If that got destroyed, then—"

"At least we're alive."

"For now," Wiki said, still staring toward the horizon. His face looked different in Earth's gravity, more expressive. "It looks like the sun is setting. We could spend the night in the pod, safe from whatever's out there." He gestured toward the forest. "It's the beginning of summer, so the night won't be too long."

"I didn't come to Earth to spend another night in a metal box." Liam turned toward the smoke. "Let's go to the shipwreck, see if we can salvage anything useful before it burns up."

"But—"

"We'll camp there." He started walking, knowing that Wiki wouldn't stay behind. "Come on. It doesn't look too far. Maybe some of the others are already on their way."

"I don't like this," Wiki said, but he followed anyway.

Twigs and pine needles crunched beneath Liam's feet as he and Wiki traversed the forest. Boulders littered the forest floor, great heaps of granite that had once been part of the nearby mountains. Living things scurried away from them as they walked, birds and rodents moving too quickly to be identified.

The hike proved difficult, but the exertion felt great after being cooped up in the pod. Liam knew he would sleep well that night, that he would wake up with a pleasant pain in his muscles, soreness that would become strength. He had trained hard for this world, and he looked forward to adapting further.

They came around a boulder into a small clearing. Liam stopped and put his arm out to stop Wiki. He pointed ahead at a heap of brown with a branch of spikes jutting out of it.

"What is that?" Wiki whispered.

Liam moved closer. His eyes narrowed. The thing stayed still, but he remained cautious, doing his best to see in the branch-filtered twilight.

"Maybe some kind of animal." Liam snuck forward, avoiding anything that might make a sound beneath his feet. "I think it's dead."

When they got close enough, Liam could see a stream of blood leaking out of the thing's neck.

"I think it's called a moose, maybe?" Wiki knelt beside the

carcass, touched the things branching from its head. "No, we're not far enough north. It must be some kind of deer. This one's a male. These antlers—"

"They look deadly," Liam said. "It makes me wonder what could have killed it."

Wiki shook his head. "I'd rather not stick around to find out."

Liam took a closer look at the deer's neck. He found a pair of deep puncture wounds there, still gushing blood. Teeth or claws had ruptured the fur, recently by the look of it.

"Let's go," Wiki said. "It's almost dark. I don't know how much longer I can stay vertical in this gravity."

Heat rose from the deer's body—a body built for running, for surviving.

"What could have killed you?" Liam whispered.

He shook his head and turned to leave. Two steps from the carcass, he heard a sound coming from the nearest boulder, a guttural growl that made his skin tingle.

The answer to Liam's question stood no more than ten meters away, perched atop a massive boulder. The predator bared its fangs and crept forward with its head low to the boulder's surface. Blood dripped from the fur and whiskers surrounding its mouth.

"Cougar," Wiki whispered. "Don't run, or it'll attack."

Liam scanned the ground for a weapon, wishing he had time to pull the knife from his backpack, but the cougar was coming closer. Its black-tipped tail whipped from side to side as it approached. Its gaze never left Liam's face. He picked up a fallen branch and backed away slowly, arms in the air as if the cougar understood surrender.

"Easy now," he said.

The cougar growled again, pausing when it reached the sheer edge of the boulder. Its eyes darted from Liam to Wiki, to the dead deer, then back to Liam.

"Eat your dinner," he said, pointing his stick at the deer carcass.

Then again, the cougar had probably never tasted human meat before—and it seemed eager to. It descended from the boulder in a single leap.

Wiki yelled, but his scare tactics hardly made the cougar look away from its target. Its gaze remained locked on Liam as it continued to creep forward.

Liam could smell it now, wild and foul like condensed urine. He gripped his stick with both hands, raised it in the air, and—

The cougar charged forward, moving faster than anything Liam had ever seen, even in the Earth Sim.

With no time to aim, he swung his weapon downward with all his strength. A loud crack sounded through the clearing, and Liam became vaguely aware of sharp pain in his right leg. The momentum of the beast pushed him backward, and he flailed to the ground, clutching what remained of his stick.

The cougar rolled straight over him, made a sharp turn. Stunned by Liam's blow, it backed up, hissing and crouching. Liam stood and brandished the splintered end of the branch. It was sharp, but it would take a fair amount of force to do any damage. He shouted and stomped one foot into the dirt to scare the beast away.

But the cougar stood fast, unafraid, and Liam had time to take a better look at it. It stood no taller than his thigh, but that didn't matter. Beneath sandy fur, the big cat's muscle definition bulged, an impressive display of pure strength. Its fangs glistened like knives.

They danced around each other, neither attacking nor retreating. The forest and everything in it seemed to disappear until nothing remained except Liam and the cougar.

It growled again, taunting him, daring him to make a move.

But he couldn't.

Terror froze him in place. One wrong move and the cougar would shred him, devour his flesh, clean its teeth with his bones.

Liam had come face to face with violent monsters before. But this was no simulation. This was real life. And if he died, he wouldn't get another chance the next day.

He looked down at the dead deer, wondering what its last thoughts had been. He only looked for a split second, but by the time he looked back up, the cougar was crouched low, preparing to pounce.

Not on Liam, though.

On Wiki.

11

GRAVITY

Side by side, Glo and Quinn trudged through the forest toward a pillar of smoke far in the distance, each step a milestone in the strong gravity. Glo knew the math. She and Quinn were six times heavier on Earth than they had been on the moon. She felt every ounce of the extra weight, a homogenous heaviness in her bones and flesh. The backpack made it worse. Sweating profusely from the exertion, she wondered how her ancestors had carried such mass.

Quinn sighed. "How much longer?"

Glo shrugged and looked down at the girl. She had a natural beauty about her that Glo might have once envied—before she learned the price of such beauty. Youthful skin, bright blue eyes, and perfectly symmetrical features. Somehow, the dappled sunlight filtering through the trees made Quinn shine even brighter. Glo shuddered, thinking about the night the girl was forced to spend with Commander Killion.

"Let's take a break." Glo dropped her backpack to the ground and pulled out what remained of her blanket. "Help me spread this out."

They lay on the blanket, chests rapidly rising and falling as they caught their breath. The sky was beginning to darken, but Glo figured they could spare a few minutes.

"It is beautiful here," Quinn said, her pupils reflecting the forest canopy. "Not like I thought it would be."

Glo silently agreed. Earth always looked so dreary in the simulations, filled with flesh-eating subhumans and decaying landscapes.

"Maybe all the monsters are dead," Quinn said.

"Not if Reagan's still alive."

And Killion, she almost said, but something stopped her. Motion in the canopy caught Quinn's attention, a blur of black and white streaked with red.

"Is that—"

"A bird," Glo said. "Like the one that tapped on our pod."

The bird landed on the side of a tree, its talons gripping the bark, then it pecked at the trunk repeatedly. A crimson crown of feathers adorned its head.

"It's so pretty," Quinn said. "I wish I had my Halo."

"To take a picture?"

"To identify it," Quinn said.

"Halo or not, I bet Wiki could tell us exactly what species it is." Glo frowned, suddenly anxious to continue their trek through the forest. "I hope he and my brother are okay."

"Me too," Quinn said, still staring at the bird. "And Nikolai."

"Nikolai?"

"Commander Killion," Quinn said as if it were obvious.

"You hope he's okay?" Glo turned her head until she could see Quinn's face. "Why do you say that?"

"Because," Quinn said, her cheeks growing pink. "He's a nice man. He cares about me."

Glo sat up. "Why do you think that, Quinn?"

"He told me." She folded her arms. "Why are you getting so mad? We just—"

"Men will say anything to get what they want."

"What is that supposed to mean?"

Glo forced her voice to calm, ran her fingers through Quinn's blonde locks. "You two don't even know each other. He's twice your—"

"You don't understand," Quinn said. She rose to her feet and donned her backpack.

Glo stood up from the blanket. "You're too young to—"

"What are you?" Quinn asked. "Eighteen? How much more could you possibly know?"

"Almost nineteen," Glo said, following Quinn as she stormed off into the forest. "Hey, wait up!"

"No." The word rolled off Quinn's tongue with a well-rehearsed edge. "Leave me alone."

Her poor mother, Glo thought. She had to jog to keep Quinn in sight, and jogging was no easy task. She needed to talk some sense into the girl, but what could she tell a hormonal fifteen-year-old about love that wouldn't go through one angsty ear and out the other?

"Quinn," Glo said, the answer hitting her like a falling ejector pod. "Listen. I was your age when—"

Glo hesitated. She couldn't say the words that nearly escaped her mouth, could hardly get herself to think them.

But she had to.

She took a breath, tried to catch up to Quinn so she wouldn't have to yell her truth. But her knees buckled, and she fell to the ground. Dirt scraped against her elbows.

"Quinn!" She struggled to stand up, to see Quinn through the trees. "Quinn!"

12

RED HANDPRINT

Liam lunged forward, arms outstretched to tackle the cougar before it could get to Wiki. As soon as he dove, he knew he wouldn't make it. He was fast, but the cougar was much faster. If he missed the target, Wiki would die, and he would be next. Perhaps he had underestimated the dangers of Earth.

The bulk of his body thudded against the hard ground.

He missed the cougar's torso, but somehow he managed to get both hands around its tail and yank it. Angry, spitting animalistic profanities, the cougar whipped around and slashed at Liam's torso. He veered to the side, dodging razor-sharp claws by mere centimeters.

Wiki threw a fist-sized rock at the cougar's ribs, which granted Liam a precious second to dodge a second attempt to lacerate him.

Now on his back, Liam elbowed the cougar in the mouth, breaking skin on fangs. When the cougar recoiled from the blow, Liam managed to pull his leg back, loading it with as much tension as possible.

He kicked.

Hard.

Hard enough to jump ten meters in lunar gravity. Maybe higher.

The heel of his boot collided with the cougar's shoulder joint, and the crack of snapping bone rang like music in his ear.

Now wounded, the cougar backed away.

Liam stood between the predator and its prey, between the living and the dead, wondering how much longer he would walk that line. Making himself as big as possible, he limped forward, blood soaking his pant leg, dripping into the dirt.

"Go," he said. He could taste the blood now. He felt no pain but thought he might have bitten his tongue in the scuffle. "Go away."

The cougar made a sound, something between a growl and a moan, and for a moment, Liam thought the fight was over.

But it stared him down, unrelenting, dug its rear claws into the earth, and pounced again.

This time Liam was ready.

He sidestepped and watched the cougar turn in midair as it flew past him, one limb bent at an odd angle, paws reaching out in an attempt to change its trajectory. But the motion had already been set. Carrying that much mass, traveling at that speed, the cougar had momentum that no amount of flailing could stop. The situation was Newtonian, a force of nature. An object in motion will stay in motion until—

The cougar's body hit the ground with enough force to send clouds of dust into the air. And carrying the same amount of force, its head hit one point of the deer's antler.

•|•

Wiki poured antiseptic onto Liam's wounds—a trio of cuts across his calf.

Liam winced. "Stings," he said through gritted teeth.

"Better than getting an infection," Wiki said. He wrapped Liam's leg in gauze. "These are deep. You might need stitches, but this should work for now. Hopefully, we have enough."

They sat in a hollow of the nearest boulder, more of a crack in the stone than a cave. Still, it was better than being exposed. Less than fifteen meters away, the cougar stared blindly into the dark forest, its head impaled like some ancient traitor's. Wiki had managed to start a small fire, and the heat reflecting off the face of the boulder made their shelter bearable, if not comfortable.

"I'm starving," Liam said.

"We've got some algae paste in the pack."

"Gross." Liam peered at the silhouettes of the two dead animals.

"Can't we eat the cougar?"

"Really?"

"What? He tried to eat us."

"She," Wiki said.

"How do you know that? You know what, never mind."

"We could eat the deer." Wiki tightened his blanket around his shoulders, stoked the fire with a tree branch. "Probably tastes better than the cougar. But I'm not butchering it."

Liam dreaded the task, but his hunger didn't care. He had dealt with plenty of nasty things in the Farm Module. After finding his knife, he limped over to the two carcasses. A few stray flies buzzed around them in chaotic orbits, but most of them congregated around open wounds, mouths, and eyes. He knelt, avoiding the deer's vacant stare, the cougar's accusatory scowl.

Liam decided the best option was to chop off a limb. He cut through the apex of the deer's exposed hind leg. Once he got through the fur and skin, the muscle cut easily, but the bone…he had to stomp on the deer's hip, snap the bone to free the leg from the torso.

He came back to the fire, breathing heavily, his red-painted hands wrapped around his dinner. Slinking into his rocky shelter, he felt like a human from an era long gone, a caveman returning home. The thought made him smile. He dropped the meat on a flat rock beside Wiki. Then he walked over and pressed one hand against the face of the boulder.

"What are you doing?" Wiki asked.

Liam shrugged. He pulled his hand away from the wall, leaving behind a red handprint—his mark on the world, the first of many. Having killed something that tried to kill him, he felt invincible, like he could conquer any challenge thrown his way. Then he thought about Reagan, what he had done to Glo. A monster without claw or fang. Old. Sick. What chance did the Admiral stand against Liam?

"Tomorrow," Liam said, "we'll find Glo and the others." He skewered the deer meat on a spit that Wiki had constructed, gave it a single turn above the flame, and smiled. "Then, this world is ours."

•|•

Liam awoke in the black of midnight to a strange sound. In the haze of waking, he couldn't identify what it was. Shuffling? Scratching? No, that wasn't right. It was a wetter sound than that, like a mouth opening and closing. Chewing?

His eyes cracked open to investigate. The canopy above blocked the moonlight, but the embers of the dying fire illuminated the shelter just enough. Liam sat up slowly.

A small animal stood by the fire, its back to Liam, chewing on what remained of their dinner—a few bones that he and Wiki had practically stripped clean. The creature looked harmless, helpless even, so Liam didn't bother trying to scare it away. He just watched, wishing he had paid more attention in biology. It had four legs, dark spots, and a tail that whipped back and forth as it chewed on the bone. It moved clumsily, almost playfully.

When Liam shifted his position to get a better look, a twig snapped beneath his palm. The animal recoiled from the sound and sprang up from the dirt. Liam thought it would run, but it just crouched low and began to back away. The motion seemed familiar, and Liam immediately understood why.

"Cougar," he whispered.

It was probably the offspring of the one he had killed. It had to be. Looking at the cub, he stifled a rush of guilt.

"It's okay." Liam reached out with one hand. "Come on."

The cub tilted its head as it regarded Liam. Its hair, which stood erect on its back, began to relax.

"That's it," Liam said softly. "I won't hurt you."

The cub took a few cautious steps forward, then stopped and sniffed the air. Liam made some kissing sounds and wiggled his fingers.

"A little bit closer." Looking into the cub's blue eyes, which reflected orange embers, Liam began scratching at the ground. "That's it, buddy. Almost—"

The cub pounced, and Liam almost jumped out of his skin. It nibbled playfully before beginning to lick the dried blood from Liam's hand with a tongue equally soft and rough. Liam couldn't help but laugh. Growing up, he had seen images and watched videos of all kinds of animals, but Omega had none—unless you counted shrimp and other tiny, stupid creatures that he and the androids farmed for nutrients. No one had pets, except the bioluminescent jellyfish that every third-year class got to raise.

"You can stay with us," Liam said, petting the cub's back with his free hand.

It crawled onto his lap and curled itself into a fluffy ball. Stroking the softest fur—the only fur—he had ever felt, Liam yawned. Soon he fell asleep to the sound of the cub's purring.

13

CAMP RESURGENCE

Glo's eyes shot open. The echo of a high-pitched scream rang out in her mind. She peered into the forest, unsure whether the sound was real or just a remnant of her sleeping terror.

The first inklings of daylight illuminated the landscape, displaying nearby rock and wood in vivid detail. Countless birds performed their songs, a wild and chaotic symphony.

Maybe it was just a birdcall, Glo thought.

She let her eyelids fall shut and reclined in the crux between the two gnarled tree roots she had slept between. Shivering, she wished she still had her blanket. The roots sheltered her from the breeze, but the chill of the earth still seeped in through the backs of her legs.

"Help!"

The cry came from far away, barely audible but out there. Somewhere. Strange noises came from every direction, the calls of rodents and birds that Glo couldn't identify. Every sound made her body tense up.

"Somebody help!"

It sounded like Quinn. Adrenaline warmed Glo's skin, made her rise. Nausea threatened to make her lose the algae paste she had swallowed before bed. She knew from experience that it tasted much worse coming back up. She took a few breaths to settle her stomach. Gravity sickness was a mean bitch.

Feet heavy, she left her things behind and started jogging through the trees. Twilight filtered through the canopy, making some spots more visible than others, playing tricks on her mind. She clutched her knife, the only thing that made her feel remotely safe.

"Please!"

The voice sounded louder now. Glo doubled her pace. At least she was going in the right direction. Dripping sweat, stomach heaving, she carried on as fast as she could.

"Quinn!" she yelled.

Glo crossed a path where a meter or two of underbrush and natural mulch disappeared. She wondered what animals might have carved the trail—or if it had once been a road.

"Over here!"

Through a gap in the green and brown, Glo saw a smudge of yellow. Quinn's hair. She ran to the girl, who sat on the ground with her back reclined against a tree.

"My ankle," Quinn said. Rivers of red crossed the whites of her eyes, and dirt clung to dried tears beneath them. "I think it's broken."

"What happened?"

"I fell," Quinn said.

"You climbed this tree?"

"I slept up there."

Glo examined Quinn's ankle. It was swollen and purple in a few places, but it didn't look bent out of shape.

"Any numbness?" Glo asked.

Quinn winced. "Don't touch it."

"Did you hear it break?"

"I don't know, it just hurts really bad."

"Flex your foot. Now wiggle your toes. Good. Where's your backpack?"

Quinn pointed to a large branch a few meters above. The backpack hung from a smaller offshoot. Too high to reach.

"Stay here," Glo said.

"What am I going to do? Walk away?"

So much attitude, Glo thought. Was I like that at fifteen?

Despite the gravity, the tree didn't prove too challenging to climb. Quinn had chosen a good one. It had plenty of evenly spaced holds. When she got high enough, Glo dropped the pack to the ground, careful not to hit Quinn.

Back on the ground, she found the first aid kit and began sorting through it.

"Swallow these." Glo handed Quinn a pair of white pills and what remained of her water. "They should help with the pain and swelling."

"Thanks," Quinn said. The panic had left her face, but she still looked upset—embarrassed, maybe.

"Why did you run away? You know it's not safe out here."

Quinn avoided eye contact.

"I'm not mad," Glo said. "I just—"

"You sound like my mom, you know that?"

Glo couldn't argue with that. Her friends had always called her the mom of the group.

"I wasn't trying to lecture you, Quinn, I—"

"You were worried about me." Quinn swallowed the pills. "I get it. I don't need you to look out for me, but I get it. You think you know better than me because you're older."

"I don't think that, I just—"

"Then what is it?"

Glo's mouth went dry. The day before, she had almost told Quinn her story out of desperation, to keep her from running away, but now the thought of sharing it terrified her. She gulped, preparing to speak the words she had never spoken out loud, then took a calming breath.

"Listen. I was your age, only fifteen, when I got drunk on moonfire with my boyfriend. Well, he was the one who got me drunk." Glo hesitated, already embarrassed. "It was after the annual dance in Armstrong Garden. We'd been dating for months, and I thought I was ready. I really did. But I wasn't, and he wanted me to— He convinced me to—"

"To have sex with him," Quinn said. Her eyebrows rose a notch. "I'm fifteen, Glo, not ten."

Glo wished she had some more water. "He said he loved me. He said if I loved him, I would do it. But I wasn't ready. That night we drank so much— Well, I drank so much that I couldn't even walk home. I don't think he had more than a few sips. He said I should sleep in his pod, that my mom would be mad if I came home drunk. I believed him."

"That's different," Quinn said, but the way she spoke made it sound like she didn't believe her own assessment. "Nikolai is a nice man."

"This boy was someone I knew," Glo said. "Someone I trusted. Someone I thought I loved. And he was only a year older than me. If a boy could take advantage of me like that, imagine what Commander Killion could do. He's a man, and he's powerful."

"But he said—"

"It doesn't matter what he said, Quinn. That's what I'm trying to tell you."

"We stayed up all night and talked." Her lip quivered. "That's all. Nothing bad happened."

The news granted Glo some relief, spiked with a bit of jealousy. Instead of polite conversation, her night with Reagan had consisted of silence on her part and not-so-gentle coaxing on his. And that time, she didn't have the luxury of alcohol to blur out the memory. The details of the encounter were still sharp and painful, like splinters of glass too small to see. She couldn't remove them, and so the skin would grow around them. They would be a part of her now, festering beneath the surface. Still, she would have taken a thousand splinters to keep her brother safe.

"Okay," Glo said. "I'm sorry for yelling at you. I just didn't want what happened to me to happen to you. I don't want it to happen to anyone."

"I'm fine," Quinn said. "And I'll be careful. I'm young, but I'm not dumb. I've had to deal with unwanted attention before."

Glo had to admire Quinn's character. She had a strength about her that fifteen-year-old Glo had lacked. She put an arm around the girl, pulled her closer.

"Still friends?"

"I think we have to be." Quinn looked forward through the trees. "I mean, there aren't too many options around here."

Despite the pain she felt inside and out, Glo smiled. The strangeness of the setting provided a comforting distraction from the regret and worry nagging her heart. She squeezed Quinn a little tighter, a silent promise to protect her.

"I'll take that as a yes."

•|•

"Do you think you can walk?" Glo asked.

Quinn stood, one arm draped over Glo's shoulder for support, the other pressed against the tree she had fallen from.

"Maybe," she said, "but not very far."

Glo had no idea which direction to go. Her mad dash through the forest to find Quinn had disoriented her, and the distant plume of smoke that marked the shipwreck had disappeared overnight. Still, she felt the need to do something other than wait. She wanted to get Quinn to safety, whatever that meant on this planet, and she needed to find Liam.

"There's a road," she said, "or a path or something. It's not far from here. Maybe we should follow it."

"Worth a shot," Quinn said, "but what if we go the wrong way?"

"You won't," a male voice said.

Glo looked toward the source of the sound. Commander Killion stood among the trees. He had a plasma rifle slung over his shoulder and wore a perfectly white smile that seemed out of place in the environment.

"I know the way."

"Nikolai," Quinn said, her voice higher than usual.

"We've been looking for you." Killion came closer, put his hand on Quinn's shoulder. "Are you hurt?"

"Sprained ankle," Quinn said. "It's not too bad."

Glo understood why Quinn might have a crush on the guy. He had a muscular build and a handsome face with a strong jawline.

"Where's my brother?" Glo said. "Liam Stone."

Killion shook his head. "When I left camp, there were sixty crew members accounted for, and I don't remember seeing that name on the list. I don't remember seeing that name on the manifest, come to think of it."

"He wasn't on the manifest," Glo said.

Killion shot her a confused look.

"Long story," she said. "But we need to find him, and his friend Wiki— I mean Richard Abbot. They might've been in the same ejector pod. Deck Eight."

"We're doing our best to locate as many survivors as possible."

His words sent a wave of panic through Glo's body. "Survivors?"

Killion drew in a sharp breath. "Out of the sixty accounted for, only forty-three survived the landing."

Glo did the math. If what he said was true, over a quarter of the people they had found so far were dead, and more were missing. She didn't like thinking about those odds when it came to her brother.

"How?" she asked. "How did this happen?"

"I don't know," Killion said. His eye contact broke as he spoke. "My best guess is that our engineers made a miscalculation. Or the instruments were improperly calibrated. Small discrepancies have big consequences for spaceflight. This was the first rocket launch in—"

"We need to find my brother."

Killion nodded. "I'm not the only one scouting the forest. If Liam is out there, we'll find him. He might even be at camp when we get back. The wind carried you two pretty far."

"Can you carry her?" Glo said, leaning her head toward Quinn.

"I think so," Killion said.

"Then let's go."

•|•

Camp Resurgence, as Killion called it, was hardly worthy of the title. A bonfire blazed in the middle of a clearing, surrounded by men and women performing various tasks—from carrying felled trees from the forest to cutting and rolling parachute fabric. Four or five ejector pods made up the perimeter, each with an armed officer on top.

"We've got a lot of work to do," Killion said. "We're building walls today, and an infirmary tent. Luckily, one of these pods had a medkit. Tomorrow we'll go searching for more supplies at the crash site."

Glo nodded, looking around for Liam.

A couple of guys rushed over from the center of the camp. "Commander," one of them said.

"Get these girls some water," Killion said. "And Quinn needs a cot."

"I'm fine," Quinn said, standing on one foot with her arm draped over Killion's shoulder.

"You can't walk on that." He transferred her weight to one of his men before looking at Glo. "You two get settled in."

When Killion left them, Glo wandered through the camp and searched the sparse crowd.

"Liam!" she shouted. "Where are you?"

Many faces turned her way, some of them familiar, but none of them belonged to her brother. Glo tried to stay calm, to keep her panic at bay.

"Liam!"

A hand gripped her shoulder, and she twisted around hopefully. But hope became dread when she saw Reagan's face.

"Gloria," he said. "I'm glad you made it."

Glo stared at the ground, where some kind of beetle scuttled under a rock. She wished she could follow it.

"I know you're scared," Reagan said, his hand still on her shoulder, "but look around. Earth's a beautiful place, and now it's our home. You don't need to be afraid anymore."

It wasn't Earth that scared Glo. She took a step away, shrugged Reagan's hand off her.

"I hope you know I would never hurt you, Gloria."

You already have, she thought. I already let you, and now it might have been for nothing.

"Have you seen my brother?"

"Not yet." Reagan touched her back. "We're still—"

"Admiral!" Killion's voice came from the other side of camp. Glo looked up and saw him coming closer. "It's time for another sweep of the perimeter."

"Duty calls," Reagan said as his hand left Glo's back.

14

THE RIVER

"Is that what I think it is?" Wiki asked.

His shadow fell on Liam, who lay on the ground, the cougar cub still asleep on his lap.

"It came here last night," Liam said, his voice raspy. "Any water left?"

"We need to find more."

Wiki tossed Liam what remained of their water, and Liam drained the rest of it into his mouth.

"Are we going to the shipwreck?"

"Priorities. Without water, we die." Wiki eyed the empty water bottle. "Do you want to die?"

"That's a dumb question." Liam pulled the blanket over his shoulders and closed his eyes. Despite the hardness of the ground, he felt cozy there. Gravity held him down like a heavy blanket.

"Come on," Wiki said. "We've got a lot to do today. We have to find that river."

The cougar cub made a tiny snoring noise. "What should I do with—"

"I don't know, and I don't really care."

Liam's eyes narrowed. "Why are you acting like this?"

"Like what?"

"I don't know. You seem cranky."

Wiki didn't open his mouth, but released a short, unamused laugh. "How should I be acting?"

"You could start by thanking me for saving your life yesterday."

"My hero," Wiki said, doing nothing to hide the sarcasm in his voice. "Excuse me for being upset about our current situation."

"Whatever." Liam stood up. "Let's go, then."

Wiki started to leave but stopped at the threshold of their shelter. He stared into the clearing beyond.

"What's the holdup?" Liam asked.

Wiki shushed him.

"What is it?"

"Did you do something with the bodies last night?"

"Just chopped off a leg," Liam said, confused. "You're welcome for dinner, by the way."

"I mean, did you move them?"

"Why would I?"

"They're gone," Wiki said. He made room for Liam to pass and take a look for himself. Sure enough, neither the cougar nor the deer was in the clearing anymore. Wiki shook his head slowly. "Someone must have taken them."

Liam couldn't believe what he saw. If someone had passed through in the night to take the animals, how did they do it without waking him? Without seeing their shelter?

"Someone?" Liam asked.

There were no obvious clues about what happened while they slept. They saw the discolored earth where blood had seeped into the ground, a few tufts of fur, but no other trace of the two dead animals.

Wiki stroked his chin. "What could be big enough to do this? A bear, maybe?"

"Don't ask me."

"A bear would have left tracks. There aren't even any drag marks. It must have been a group of people, or— Oh, no."

"Do you think it could have been the others?" Liam said. "They could have come through this way in the night."

"Not people."

"What are you talking about?" Liam asked. The answer came to him when he saw the fear on Wiki's face. "Out here? I thought their populations were concentrated in big cities."

"Maybe centuries ago. Who knows how far they could have spread out by now."

Liam imagined the subs from the Earth Sim roaming the woods, deadly packs of devolved humans searching for things to kill. He doubted such beings could be so careful, so meticulous about leaving no trace, but it was the only explanation that made sense.

"And who knows how they might have evolved," Wiki said, mirroring Liam's thoughts.

Liam paced back and forth, the cougar cub at his heels the whole time. "We need weapons. I'm not wrestling any more cougars, and we can't run into a pack of subs unarmed. Let's head to the shipwreck. We'll find water on the way."

"Fine," Wiki said. He watched the cub following Liam around and smiled. "That thing's pretty cute, actually."

Liam nodded. "Not so scary when they're small."

"He seems to like you. Even though you"—he looked at the spot on the ground where the dead cougar had been—"Well, you know."

"Even though I made him an orphan?"

"It's not the worst thing, I guess. I turned out all right." Wiki started packing up his things. "What are you going to call him?"

"I haven't really thought about it." Liam reached down, scratched the head of his furry shadow. It was strange how quickly the cub had bonded with him. "Any ideas?"

"How about Simba?"

The cub walked a figure eight around Liam's ankles.

"What does it mean?"

"Not sure," Wiki said. He hoisted his backpack onto his shoulders and started walking toward the tree line, a knife in one hand and an empty canteen in the other. "It's the name of a lion cub from an ancient movie I watched. Simba's dad is murdered by his uncle, then Simba ends up becoming king."

"Fitting," Liam said. He didn't feel too bad about killing the adult cougar. After all, he had done it in self-defense. However, he did suffer a twinge of guilt for making the cub an orphan. He knew what it felt like to lose a parent. "I like the name King better, though."

•|•

They hiked in the general direction of the shipwreck and followed the distant sounds of moving water until they came to a roaring river. The air coming across the water smelled like nothing Liam had ever experienced before. He knelt on a log jutting out of the riverside and dipped his hand into the frigid water.

"So, we shouldn't drink this?"

"It looks clean," Wiki said, "but anything that might harm us is invisible to the naked eye. We should boil it to be safe."

Liam filled his metal canteen to the brim, resisting the urge to chug it. The cold water looked refreshing, but the last thing he wanted was to get infected by some invisible parasite. He filled Wiki's bottle as well. They gathered wood, started a small fire, placed both bottles as close to it as possible, and waited.

"It's weird that we haven't run into anyone else yet," Liam said.

Wiki stared into the fire. "For all we know, they could be dead."

"Don't say that. We haven't found any bodies or debris."

Wiki sighed. "I'm just being realistic."

"More like depressing. There's no way we're the only survivors."

Wiki's gaze strayed from the fire and rested on Liam's face. "This isn't another day in the Earth Sim."

"You think I don't know that?"

"We were lucky to land in an open field. The others could have crashed into cliffs, sunk into the river, or—"

"Just stop. We need to stay positive."

Wiki shook his head. "It wasn't supposed to be like this."

The canteens boiled over, stopping the conversation. Liam scooped handfuls of river water into the fire to put it out. Shielding his skin with the corner of a blanket, he picked up the steaming canteens and buried them halfway in the mud so they could cool. When he returned his attention to Wiki, he saw moving water reflecting off still eyes.

"You okay?"

Wiki scoffed. "What do you think?"

"You look miserable."

Wiki poked the ashes with a stick. "The odds of this mission succeeding were low enough to begin with, and now—"

"Who cares about the mission?"

"Everyone but you."

Liam stood up and walked to the riverbank. It wasn't that he didn't care about the future of humankind. It just seemed like others were more capable, more willing to lead the charge.

"I just want to keep us alive long enough to find my sister and—"

"And what, Liam? Run away? Live the rest of our days out in the woods?"

Liam's temper flared. "You don't have to come if you don't want to."

"You're underestimating what Reagan is capable of. He spent centuries in and out of cryostasis planning this mission. Going against whatever he wants isn't going to be easy."

"The world's a big place," Liam said, looking over the water. "You worry too much."

"And you don't worry enough. You think Reagan will let you leave with Glo? That he'll let you disrupt the mission? You're a criminal, remember?"

"Maybe according to his rules. But here on Earth, I make my own rules."

Wiki kept speaking, but Liam managed to ignore it, focusing instead on a curious shape bobbing around upriver, reflecting the sunlight. He started walking up the riverbank toward the object.

"Where are you going?" Wiki said.

Liam quickened his pace as the object came into focus. King followed but couldn't keep up. The object almost blended in with the environment. It disappeared below the water and reappeared every few seconds. By the time Liam got close enough to see what it was, he no longer heard Wiki's voice. He removed his shoes and shirt then stepped into the shallows.

Wiki showed up moments later, breathing heavily. "What are you doing? Wait. Is that—"

"An ejector pod," Liam said. Heart pounding, he waded into the cold water. "Let's get it to shore."

"You don't even know how to swim."

Liam shrugged. "It can't be that hard."

"And you have no idea how heavy that thing is."

"I have to try."

The roar of the river drowned out Wiki's voice. When the water reached Liam's stomach, he shivered. The current threatened to knock him over, but he leaned against it and dug his bare feet into the muck below. Each step became more treacherous as he descended the slope of the riverbed.

He waded forward until the ejector pod floated only a couple of meters ahead. The current grew stronger, the water deeper. Liam took another step forward, but his foot failed to connect with the riverbed.

He toppled over, head sinking beneath the water, and lost his footing completely. Underwater, the buoyancy took some of the weight off him, giving him temporary relief from Earth's harsh gravity. He kicked off the bottom.

When his head broke the surface, he was surprised at how far the current had pushed him downstream. He paddled and kicked, a chaotic and desperate attempt to get closer to the ejector pod. Miraculously, it worked, but every time he got closer, the current erased his progress. Pace-wise, they were an even match. The only difference was that the river would never run out of stamina.

His head went below the water again. This time, he mistimed his inhalation and took in a mouthful of water. He sputtered and choked, swallowing some in the process.

So much for not drinking parasites, he thought.

The mistake brought him farther from the pod, and though he was beginning to understand the act of swimming, he didn't have much strength left to test that knowledge.

Still, he carried on, picking up his pace as much as possible. His elbow crashed painfully into a piece of driftwood, and the wounds on his leg burned in the wetness, but he kept swimming.

Almost out of breath, he saw his salvation. Beneath the dark water, the ejector pod's parachute undulated like some grotesque jellyfish.

Liam altered his course, dove, and reached for the parachute. He gripped the paracord in both hands and floated back to the surface, where he let his limbs rest and took in several soothing breaths of air. His muscles already burning from the exertion, he decided that he liked swimming. It was a full-body workout that had no match in Omega.

"You're insane," Wiki yelled.

Liam smiled and pulled himself closer to the ejector pod. With some struggle, he managed to get his body on top of it. Though it wobbled a bit, it seemed to be firmly stuck between two submerged boulders. He peered through the pod's silica strip, looking for signs of life.

"I doubt they survived," Wiki said, his voice distant. "It must be full of water by now."

Liam put his ear against the metal, tapped on it with his knuckles, and waited.

A response didn't come.

"Swim back," Wiki said after a minute or so.

"No," Liam said. "We have to be sure."

"What if they're dead?"

"Then we could use whatever supplies are inside."

"It's not worth the trouble."

"This could be Glo's pod!"

Wiki winced. "But—"

"We have to check, Wiki." Liam surveyed the situation, quickly deciding on a course of action. "Throw me a knife."

"What if I miss?" Wiki asked. "What if you miss?"

"We have two knives."

"Well, what if—"

"What if you stopped worrying for five seconds?" Liam stood, widened his stance, and spread his hands in preparation. "Either throw me a knife or swim one out to me."

Wiki glanced at the moving water, sighed, and pulled out his knife.

"Count of three," he said. "One, two, three."

The knife arced through the air, its blade flashing as it spun through beams of sunlight, until it landed in the water a meter or two in front of Liam.

Wiki groaned. "I told you—"

"Just try again," Liam said, frustrated about the loss but

determined to get the job done. "And put the sheath on it this time. You know, for safety reasons."

Wiki did as instructed. He usually did, but Liam tried not to abuse that fact too often.

"Don't think too much," Liam said. "You know what the gravity's like now. Your eye knows where it wants the knife to go. You've got this."

Wiki nodded. "Ready?"

"Yes," Liam said.

Wiki took a deep breath.

"One."

He drew his arm back.

"Two."

His muscles tensed.

"Three."

Wiki threw the knife harder this time. It soared above the water, barely spinning as it came closer to Liam, who reached both hands above his head—and caught it. After a silent celebration, he fished a length of paracord out of the water and cut it where it connected to the parachute. He pulled as hard as he could to test its connection to the pod, tied the knife onto the end, and tossed it back to Wiki. Then he dove into the water and swam back to the riverbank.

Water gushed from Liam's drenched pants when he stepped out of the water, then he slapped Wiki on the back and smiled. "Ready to haul it in?"

They had to pull from several different angles before they found one that made the ejector pod budge. After that, it was a matter of strength and stamina, two things Wiki lacked. Sweating profusely, he let go of the paracord and dropped to the ground.

"I give up," he said.

"No, you don't."

"It's hard enough for me to stand right now."

"We'll take a break, then." Liam joined Wiki on the ground and took a sip of water. "What are the odds that Glo is in this pod?"

"I don't want to think about that."

"If she's in there, if she's alive, just think how grateful she'll be that you saved her life. She might even—"

"I know what you're trying to do."

Liam shrugged. "Is it working?"

The fact that Wiki had a crush on Glo had been an undeniable truth for as long as Liam could remember. As a young child, Wiki would follow her around and do whatever she asked him to do, often to Liam's amusement. Liam didn't love manipulating Wiki, but potentially saving Glo's life called for pulling his heartstrings.

"Unfortunately," Wiki said, rising to stand, "it is working."

•|•

The ejector pod didn't make it to land, but Liam and Wiki did manage to drag it into the shallows, where they could take a closer look. At least half of it had filled with water through some leak they couldn't find.

"We didn't think this through," Wiki said, one hand on his chin.

"Why?"

"Because these things only open from the inside."

"We'll see about that."

Liam found the outline of the hatch. He managed to wedge the tip of his knife between the threshold and the door. Then he pulled hard, trying to pry it open. His efforts only snapped the end of the blade off.

"I told you," Wiki said. "And now you broke our only knife."

Frustrated, Liam stormed upstream and found the largest rock he could carry. He brought it back to the pod, raised it above his head.

"What are you—"

The sound of stone hitting metal rang through the valley. The hatch dented but didn't open, so Liam tried again—and again—and again. Sweat poured from his temples and dripped into the water.

"Stop!" Wiki yelled.

Arms exhausted, Liam raised the rock as high as he could, preparing to smash the door in once and for all. But as he was about to release the final blow, something stopped him. The hatch door moved, up and down, just barely. It slowly tilted open, revealing a terrified but familiar face.

15

SHIPWRECK

Zara squinted in the bright light as Liam pulled her through the hatch. Once on the riverbank, she shivered, her clothing drenched. Her round face looked sickly, as if she might vomit at any second.

"Are you hurt?" Liam asked.

"Water," she croaked. "Please."

He brought her to a patch of grass, sat her down, and handed her his bottle, which she put to her lips with shaking hands before chugging the entire thing. They would have to boil more soon. Wiki came from the pod toting a pair of backpacks, his lips set in a straight line.

"Zara," he said gently. "The other girl in the pod, she's—"

"Dead." Zara spoke in a monotone voice. "She hit her head when we crashed."

"How is that even possible?" Liam said. "We had neck braces."

Zara scanned the alien landscape. "How is anything possible?" she asked, her voice nearly a whisper.

For a moment, Liam wondered if she had hit her head too, the way she stared dreamily at everything she saw. Just then, King sprinted out of the forest, straight toward her. She screamed and scrambled to get away.

"It's okay," Liam said. He dove to catch King before he could touch her. "He's friendly."

Zara nodded but didn't speak. She seemed more alert, as if the scare had snapped her out of her daze. Liam figured that spending a day in close quarters with a dead body had consequences.

"Where is everyone?" she asked. Wiki and Liam looked at each other and hesitated, silently deciding who would break the bad news. "Everyone's dead, aren't they?"

"We don't know," Liam said. "We were on our way to the shipwreck when we found your pod."

"Thank you," she said. "For finding me. I thought— Well, for a while, I thought I was dead. I tried to get out, but the water"—she drew in a sharp breath—"the water, it came so fast, and it was dark. So dark. I—"

"It's okay," Wiki said. He put a hand on her shoulder. "You're safe now."

"I would have died. I would have"—she hugged Wiki so tightly that Liam thought he might snap in half—"You saved my life."

"No, it was all—"

"We should go," Liam said, already gathering his things. He threw Zara a blanket.

"What about"—Wiki gestured toward the pod—"What was her name?"

"Nova." Zara sniffled. "She was nice."

"We should"—Wiki gulped—"We should bury her, shouldn't we? We can't just leave her here."

"We have to go," Liam said.

"But you said—"

"I know what I said, but half the day is gone already, and we can't be out here at night again."

"It just seems wrong," Wiki said. "To leave her body here."

Liam knew what Wiki meant. The last dead bodies they left out overnight—the cougar, the deer—had likely ended up as food for whatever else lurked in the forest. Still, he didn't need to waste any more time.

"We can come back for her. For now, we'll close the hatch, so she doesn't"—he hesitated, unsure whether Zara could handle any more trauma—"Never mind."

"So she doesn't what?" Zara asked.

"Nothing," Liam said. "It's nothing."

"Tell me."

"I don't think you—"

"Just tell me what's going on, Liam. I can handle it."

"Fine," he said, marching over to the pod. "So she doesn't get eaten."

Zara remained silent. Without looking inside the ejector pod, Liam slammed the battered hatch shut.

•|•

Despite Zara's slow pace, they made it to a ridge overlooking the shipwreck in about an hour. Debris littered a clearing burnt into the forest, where embers still smoldered among the blackness. Peering down at the wreckage, Liam doubted they would find anything useful. Still, he led their descent into the wasteland. They wound their way through twisted spires of metal that poked out of the ground at odd angles, toward a large, cylindrical object that leaned slightly to one side.

"If there's anything useful here," he said, "it's inside that."

"There's no one here," Zara said. "I thought—"

"There's no one here *yet*." Liam sidestepped to avoid a burning log. He carried King in his arms. "They'll come."

"We were the last to eject," Wiki said. "Everyone else might have landed farther out."

The smell of burnt wood invaded Liam's nostrils, which made him salivate for some reason. "Is it weird that this is making me hungry?"

"Hiking?" Wiki asked.

"No, the smell. The smoke."

Wiki inhaled. "Our distant ancestors would have associated the smell of burning wood with dinnertime. It meant something was cooking."

Liam smiled, thinking about all the novel experiences he had enjoyed over the last day. "We missed out on a lot up there," he said, glancing at the sky.

"We did."

"Have you seen the moon yet?" Zara asked. "From down here, I mean."

"I did," Wiki said. "Last night. It seems so far away now. Almost like we were never there. Like it was a dream or something."

Zara sighed. "I always wanted to come to Earth, but I never really thought about what I'd be leaving behind. When I was stuck in that pod, my family was all I could think about."

Guilt bubbled up in Liam's chest, threatening to boil over. It dawned on him that he had forgotten to say goodbye to his mother before stowing away. He wanted to change the subject, anything to avoid that heart-nagging feeling.

"What part of the ship do you think this is?" he asked as they arrived beside the cylinder.

Wiki examined it. "It doesn't look wide enough to be part of the hull."

"I thought you had the schematics memorized or something."

"I do, but that's hardly helpful with the ship ripped apart." Wiki walked around the object, which was about two meters across in the middle and twice as tall. "It looks like a tank, maybe a fuel tank?"

Liam rapped it with his knuckles. "Why didn't it blow up?"

Zara plopped down into the dirt and leaned against the tank. "While you guys figure it out, I'm going to take a break."

"We should wait here anyway," Wiki said. He dropped his pack to the ground. "Good visibility. Nothing can sneak up on us."

Already, the sun was beginning to set behind the monolithic peaks and vibrant hillsides that towered in all directions. Wherever they were, Liam thought, this valley had to be among the most beautiful places on Earth. He set King down and cleared a place to sit.

"I guess we're camping here tonight."

•|•

Gathered around a fire started from the embers of the crash site, Liam, Wiki, and Zara slurped down tubes of bland algae paste. They sat silently, ears trained on the surrounding wilderness. Moonlight illuminated the sky, creating silhouettes of the landscape in all directions.

"Disgusting," Liam said.

He offered King his leftovers. The cat sniffed the algae but refused to eat it. Liam threw the tube into the fire, silently promising to find something better for them to eat in the morning—maybe a fish or a turtle, something easy to catch.

"We should sleep in shifts," he said. "Take turns keeping a lookout. And keep the fire going."

"I don't know," Wiki said. "A fire will put a spotlight on us."

"Would you rather sleep in the cold?"

"If it means waking up in the morning, then yes."

"I think we'll be okay." Liam yawned. "So, who's taking the first watch?"

"I can," Zara said. She wore her blanket like a hooded robe, the firelight casting eerie shadows on her face. "I don't think I'll be able to sleep out here. It's too strange. Too open."

"Great," Liam said, lying as close to the fire as he could without burning himself. "Wake me up in a few hours?"

Exhausted from spending over a day fighting Earth's gravity, Liam stopped resisting and quickly sank into a deep sleep.

•|•

A strange sound tore Liam from his slumber. The first thing he observed was that the fire no longer burned beside him. Then he noticed the silence, a stillness so complete it seemed manufactured. Whatever it was, the source of the sound had been muted abruptly, as if a switch had been flipped.

He scanned the area. Clouds now covered the moon, ushering in near-total darkness, a land of shadows. Then all at once, the stillness vaporized. Some of the shadows danced.

"Who's there?" Liam asked.

Wiki snored nearby, but Zara was no longer at her post.

"Z," Liam said. "Are you out there?"

The shadows stopped moving, and Liam examined the fire pit. He held his hand over the ashes and dead charcoal but felt no residual heat. He touched a piece of charcoal, which was not only cold but wet. The fire hadn't burned out in the night. Someone had put it out.

"Wiki," he said. "Wake up."

Wiki groaned. "What is it?"

"Zara. She's gone."

"Gone?" Wiki sat up. "She probably just went to pee or something."

"Why would she put out the fire first?"

Wiki glanced at the ashes. "I don't know, safety?"

"I'm going to look for her." Liam gripped his knife. "You coming?"

"Yeah," Wiki said.

A gust of night-chilled wind nipped at Liam's ears as he crept into the darkness. He walked blindly, avoiding debris by touch alone. The lack of light played tricks on his mind. The calls of insects and nocturnal birds filled the soundscape, but Liam heard something else there too—footsteps. He came to a sudden stop, and Wiki slammed into him.

"What are you—"

Liam shushed his friend and listened more closely. The footsteps ceased, replaced with whispers that he couldn't comprehend—not because they were too quiet, but because the words made no sense, like they weren't words at all.

"Zara?" Liam said. "Are you there?"

As if summoned by Liam's voice, shafts of moonlight spilled out from fissures in the dark clouds, bathing the scene in monochromatic light. The sight ahead made Liam gasp and grip his knife a little tighter. Among the burnt wreckage stood Zara, her face bent in terror, a rugged blade pressed against her neck, and a dark hand cupped over her mouth.

16

SUBHUMANS

Glo lay on her bedding, battling the restlessness that had plagued her since her arrival at Camp Resurgence a day earlier. The first glimmers of daylight were beginning to brighten the sky. All but the earliest risers still slept in the tightly packed rows that made up the center of the camp.

Unable to relax any longer, Glo rolled out of bed and trod lightly through the camp, careful not to step on anyone. When she passed Reagan's tent, the only completed shelter in camp except for the infirmary, she softened her footsteps. She had been able to avoid Reagan since her arrival, and she intended to keep it that way.

In less than twenty-four hours, the camp had already evolved dramatically. Under Killion's command, the chaotic shambles had transformed into an organized encampment, complete with communal latrines, a central square for meetings, and a secure perimeter made of fallen trees. Wooden cots and tents made of parachutes were also being built to make the sleeping arrangements more comfortable.

There would be plenty more work to do, but first, Glo wanted information. She walked over to the camp's designated entrance, where Tai sat on a stump, keeping watch, his muscles tense for seemingly no reason at all.

"Morning," she said.

Tai nodded, but his gaze never left the tree line.

When it became clear that he wouldn't reply, Glo said, "Any news?"

"Negative," he said.

Glo sighed. Scouting party after scouting party had trickled into camp throughout the previous day, most bringing back no news, the rest carrying bodies—or pieces of bodies. The thought of her brother coming back like that made Glo sick. Somewhere out there, one group still searched the valley, her only hope of finding Liam and Wiki. Frustrated, she made her way to the infirmary tent to care for the wounded, anything to pass the time.

•|•

"How's your ankle?"

Glo knelt beside Quinn and pulled her blanket up to take a look.

"You tell me, Doc."

Glo laughed. "I'm no doctor."

The real doctor was still missing. Probably dead.

"How did you get so good at this stuff, then?"

Glo gently squeezed the swollen flesh surrounding Quinn's ankle. "I spent a lot of time in the infirmary growing up. You can learn a lot by watching."

"You were sick?"

"My mom," Glo said, and it took everything in her to hold back a flood of emotion. "It was the radiation."

Quinn nodded. "I'm sorry. Is she—"

"Not yet," Glo said, though she honestly had no idea if her mother still lived. She made a mental note to ask someone about the state of the communication systems.

"Do you think Nikolai will come see me today?"

"He's a busy man," Glo said.

"And your brother?"

"Still missing." Glo pulled the blanket back over Quinn's feet. "Your ankle doesn't look any worse. You should probably take it easy for a few days and only walk when you have to, but it should heal fine on its own."

Quinn rolled over and came onto all fours, then she rose to a standing position.

"Didn't I just say to take it easy?" Glo said.

Quinn tested her ankle by shifting some weight onto it. "You also said I can walk when I have to."

"Oh yeah? And what do you have to do? You haven't been assigned a job yet."

Quinn beamed. "I'm going to look for Nikolai."

"I really wish—"

"I know how you feel about us," Quinn said. "But I'm basically an adult, so I don't really have to listen to you. You really need to relax. I just want to say hello."

"Fine." Glo folded her arms. "But I'm coming with you."

Quinn groaned. "I don't need a chaperone, Glo."

"And I don't want to babysit you." Glo followed Quinn out of the tent. "I need to talk to him, too."

•|•

They found Commander Killion outside the walls. He stood, arms folded, overseeing a group of young men unloading cases from a crate. As Glo and Quinn passed, a few of the boys stared, filthy where the dirt clung to their sweat. Nothing stayed clean in the forest.

"Nikolai," Quinn said, her voice electrified with excitement.

Quinn limped over and pulled him into a tight hug. Dark stubble had formed on his chin, making the age gap between him and Quinn more pronounced.

"Good to see you walking around," he said.

"What are you working on?"

"Taking stock of our supplies. One of the search parties came back with the rest of the guns this morning."

"Need any help?"

"Are you trained to handle weapons?"

"Not yet," she said. "Teach me?"

He grinned. "Maybe another time. Shouldn't you be resting?"

"I can't stay still. Put me to work?"

Glo rocked her weight from side to side as she listened to their conversation. After a few moments of meaningless chatter, she decided to interrupt.

"Commander," she said.

He dipped his head in greeting. "Miss Stone."

"The search parties," she said. "They still haven't found my brother."

"I'm well aware."

"Of course." The conversation started to make Glo sweat, and she didn't know why. "I was just wondering if there's anything I can do to help."

"You can tend to the wounded, as you were assigned."

"But—"

"The team I sent out there is entirely capable of locating the survivors…on their own. I told you, if he's out there, we'll find him."

"I'd like to go out with the next search party."

Killion laughed, a sound that might have seemed charming in any other situation, but at that moment, it reeked of condescension.

"What's so funny?" Glo asked.

"You're not allowed to leave camp. Not without a proper escort, at least."

"Why can't she?" Quinn asked. "We're outside camp right now."

"Not just her," he said. "None of the women can leave camp. Reagan's orders. You're all too valuable. Without surrogates, this entire mission fails. Besides, it's much safer inside the walls."

Once again, Glo felt like an object designed for men to use. Her existence had been reduced from *woman* to *surrogate.* No matter what Killion said, she didn't feel safe locked in a cage with men like him and Reagan. Instead of letting this anger her, though, she tried to use it in her favor.

"And what good is my womb without the biorepository? It's still out there, too."

Killion's smile relaxed into an emotionless line. "We're working on it."

"Without it, we'll have nothing but a colony of inbreds as our legacy. You know that."

"Yes, I'm—"

"And you know the fuel cells won't last much longer. I should be out there looking for it."

"Get back to the infirmary," Killion said sternly. "You too, Quinn."

"But—"

"That's an order. These boys are easily distracted."

Quinn saluted, barely concealing her sarcastic tone as she said, "Yes, sir."

Too angry to speak, Glo shook her head. She couldn't believe Killion's resistance to even acknowledging her argument. Why wouldn't he listen? Why didn't men ever listen?

As she turned to leave, motion beyond the tree line caught her attention, a flash of black slipping in and out of sight between tree trunks. Killion traced Glo's gaze until he saw what she saw.

"What is that?" Glo asked.

"Get inside," Killion said. "Now!"

Glo froze, unable to look away from whatever it was that approached. She squinted until it came into focus—a person running, not at a relaxed pace like someone exercising, but with the frantic, terrified gait of someone being chased. And by the look on the man's face, the way he flailed his arms, the tattered clothes that hung around his lean frame—whatever chased him was terrifying.

Killion knelt beside one of the crates and pulled a large plastic case out. He set it on the ground, fumbled with a pair of latches until the case opened.

In the distance, the running man tripped over a root and fell hard on his elbows. Struggling to get back up, he screamed—a sound that made Glo's heart race.

She gasped. "Help him!"

Killion picked up two parts of a plasma rifle, put them together, and twisted. When the mechanisms clicked into place, he raised the barrel and held the butt against his shoulder. Ionic gases churned in the rifle's tank, preparing for release, glowing softly through transparent stripes of glass.

More people came out of the forest. Glo immediately noticed that something seemed off about them. They stood over two meters tall and ran with their backs hunched, their hands nearly reaching the ground at the end of arms that looked far too long. Instead of clothes, they had shaggy hair covering large portions of their bodies. Even from afar, Glo could see their strength—muscled and scarred arms outstretched to catch the running man, to pull him toward their gaping mouths.

"Oh no," Glo said under her breath.

Throaty growls accompanied the running man's cries for help.

"Get inside!" Killion yelled again.

Terror froze Glo in place. In a daze of fear, she counted three subs, at least two of which appeared male. The third one looked more androgynous. They tumbled forward, a storm of limbs and teeth. The distance between them and their prey shrank quickly. Limping forward, the running man tried to outpace them, but his situation didn't look hopeful.

Killion aimed and squeezed the trigger. A bolt of plasma fired silently, hit one of the subs, and burned a hole straight through its chest. It screeched its last breath, crumpled to the ground, and spasmed violently before falling still. The others barely glanced at their fallen brother as they advanced.

One of the boys fired his weapon but missed. Vaporized by the plasma bolt, branches fell from trees. Puffs of steam rose into the air. The smell of ozone singed Glo's nostrils.

The remaining subs caught up to the man and pounced on him. They broke his neck so quickly that he didn't even have time to scream, but Glo couldn't look away. She expected them to start devouring him like they would in the simulations. Instead, they leaped over the body and continued running toward the camp.

Killion fired his rifle again, which vaporized an ear and a large chunk of flesh off the side of a monstrous head. Another bolt of plasma tore one of the sub's arms off at the elbow, but neither injury slowed its pace. It stormed forward.

Glo reached into the crate and found a small case, which she quickly opened. The plasma pistol heated her hand as it charged.

Killion fired again. Blasted through the torso, the wounded sub fell to the ground. Half-cooked guts oozed out of a fist-sized hole in its stomach.

Ten meters from the wall, the last sub stopped running. It stood taller, turned its nose toward the sky, and sniffed the air. The wild, ravenous look on its face transformed into something more intelligent—anger. Perhaps sensing that it stood no chance of surviving, it backed up and straightened its spine. For a moment, it looked frighteningly human.

Glo released her finger from the trigger. She dropped the pistol to her side and hid it in her waistband.

"Someone shoot it!" Killion yelled, his rifle still recharging.

Several plasma bolts shot through the air. The sub twisted and ducked, blood-blackened teeth gnashing. Crouching in the undergrowth, it jerked its head toward camp, revealing a bloody stripe from chin to forehead.

A pained howl escaped the sub's mouth before it vanished into the forest.

17

MOON PEOPLE

Despite the threatening postures of the men surrounding Zara, Liam couldn't help but marvel at their existence. The fact that human beings stood before him completely shattered his understanding of reality. Save for a small city on the moon, humankind had perished centuries earlier. At least that was what he had been told his entire life. Speechless, he stared at the impossibilities before him.

He counted four of them. Even in the darkness, he could tell they had skin a few shades darker than his own, and that they stood several centimeters shorter than he did. They wore robes made of animal fur and held weapons of strange design, with rough metallic blades and handles made of wood. The blade pressed against Zara's neck had a dramatic, hook-like curve to it.

Two of the men approached Liam and Wiki, their blades glistening in the moonlight. Liam backed up a few paces. His ankle collided with something hard, and he fell to the ground, losing his knife in the darkness. Terrified, he searched for his weapon, gripping handfuls of dirt and charcoal.

One of the men came closer. He wore similar furs to the others, but with the addition of a hood. A multitude of antlers and bones were interlaced over the hood, creating a crude armored helmet. He wore a necklace of canine teeth around his neck. Up close, Liam saw deep wrinkles carved into the man's face. He frowned, which accentuated his wrinkles even further, and he raised his blade.

"Stop," Liam begged. "Just stop. I can—"

The wooden end of the man's weapon smacked Liam on the side of the head, just hard enough to silence him without breaking skin. Liam put his arms up to block his face, but the man didn't attack again. He stared at Liam, his face revealing not even a hint of emotion.

"Who are you? How is this—"

The blunt wood hit Liam's skull harder this time. The man held a single finger up to his lips. Liam wanted to scream, but he didn't try to speak again. He looked over at Wiki, who wasn't bothering to struggle against the large man tying his wrists. King hissed as a different man picked him up by the scruff of the neck and threw him into a leather bag.

His head now aching, Liam knew there would be no fighting these natives, whoever they were.

His attention returned to the hooded man, who did something he didn't expect. The man's lips curved upward, revealing a smile that lacked more than a few teeth. He reached forward and offered Liam a withered yet strong hand. Hesitantly, Liam let the stranger help him up.

Then the man looked over Liam's shoulder and nodded. In a flash of motion, something came over Liam's head and shrouded him in darkness.

•|•

For hours, Liam marched blindly, his wrists bound in front of his body so one of the strange men could lead him. Foliage tickled his bruised and bloody skin. He followed silently because every attempt to speak ended with a blunt object hitting his head.

The blindfold ruined his balance, making it hard to walk in a straight line, but the procession never slowed. Even when the landscape began to slope upward, his captors kept a brutal pace. Eventually, the incline doubled in intensity before turning into stone steps, each tread a different height.

Liam did his best to keep up, every step up the never-ending staircase pure agony. He tripped several times, banged his knees on stone. The exertion destroyed his leg muscles. Bolstered by the dark hood over his face, sleep tugged at his eyelids. He wanted nothing more than to rest, to have some time to process everything. Where were these people taking him? And who were they?

Though he had seen them briefly with his own eyes, he still couldn't believe there were humans living on Earth. But there they were, living proof that the Terminal Plague hadn't been so terminal after all.

How have these people been able to survive what no one else could?

With this question repeating in Liam's head, he carried on. Up they went until the sunlight warmed his skin and the terrain leveled out. He heard rough waters rumbling in the distance. His captors ended the strict silence and began to speak to one another.

Their language sounded like nothing Liam had ever heard. They spoke a gentle tongue, some of the consonants softened, and others almost entirely muted. Some words sounded vaguely familiar, as if the pronunciations had been warped by time, but none of them made sense. Though he couldn't understand the meaning of their speech, their tone sounded tense, as if they were arguing— deciding his fate.

Had they walked him up a mountain just to throw him off? Would they cut his neck open with one of those jagged blades? Make him a slave? He had no way of knowing what might happen to him and his friends, which frustrated him more than anything.

Liam didn't remember seeing a woman in the group that captured him, but a female voice entered the discussion. She spoke frantically, in quick, choppy sentences, repeating the same thing over and over. After a few minutes, the conversation came to an abrupt end.

Someone yanked the shroud off Liam's head. When his pupils adjusted to the harsh light, he saw Wiki and Zara beside him. They looked exhausted. Wiki stared ahead in wonder while Zara lay on the floor, breathing heavily.

A small crowd surrounded them. They watched the newcomers curiously. In the daylight, they appeared even more foreign to Liam. Everything about them—their clothes, their hairstyles, the way they stood—was wild and strange. They all looked strong, but it wasn't only their lean and well-fed muscles that signified this strength. Each of their expressions had a steely edge, like they were ready to face anything.

Beyond the crowd stood row upon row of single-story buildings, each one a different size and shape. Some were made of wood, others of stone. The rows continued up a steep incline, with many dwellings built directly into the cliffside. The village looked like it could house hundreds, maybe a thousand people. Humankind wasn't just surviving here. It was thriving. Head shaking, Liam returned his attention to the crowd.

"Hi," he said, putting more emphasis on his tone than the word itself. He mentally prepared for a stick to smack his head, but it never came. "My name is Liam."

He looked from face to face, searching for any sign that they understood him—if not his words, then at least his intention to greet them. Where he didn't see curiosity, he saw pure confusion.

"Liam," he said, touching his chest.

He scanned the crowd again until his gaze settled on a young woman, maybe a little older than his sister. She wore a short dress composed of small fur squares stitched together. Her dark hair hung in tight curls, kissing her bare shoulders. Her head tilted to the side, and the skin around her brown eyes tightened. She approached until she stood less than a meter from Liam, paused for a breath, then reached forward and poked his chest.

"Liam," she said.

"Yes," Liam said.

She put a hand on her chest and said, "Skai."

Liam smiled. The man with the antler hood hovered behind Skai. He appeared much older in the daylight, his skin ravaged by time and too much sunlight. Skai turned to him, and they had a brief conversation in their language, their tones argumentative. Then she pulled a small dagger from somewhere beneath her clothes.

Liam recoiled when she came forward. Surrounded, he had nowhere to run.

"Wait." He backed up and nearly tripped over his own feet. "I mean no harm."

She smiled, then glanced at the ropes binding Liam's wrists.

"Oh."

Skai cut the ropes, freeing him from his restraints. Liam shook his wrists and bowed his head. Others came forward to cut Wiki and Zara loose. The old man shouted a single word, and the crowd parted to create a path toward the buildings behind them.

"You speak the old language," Skai said, her voice soft and low. The words rolled off her tongue slowly, carefully. She beckoned Liam and his friends toward the path. "Come, moon people. There is much to tell."

Speechless, they followed.

•|•

They walked on narrow streets between buildings. Children roamed the area, playing games that Liam didn't understand while their parents stared through glassless windows.

Smoke rose from some of the buildings, carrying the scent of cooked meat. Liam's stomach growled. The scarce meal of algae paste from the night before had long since burned up during the hike. He needed food and sleep—in that order—but curiosity kept him from complaining.

"Skai," Wiki said, walking beside her. "How do you know our language?"

Skai sidestepped to avoid stepping on some kind of domesticated bird pecking at the dirt. "It is my choice to know."

"I mean, how did you learn it?"

"Someone taught," she said, as if it were obvious. "I learn."

We're lucky she did, Liam thought.

"Do you have books?" Wiki touched his palms together and hinged them open.

"You ask many questions. A busy mouth."

"Sorry," he said.

"Eat more." She looked down at his thin legs. "Talk less."

"Good advice," Liam said. "You should listen to her."

Wiki blushed. "We didn't think that anyone survived the plague. I'm curious how you did it. That's all."

"Answer questions." Skai gestured toward a doorway that led into one of the larger buildings with red clay walls. "Then ask."

They followed Skai inside. A fire crackled in the corner, its smoke rising through a narrow gap in the ceiling. Sunlight spilled through multiple high windows of various sizes, each no bigger than a person's head. The room smelled like smoke and earth.

The old man settled into a seat built of stacked stone, then he waved his arm toward a scattered semi-circle of tree trunks that stood on the perimeter of a woven rug in the center of the room.

"Sit," Skai said.

She didn't need to tell Liam twice. Even the hard surface felt comfortable after hiking for so long. Sitting there with his legs throbbing, he thought he might never stand again. Once everyone had a seat, the old man spoke.

"Greetings, moon people," Skai translated. "I am Fang, leader of this people. We are called the Suvi."

Liam bowed his head because he didn't know what else to do. He hoped that the gesture didn't mean something offensive in the Suvi culture. Fang didn't seem to notice Liam's hesitance.

"There was a world before this world. Countless peoples once lived beneath the sky. They tamed the wildness and built cities as tall as mountains. Do you know this truth?"

Liam and Wiki nodded while Zara stared at the rug. With a calmness bordering on reverence, Skai continued to translate the conversation.

"When the wildness returned, it destroyed everything. Cities crumbled, and ghouls now rule the ruins."

"Subs," Liam whispered.

"I know stories of people who fled to the sky, who left everyone to die. Legends. Myths. I never dreamed the moon people would return." Liam detected a hint of anger shifting Fang's wrinkles into a less-than-inviting expression. "Yet, here you are."

"How did your people survive?" Wiki asked.

Skai ignored his question and continued her solemn translation.

"Your arrival has caused much trouble. Great herds of ghouls wander from the highlands. They follow the thunder of your arrival."

The crash, Liam thought.

"The Suvi cleared the valley below long ago. Our ancestors killed every ghoul, slew every giant. They made it safe there. But it is safe no longer."

Liam took some time to process everything the man said. How bad could it be out there? He thought he knew what Fang meant by ghouls, but giants? He had so many questions.

"You did this," Skai translated. "Brought this upon us."

Whether that was true or not, Liam didn't want to test the patience—or the violence—of his hosts.

"We can fix it," Liam said. "My people. The moon people. We have weapons."

"There are more of you in the valley?" Skai asked, now speaking directly to Liam instead of translating.

"I don't know where the others are. But if you help us find them—"

"We cannot help you. The valley is too dangerous now. We must wait, and the Watchers must see."

"But—"

"No," Skai said sternly.

Liam sighed. "We'll find them on our own, then."

"It is forbidden," Skai said.

"What? Are we prisoners?"

"Obviously," Wiki said.

Skai tilted her head to the side, which made her hair bounce. "Only the strong may descend to the valley. You are too weak. You will die."

"I'm not weak," Liam said, even though the way his body felt contradicted those words. "I killed a cougar with my bare hands."

"Kind of," Wiki said.

Skai raised an eyebrow. "What is cougar?"

"I don't know, like a big cat."

Liam made a claw-like gesture and hissed. He felt ridiculous, but he didn't know how else to get the message across.

Skai giggled. "I see. So, it was you who killed the lion?"

"That's right," Liam said. "It was easy."

"Lion Slayer," Skai said. "A good start, but lions are not all you should fear. Lions can be tamed. Lions are small. Lions hunt alone. There is much you need to learn."

"Will you teach us?" Wiki said.

Skai smiled. "Now, you ask the right questions."

"We can't just sit here and take notes," Liam said. "We need to find Glo."

"I'm not doing anything until I sleep." Wiki yawned. "They won't let us leave, anyway."

"That's right." Skai walked toward the exit. "Now come. Fang wants me to show you something."

•|•

Skai led Liam, Wiki, and Zara out of the village to a grassy field, where the shadow of a mountain covered the landscape like a blanket. As he walked, Liam swept his hand across the tallest blades of grass, felt a light breeze on his skin. The place was so tranquil. He wanted to lie down and sleep there.

"Will this take long?" he said.

Zara yawned. "I hope not."

"We are almost there," Skai said.

Minutes later, they approached what Liam could only describe as a pen, a roughly square piece of land enclosed by a wooden fence. But in the middle of that square, he didn't see sheep or goats or chickens. There was no grass there, either. Just a hole carved into the earth, so deep that he couldn't see the bottom from his vantage point.

"What is—"

Skai shushed him, then she touched one ear with her finger. Liam listened but heard only wind and bird songs. He closed his eyes and attempted to focus on the sounds hiding beneath the others. Then he heard it—a low rumbling coming from the pit. The sound grew in volume until it came to a peak, then stopped altogether.

Skai smiled mischievously and crept forward. She opened a gate into the enclosure and beckoned the others to follow. Curious, Liam glanced over the edge of the pit. At first, he thought he saw nothing—just muddy ground and an enormous pile of dirt in the center of the pit. But as the mound of earth rose, the rumbling came again, and Liam noticed that it wasn't a featureless lump after all. It was alive. Zara gasped at the sight.

"No way," Liam whispered.

Focusing beyond the odd proportions, he saw a leg as thick as a tree trunk, a pair of arms as long as his own legs, and a head like a boulder—all caked with layers of dirt. Long hair surrounded the sleeping giant's head, soaking in the mud. Only then did Liam understand the rumbling sound. The giant was snoring.

"How is this possible?" Wiki said.

Liam stared, marveling at the sheer improbability of the lifeform sleeping at the bottom of the pit. It was maybe three meters tall, definitely male, and had muscles like iron. How many generations of the infected had it taken to produce such a monstrosity of virus-aided evolution?

The giant snored again, and Skai pulled something out of her satchel. The smell hit Liam before he realized what she held. Skai swung the dead fish once, twice, then tossed it into the pit, where it hit the giant's belly with a thud. Bending into a sitting position, the giant reacted faster than something of his size should—not violently, but quickly nonetheless.

Adrenaline heated Liam's skin. Skai hadn't been kidding about cougars being the least of his worries. This beast could snap him in half if he got close enough, swallow him in chunks if he chose to—with room for a second helping. It felt wrong to be standing so close to such a wild creature.

The giant looked directly at him, but where Liam expected to see ferocity, he saw only boredom, a passing glance at the people who brought him food. The giant crunched down the fish, bones and all, then Skai tossed him another.

"Why keep him here?" Liam asked.

"Fang believes he can be tamed."

Liam almost laughed, but it came out as a short burst of air. "How's that going?"

"He is less angry than before."

Wiki came to stand beside them. "How did you catch him?"

Skai threw more food into the pit. "Many fishes," she said.

Liam laughed this time. It felt like he was dreaming. He always knew he would encounter strange things on Earth, but he never expected to be standing next to an Earthborn human at the edge of a giant trap.

When the last fish left Skai's bag, she turned to leave.

"Come," she said. "You are tired and hungry."

"Truer words have never been spoken," Wiki said.

In a daze, Liam lingered at the edge of the pit and stared at the behemoth below.

18

TEN AND SEVEN WINTERS

Skai brought Liam, Wiki, and Zara back to the village. Zara hadn't spoken much since their abduction, and that trend continued throughout the short hike. Liam chalked it up to fear and exhaustion, but every time he looked at her, she had a vacant, foggy look in her eyes. Perhaps she was still reliving those twenty-four hours in the ejector pod? He didn't bother asking.

On the other hand, Wiki seemed delighted. Somehow, he had managed to keep his wearables on him during their abduction. Throughout their walk, he occasionally tapped out notes on his thighs and took photos with his over-ear camera, but he mostly observed and asked Skai every question that came to his mind.

"Are there other people out there?" he asked once they settled down beside some kind of outdoor kitchen. "People like you?"

Skai sat cross-legged across from him.

"I don't know." She frowned. "Fang once told stories about other villages, but getting to them is too dangerous now. No one has left the valley in my lifetime."

"How old are you, anyway?" Liam asked.

Skai had a youthful face, but everything else about her seemed more mature—her attitude, her voice, the authority she clearly had. At that moment, though, she did something extremely childish. She started counting on her fingers, biting her lip as she did so.

When she finished, she said, "I have lived ten and seven winters."

The moon didn't have winters, but Liam said, "So have I."

Skai smiled, a beautiful sight. "We are the same."

"We are," he said, knowing that they actually couldn't be more different.

Skai's was a completely different world, a world that Liam had only experienced in dreams and simulations. It was a place much stranger and far more magnificent than he could have ever imagined.

Liam closed his eyes for a moment and thought about his old home. A barren grayness filled his mind—cold, hostile, uninviting. The moon had never been and would never be a place for humans. The city of Omega was fighting a constant uphill battle against nature. Eventually, it would lose. Everyone knew this, but no one wanted to admit it.

When Liam opened his eyes, he saw color—the reds and browns of buildings, gradients of blue and purple and white in the sky, and flashes of greenery swaying in the wind. Natural and manmade beauty struck him everywhere he looked, flowing seamlessly, one into the other. The Suvi were people of the Earth, and this fact was reflected in their architecture, their clothes, even their attitudes.

Soon the smell of food drew Liam's attention away from his silent observations. His mouth watered. Something sizzled on a sheet of metal suspended above open flames. A shirtless man brought over a platter of food and set it in the middle of the group. Skai said something to him in her language. Then the man sat down among them.

Liam smiled at him, and he smiled back. He had no hair, and his two front teeth were missing. Liam bowed his head. He didn't need verbal language to say thank you.

"Eat." Skai gestured toward the platter then looked at Wiki. "Especially you."

Zara snapped out of her daze and eyed the steaming sustenance. "What is all this?"

Liam didn't have words for each ingredient. None of these vegetables grew in Omega, and he had no way of telling what kind of meat he smelled. He just knew it all looked delicious—more than just edible.

"It is a feast to welcome you," Skai said. She reached forward and grabbed a chunk of meat right off the bone. "It will make you stronger."

Liam's hunger didn't require further explanation. He picked up a piece of something orange and put it in his mouth. It had a soft consistency and tasted sweet and earthy, even better than the deer meat he had the other day. The flavor touched on his sense of taste, exploring unknown depths, activating tastebuds that had never been used back home.

"You have to try that," he said to Wiki, his mouth full. "Wow."

They dug in, sampling everything on the platter and relishing all of it. Liam was so consumed by hunger, it took him a few minutes to notice that Zara wasn't eating. She sat there, staring into the distance.

"You good?" Liam asked.

She glanced at the meal and shrugged. "Do we have any more algae paste?"

"It's back at the crash site," Liam said between bites. "Believe me, this is much better. Try some."

"Honestly, I'm kind of afraid to eat it."

"Seriously?" Liam scoffed. "More for me, I guess."

Liam returned to the feast. The diversity of the food amazed him. Everything had a distinct and interesting flavor and texture—nothing like the unvarying Omegan diet that favored nutrient content above all. He nodded to the chef enthusiastically, making sounds to show how much he appreciated his cooking.

"Seriously, Z, you have to try this." When she didn't respond, he looked over and saw tears forming in the corners of her eyes. "What is it? Are you still thinking about— What was her name?"

Zara stood, her eyes glazed. She turned and walked away.

"What was that about?" Liam asked.

"Her name was Nova," Wiki said.

Liam swallowed another mouthful. "I forgot."

Wiki stood, shook his hands to get the food drippings off. "I'll go talk to her."

"What's the point? She's done nothing but cry and slow us down this entire time."

"Are we in a hurry?"

"Kind of," Liam said. He leaned forward to grab more food.

Wiki stared, his gaze narrow, and said, "I don't know why you hate her, but now's not the time to be rude."

"I don't hate her, I just—"

"You think you're better than her." Wiki's mouth became a straight line. He exhaled sharply through his nose, then he shook his head. "You think you're better than everyone."

Anger pumped through Liam's blood. "And you think you know everything."

Both of them became silent then, each one anticipating another verbal strike. Only then did Liam notice that some of the Suvi were watching their argument, through distant windows, from the corners of buildings. They couldn't understand the words, but clearly, they recognized a fight when they saw one.

Liam turned to Skai, who looked more concerned than angry. When he looked back, Wiki was gone, a small plume of dust the only sign he had been there. Liam sat down, though he didn't remember standing in the first place. Fatigue hit him full force.

"I think we're all just tired," he said. "Is there somewhere I can sleep?"

Skai stood and gestured for him to follow.

•|•

Liam woke with a start. Firelight danced on the low stone ceiling, chaotic waves of orange and brown. Joyous sounds came through the open-air windows, laughing and talking and singing. He sat up, stretched his arms. His achy muscles crackled beneath his sunburnt skin. His hunger had been satiated, but now he craved water.

Wiki snored beside him, his thin chest rising with each inhalation. Liam saw no sign of Zara. He had fallen asleep before them both, too tired to worry about what happened.

Do they really think I have a superiority complex?

Sure, he compared his stats in the Earth Sim to those of the others and drew conclusions, but he tried not to brag about it. And if he did, wouldn't it be justified? He shook off the thought and rose from his bed, careful not to hit his head on the ceiling or wake Wiki. The last thing he wanted to do was talk about their little fight. It would blow over in time.

The wounds on his leg still throbbing, he hobbled to the exit and stepped into the night. The lukewarm winds of early evening brushed against his face, a gentle reminder of his place on Earth, his relationship with nature. With enough time, nature could destroy or change things. It could carve valleys into the earth and make men grow into giants. Nature had power that no man could ever aspire to.

Liam walked on. Obstructed by only the highest peaks, the sky appeared as a canvas of stars, not as full as the view from Omega, but much more impressive. Without an atmosphere to disrupt their light, stars didn't twinkle back home. The effect gave the scene a glimmering quality that Liam had never witnessed before.

The soundscape led back to the place where Liam and the others had eaten lunch earlier. In the center of the circle, a bonfire now blazed, shooting sparks into the sky. The Suvi stood and sat in small groups around the circumference—on logs and stumps, arms draped over each other, mouths busy talking or laughing, singing or drinking.

Liam found Skai in the crowd. She stood across the fire from him, a ceramic bottle in her hand. When she noticed him, her teeth gleamed in the firelight. She had her hair tied back, wild curls tamed into something more manageable—as if the night had transformed her. Sun to moon. Clouds to stars. Her appearance mimicked nature.

Still smiling, Skai beckoned him to join her.

The villagers stared as Liam passed. Some regarded him with guarded expressions. Most just grinned. He couldn't tell whether their smiles came from their hearts or the bottles in their hands, but he decided it didn't matter. He would take cautious, ethanol-fueled kindness over outright hostility any day, especially from a group that blamed him and his people for making their home less safe.

"Good evening, Lion Slayer," Skai said when he made it to her. "Could not sleep?"

"I slept okay."

"We thought you would sleep all day and night." She swayed toward him. "Did the people wake you?"

"No," he said. "Well, kind of. But it doesn't matter."

"And your friends?"

Liam shrugged. "I don't know."

"They are sad? Angry?"

"We don't always get along." Liam sighed, didn't want to think about it anymore. "It'll be fine."

That seemed to be a sufficient explanation for Skai. She bounced her weight from side to side, matching the rhythm of the strange music. Admittedly, all music was strange to Liam. Musicians had always been a rarity in Omega. Music was deemed nonessential, so the study of it had been relegated to the disabled and elderly, those who couldn't help with the real work. Sure, Liam listened to computer-produced focus tracks on his implant every day, but it wasn't the same as hearing lungs and vocal cords turn air into sound. It lacked that magical quality. He remembered his dad singing to him, the sweet tenor of his voice, though he couldn't remember the songs.

"Do you thirst, Lion Slayer?"

She held out her bottle, and Liam took it. "What is it?"

Skai scrunched her lips to one side. She closed her eyes for a second. "I don't know the word in the old language." She held the bottle up, made intense eye contact. "It is very good. Makes you brave."

Liam smiled and took the bottle. He swirled the contents, sniffed it, and took a sip. The drink definitely had ethanol in it, but it didn't burn as intensely as the corn-based moonfire back home. Slightly sweet, it had a bitter, bubbly quality to it that Liam couldn't compare to anything available in Omega. He didn't expect it to be so cold and refreshing. One sip, and he no longer felt the stares of the villagers quite as much.

"Is this beer?" he said. "Like actual beer?"

Skai shrugged. "Maybe that is the word. Drink all you want."

After a few more swigs, the intoxicating effects hit Liam like a crash landing. It had been a while since he had a drink. Omega didn't enforce a legal drinking age like the governments of old, but most people couldn't afford alcohol. His body didn't sway like Skai's, but his eyes felt looser in his skull. They slowly drifted from side to side, up and down, taking in all the sights. The fire glowed a little brighter than before.

Liam had never seen so many strangers in one place, people made even stranger by the effects of the drink. Wondering if it had something in it other than ethanol, his gaze lingered on Skai's left collarbone. It had a pair of circular scars above and below it, bigger in diameter and spaced farther apart on top. He squinted, trying to understand the scar.

A light slap to the cheek brought his attention back to Skai's face. "My eyes are here."

"Sorry, I wasn't looking at your— I was just—"

"I joke," Skai said, her mouth stretched wide in an exaggerated grin. "Relax, Lion Slayer."

Liam couldn't tell if she had been using that title to mock him, but he decided not to press the issue. "How did you get that scar?"

She walked away from the fire, tilted her head to the side to summon him.

"There are too many noises here for this story," she said. "We will walk."

Liam took another swig from the bottle and followed her. They walked away from the crowd until the sounds from the bonfire faded to a manageable level.

"When I was young," Skai said, "my family lived in a hut near the river. My father was—how do you say—a fisherman?"

"That's right," Liam said.

"Every morning, my father rose before the sun. I stayed in the hut, helped my mother sew skins for clothes. My mother always started the fire before my father came home, boiled the roots. Together, they would cut the fishes and cook them—some fried, some with smoke to trade."

They sat down on a log, and the murmur of the crowd faded. Liam tried to imagine Skai as a child, what it would be like to grow up in a forest on Earth.

"One day," Skai said, "my father took me to the river with him. We woke up before the sun and went to all the best fishing places.

We caught many fishes that day. When the time came to return home, I ran ahead of my father to the hut. I couldn't wait to show my mother our catch." Skai squeezed her hands into tight fists. "But when I got there, wolves surrounded our home—black and gray and angry. One turned to me, blood falling from its mouth."

Liam gasped softly, which stopped the story for a moment.

"My father yelled and charged the wolves, but they did not flee. I remember falling to the ground, crying. I could not see her, but I knew my mother was gone. It was her blood. I knew it."

Liam shifted uncomfortably. He felt the urge to comfort Skai, but he didn't know how.

"My father yelled and ran to her. The wolves pounced on him. I wanted to help, but I was only a girl. How could I fight a wolf?"

Liam thought about Glo, how he wanted to save her from Reagan but couldn't.

"I saw the wolves bite my father." Skai's gaze found the dirt. "I ran away. I had no choice."

Neither did I, Liam thought.

"Did the wolves—"

"One saw me running. It chased me into the forest. So fast, it ran. My legs were too few. I knew it would catch me. Four-legged things run twice as fast."

"How did you get away?"

"The wolf chased me to the river. I wanted to dive into the water to escape, but I was too late. It jumped on me and bit my shoulder. I can still feel it." Skai ran her fingers across the scars on her collarbone. "The wolf dragged me away. I thought it would kill me, but it carried me back to my home. I closed my eyes. I did not want to see my mother and father like that. I remember silence. I remember fear. Everything was quiet."

Liam reached out but stopped himself from touching her back.

"I don't know why, but the wolf released me. It laid me on my back and watched me. I thought maybe I died. Then the other wolves came, covered in blood. They surrounded me, and"—she took in a deep breath—"spears flew above me, sliced through the pack. The wolves scattered, but they were too slow to escape. Most of them died."

Liam shook his head.

"The hunters saved me," Skai said, "but could not save my parents. That whole time, I kept my eyes closed. I couldn't move. I felt—how do you say—frozen?"

"I know the feeling."

"One hunter tracked the surviving wolves. He brought me their skins. He burned their flesh and made a necklace of their teeth. But I did not want these gifts. I wanted my family back. I wanted to open my eyes and see my mother and father again. I wanted safety."

Skai paused, and Liam traced her gaze back to the bonfire, specifically to the old man with the hood.

"From that day," Skai said. "The hunter called himself Fang. He wears the furs and teeth of the wolves, a reminder to always protect me—to protect all of us—from danger. For his bravery that day, he became our leader."

Liam had no love for the Suvi leader, especially after getting smacked in the head multiple times by the man, but he felt some respect for him after hearing Skai's story.

"When we came here," Liam said, "what did you say to Fang?"

"I called for mercy. I asked him to spare your lives."

"Spare our lives from what?"

"Punishment for drawing the ghouls from the highlands." Skai's shoulders tensed, drawing closer to her ears. "Fang wanted to throw you in the giant's pit."

"Oh," Liam said, unsure of how to process that news. "Well, I'm glad he didn't."

"So am I," Skai said. "Just do as you are told, and no harm will come to you. It is the way of our people."

Liam looked back at the bonfire gathering, where he found Fang staring straight at him, his eyes piercing despite their age—a silent warning to stay in line.

•│•

Even after the bonfire burned to embers and the majority of the Suvi retired for the night, Liam and Skai still sat on the same log. They had no lack of things to talk about. After her tale of childhood trauma, he told her about his own father, how he had died when one of the mines collapsed, how his body had never been found. He educated her about the Resurgence Mission, and she shared an oral history of her people. It took hours, but eventually, the conversation lulled and died off.

"I guess we should go to sleep," Liam said, fighting to speak through a yawn.

Skai shrugged. "Why?"

"I don't know, because it's the middle of the night?"

"It's no matter," Skai said. "I stay up late and sleep through the hot hours."

"That makes sense," Liam said. "I guess I can stay up a little longer."

"Come." She stood. "I will show you something."

Liam stretched his legs, which had almost gone to sleep from sitting for so long. This had never been a problem in lunar gravity. They walked away from the village and started on a tree-lined path that led uphill.

"Where are we going?"

"You will see."

Moonlight trickled through the leaves and branches above, casting eerie shadows on the forest floor. Though nighttime had descended, the forest was far from asleep. Insects chirped from their hideouts while nocturnal rodents scurried to catch them. When they made it to a small clearing, Skai stopped.

"Do you see that?" she asked.

Liam swiveled his head around, looking for some kind of threat—a giant, maybe? He glanced at Skai, who inclined her head toward the horizon. An odd-shaped silhouette blocked a large section of the starry sky, a mountain with three peaks. They leaned in one direction, as if they might one day topple over.

"The tall one," she said. "It's called the Eagle."

Though many things had changed on Earth, Liam imagined that this mountain had looked the same for millennia. "Have you been up there?"

"Yes," she said. "You can see much of the valley there. It is beautiful."

"How do you get to the top?"

"There is a trail." She pointed toward the base of the mountain. "That way."

They hiked until they came to what looked like a dead end, a hillside of massive boulders sloping up and out of Liam's visibility.

"Where are we—"

Skai scurried up one of the boulders, agile as a squirrel. When she reached the top, she stood tall and tossed her head to the side. "Are you coming?"

"Yeah," he said, trying to remember what path Skai had taken to ascend the boulder. "I'll be right up."

"Don't think," Skai said. "Just climb."

She leaped across a narrow ravine to the next boulder. After a running start, Liam made it to the top of the first boulder in a few bounds. By the time he got there, Skai had moved on.

"Hey," he shouted. "Wait up."

When she didn't, he decided to commit to the chase. He followed as closely as possible and did his best to memorize her path. His time in the Earth Sim had not prepared him for such an intense and varied workout, but he managed to stay two or three boulders behind her the whole time. After a while, the rocks leveled out, and Liam noticed that some of them were wet. Careful not to slip, he slowed his pace. Only then did he realize they were approaching the base of a waterfall. He couldn't see it clearly, but he heard it now.

Unlike Liam, Skai didn't let the slippery surfaces slow her down. It only took him a minute or two to lose her completely. Still, their destination was clear. He followed the growing roar of the waterfall until he stood above a natural pool, the surface of which rippled out from the water's source. He sat down to catch his breath.

"Over here!" Skai shouted, barely audible through the noise.

She stood a few boulders away from Liam, on the edge of a sheer cliff overlooking the pool. He started moving toward her.

"No," she said. "I'll come to you."

Skai took off her leather shoes and dropped them behind her.

"What are you doing?" Liam asked, but she didn't respond.

He didn't have to wonder for long. Skai removed the dagger

from her hidden pocket and placed it on top of the shoes. Then she looked over at Liam, untied the front of her furs, and dropped them to the ground. He expected to see another layer—a slip, a bra, at least some kind of underwear—but she just stood there, completely naked, and apparently unashamed. The rippling water reflected the moonlight, which shimmered on her tan skin. The light undulated across her body, illuminating it piece by piece, providing flashes and glimpses but never a full picture. Liam turned his head slightly away, but he couldn't stop looking at her.

"My face is here, Lion Slayer," she said, and though he couldn't see her clearly, he could almost hear her smiling.

Skai dove from the cliff into the water and entered it so smoothly that she barely made a splash. Her body disappeared beneath the dark surface. When she didn't come back up immediately, Liam stood, worried. He stared at the spot where she had jumped in, debating whether he should dive in to help her. As he was about to do so, she returned to the surface near the base of a different boulder. She treaded water there, with only her shoulders and head visible.

"Jump," she said.

Liam laughed. "I don't know. It looks pretty cold."

Skai reclined in the water and floated on her back. She twisted and rolled onto her stomach, then dove again. When she resurfaced, she whipped the hair out of her face and hugged her arms around herself, her chest rising above the water. Was she doing that on purpose?

"The water is cold," Skai said and started swimming away. "But I am warm."

Liam hesitated. He had gone swimming in the river, but only out of necessity, and it had been far from graceful. He didn't want to embarrass himself. What if he started to sink? What if she needed to rescue him?

"Are you afraid?" she asked.

"No, I—"

"You dove from that rock?" Skai floated on her back and pointed up at the moon. "And you're afraid to jump off this one?" Bobbing up and down, she flashed more than a smile. "Even for a girl?" A few kicks sent her farther away. "Don't you want to feel the water?"

In truth, Liam wasn't afraid of jumping or hitting his head or drowning. It was Skai's intensity and straightforward attitude that frightened him. He had never met anyone like her. Swallowing his nerves, he removed his shoes and shirt. Then he filled his lungs and dove in.

19

MONSTERS

Monsters everywhere.

The thought swarmed Glo's mind, burrowing deep, keeping her from sleep. She lay beneath the parachute ceiling of the infirmary tent, the darkness forcing her to recall each encounter with monsters since leaving Omega.

With a shudder, she remembered the inhuman gaits of the subs that came from the forest, how they sniffed the air like animals, howled like ravenous beasts. More chillingly, she recalled the human-like anger on the scarred one's face. Even now, in the relative safety of Camp Resurgence, his gaze still haunted her.

Glo shook her head to clear the visions, and her mind drifted to memories of Reagan's hand on her shoulder as they made their ascent to his cabin on the ETS Resurgence. She recalled his acrid smell and the threatening way he said, "Don't forget who has the guns."

Glo slid a hand into the waistband of her pants, where she felt the metallic barrel of her stolen plasma pistol, warm from its contact with her outer thigh. It didn't make her feel safe, exactly. Only less exposed, less vulnerable. She pulled the gun out and examined it in the dim moonlight that poured through openings in the shelter. She had never fired such a weapon, but having it as an option felt right. Human or not, monsters could still be fought.

Don't forget who has the guns, she thought.

One of the cots creaked, which nearly made Glo drop the gun

onto her face. Hands shaking, she quickly hid it beneath her bedding, careful to keep her finger off the trigger.

"Glo?" Quinn said, her voice soft and low. "Are you awake?"

"Yeah," Glo whispered. "You need something?"

"I can't sleep." Quinn rolled over, and Glo could see her eyes reflecting like a pair of blue lakes.

"Is it the pain? I can—"

"I can't stop thinking about the subs."

Glo sighed. "I know," she said, still holding the gun against her lap. "Me neither. But you're safe here. The guards will protect you."

And if they don't, I will, Glo thought.

"What if our children come out like that? What if they're hideous and violent? What if they're monstrous?"

"We're not infected, Quinn. And we can't be. We've all been injected with the antivirus. Doctor Collins made sure of that. She—"

"She's still missing."

"She could be alive," Glo said. "And besides, as much as I hate saying this, we don't really need her. We only need what she created, and it's already in us. Our children will inherit our immunity."

"I hope so," Quinn said.

The girl was right. Theoretically, what Glo said was true, but the antivirus hadn't been proven to work. It had been modeled and simulated, but never tested outside a virtual environment.

"Everything will be fine," Glo said. "You need to rest."

Even after Quinn quieted and went back to sleep, Glo couldn't shake how similar she sounded to her mother, how she stayed positive in times of great distress. Peering at a shaft of moonlight piercing through the dust and residual smoke of camp, she tried to take comfort in the fact that the light she saw came from home. She imagined her mother standing on the moon, holding a mirror to reflect the sunlight, delivering it through the darkness to her only daughter…to her only son.

Liam, Glo thought, as if her mind could project his name. Where are you?

She squeezed the handle of the gun, wondering if she dared to get out there and find her brother alone. But the scarred sub's

ANDY GORMAN • 151

face hovered in her mind, smothering all hope of escape or rescue. What chance did she have against a forest crawling with monsters like that?

The rasp of a wet cough tore through the night air. Glo sat up and tried to figure out which patient the sound came from, but no one in the infirmary tent had moved. Then the tent flaps parted. A man's silhouette approached, his face veiled by darkness.

"Who's there?" Glo whispered.

Subconsciously, she already knew who stood there—and what he had come for.

"Get up, Gloria," said the raspy, timeworn voice of Admiral Reagan. "Come with me."

Too late to feign sleep, Gloria froze. "What? I—"

"That's an order."

Glo's index finger wandered to the trigger of her plasma pistol. One squeeze, and she could eliminate at least one monster from Earth. But what if she missed? What if he had a gun and reacted faster?

"Where are we going?" Glo asked, trying to buy more time to decide her best course of action.

"With the biorepository missing," Reagan said, "it's time to begin Earth's repopulation the old-fashioned way."

Glo thought she felt plasma churning in her grip, but it was only the heat of her own hand, fear and anger turned thermal. She had a sudden urge to return the pain that Reagan had dealt her, but something held her back. She couldn't ruin her only chance of finding her brother by getting executed for treason.

"I'm tired," she said.

More mechanical than organic, Reagan's throat imitated a laugh. "It won't require much work on your part, Gloria. Come on."

Glo's walls came up. Numb, fighting her own will to fight or flee, she stood and followed Reagan out of the infirmary tent. She left the plasma pistol behind, safe beneath her covers. The time might come for violence, but now she would have to fight with a different weapon. Perhaps she could use Reagan's perversions against him, get what she wanted tonight.

"You made the right choice," Reagan said, walking beside her.

"My bed is much more comfortable than those cots. Perks of being in charge."

Hiding her revulsion, Glo smiled. "I'll be the judge of that."

Another laugh. "I'm glad to see you're finally warming up to me, Gloria."

"It's Glo," she said. "Everyone calls me Glo."

"I like it," Reagan said. "So, what changed your mind about me, Glo?"

For a moment, the breeze through the trees was the only sound as Glo decided how to respond.

"When our ejector pod came down," she said, "and I took that first step out, something changed. When my feet touched the ground—I don't know—I felt different."

"Like the past no longer mattered?"

"Kind of," Glo said. "I guess setting foot on Earth made me feel smaller but somehow more important. I realized that we all need to do our duty, regardless of how we feel about it. That we're all part of something bigger than ourselves."

"That we are." Reagan parted the opening of his tent. "Make yourself at home."

His quarters weren't elegant by any standard, though he did have luxuries that the rest of the survivors didn't: electric lights, his own store of rations, and some privacy. The rest of the camp slept communally. An orderly arrangement of objects lined the walls of the space—a cot larger and more cushioned than the rest, a plastic crate that served as a nightstand, and fresh sets of vacuum-sealed clothing hanging from the ceiling. He didn't have much, but he still had more than everyone else.

Glo gulped down some air. "Do you have anything to drink?" she asked.

"Water?" He gestured toward a vessel on his nightstand. "It's filtered from the river."

"Do you have anything"—she faced him, hesitated, then put her hand on his shoulder—"a little bit stronger? I could use a bit of fun."

A youthful mischievousness lit up Reagan's face, and Glo wondered how old the man actually was.

He pulled a bottle from the crate beside his bed and handed it to Glo.

"I'm glad the shuttle had space for liquor," she said.

Even though they could have filled that space with more food or people, she thought. Breaking eye contact, she held the bottle to her nose and sniffed.

"People need a way to keep their spirits up, especially in situations like this one. The strangeness of a new setting can get to people. It can break them."

Glo sat on the bed, took a small swig from the bottle. It burned, but not in a terrible way. "Is it strange to you?"

"It's more nostalgic," he said, chewing the final word. "Tell me, Glo, did your history courses teach you much about me?"

"They mostly taught us about your role in the Resurgence Mission."

"Yes?"

Glo's eyelashes fluttered. "They didn't mention how charming you are." She had to dam the vomit threatening to escape from her body. "I'm curious. When were you born, Arthur?"

He smirked. "Let's just say I wasn't much older than you when we left Earth."

Glo knew the man had spent more time in stasis than out of it over the generations, but almost seven centuries? It seemed impossible, even with advanced cryonics.

"By my calculations," Reagan said, "I'm the oldest man in the universe—according to calendar years, anyway."

"Good thing I like older men." Glo couldn't tell whether it was the lie or the impending vomit tickling her throat. She took another sip.

"I don't feel that old," Reagan said. "There's much more life to live, and I intend to live it. I'd like to watch my children inherit their birthright. I want them to rediscover the beauty of this planet and claim it as their own."

"That sounds nice," Glo said, though she didn't want men like Reagan to inherit the Earth.

"Why don't you lie down, Glo? Make yourself a little more comfortable."

The smirk on his face said, *"And by comfortable, I mean naked."*

Glo took a long drag from the bottle, drawing whatever courage she could from its contents. She turned to set the bottle down, took one more gulp, then placed it on the crate. With an empty stomach, she instantly felt her mind buzzing. The feeling didn't eliminate her anxiety, but it buried it just enough.

"Why don't you lie down?" she said.

Reagan took the bait. At a pace bordering elderly, he unbuttoned and removed his shirt. Spotted with discolorations, his skin shone a pale gray beneath the electric lights of the tent. He sat down on the edge of the bed, and Glo helped him unstrap his boots. She stood before him and unzipped her jacket from her neck to the rise of her chest.

"So beautiful," Reagan said. "Why don't you—"

"I can do whatever you want, Arthur," she said, inching closer. "I can be whoever you want me to be." She touched the shimmering circle of his lung vent, then lightly caressed his collarbone. "But"— her hand slid down his torso until her fingers touched his belt buckle—"I need you to do something for me in return."

"And what's that?" Reagan asked, and Glo could sense his heartbeat quickening. Oh, the power of the fairer sex, she recalled him saying. Even he, who knew to beware of this power, could fall victim to it.

"I need your help." Without breaking eye contact, Glo unclasped his belt buckle. "It's something only a man of your authority can help me with. And I'd be so—very—grateful for your help."

"What is it?" Reagan glanced at Glo's hand on his belt, then back at her eyes. "If it's in my power, I'll make it happen."

"I want you to find my brother. Liam. He's still out there."

"The stowaway," Reagan said. The excitement drained from his face. "I nearly forgot about that little shit."

Glo frowned. "He's not—"

"Of course, we're looking for him."

Reagan, who had been staring intently at Glo, looked at the wall. "Are you really?"

"Yes."

Men will say anything to get what they want, Glo thought.

"I don't believe you." She pulled away, took a few steps back, and zipped her jacket back up. "Tell me the truth."

"Fine." Reagan took a deep breath through his vent. "We already found your brother."

"Where?" Now it was Glo's heart racing. "Where is he? Can you take me to him?"

"He's dead," Reagan said plainly, with no hint of remorse on his face.

"No." The word came as a toneless whisper, then the repetition of it crescendoed into quiet moans of pain. "No, no, he— No, he can't be."

"He is."

Glo wanted to run away, but her body wouldn't move. She couldn't even cry. The only family member she had left on this planet couldn't possibly be gone. It made no sense.

"You're lying," she said. "Why are you lying to me?"

"Oh, Gloria."

"It's Glo! Only my mother calls me Gloria." Thinking about her mother only worsened her emotional state. "Liam, he never—"

"Glo." Reagan took her hand. "I wish I was lying. My men should have—"

"I don't believe you. Show me his body. Was he— Oh, was he with Wiki? Are they both— Where are they? Take me to them. I need to see them. I need to—"

The tent blurred behind a flood of tears, and Earth's gravity became too much. The alcohol peaked in Glo's system. Her body swayed, unsteady, as if some vital part of her had disappeared. Maybe it had. Taking care of her mother, protecting her brother— those had been the pillars of her existence for as long as she could remember, and now both pillars had crumbled in a matter of days.

"I'm sorry, my dear." Reagan stood and wrapped Glo in his arms, and she didn't have it in her to resist. "The boys had a rough landing," Reagan said, stroking her hair. "I would show you their bodies, but both of them burned up in the ejector pod."

20

THE WORLD BEFORE THIS ONE

Liam found it hard to remove his lips from Skai's, to break the chemical bond between them for even a second, but his lungs needed air. When he tried to pull away, her grip on the back of his neck kept their faces fused.

"Hold on," he said between breaths, but she didn't let go.

"I am"—she kissed his cheek then his neck—"holding on."

Liam pushed himself up from the pile of furs beneath them, but still, she held him in her gravity.

"I didn't mean to literally hold on." Liam laughed. "It's just an expression, a saying. It means stop for a minute."

"This saying is—what do you say—fucking stupid?" She smirked. "You really want to stop?"

"Just for a minute."

When Skai released him, he rolled onto his back beside her. The fur felt hot against his bare skin, but he didn't mind.

"You are sweating," Skai said, her fingers like feathers on his chest.

"It got kind of hot in here."

"Yes," Skai said, "it did."

Liam took a moment to catch his breath, but mostly to calm his nerves. Skai was intense, and that made him nervous.

They lay in an abandoned cliffside dwelling on the outskirts of the village, a place analogous to the dead sectors in Omega. Cracks meandered across the earthen ceiling, some spilling light, others repaired with mud and dried grass. The structure didn't look sturdy, but Skai had assured Liam it would hold. This was her hiding place, her secret getaway, but most importantly, her museum. A collection of artifacts sat on a shelf opposite the entrance: chunks of glass sanded opaque by time, bolts and screws nearly rusted beyond recognition, and a plethora of plastic bottles in various shapes and sizes.

"Where did you find all this stuff?" Liam asked, rolling onto his side to face Skai.

"Some in the valley. Some were given to me." Staring at the ceiling, Skai frowned. "Most my mother left me."

Liam's fingers traced the scars above and below her collarbone, a permanent reminder of her loss. "Is she the one who taught you to speak our language?"

"Yes. Mother knew much about the world before this one," Skai said. "More than I ever will."

"That's not true," Liam said. "We can teach you. I don't know everything about what the world was like before, but Wiki might."

Skai sat up, draped one of the furs over her bare shoulders. "Tell me. Do you know what United States of America is?"

"Yeah," Liam said. "It's a country. Well, it was a country. We're in it right now."

She stood and wandered over to the shelf. "What is country?"

Liam had to think about that for a moment. How could he explain the ancient concept of borders and nationality in a way that Skai would understand?

"It's like a village, but bigger," he said, "Much bigger. How did you hear about the United States, anyway?"

"It is written on all the circles." Skai grabbed something small from the shelf and tossed it to Liam, who caught it by instinct before examining it. Even through the corrosion, he could still make out the shape of a head.

"This is a coin," he explained, but Skai only shrugged in response. "It's currency. Money."

"What does it do?"

"Nothing now." Liam chuckled and handed the coin back to her. "It's worthless."

"I think it's beautiful," Skai said, her tone defensive. "Are beautiful things not worth something?"

"They are," Liam said, watching the scattered shafts of sunlight illuminate her body as she passed under them. "Especially you."

He reached up to grab her hand, to pull her closer, but the artifacts held her attention.

"Can you keep a secret, Lion Slayer?"

"I can try," he said.

"Someday I wish to leave this place," Skai said, "to explore the lands beyond the valley. I have dreams about it."

Liam stood and joined her beside the shelf. "Why don't you?"

"It is forbidden."

"Who cares?"

She faced him then. "To leave would dishonor my mother."

Skai's words struck Liam, filling him with a sudden rush of guilt. Was that what he had done to his mother by leaving Omega without saying goodbye? He put his arm around Skai, partially to comfort her but mostly to comfort himself, and kissed her hairline.

"I understand," he said. "I think I might have dishonored mine, too."

"How?"

"I came here, to Earth, without saying goodbye. I don't know. It all happened so fast. I didn't think about it." Liam stopped speaking, woefully aware that Skai never had the chance to say goodbye to her mother, and he did. "I don't even know if she's still alive."

He stared at some of the items on the shelf, focusing on the rusted and timeworn objects instead of the guilt corroding his conscience.

"If she is alive," Skai said, "maybe you will see her again, and you will say something better than goodbye." She laced her fingers through his. "You will say hello."

The thought washed away some of the guilt. "I hope so," he said.

They stood together for a minute, eyes trained on each other instead of Skai's collection of ancient curiosities.

"Now, Lion Slayer." She squeezed his hand, pulled him back toward their pile of furs. "Did I hold on long enough?"

•|•

A voice in the distance, no louder than a dropped pebble or some windblown twigs, came from outside Skai's museum. This time, Liam had no trouble removing himself from Skai's arms. They both heard it.

"Who is that?" Liam asked.

"I don't know."

"What's he saying?"

Skai shushed him. The voice grew louder, repeating the same phrase, until Liam noticed more than one set of footsteps accompanying the voice.

"They are looking for me," Skai whispered. "I am not supposed to be here."

Liam knew she had abandoned her fishing duties for the day, but he didn't think it would warrant a search party. Skai rose silently from the floor, aimed one ear at the nearest window. The last remnants of daylight brightened her forehead, which was creased in worry.

"I must go," she said, already beginning to put her shoes on.

Liam sat up. "I'll go with you."

"No," she said. "If Fang knows you came here, he will punish you."

"Punish me? I'm not afraid of—"

"You should be." Skai finished tying the laces that held her furs on. "Stay until dark, then sneak home."

"But—"

She kissed him. "Just do it. Trust me."

Skai left the museum without another word—before Liam could ask if she would be punished as well.

21

THE GIANT'S PIT

"Come," she whispered.

Liam rolled over and found Skai sitting beside him on his bed, hardly visible in the dark dwelling.

"Hey," he said. "Are you okay?"

"I am fine," she said. "Now come with me. I need your help."

Liam yawned. "But the sun's not even up yet."

She leaned over him, bringing the scent of flowers and smoke with her. The ends of her hair grazed his cheek as she brought her lips to his ear.

"Your friends are awake."

Liam hadn't seen Wiki or Zara much since their argument. Except for some stilted and awkward conversations at the communal meals, they had hardly spoken in days. He had plenty of things to do to fill his time, and so did they.

"Good for them," Liam said. "But I'm tired. I was up late worrying about you."

"Fine." Skai kissed Liam's head, ran her fingers through his hair. Her touch woke his every nerve. "I will go alone then."

She stood and turned to leave, but Liam grabbed her hand.

"Wait," he said.

A mischievous smile came to her lips. "I knew you would come."

Liam stood, stretched his sore legs, and followed her out of the dwelling.

"You never wake up this early," he said.

"You have only known me for a few days."

"Still…"

"I have not slept, Lion Slayer."

"Why not?"

Skai shook her head.

"Come on, tell me."

She sighed softly, sadly. "A child went missing last night," she said. "Her parents said she went to get water. She never came back. I helped look for her."

Liam didn't know what to say to that. Children didn't go missing in Omega. There was nowhere they could go that wasn't tracked by cameras, and hardly anyone had airlock clearance.

"They should not have let her go alone," Skai said.

"What happened? Did you find her— I mean, was there a—"

"No." Skai paused, stared ahead as she walked between buildings. "We only found scraps of her clothing."

Liam grabbed her hand. "I'm sorry."

Skai nodded. "No one escapes death. I only wish she could have run a little longer. Fang will not be pleased to hear about this."

"I hope he doesn't blame me for her death."

"I will talk to him," Skai said.

"Speaking of Fang," Liam said, "are you in trouble?"

"I should not have taken you to the museum, but my debt will be paid."

"What does that mean?"

"We must be more careful, stay where it's safe. No more leaving the group."

"Okay," Liam said. "If you say so."

She stopped and turned to him. "I am serious, Lion Slayer. If we obey, we live. If we disobey, we die." Even in the twilight, her eyes blazed, pleading. "I do not want you to die."

"I don't want to die, either."

"We could have drowned beneath the waterfall. We could have been attacked like the girl."

"I get it," Liam said. "But if we can't leave the group, where are we going now?"

"To pay my debt." Skai continued walking, and Liam followed.

"The river is safe, and there are many fishes to be caught."

After reaching the edge of the village, they turned toward the river. They set out traps and lines—nets woven from a material Liam had no name for, and hooks tied to strings. They spent hours there, from sunrise to lunchtime, and Liam discovered that fishing was synonymous with waiting. He wanted to try something more active next, maybe spear hunting—on whatever had killed that little girl.

•|•

Liam stood at the edge of the giant's pit, swinging a fish in his hand—his only catch of the day. Skai sat nearby, gutting and salting a pile of fish that she had caught, enough to make up for a lost day of work.

"You sure I can't eat this one?" Liam said, watching the giant's eyes as they tracked the swinging fish.

"You can," Skai said. Liam looked over his shoulder and saw her sun-darkened lips curve into a wry smile. Fishing all morning had improved her mood. "If you like the flavor of excrement."

Liam laughed so hard that he nearly snorted.

"Are you saying it'll taste like shit?" he asked.

"If it's you who cooks it," she said, "then yes."

"And how do you know what that tastes like?"

She smiled. "Silence, Lion Slayer."

Liam laughed again. He took a step forward to toss the fish into the pit. "All right, big guy, are you ready for your—"

His ankle rolled on a loose stone, and he stumbled forward.

"Liam!" Skai shouted.

By the time her call reached him, he had already gone over the edge. Elbows and heels scraping against the slanted rim of the pit, he managed to slow his descent to the bottom. The dead fish slapped against the mud first, followed shortly by Liam. Using the momentum from the fall, he rolled forward and lunged into a squatting position, then quickly scanned the area for the giant's approach. He didn't have to look far.

The giant dug his fists into the mud. His arm muscles rippled as he pushed himself up to a standing position. If he appeared large from above, he looked colossal standing on the same ground—even with his back hunched.

Liam imagined that the giant could run faster than any man, that the fight would be over as soon as it began. But the giant just stood there, his gaze moving slowly between the fish and Liam—as if deciding which to eat first. Would he skip the appetizer and go straight for the main course?

One small step brought the giant a couple of meters closer. Liam retreated toward the wall, his focus never leaving the giant's face. Fear activated every cell in his body, as if each one knew it would soon be dissolving in stomach acid.

Another footfall splashed dirty water through the air, sending a few drops to collide with Liam's shins. Buried beneath his fear, another emotion simmered—anger. Anger that he had worked so hard for so long, that he had committed an unpardonable crime, that he had traveled through space, only to die from the consequences of one clumsy motion. On this planet he had risked everything to reach, this world filled with wonder, would his last emotion be self-pity? Would his last sight really be a muddy pit instead of some beautiful expanse of hills and trees? And what would happen to his sister if he died now? His body raged against the notion, tensing for one last fight.

Within a split second, he decided to attack first. His fist gripped the knife handle at his belt. It was a small blade that Skai had given him to gut fish, but it was sharp. The giant had to have a weakness. Liam just needed to find it. He glanced at the shroud of hair covering his opponent's genitalia. Perhaps he could strike there first, make the beast curl over in pain. Or maybe that would just anger it into a frenzy. A giant elbow or knee to any vital part of Liam's body could be fatal.

Skai shouted something in her language, and the giant's head creaked upward. Liam took the opportunity to sprint to the far side of the pit. Fish in hand, the giant turned back around slowly. At least Liam had the advantage of speed. Smaller limbs could pivot faster. Maybe he could find a way to jump on the giant's back, stab the knife into his neck. That way, there would be no flailing limbs or retribution to worry about.

The giant dropped the whole fish into his mouth and chomped through bones.

Appetizer first, then, Liam thought.

Bones crunching between his teeth, the giant stepped forward— then stilled again. He stared at Liam the whole time, his expression sitting on the border between curiosity and hunger. Though the rest of his enormous body hid in the shade, the giant's face appeared in vivid detail, illuminated by direct sunlight spilling over the edge of the pit. Not a single square centimeter of his face appeared clean. The shoulder-length mop hanging from his scalp seemed more dirt than hair. He wore a permanent frown, framed by filthy wrinkles etched into his face.

Skai shouted again, the same word as before: "Jarok."

The giant's head twitched toward the sound of the word. Liam wondered what it meant. Sit? Stay? Stop? No, the giant's reaction to it was more instinctual, as if the word had a deeper, more personal meaning, as if—

"Jarok," Liam said and watched the giant react to his name.

Peering at Jarok's filthy and bruised skin, the scars around his neck and wrists that suggested a violent capture, Liam wondered how long Jarok had been forced to live in such conditions—and what he had done, besides merely existing, to deserve the abuse.

The knife shook in Liam's hand, his grip fierce around the handle. Even if he could get behind Jarok, he doubted he could jump high enough to land a deadly blow. Truthfully, even if the opportunity presented itself, he no longer wanted to attack.

Liam's eyelids sealed like airlock doors, the image of Jarok burned into his mind. His last sight would not be a blur of sky and filth, but a pair of eyes twice as large as his own, filled to the brim with pain. He didn't know how long he stood there. Adrenaline distorted his sense of time, and he grew oddly impatient about his impending death. Then a terrible thought came to mind—of Jarok devouring him slowly, limb by limb, instead of providing a quick death. But the giant didn't approach.

Confused about how he was still alive, Liam opened his eyes.

Jarok still stood in the same spot, waiting patiently, but for what? Why won't the monster attack?

The answer crashed into Liam's mind.

"Because you're not a monster," he said, his voice almost a whisper. "Are you?"

Jarok stepped forward, his motions almost intentionally slow, as if he knew any sudden movement might startle the tiny man standing before him. He pointed four fingers at Liam, moved his arm up to indicate the edge of the pit, then spread his hands apart at the waist—summoning Liam to come forward.

Already prepared to die, Liam had no reason not to heed the giant's call. He took a hesitant step toward Jarok.

"Liam, no," Skai said from above. He had almost forgotten she was still there.

"It's okay," he said, now standing within reach of Jarok, his eyes level with the giant's great belly.

Jarok bent lower and placed his hands beneath Liam's armpits. His cold fingers met at the spine with uncanny gentleness. The ground made a sucking noise as Liam's feet escaped its viscosity. Jarok lifted him to eye level, and for a split second, Liam thought he saw the giant's permanent scowl straighten into something less menacing. Jarok carried him to the slanted wall of the pit. Then, using almost no effort at all, he lifted Liam above his head, where Skai waited, her arms outstretched to pull him up to safety.

•|•

"You are lucky, Lion Slayer."

Liam winced as Skai applied a sweet-smelling ointment to his elbow, which had split open from the fall—the worst of his injuries. Otherwise, he only suffered a few scrapes and bruises. He could tell he would be sore later, but then again, he had been sore every day since his arrival on Earth, especially the morning after bouldering with Skai. He wondered if life on planet Earth would always be so painful or if he would get used to it over time. At least he had Skai to soothe him. It made the pain worth it.

"Almost dying is lucky?" he said.

Skai giggled, medicine to Liam's ears. "More lucky than dying."

They sat in silence for a while. A small fire crackled in the corner of Liam's assigned dwelling. He doubted the place would ever feel like home, that anywhere on Earth would ever feel like home, but a few days had dulled the novelty of living there.

"I can't believe Jarok didn't kill me."

Skai tended to Liam's wounds with careful hands. "Fang will be happy."

"That I'm alive? I thought he hated me."

"Happy that Jarok is tamed."

Liam recalled how the giant had looked at him, the empathy that couldn't have been taught. "I don't know about that."

"And Fang does not hate you."

"He acts like it."

"He doesn't trust you yet," Skai said. "And trust is survival. It binds us."

Wiki entered the dwelling, King bouncing at his heels. The cub had latched onto Wiki in Liam's absence, but Liam didn't mind. Someone had to take care of the cougar, and Fang's instructions had been clear: "If the cub kills any of our livestock, you will have to pay the price."

Wiki regarded Liam's battered body. "Did you get in a fight or fall off a cliff?"

Liam stretched his legs, and King pounced gently on his foot. "A little bit of both, I guess."

Wiki raised an eyebrow, then Liam told him the whole story. Skai interjected now and then to narrate what she had seen from above.

"Incredible," Wiki said. "I can't wait to tell the others about everything we've seen."

"Same here," Liam said.

"I wish we could go find them."

"You can't," Skai said. "It is forbidden."

"But his sister is with them," Wiki said. "She could be in danger."

Skai shrugged. "Everyone is in danger."

"I know it's rough out there right now," Liam said, "but Wiki is right. We've been here for days. I really need to go and find—"

"No," Skai said sternly. "Not yet."

"Then when?" Liam said, his voice projecting more than he intended. "This is my sister we're talking about, possibly my only living family member. I need to get her away from Reagan. If your parents were out there, wouldn't you break the rules to find them?"

"You know I would."

"And don't you want to leave and explore? We can go together."

Skai backed away. "You are not ready."

Liam didn't know where his sudden rush of anger came from, whether nearly dying had drawn it out of him, but it erupted without warning.

"I've been ready."

"You're wrong. You have to obey—"

"Where I come from," Liam said, "we weren't allowed to leave because we couldn't breathe if we stepped foot outside. We would asphyxiate and freeze to death. Those rules made sense. The danger outside was unbeatable. But Fang won't let us leave because— Because why, exactly?"

"He's punishing us for the crimes of our people," Wiki said.

"Because it was our choice to crash here?" Liam took a step toward Skai. "Does he think I can't defend myself? Because I'm not a little girl, Skai. I know it's dangerous out there."

"There are more to defend than yourself." Skai's lips straightened. "There is still much you need to learn."

"You said that already. But so far, I've only learned how to climb boulders and catch fish."

"And still the children know these things better than you." Skai stormed away, toward the fire's dying embers. "I have only protected you."

"I don't need your protection," Liam said, fuming.

Wiki grabbed his arm, gestured toward the door with his head. "Calm down. Fang might hear you."

"What's he going to do?" Liam jerked his arm out of Wiki's grasp "Kill me?"

"Our laws may be cruel," Skai said, her back to Liam, "but they are necessary. I trust you, but Fang does not."

"Then fuck Fang!"

As soon as the words left Liam's mouth, he knew he should have kept them there—even though he meant them.

"I owe Fang my life." Skai turned and faced Liam. "But you—I hardly know. Perhaps I shouldn't trust you."

"You don't understand. By keeping me here, Fang is endangering my people."

"Why do you care only about you and yours?"

Skai crouched down beside a pile of firewood.

"What are you doing?" Liam said.

She turned and displayed a fiery expression. "Listen to me," she said. "Only listen."

Liam took a deep breath. "What is this?"

"You want to learn? Here's a lesson." Skai plucked a piece of kindling from the pile and held it out between both hands. "One stick." She snapped it in half. "Breaks."

"Okay?" Liam said.

Next, Skai grabbed a handful of sticks and bundled them. "Many sticks." The bundle slightly curved as she attempted to break it. Some of the smaller twigs cracked and splintered, but as a group, they held. "Hold strong." She tossed the wood onto the hot embers behind her. A sudden blaze lit up her face. "Do you understand?" She stared him down for a moment, her brown eyes reflecting waves of firelight. "Do you?"

A tense silence filled the dwelling, interrupted only by King's quiet meowing and the crackle of burning wood. Liam walked past Skai to the pile of firewood, knelt, and selected the thickest, heaviest log he could find. He held it out above the dying flames.

"I understand," he said, "but I'm not a twig."

Liam dropped the log, sending sparks and ash flying up to the low ceiling. He exited the dwelling before anyone else could speak.

22

FREE MEN

If I only cared about myself, Liam thought, then I wouldn't be doing this.

"Thanks for letting me live," he said.

He stood above the giant's pit, making eye contact with Jarok. Moonlight illuminated the pit's muddy floor, where nocturnal insects buzzed incessantly above piles of feces and discarded fish bones. It smelled worse than a thousand shrimp barrels. Liam didn't understand how anything could survive in such a cesspool—and how he hadn't noticed the stench before.

"Consider this payback."

Liam hoisted Jarok's salvation over the edge, a length of fence just long enough to reach the bottom of the pit. Jarok backed up as Liam carefully lowered the makeshift ladder down to the swampy surface below. Hands filled with splinters, forehead sweating, he stood back and watched Jarok regard the new addition to his world.

"Go," Liam said. "You're free now."

Jarok hesitated, and for a moment Liam thought he would ignore the ladder and plop back into the muck. Maybe he was too dumb to understand freedom, too conditioned to his captivity. But after a few minutes, his distraught and confused expression softened. He nodded slightly at Liam before wrapping his massive fingers around the first rung.

•|•

Liam found Wiki sitting in their dimly lit dwelling, his back pressed against a wall. When Wiki noticed Liam, his fingers stopped tapping out notes on his projected keyboards.

"Where have you been?"

Liam walked past Wiki. "It doesn't matter."

He removed the furs that the Suvi had given him, and he hung them by the fire. Water droplets fell from the clothes, boiling and evaporating upon collision with the hot stones below. He changed into the undergarments from his pressure suit, which were much more comfortable and absorbent than leather.

"Did you talk to Skai?" Wiki asked. "Is she still—"

"I don't want to talk about it." With his back to Wiki, Liam started laying out a few belongings on his bedding. He didn't have much.

"You don't want to talk about anything lately. It just seemed like you two were getting along until today."

"We've been wasting time," Liam said. He picked up his belt and wrapped it around his waist. "We should have been out there looking for Glo."

"I don't disagree with you, but we haven't really had a choice."

"We always have a choice." Liam cinched his belt and strapped a canteen to it. "I'm not afraid of these people."

"Clearly, but—"

"And I didn't come all the way to Earth just to follow more rules." Liam stopped packing and turned to his friend. "We're free men, Wiki. We have to start acting like it."

"Free men who can't leave," Wiki said.

"The Suvi just want us to think that we're trapped here." Liam shook his head. "But we're not. I've been out of the village with Skai plenty of times."

"So, you're trying to leave tomorrow?"

"No." Liam went to check if his furs had dried. "I'm leaving tonight."

Wiki sighed. "You have to think this through. Remember those stone steps we hiked up? It's the only way down to the valley, and the Suvi have guards posted there day and night. I've been keeping a pretty close eye on things while you've been— Well, never mind."

Liam decided his furs were dry enough and wrapped them around his shoulders. "While I've been what?"

"Well, you know."

"Would you just tell me?"

A tiny smile appeared then vanished from Wiki's face. "While you've been swimming with your new girlfriend."

Liam felt blood rushing to his cheeks. "How would you even know about that?"

"Information is available—"

"To those who seek it." Liam scoffed. "So, you've been spying on me?"

"I'm just observant."

"Whatever." Liam started toward the door.

"Wait." Wiki stood. "What about the guards?"

Liam stopped in the threshold and turned around. "I never said I'm going down to the valley, not yet anyway."

"Then where?"

Liam considered telling him, but he didn't need Wiki tagging along.

"I'll be back." He tried to calculate how long the trip would take, but he honestly had no idea. "Sometime tomorrow, hopefully."

With that, he exited. However, the solo portion of his journey only lasted a few minutes before Wiki came scrambling after him, followed closely by King.

"Wait," Wiki said. "Shouldn't we find Zara and bring her with us?"

Liam groaned. "She'll slow us down."

"But we're coming back for her, right?"

"Yes," Liam said. "We'll have to come back through here, anyway."

Wiki hurried to keep up. "Zara's a great marksman, you know. She's been practicing archery with Fang, and she's a natural. I guess she always has been."

Liam marched onward. "I wouldn't know."

They passed the last row of buildings and left the village behind.

"Are you kidding?" Wiki said. "She saved your life in the Earth Sim so many times."

Liam shrugged. "Did she?"

"You had no idea, did you?"

In truth, he didn't, though it did explain a few miraculous escapes he had made during training. How many times had the packs shrunk—or disappeared—chasing Liam around a corner? He always chalked those moments up to glitches or his own ability to throw the subs off his trail. It didn't matter now, though.

"Does this look like a simulation to you?" Liam spread his arms to indicate the forest. "I'm not expecting any fights, so I doubt we'll need an archer."

"Were you expecting *that*?" Wiki pointed at the trio of scars on Liam's leg, visible through a large gash in his pressure suit leggings. "All I'm saying is that you could give her a little bit of credit."

"Did you come here to criticize me? Or did you come to help me?"

"Sometimes a little bit of criticism can be helpful."

"Speaking of criticism, I've been meaning to ask you something." Liam sidestepped to avoid tripping on a rock. "Do you really think that I think I'm better than everyone else?"

"I mean, am I wrong?"

Liam didn't answer that. He knew he could be a little bit cocky, that he felt superior to many people in a few specific areas, but no one had ever called him out on it. He took the criticism like a handful of dry algae pellets—hesitantly and with disgust. But like algae pellets in the Omegan diet, was the criticism also necessary?

"Look, Liam. I'm not saying it's bad to think like that. In fact, I wish I had your confidence sometimes. It's just that thinking so highly of yourself affects how you treat people, and not everyone can handle it."

"Like Zara?"

"Exactly." Wiki had to hurry to catch up to Liam, who had quickened his pace to avoid the conversation. "And me, I guess. It's been harder for us to adjust to this place. Maybe you were always meant for it, but we're struggling. Zara's having an especially hard time. When you act like everything's so easy, it makes us feel weak. Useless. It hurts a bit. That's all."

A tense moment followed as Liam processed his friend's feelings.

Wiki's words hit him harder than he thought they would. Frowning slightly, he slowed down. "I didn't know."

They took a few more steps without talking. Liam almost said he was sorry, but the apology got stuck somewhere between his brain and his mouth.

"It's okay." Wiki slapped Liam's back. "Not all of us can know everything."

Liam laughed softly, the closest thing to an apology that he could muster. It was the first time he had felt comfortable talking to Wiki in days. After all that time avoiding the issue, they had finally met on level ground with their friendship still intact. Even on an alien planet, some things never changed.

•|•

They reached a small clearing in the forest, where Liam stopped and pointed up at a trio of mountainous silhouettes.

"There it is," he said. "The Eagle."

Wiki squinted in the moonlight. "We're climbing all the way up there? Tonight?"

"That's right." Liam stroked King's back. The cub snored gently in the crux of his free arm. "If we hurry, I think we can make it before dawn."

Wiki groaned. "Now I wish I'd stayed in bed."

As if on cue, King yawned, displaying his not-quite-deadly incisors. Liam scratched the cougar cub between the ears.

"Maybe you should go back," Liam said. "You could take King and start prepping Zara for our escape. Once I figure out the location of the others, we can jet."

Scratching his chin, Wiki paused for a moment. "I've already come this far."

"We've only been walking for half an hour."

"Yeah, and I don't want to waste it. I could use the exercise anyway. I've been spending too much time sitting and writing."

"Really, you should go back." Liam avoided Wiki's questioning gaze. "When I come back, I don't want to stay any longer than necessary. Actually, if I could bypass the village completely and meet you two somewhere, that would be perfect."

"Avoiding Skai?"

"Right."

Wiki's eyebrows inched closer together. "What aren't you telling me?"

"Nothing."

"I can tell it's not about Skai. Why don't you want to go back?"

"I told you." Liam shifted his weight from one foot to the other, then back again. "I can't follow their rules."

"Liam," Wiki said, his tone approaching motherly. "I've known you for how long?"

Liam didn't have to think hard to come up with the answer. "Since first year."

"And ever since then, I've been able to tell when you're lying." He exhaled dramatically. "Just tell me what's going on."

"Okay, fine." Liam swallowed hard, considering the best way to approach the subject. "I may or may not have done something that Fang won't be too happy about."

"Elaborate."

"I was angry, and it kind of just happened."

"Spill it," Wiki said. "How bad could it possibly be?"

"It's bad." A nervous chuckle escaped Liam's tight chest. "Pretty bad."

"I'm definitely not going back now, so you might as well tell me." Wiki started toward the Eagle, as if to prove his devotion to discovering the truth. "Let's walk and talk."

"Fine." Liam walked beside him. "Just promise to keep an open mind."

"I always do."

"All right," Liam said, more to himself than Wiki. "After what happened with Skai, I swung by the giant's pit."

"Why would you go back there?"

"I just wanted to thank Jarok. You know, for not killing me."

"You know he doesn't speak, right?"

"There are other ways to express gratitude."

"Like a pile of dead fish?"

"I thought about that, actually." Liam stared ahead, subconsciously scanning the tree line for signs of danger. "You should have seen the way Jarok acted in that pit, Wiki. He looked so…human. It didn't feel right to see him treated like an animal. Locked up like that."

"Oh, no," Wiki said, his mind clearly arriving at the most logical conclusion. "I'm guessing you didn't feed the giant."

"No." Liam picked up his pace, as if he could outrun the consequences of what he had done. "But at least he can feed himself now."

"You know if he goes back to the village and kills somebody, that death is on you, right? They kept him in that pit for a reason."

"He went the other way," Liam said. "I watched him go. Away from the village."

Wiki gulped air. "You mean the same way we're heading?"

•|•

The trail to the top of the Eagle was easy enough to find, and though they lost it a few times, Wiki managed to get them back on track. The slow climb in elevation drained Liam's energy, but the will to find the other Omegans kept him motivated to carry on. They didn't stop until the stars began to fade, replaced by the glow of early morning.

"I think we're close," Liam said.

Wiki's mouth stretched open so wide that it looked like his jaw might separate from his head. "We're almost out of water," he said.

Liam shook his canteen. Only a few sips sloshed within it. "We can find more."

"We should have packed more to begin with. If you told me we'd be climbing a mountain, I would have brought a pack."

King rubbed up against Liam's heels. "It's a little late for that."

They hiked on silently, both of them too exhausted to speak. The path narrowed as it skirted the mountainside. Liam and Wiki stopped at every clifftop vista to search the valley floor for signs of life, but they could only see small sections of the valley from each overlook.

"We just have to get to the top," Liam said.

"And what if we can't see them from up there?"

"Skai said you can see the whole valley from the peak. We just need to find some smoke from a fire or something like that. Doesn't your cam have a zoom option or something?"

"It's only four times magnification." Wiki smiled. "But yes, it does help with all of my spying."

"You didn't really follow us to the waterfall that night, did you?"

Wiki smirked. "Which night?"

"I thought you were sleeping."

"Don't worry." A dry chuckle came from Wiki's mouth. "Skai told Zara, and Zara told me. Nobody saw anything. I mean, besides you and Skai."

"It was dark," Liam said through a smile, but that smile quickly faded when he remembered he might never see Skai again. He shook the thought away.

They continued, the silence between them filled by a crescendo of birdsong. Soon the path narrowed as it reached a treacherous ridge, like a gash in the mountainside. On one side stood a steep sheet of rock that stretched toward the sky. On the other side— nothing but air and a long fall to the bottom. Liam began to tread more carefully, knowing that one wrong step could quickly become fatal.

"Wait," Wiki croaked. He had stopped several meters behind Liam, where he leaned on a boulder jutting out of the mountain's face. "I don't think I can do this."

"What do you mean?"

"I think I've suddenly discovered that I'm acrophobic."

Liam raised one eyebrow.

"I'm afraid of heights," Wiki said, his hands beginning to shake violently. "Well, afraid of falling, at least. Or maybe it's just gravity. Whatever it is, I would rather not die this way."

"You're not going to die." King came from behind Wiki and trotted along the ridge to where Liam stood. Liam indicated the cub by tilting his head. "See, King's not afraid, and he's still a baby."

"He's a cougar, also known as a mountain lion. His body is built for balance. It's in his evolution. My body, on the other hand, is built for—"

"Overthinking."

"Hey, it's kept me alive so far."

Liam stopped to think, not without silently acknowledging the irony of doing so. He had to appeal to Wiki's pride, and he knew of one surefire way to do that.

"When we find Glo," Liam said, "do you want to tell her that you hiked to the peak of the highest mountain to rescue her?"

"That's not—"

"Or that you shat yourself when the path got a little bit narrow?"

"I didn't— I haven't—"

Liam activated his story-telling voice, a deeper, more enunciated way of speaking. "I could smell his fear from the peak, Glo. It was disgusting—and a little bit pathetic."

"Stop," Wiki said, clearly unamused. "Just give me a sec, okay?"

"No. No more time to think about it. Just do it."

"I'll come, I just—"

"Do it now. Take one step."

After a slow breath, Wiki took one hesitant step forward.

"Another one."

"I'll get there."

Liam glanced over his shoulder. "Guess what I found around this bend."

Wiki's fingernails clutched the stone wall. He stood there, his whole body frozen in place.

"There's water trickling out of a crack in the mountain. Clear. Cold. All you have to do is get here."

Wiki's eyebrows came closer together.

"What?" Liam asked. "You think I'm lying? Hold on."

Liam took the empty bottle from his belt and showed it to Wiki. Then he walked over to the natural spring and filled it with water. When he came back, he shook the bottle in front of him before chugging half of it. It was as pure and cold as it looked.

"So refreshing," he said.

Wiki swallowed some air and took another step. The wind made his hair stand straight up. At that moment, Liam wondered if a strong gust would be enough to push his friend over the edge.

"See? The fear is all in your head, Wiki."

"Technically, all sensory perceptions and emotions are in your head."

"Whatever gets you here."

A few more slow steps brought Wiki to the narrowest part of the ridge. Every time his foot connected with solid ground, his tremors lessened in intensity.

"The worst is over," Liam said.

This seemed to invigorate Wiki. He took the last steps more quickly, with renewed confidence. Finally, he arrived on a wider landing, where he immediately fell to all fours and nearly kissed the ground.

"I'm never doing that again," he managed to say after savoring a few breaths of mountain air.

"You know," Liam said. He handed Wiki what remained of his water. "I've heard going up a mountain is the easy part."

By the time the Eagle's summit came into view, the sun had been up for well over an hour. Too fatigued to celebrate, Liam and Wiki approached the end of their journey quietly, their bellies and canteens filled with ice-cold spring water. They rounded the final curve, and all at once, the landscape came into view.

Liam had no words. Staring across the vast expanse of nature from this vantage point filled him with wonder. Beautiful though they were, the surrounding mountains had limited his view. Now he could see the tops of those great monoliths of stone. Below them, the valley floor stretched out in its entirety, dotted with clearings, bursting with vibrant greenery, etched by rivers and streams. Beyond the mountains, the rolling hills and highlands sprawled along the distance until the horizon swallowed them up.

Overwhelmed by the sheer magnitude of it all, Liam couldn't focus on any single detail for long, though he did quickly register the dark scar on the earth that marked the crash site. He pointed it out.

"There."

Wiki nodded and closed his jaw, which had fallen open. "Wow, we really left a mark."

"It looks like"—Liam squinted, though it didn't help—"Is there movement down there? I can't tell."

"Maybe," Wiki said. "It's hard to see, but it could be—"

"Zoom in, already!"

"I'm trying." Wiki adjusted his over-ear camera, then blindly tapped in a sequence on his thigh—no need to project the holographic keypad. "There's a glitch. No, wait. Unable to process your request. Oh, I know."

"What's wrong with it?"

Wiki scratched his sunburnt neck. "Fair warning, I'm about to talk nerdy to you."

"I'll try to stay awake," Liam said.

"Okay, so my tech usually relies on the computational power of Omega to do the heavy lifting."

"How is zooming in considered heavy lifting?"

"The optical zoom is limited on such a tiny camera, so zooming in requires a digital enlargement enhanced by a complex algorithm. It's actually a fairly high-performance task. Since I'm no longer linked to Omega's systems, we might be out of luck." Wiki displayed the bands around his wrists. "My local systems were designed for word processing, not augmented reality."

"Of all people, why would they limit you?"

Wiki sighed. "Thing is—I kind of limited myself. I didn't want to get distracted while revising the Archives, so I opted for a simpler unit to remove all unnecessary functions. It's more reliable."

"Can't you reverse the limit or something?" Liam asked.

"Maybe if I terminate a few high-resource processes, I can reallocate enough processing power for the task. Hold on, I'll try it."

While he waited, Liam focused on the teardrop-shaped crash site, the enigmatic way the dark wasteland there seemed to ripple with movement. "It must be the others," he said. "It has to be."

Wiki continued his work for another ten minutes or so, the only interruption a gust of wind that nearly knocked him off his feet. He sat down after that, careful and cross-legged.

"Maybe we should go back," Liam said.

Wiki ignored him. Growing impatient, Liam walked away.

"Wait," Wiki said, typing twice as fast now. "I think I did it. Well, not the way I planned to, but this way might be better."

"What do you mean?"

"I don't know if it's because of our elevation or what, but I managed to establish a mobile connection to Omega's systems." Wiki tapped his over-ear camera. "I can't believe this tiny antenna was enough."

"Does that mean we—"

"We can use Omega's processing power. There might be some lag, but we can"—Wiki looked directly at Liam—"We can send a message home, too."

"Really?"

Wiki grinned. "With only a couple of seconds of delay. But we better hurry." He pointed at the moon, which sat above the horizon, nearly invisible in the daylight. "I estimate less than thirty minutes before we lose the signal for the next twelve hours—give or take."

"Let's do it."

Wiki displayed the band around his wrist, which Liam knew hid a tiny microphone. "Would you like to do the honors?"

Liam thought about it for a moment. "I don't even know what I would say. This one's all you."

Wiki closed his eyes and kept them shut for so long that Liam thought he might have fallen asleep, then he held the band to his mouth and recited the message he had just rehearsed in his head.

"This is Ensign Richard Abbott of the Resurgence Mission, transmitting from Earth. I am here with Ensign Liam Stone. Does anyone copy?" He paused. "Over."

Two seconds passed.

Then another ten.

Liam doubted that the message had gone through, but then a burst of static exploded in his ear. He jumped, having forgotten all about his aural implant. Apparently, Wiki had linked him into the audio stream.

"Hold on," Wiki said, typing furiously. "Adjusting for interference."

The static sounds buzzed and shifted into something less obnoxious, then a voice came through, barely audible under the fuzzy soundscape.

"Please repeat. Over."

Liam and Wiki glanced at each other, amazed, then Wiki cleared his throat and began again.

"This is Ensign Richard Abbott of the Resurgence Mission, transmitting from Earth. I am here with Ensign Liam Stone. We are alive and well, but we have been separated from the rest of the crew. We require assistance finding the remaining survivors of the ETS Resurgence. Over."

The monotonous drone of the operator returned after a few tense seconds. *"Not funny, kid."*

"What?" was all Wiki could manage.

"You're transmitting on a private channel reserved for official use only. I suggest you stop this nonsense before I report you."

"What do you mean *nonsense*? This isn't a prank. Why don't you triangulate—"

"And the moon is made of cheese, kid."

Over the course of their short conversation, the operator's voice had shifted from bored to conversational to unamused. Liam wished he could throw a rock into orbit to pelt the guy with. Who was he to belittle them by calling Wiki a kid? A kid?

"Wait a second," Liam said. "I recognize that voice."

Wiki shot him a questioning side-eye. Liam grabbed his friend's wrist and held the device up to his own mouth.

"Is it transmitting?"

Wiki tapped his fingers against his leg and said, "Now it is."

"Come in, Smythii. It's me. It's Liam. So, your transfer went through after all?" Then, doing his best to impersonate the man's rugged voice, he said, "I heard radio operations is a pretty sweet gig."

Once the infuriating delay passed, Smythii's response came through loud and clear.

"Well, I'll be damned." Another pause. *"We thought you were dead, kid. We thought that all of you were dead."*

23

HOLE IN HER HEART

Glo's grief made the days pass slowly. It dulled the flavor of what little food she could stomach, and colored the clouds a darker shade of gray. Her only brother—dead. The mission to restore life on Earth—dire. What did she have to live for now? More than once since learning about Liam's death, she had held the stolen plasma pistol in her hand for long periods, teasing the trigger, searching her mind for a reason not to take the easy way out. One single question continued to haunt her, manifesting itself in various forms: Why? What reason did she have to go on? What purpose could she possibly aspire to now?

Contemplating this question, Glo rolled over in her cot for what felt like the hundredth time. It was mid-day, but the bed still held her in its magnetic embrace. It hurt to move, and not only because of the higher gravity. Staying still hurt as well. Life hurt.

Glo silently justified her laziness. She had nothing better to do. Several days after the crash, most of her patients had recovered enough to care for themselves, leaving her with zero work on her agenda. She supposed she could get up and help with the communal chores, but again, what was the point? No one seemed to notice her absence, so why go asking for work to do? Even Reagan had left her alone.

The tent flaps parted, and Quinn limped in, her hair soaking wet and her body wrapped in a large piece of white cloth. Glo didn't bother greeting her.

"Good *afternoon*," Quinn said. She came over and sat down on the corner of Glo's cot. "It's about time to get up, don't you think?"

Glo groaned softly into a bundle of clothes that she used as a pillow. "Why?"

"Because the sun is shining. Because the day is half gone already. But mostly because you need to bathe." Quinn touched Glo lightly on the back. "You stink."

"Whatever, Quinn. I don't feel like a bath." She sniffed the collar of her shirt. Definitely not fresh, but not yet rancid either. "I'm clean enough."

"Now you sound like one of the nursery kids. Seriously, Glo, get up. You can't just stay in bed all day."

Glo pulled the covers over her head. "Watch me."

"It's not healthy to stay cooped up like this."

"I don't care."

Quinn sighed. "I know depression can be a bitch."

Usually, Glo would have said something about Quinn's language, but she really didn't care what the girl did anymore. She had even given up on trying to prevent her from seeing Commander Killion.

"Shouldn't you be following Nikolai around or something?" Glo asked, mocking the way Quinn said the man's name. "Can't you go annoy him instead?"

Glo's remark shut the girl up, but only for a beat. "I know you're sad, Glo, but you don't need to take it out on me."

"And you didn't need to come check on me."

"I'm just trying to help."

Glo pulled the blanket tighter around herself. "I'm fine. Really. Just go away."

"No." Quinn yanked the blanket off Glo. "You're not fine."

"Go. Away."

"Listen, Glo. I don't care what you do. It doesn't matter whether you clean yourself or feed yourself or just go for a walk. But you need to get up and do something. Anything. I promise you'll feel better. You need some fresh air—and sunlight. And please, please, if you're not going to take a bath, at least change your clothes."

Not so deep down, Glo knew that Quinn was right. She usually was. The girl had wisdom beyond her years, but that didn't mean

Glo wanted to hear it. She just wanted to be left alone.

"Fine."

Quinn perked up. "Really?"

"Sure," Glo said. "I'll get out of bed in a few minutes. I'll go for a walk. Happy?"

"Yes." Quinn set the blanket back on the bed and got dressed. When she went to leave, she paused in the threshold. "If I don't see you outside soon, I'll be back."

"I don't doubt that."

Quinn's wet hair flipped through the air as she turned away. "See you soon, then."

For a few minutes after Quinn left, Glo just lay there. She didn't want to bathe or eat or walk, but she supposed that moving around couldn't hurt any worse than staying put. She threw her legs over the edge of the cot, stretched her ankles and toes. Her lower limbs felt heavy and pliable, as if they had forgotten how to function. She took a long, slow breath, gathering what little energy she had.

There was one thing she needed to get up and do, a task she dreaded, but one she felt guilty about putting off—even under layers and layers of sadness. She avoided standing for as long as possible, but eventually, the guilt consumed her. Hesitantly, she stood on shaky legs, numbly donned some fresh clothes, and exited the tent. Her reason to continue living—for the day at least—was to get a message back to Omega. She needed to share the bad news. She needed to tell her mother about Liam's death.

•|•

When Glo stepped out of the tent, she closed her eyes and allowed the sun to work its magic. Unlike the sunshine in Omega—a poor, diluted substitute for the real thing—the sunshine on Earth actually warmed her skin. It covered her pain, buried her sorrow beneath serotonin.

The effects didn't last long enough. If things had gone differently, Glo could see herself eventually being happy on Earth. But the few people she cared about sharing the sunlight with had disappeared for good, and now that gentle warmth mocked her. It sang of brighter days that would never come.

Glo walked through Camp Resurgence, which bustled with the activities of survival. Some, mostly the younger women and the injured, sat around smoky fire pits, cooking meat brought in by the hunting parties, washing and mending clothes. Meanwhile, the more able-bodied chopped wood, carried crates of supplies, and exercised. Armed officers—all of them male, Glo noticed—manned the walls, which had grown much taller and thicker since the influx of subhumans wandering the forest.

Several more attacks had occurred, but only one casualty. Human and not-quite-human, the bodies of the deceased were now a pile of ash outside the camp, except for one sub wrapped in a plastic sheet and stored in the frigid shallows of the river. They kept it preserved, just in case the virologist ever came back and needed a specimen to study. No one Glo spoke to actually believed Viola Collins would return.

A few more survivors had wandered into camp as well, ragged and hungry, but mostly uninjured. They told stories of crash landings and close calls, and ate like they had never seen food before. This small influx of people brought the survivor count to a mere forty-nine. Forty-nine human beings left on the entire planet, only twenty-two of whom were capable of producing more. There was always a chance that additional survivors would come, but as the days passed, Glo doubted that would happen.

Commander Killion nodded at her as she passed. He had a plasma rifle slung across his back, a pistol on each hip, and his mouth set in a straight, hard line. The camp had far more guns than men, yet Reagan still wouldn't arm the women. The guns were locked up and guarded in the center of camp. Clearly, Reagan still didn't trust the fairer sex.

Glo hadn't planned on eating, but the smell of food drew her closer to one of the fire pits, where a trio of women sat, their mouths busy talking, their hands engaged in various chores. When Glo sat down and joined them, their chatter ceased. One of them—a thin woman in her twenties named Aurora—smiled and handed Glo a fire-roasted drumstick from some kind of wildfowl.

"Hungry?"

"Thanks," Glo said.

Aurora hummed and said, "Don't mention it."

Once Glo settled in and started eating, the others continued speaking to each other.

"So," one said, her voice quiet, "do you think they ran away, or do you think they were banished?"

"Oh, they definitely ran away." Aurora checked her surroundings and lowered her voice. "After what the Admiral tried to do. I mean, what would your husband do if he found out?"

The woman frowned. "I thought we agreed not to talk about home."

The gossip piqued Glo's interest, but not enough for her to interrupt. She continued to take tiny bites of the poultry while she listened.

"I'm sorry, Drea. I forgot."

"It's okay," Drea said. "If I'm being honest, Abram probably would have tried to fight the guy. He definitely wouldn't run away like that." She glanced skyward. "I miss that man."

Glo couldn't resist anymore. She usually didn't care about gossip, but she had to know. She stopped chewing, swallowed, and cleared her throat.

"Who are you talking about? What happened?"

Aurora turned to her. "Oh, you haven't heard?"

Glo shrugged. "I've been sick in bed."

"Let me catch you up," Aurora said. "You know that muscular young man, Tai, the one who's always walking around like he hit the Earth Sim too hard?"

In response to the apt description, Glo nodded.

"Well, he and his girlfriend— What's her name again? That fiery little cyborg."

"Raelyn," Drea said.

"Yes, her. Anyway, nobody has seen either of them since yesterday. We think they deserted camp, right after Reagan invited Rae to his tent the other night." Aurora folded her arms. "And *invited* might be too nice of a word for it. He basically threatened her. Said it was her duty, that she owed it to him. I overheard her going off about it to Tai afterward. Then they were gone."

Glo had never been close with Tai or Raelyn, but their

disappearance meant she would see even fewer familiar faces around camp. She sighed. Was this how things would be from now on? Would the rest of humanity get picked off one by one until no one remained?

"I'm sorry," Aurora said after a moment of silence. "Were they friends of yours?"

"Not really." Glo threw the drumstick, which still had meat on it, into the fire. "I have to go."

Forty-seven survivors, Glo thought as she walked away.

Glo stood outside Reagan's tent, listening for the telltale huff and puff of air entering his mechanical lung. She heard nothing but distant chatter and wind rustling through the trees. A sigh escaped her mouth. Her cot was calling her name, but first, she wanted to get her request over with.

She waited outside for several minutes before deciding to come back later. But as she turned to leave, something stopped her—curiosity, the first emotion besides sadness that she had felt in some time. She scanned the area to see if anyone was watching. Nobody in sight seemed to notice her presence, so she parted the tent flaps and slipped in.

Musty darkness dominated the space. Instead of finding the lights, Glo took a minute to let her eyes adjust. The tent looked the same as it had days earlier, the night Reagan broke the news about Liam's death.

Glo wandered around the tent, picking up and observing the Admiral's belongings: some clothes, various medications, and a small figurine she hadn't noticed before. It sat on the crate that served as Reagan's nightstand, right beside his bottle of moonfire. She sat on the bed, took a long draw out of the bottle, and examined the figurine. It looked like an animal, but one Glo couldn't name. She ran her fingers across the dark green stone. The figurine's fine details looked worn out, as if time had erased them, but the shape of the creature remained. It had four legs, ears that looked massive relative to its body. Two horns protruded from its mouth, one of them broken off, right below a third protuberance that looked like a section of hose. Holding it in her hand, she took another sip from the bottle.

"Put that down."

Reagan's voice nearly made Glo choke on the liquor. She swallowed hard.

"Sorry," she said. "I was just—"

"Snooping? You know you're not allowed in here."

Glo set the figurine down on the nightstand. "I didn't know where else to go." She began to tear up. "I didn't mean to snoop. I'll leave now. I just—"

"It's fine, Gloria. Stay." Reagan sat on the bed beside her, and Glo scooted away. "I was just startled, that's all. And I don't like people touching my things. Especially that."

Glo's shoulders slumped, and her head followed. "It's pretty. What is it?"

"The statuette? It's an elephant. It was a gift."

She glanced at it. "From who?"

"From someone very important to me."

"My grandmother?" Glo asked.

Reagan emitted a deep, audible breath from his lung vent. "Not quite," he said. "Elara's great-great-grandmother hadn't yet been born when I got this."

"Then who?"

"Drinking my booze, I see? If we're going to talk about this, I need some too." He picked up the bottle, took a sip for himself, then held the stone elephant in his hand and stared at it. "My wife gave this to me. A long time ago. It was her favorite animal. The Indian elephant."

"What a strange creature," Glo said.

"One of the strangest."

Glo thought about the magnificent things she had seen in the last few days. "What did she like about the elephants?"

"She loved that something so large and fierce-looking could be so sweet. Too sweet to live, apparently. Elephants were endangered then. They're probably extinct by now."

"Or they're flourishing," Glo said.

"I doubt that." Reagan shook his head. "We planned to go

to India one day. She wanted to volunteer, to help care for the elephants. We were young then, full of hope. We didn't understand the world was ending."

"So, you didn't go?"

"We were too late."

"Was it because she— Did she—"

"Die?" Reagan squeezed the figurine in his fist until his knuckles turned white. "Everyone that stayed behind died."

"I'm sorry," Glo said. She hated Reagan and everything he had done to her, but her own grief granted her some temporary empathy for the man.

"It was her choice," he said, his tone growing bitter. "All she had to do was get on the damn shuttle."

Glo paused, her mind slowly processing Reagan's words. "Why didn't she?

Reagan took another sip, and his head tilted downward. "She wanted to stay with our son, even after all the strings I pulled to get her a seat."

"Couldn't they both have—"

"He couldn't come, and she wouldn't leave him behind. It was the plague that got him." A violent coughing fit erupted from Reagan's chest. "She still loved him, you know? Even though he was born deformed, deranged, violent. Even though he bit and scratched and howled. And I loved him, too. I really did. But I knew what he would become. She didn't understand. She couldn't. Love blinded her. I don't blame her, I just—"

Another coughing fit ended Reagan's speech. Glo didn't know how to respond, so she just sat there and tried to imagine how a baby could be anything other than wonderful. How could a single virus, something so minuscule, strip someone of their humanity? It didn't seem fair.

"Ethan. That was his name." Reagan coughed again then sighed. "This whole mission. I orchestrated all of this to honor him and his mother. After all these centuries, we can finally build a world where mothers can be mothers, where they don't have to worry about giving birth to monstrosities."

Glo considered Reagan's words for a while. Their chances of

achieving such a lofty goal had diminished. "Will we ever see that world now?"

"I don't know." Reagan set the token of his past on the nightstand. He looked at it for a long time, as if gears were spinning in his head. "But there is another path I've been considering, a shortcut, really."

· He picked up his tablet from the makeshift nightstand and tapped through some menus until an image appeared on the screen.

"What is that?"

"A map." Reagan pointed at a mountain range that occupied the right side of the screen. "This is where we are." His index finger traced a line across the screen until it reached a point near the coastline. "And this facility here could be our salvation."

Glo squinted. "I don't see anything."

"It was never on any official maps, but it's there. Underground. Top secret. It's called the Life Vault."

The name intrigued her. "What's inside?"

"It was originally set up as a gene bank. Seeds and DNA samples from the world's plants and animals were stored there in case of an apocalyptic event. But it also has a large supply of medical equipment, drugs, imperishable food—even human embryos and artificial wombs. Everything is preserved in cryogenic freezers powered by geothermal generators deep in the ground."

"How have I never heard about this?"

"Not many people believe the Life Vault is real. Others speculate that it has probably already been scavenged or fallen into disrepair. Think of how much time has passed."

"And what do you believe?"

"I have no choice but to be hopeful," Reagan said. "I always wanted to get there eventually, to see for myself. Our original trajectory would have put us in range, but now…"

"Can we still make it? Is it possible?"

"I don't know," Reagan said. "It's a long journey, and who knows what dangers we might encounter on the way. I've sent a few scouts to look for a path out of the valley. It might be difficult, but if we can get the antivirus there, we may be able to see this mission through to the end. That's my hope, anyway. My last hope. I know I've made a lot of mistakes, but if I can get us there, then at least I'll know I did one thing right."

Glo nodded. It was like two versions of Reagan existed: one who used his authority for his own agenda, the other the savior of humankind. He treated women like objects, but also grieved his dead wife and son. The dichotomy confused Glo.

"I thought we lost the antivirus in the crash," she said.

"No." A grin stretched across Reagan's face. "Well, yes, we lost the payload. But the antivirus is inside all of us. It can be synthesized from our blood. We just need to get there."

"But Doctor Collins—"

"We have all of her research. It may take some time, but we can make it work. It's what humans do, after all. We innovate. We survive."

Speaking of the plan seemed to invigorate Reagan. His sickly demeanor turned into something more youthful and jovial. Glo stayed in Reagan's tent and listened to him for a long time before she got up the nerve to ask the question she'd gone there to ask.

"I've been thinking," Glo said. Reagan looked at her in a way that said she shouldn't be doing that. "Have you sent a list of the deceased back home yet?"

"Oh, Gloria," Reagan said. She still hated that he called her that. "You really have been keeping to yourself the last few days, haven't you?"

Glo's organs felt like they were fighting each other, clawing to get out of her body. She didn't know if she could take any more disappointment. "What happened?"

"Like so many other things," he said, "the comm units were all destroyed. I wish we could send a message, but it's not possible. Perhaps someday, if things work out in our favor, but not now."

As hope rose in Reagan, it drained out of Glo—like a bolt of plasma had punched a hole in her heart.

24

SPECK OF LIGHT

Liam and Wiki lost their connection to Omega almost as quickly as they acquired it. Now they would have to wait twelve hours to get the location of Camp Resurgence, which would be extrapolated by analyzing both telescopic imagery and the last known trajectory of the ship. At least that was their hope. No one truly knew if such methods would work. Why these measures hadn't already been attempted baffled Liam. It was like Omega had forgotten about the ETS Resurgence the moment they could no longer communicate with the crew.

Before losing the connection, though, Wiki managed to enhance a few local images of the valley. Having descended from the peak, he and Liam now sat beside a natural spring, drinking their fill and eating the last of their food while Wiki pored over the images on his implant, his eyelids sealed shut for maximum contrast and focus.

"This doesn't look good," Wiki said.

Liam sighed. The fact that he couldn't see the images himself frustrated him beyond belief. "What's wrong?" he said.

"I know where the others *aren't* located, which can only help, I guess. They're definitely not at the crash site. It looks like there are more bodies there than the ETS could have brought to Earth. And judging by the colors I see, none of them are wearing clothes, which can only mean one thing." Wiki shook his head. "Fang was right about the crash drawing herds from the highlands. There must be hundreds of subs down there in the clearing. Who knows how many in the surrounding forest?"

"Great," Liam said.

Wiki opened his eyes, withdrew his attention from the images, and took a sip of water. "I can look at the rest of these later, but this is giving me a headache. Should we start heading back?"

Reclining against the mountainside with King sitting in his lap, Liam yawned. "We hiked all night. How about a quick nap first?"

Wiki glanced at the edge of the cliff just meters away. "Up here?"

"Think of it this way." Liam closed his eyes and rolled onto his side. He rested his head on his furs. "You can't be afraid if you're asleep."

•|•

The nap lasted longer than Liam expected. By the time he and Wiki awoke and began their descent, the sun had passed the middle of the sky. Birds sang tired songs from the treetops and flew away in droves as Liam and Wiki passed.

"At this pace," Wiki said, "we might not get back until after dark."

Liam's feet fell heavily on the ground, crunching dead leaves. "At least it will be easier to avoid Fang in the dark."

"I nearly forgot that I'm traveling with a criminal."

"No one can prove I did it."

"You should still keep a low profile."

"I will," Liam said. "By the time we find Zara and get out of there, we should have the intel from Smythii. Then we just have to get past the guards."

It sounded easy, but Liam hadn't actually seen the guards in person.

"You're forgetting about the horde of flesh-eating monsters in the valley."

"We'll open that airlock when we come to it." Liam paused. "And do they really eat flesh? I always thought that was an exaggeration in the Earth Sim."

"From what I've been able to gather from the locals, subs definitely enjoy the taste of human meat. Didn't you hear about that little girl?"

"We'll be fine," Liam said. "This is what we trained for."

For the first time in a while, Liam had a plan. It would require stealth and a lot of improvisation, but it was still a set of actions he could control. Despite the impending danger, he felt good about what might happen next.

"Let's talk hypothetically," Wiki said. "Say our escape from the village goes smoothly, and we make it to the others safely. What then? They might welcome me back, but what if Reagan is still angry about you stowing away? You're a criminal in both of Earth's societies now."

"Don't you ever stop worrying? You should be celebrating right now. We just talked to Smythii after the entire city thought we were dead. You made that happen."

"Yeah, but—"

"I can deal with Reagan if it comes to that. I have it all planned out. If he wants me to pay for my crimes, I'll play along for a while. But when the time is right, you, me, Glo, and whoever else wants to join us—we can get out of there and do our own thing. We can carve our own path. We'll finally be free." He spread his arms to indicate the portion of the valley visible from their current vantage point. "There's a big world out there, Wiki. Don't you want to see it?"

"Sure." Wiki glanced at the nearest cliff. "As long as we're not looking at it from a mountaintop."

•|•

As the Suvi village came into view at the bottom of the hill, nervous energy blossomed in Liam's chest—partly because he feared Fang's retribution for freeing the giant, partly because of the challenges he would face should they make it past the village, but mostly because he was thinking about Skai.

What was this feeling? He barely knew the girl, yet for some reason, he ached to see her again—to touch her one more time. Sure, he and Raelyn had enjoyed some good moments together during their short-lived relationship, but he never missed her like he did Skai. A connection existed between them that he couldn't define. He felt the connection, at least. Did she? Probably not anymore, he decided, not after parting on such bad terms.

Liam did his best to evict these feelings from his mind. But as he hiked through the gradually flattening terrain, his ruminations swirled into a frenzy of thought. Eventually, he couldn't think of anything but Skai—her tight, dark curls that bounced with each step she took, the way she giggled to herself after attempting a joke, and how she looked beneath the moonlight that first night. Bare. Natural. Beautiful. Skai existed somewhere in the space between nature and civilization, and she represented both with equal grace. Thinking of her, Liam sighed.

"You good?" Wiki asked.

"Yeah," Liam said. "Just tired."

"Sun's going down." Wiki peered ahead. "We're close."

Liam nodded. "Where should I meet you?"

"I've been thinking. Maybe we should wait until later to go back. Once most of the village has gone to bed."

"Not a bad idea."

At the bottom of the hill, Liam could see the first glimmers of evening firelight beginning to illuminate the center of the village. Some fires would burn until morning, but most would go out as the night wore on. He wondered which one Skai sat beside—and whether she was thinking about him as well.

A hand on the shoulder woke Liam. After a two-hour watch while Wiki slept, he had taken his turn—a slumber that felt more like a long blink than a nap.

"What is it?" he said.

He could barely see Wiki's face in the dark.

"I think I saw the giant," Wiki whispered. "He walked right past here."

Liam rubbed his eyes with his knuckles. "Jarok won't hurt us."

"One experience is hardly enough to make that assumption, but okay. He looks so much bigger when he's not in a pit."

"How long was I out?" Liam asked.

Wiki's kept an eye on the forest. "It's probably late enough to go back."

"Any word from Smythii?"

"Not yet. Moonrise isn't for a few more hours."

Liam's stomach growled so violently that King jumped. "All right, let's go. And let's steal some food for the trip. I'm starving, and King hasn't eaten."

Liam hefted the furs back onto his shoulders, placed King into a pouch to carry him, and walked beside Wiki. Every muscle in his body protested against the motion. Instead of the pain, he focused on the chill of night, which soothed his sunburnt face. As they walked, the foliage thickened until it blocked the ambient light from the sky. The breeze became more humid.

Wiki led the way along the narrow path, ducking under branches and stepping over fallen logs. Ten minutes later, he came to an abrupt stop, and Liam nearly ran into him. The path terminated at a boulder overgrown with trees and thick foliage.

"I don't remember this," Wiki said. "We should turn around, see if we took a wrong turn."

"We're so close, though." Liam glanced at the slope of the boulder, the apex of which towered over the treetops. "Let's just go over it."

Wiki put his hand against the dark stone, looked up. "I don't know."

"We can at least go up and see if we're heading the right way." Liam found a handhold to grab, then pulled himself onto a flat ledge jutting out of the boulder. "Once you get here, it's a straight shot to the top. A forty-five-degree climb. Come on."

He reached down to help Wiki.

"I can do it," Wiki said.

Liam moved out of the way, then Wiki grabbed the ledge. He didn't ascend as gracefully as Liam, but he didn't hesitate either.

"See what happens when you face your fears head-on?"

Liam turned and crawled on all fours toward the top. The sound of leaves rustling in the wind intensified as he neared the treetops. Then the dank, earthy smell of the forest floor gave way to clear, dry air. When the boulder leveled out, Liam came to a standing position. Wiki joined him at the top. They stood close to a sheer drop overlooking the fields outside the village. Though the communal bonfires had gone out, firelight still burned in some dwellings, cascading onto the streets.

"Wow," Liam said. "It's still hard to believe."

Silence reigned for a while as they both soaked in the stunning panorama.

"This civilization," Wiki said, "this speck of light so small that you wouldn't see it from outer space—it represents so much. This is humanity. This is us surviving. I mean, we're witnessing natural evolution here. Survival of the fittest."

"What do you mean?"

"The Suvi are a product of their environment. They had to adapt to survive—the same way we did. When you think about it, we're not so different. We survived by running away, they survived by hiding. We engineered our immunity, they developed one naturally."

Liam peered beyond the horizon. "It makes me wonder how many others might be out there."

"They better hope they find each other."

"Why's that?"

"The Suvi have survived here for this long, but it doesn't mean they'll survive much longer. Their environment is changing. Their population is dwindling. A few generations back, they suffered a devastating famine. Before that, it was a drought. Now they have all those subs to contend with—invading the valley, trampling their fields, eating up all the wild game."

"Haven't they always had that problem?"

"They cleared the valley a long time ago, but we ruined that. Even without all this extra pressure, their gene pool is shrinking, which will result in inbreeding and birth defects."

"What about all the kids? I saw plenty of them."

"It doesn't matter. It's not enough. Just look at how many buildings don't have fires lit. The Suvi's speck of light is fading fast. Maybe they could avoid extinction if they left this place and found others like them. Maybe."

Wiki frowned and stared off into the distance.

"Hey." Liam patted his friend on the back. "We've got our own people to worry about."

"Yeah, I know. All of this is just dredging up my existential dread."

"At least we're heading the right way," Liam said. "Should we—"

A high-pitched noise stole Liam's attention. King had poked his head out of the carrying pouch and was hissing. Liam tracked the feline's gaze to the bottom of the boulder, where he saw nothing but darkness. He stroked King's head.

"What's wrong, buddy?"

King writhed inside his pouch. Worried that he might get free and tumble over the edge, Liam wrapped his arm around the cub to keep him contained. Claw tips poking into his skin, he turned to the boulder's base. One of the trees shook.

"Someone's down there," Wiki whispered.

"Not *someone*" was all Liam managed to say before the chaos began.

Branches snapped as their visitor jumped from the tree to the boulder. Casting a gangly shadow, its motions hardly resembled those of a human. The sub scrambled up the slope at an abnormal pace, ripping shards of slate off the boulder's surface as it went. Once it ascended high enough, Liam saw bruised, naked flesh clinging to a wasted wreck of a skeleton. Sunken circles of skin surrounded irises as black as midnight. This emaciated creature looked nothing like the subs in the Earth Sim. Not one of the virtual horrors Liam had witnessed came close to igniting the same fear reflex. His skin prickled beneath his furs. Before he could decide whether to run or strike first, the sub reached Wiki and grabbed his leg.

Liam threw an awkward punch at its face, which only stunned it for a moment. Wiki fell onto his back and tried to yank his foot free, but the sub held on. Liam kicked it hard in the chest and heard the crack of ribs snapping. When he realized it wouldn't let go, he focused all of his strength on keeping Wiki from sliding down the rock face.

Wiki pulled a small Suvi knife from his belt and attempted to stab his attacker in the head, but the tip glanced off its skull. Dark blood splashed from the wound.

With his hands now under Wiki's armpits, Liam leaned all his weight backward and pulled the fight onto level ground.

Spitting and yelling, Wiki squirmed beneath the weight of the sub, which now had a thin hand around his shoulder.

Liam grabbed a fistful of grimy hair and smashed the monster's face against the slate. He lifted its head again, caught a quick glimpse of its flattened nose, the bloody chips of teeth raining from its mouth. Then he whipped it against the stone once more, decimating what little facial definition remained. With a grunt, he hefted the body off his friend and let it roll to the ground below. Completely fatigued, he lay on his back beside Wiki until he could catch his breath.

"You okay?" he whispered.

"I think so," Wiki said between quick breaths.

Liam turned his head and saw Wiki squeezing his left upper arm with his right hand.

"What happened?"

"I think"—he lifted his hand, which was now covered in blood—"I think it might have bitten me."

25

SILENCE

Liam cut a strip of fabric from his pants and tied it around Wiki's bite wound. The sub's teeth had broken the skin, but barely.

"I guess they do eat human flesh."

Wiki glowered. "Too soon."

"It could be worse."

"Not helping." Wiki stood and winced. "Let's go. I need to sterilize this immediately."

"I think I used the rest of the antiseptic."

"Zara might have some," Wiki said.

They backtracked to where the path forked, and from there, it didn't take long for them to make it to the fields. When the outskirts of the village came into view, they stopped. Liam stood at the edge of the field, where darkness still concealed him from sight.

"Do you know where Zara sleeps?" he asked.

"A hut near the village center."

The wind rustled the tall grasses, and Liam instinctively turned his head toward the sound. King meowed from his pouch.

"You have to stay quiet," Liam whispered.

"We might be okay," Wiki said. "Maybe no one noticed that Jarok went missing."

"Fang feeds him every morning. They definitely know. Even if they don't, I'm not taking any chances. Plus, we've been gone a whole day."

"You're right." Wiki glanced over his shoulder at the dark forest.

"I wasn't thinking."

"That's a first," Liam said.

Wiki ignored the tease. "So, what's the plan?"

Liam had been thinking hard about the best way to accomplish what they needed to.

"We'll split up once we get close. You wake Zara and get her ready to go. Clean your wound. Grab whatever weapons and food you can. I'll go back to our place and get the rest of our stuff. Then we'll meet up on the opposite side of the village."

"We need an exact rendezvous point," Wiki said. "You know where they took our hoods off when we first got here?"

Liam recalled the place vividly. It was where they learned that society still existed on Earth—and where he met Skai for the first time.

"How could I forget?"

•|•

Liam and Wiki took their time and made it to the village center without incident. What Wiki lacked in strength and stamina, he made up for in stealth. His footsteps made almost no sound at all as he snuck away toward Zara's hut. Meanwhile, Liam veered off and went to the dwelling he shared with Wiki.

Once he stepped inside, he set King down, willing the cub to stay quiet. The fire in the corner had long since burned down to ashes. With the moon still behind the horizon, Liam could hardly see. He would need to start the fire again or pack in the dark.

Before he could make up his mind, distant torchlight entered through the high windows and danced on the walls, illuminating the space enough for him to get his bearings. He saw the silhouettes of the tree stumps they used as chairs, beds still messy from the night before, King curled up on a pile of clothes. Then, all at once, he heard footsteps and a burst of unintelligible whispers.

Liam crept to the wall beside the entrance and pressed his back against it. The room brightened slightly as the footsteps came closer. His nerves churned like boiling water, and his fingers began to twitch. The thought of coming this far only to get caught sent waves of anger through his body.

He scanned the room, looking for another way out or something to hide behind, but the windows were too small, and there was nothing big enough to conceal him completely. Hiding under the blankets like a scared child wouldn't work. He found a weapon hanging by the door, one of the Suvi's curved blades, then he homed in on the footfall outside. Listening carefully, he counted at least three pairs of feet. The weapon in his grip would be no help against so many—especially considering he had hardly practiced using it. He didn't want to hurt anyone, anyway. For a moment, he considered turning himself in.

Light traveled across the walls as the people outside neared the entrance. Once the light spilled through the door, it stopped. Whispers echoed through the room. Liam held his breath. If he stayed quiet enough, maybe they would leave. It seemed to be his only hope, so he waited. His pursuers remained outside the door, completely silent, until Liam's lungs burned. He exhaled as slowly and quietly as possible before drawing in a fresh breath of air.

He considered making a run for it, but he didn't think he had the energy to outpace them. What if they had bows or spears? And what would happen if they caught him? All hope of talking his way out of the situation vanished when he remembered the language barrier. Unless Skai was standing outside the door, no one there would understand him. As Liam prepared to surrender, one of them muttered something in their language. The light began to retreat.

With his back pressed against the wall, Liam waited for the villagers to leave. Soon the moment would pass, and everything would go according to plan. It had to.

But as they walked away, King rose from the pile of clothes to stretch. One soft meow made Liam's pursuers stop in their tracks. Before Liam could react, all three people rushed through the threshold, one after another. They stepped past Liam until they stood in a semi-circle around King. One of them picked the cub up by the scruff of his neck, a confused expression on his face.

Liam hesitated, reluctant to leave King behind, but he doubted another opportunity to escape would come. As silently as possible, he snuck out the door and ran.

•|•

Liam crouched in an alley, his stomach in knots and his breath heavy from running. Sprinting away from the dwelling had completely worn him out. He wiped the sweat from his brow and took stock of the situation. He didn't think the villagers looking for him heard him leave, but he couldn't be sure. Gathering what little strength he had, he hobbled to the end of the alley, leaned against the wall, and waited for Wiki and Zara to arrive at their rendezvous point.

For a while, he saw nothing but a dark emptiness at the edge of town, a field barely illuminated by indirect moonlight. He heard nothing but the songs of crickets and the whistle of wind passing between buildings and trees. But eventually, another sound entered the soundscape—a female voice shouting.

"Liam," she said. "Where are you?"

Liam recognized the voice instantly. He had been thinking about it often enough—the tone, the timbre, the inflection. The voice calling his name belonged to Skai. He saw her come from the village into the field, a cohort of torch-wielding Suvi following close behind. They marched to the spot where Liam planned to meet his friends, and they had Wiki and Zara with them. Both prisoners had hoods over their heads and their wrists tied together behind their backs.

"Come out, Liam," Skai said sternly. "I know you are here."

Liam didn't know what to do. All signs pointed to failure, but giving up didn't seem like a viable option. It never had. From this angle, he couldn't tell if the villagers held weapons, but he had to assume they did. What now? There had to be some way out. He thought about running away, about leaving Wiki and Zara behind. He could find the others on his own, get reinforcements, and come back for them.

"If you don't come out," Skai said as one of the villagers hefted a spear above his shoulder and aimed it at Wiki, "there will be consequences."

Wiki stood there, oblivious to the spear pointed directly at his head. At that moment, Liam wished he had a plasma pistol. That would make quick work of the situation. But now he had only one card left to play.

"Stop!" he yelled. He stumbled from his hiding place onto the dirt road. "Don't hurt him."

The man with the spear turned and aimed at Liam. His mouth stretched into an almost toothless grin, a sight made all the more disturbing by the firelight dancing on his face. Liam recognized him. They had shared a meal in the village center on his first day there. The chef. He had seemed friendly then, but now his countenance was a mask of wildness and threat.

"You have caused much trouble, Lion Slayer." Skai's voice projected clearly through the midnight air. "Come. It is time to pay for your crimes."

Liam raised his hands above his head and stumbled forward. Acidic bile still burned in his throat. Two of the men took away his furs and his weapon. They grabbed his hands roughly and tied them together behind his back.

"What's this about?" Liam asked. While he spoke, he tested the strength of the leather cords around his wrists. They held. "What crimes?"

"Do not pretend you are innocent," Skai said, staring him down. "You know what you have done."

Liam noticed Fang standing near the back of the group. His antler-adorned hood hung on his back, and his expression wavered between tired and enraged. He held something in his arms, a bundle that Liam couldn't distinguish in the faint light.

"I have no idea what you're—"

"No," Skai said. "No more lies."

"What am I being accused of?"

"You think we are stupid?" Skai glowered at him. "You think our rules are stupid?"

Liam glanced at Wiki. What had he told them? Skai moved closer to Liam. In the smolder of midnight, her anger visibly burned. Unable to handle her disappointment, Liam avoided her gaze.

"You watched Jarok lift me out of that pit," he said. "You know I didn't do anything wrong. He deserved to be free."

Liam's words didn't seem to affect her at all. She yelled out a command in her language, and the villagers dragged him and the others away.

"Where are you taking us?" Liam asked.

"Silence," Skai said. "You are not to speak."

They moved away from the village, toward a nearby cliff that overlooked parts of the valley. Liam imagined a long fall over the edge. At least his death would be quick.

"So, this is it, then? You're just going to kill us?"

Skai didn't answer. The procession turned away from the cliffs and headed toward a part of the village that Liam had never been to before. Fang stepped forward and spoke. The bundle in his arms moved.

"You have endangered all of us," Skai translated. "As punishment, you will be imprisoned until Jarok is found and captured. If the giant hurts anyone, you will suffer equal pain. If he kills anyone—"

Skai didn't finish the sentence. The message was clear. Fang stepped forward, unwrapped the bundle, and picked up King by the scruff of his neck. The cub meowed in pain and tried to wiggle itself out of Fang's grip.

"No!" Liam shouted. "You can't—"

The blunt end of a spear hit Liam's head.

"If Jarok kills anyone," Skai said, "you will be put to death. Let this be proof that we are serious."

Fang grabbed King's head with his other hand, as if preparing to wring out a wet towel. King growled and scratched at the air. Liam watched in horror, unable to do anything. Would these savages kill an innocent animal to prove a point? Liam couldn't believe it. They really were cruel.

When Fang started twisting King's neck, the cub yanked his head free and bit Fang's wrist. He thrashed around until the man dropped him, then bolted away between buildings.

Blood dripping from his wrist, Fang pointed at the fleeing cub and yelled something. One of the Suvi chased after King, but Liam doubted any man could run fast enough to catch him now that he was frightened.

"See?" Liam said. "That's what happens when you mess with a wild—"

Another smack to the head, harder this time, shut him up.

The group moved on. The mood in the air grew tenser with each step. Soon they came to a building that Liam could only describe as a jailhouse. A single cell made up the entirety of the structure. It had three packed earth walls like the other buildings. The fourth wall, which faced an open field, was made of thick logs arranged vertically—so close together that not even Wiki's thin frame would be able to squeeze through.

One of the men pushed Liam through the door, then his friends. He pulled out a blade, cut their restraints, and yanked the hoods off Wiki and Zara. Wiki shook his head and rolled his shoulders forward and back a few times. His hair was soaking wet. Zara stared at the dirt floor, her bottom lip trembling.

"She's innocent, Skai. So is Wiki. They didn't do anything. I let Jarok out by myself. No one helped me."

"Silence."

"Do whatever you want to me, but you have to let them go. Wiki's injured."

Skai glanced at the blood-soaked bandage around Wiki's arm. "You and Wiki left the village. All three of you were caught trying to leave again. These things are forbidden."

"Why can't we leave?"

"Because you can't be trusted. You could lead your people back to us, and your people are reckless."

"If you let us go, you'll have fewer mouths to feed."

"Who said we are feeding you?"

"Skai," Liam said. "You have to listen to me. I can explain everything. We only went—"

"Speak to me again, and you will no longer have your tongue."

"But—"

"Silence," she said. "This is your last warning."

Everyone but the prisoners exited the jailhouse, then four of the stronger villagers dragged a large slab of stone in front of the only opening. Skai came around the building and stood in front of the wooden bars. Liam had seen her angry before, but never like this. It looked like the wrong word could set her on fire, like her skin might ignite at the slightest touch.

"I fought for you when no one else would," Skai said. "I convinced Fang to spare your life, to let you become one of us. I told you to be careful. And this is how you repay me?"

She shook her head and disappeared into the night before Liam could utter another word.

•|•

That night in the jailhouse proved to be one of the worst nights of Liam's life. After repeatedly trying to move the slab door, kicking the wooden bars with all his strength, and shouting every curse word he knew, he paced around the cell for hours while the others fell asleep. His throat burned, and he had a headache from both the beating and dehydration. On top of that, every muscle in his body ached, and his stomach felt like it was eating itself. They had no food, no water, and no beds—just a clay basin in the corner, heavily stained from years of use.

When the anger finally tired him out, Liam curled up in a corner. Eventually, he fell into a fitful sleep, dozing in and out of consciousness every few minutes. He had slept much better on that cliff near the peak of the Eagle. How the Suvi had managed to make a floor less comfortable than stone baffled him. The night passed at an agonizing pace. When sunlight began to spill into the cell, Liam still felt like he hadn't slept. He rolled over and groaned, hating himself for letting Skai down, hating the Suvi for imprisoning him—hating everything.

"You awake?" Wiki said.

"I don't think I went to sleep." Liam sat up and rolled his head from side to side. Cracks and pops sounded from his neck. "I still can't believe this."

"They did tell us not to leave."

A grumbling sound came from Liam's throat. "Not that it matters now, but did you hear from Smythii yet?"

Wiki displayed a white tan line around his wrist. "They took everything."

"Damn it," Liam said, pulling his own hair. "What are we going to do now?"

"We'll probably die of thirst before we starve to death."

"Not what I meant." Liam's stomach did a backflip. "They have to feed us."

"They don't have to do anything. I doubt the Suvi have any laws against inmate mistreatment." Wiki yawned. "Everything is an eye for an eye with these people."

"I can't believe Fang almost snapped King's neck. Brutal."

"I guess it takes a cruel kind of humanity to inherit the Earth."

Liam groaned. "We were so close."

"There's still hope. All we have to do is wait for them to capture the giant—and hope nobody dies in the process."

"That could take forever."

"All we have is time. It's not like the others are going anywhere."

"If I have to spend another night in this cell, I'll actually lose my mind."

Liam meant it. He had always hated the crowded halls of Omega, the tight spaces that suffocated him. After having a taste of wide-open space, after swimming beneath waterfalls and standing on top of mountains, being trapped once again felt awful. This was the exact opposite of the freedom Liam so desperately craved. He stood, walked over to the wooden bars, and put his hands around two of them.

"We have to escape," he said.

26

DESPERATE TIMES

A commotion outside the infirmary tent tore Glo from her slumber. Sitting up in her cot, she heard a cacophony of voices and footsteps. The unintelligible sounds crescendoed and became clearer as their sources neared.

"Get him inside!"

The tent flaps parted, and two ragged-looking armed officers entered. They supported a third man between them, his head slumped forward. One of them, a tan young man with shoulder-length hair, held a blood-soaked rag to the patient's neck.

"We need help," he said. "He's bleeding out."

Glo stood and took in the scene. "What happened?"

"We got ambushed out there. He got bit in the neck."

"Lay him down." Glo pointed at an empty cot. "And keep pressure on that wound."

He nodded. "I'm Tristan, by the way. This is Axel. Just tell us what you need."

Glo had seen them around camp but had no time for pleasantries. She generally avoided the men, anyway. "Are either of you injured?"

"Negative," Tristan said. "Well, not as bad as he is."

They laid their human cargo on the cot. Glo glanced at some wounds visible through holes in the unconscious man's torn pants. These could wait, she decided. She opened his shirt and checked his torso. There she found only scrapes, bruises, and a possible broken rib. Then she looked at the man's face. Dirt and blood concealed most of it, and he had a black eye, but she still recognized him. Commander Killion. Panic welled inside her, but she didn't allow it to overflow. She needed to stay calm.

"One of you go see if you can track down the Commander's Halo. I need to know his blood type."

"On it," Axel said, already heading toward the exit.

"And if you see Quinn out there, try to keep her away. She doesn't need to see this."

Axel nodded his acknowledgment of the command and rushed out.

Glo checked Killion's breathing, which sounded normal. "Was he hit in the head?"

"He must've been." Tristan displayed a zen-like calmness despite the situation. "We got attacked from above. The subs jumped down from the trees. It was almost like they'd planned it, like they were waiting for us."

Glo went to the supply crate and found a few packages of hemostatic gauze, some antiseptic, and a clean piece of cloth.

"I need to see how bad it is," she said as she knelt beside the cot.

When Tristan removed the rag, Glo wiped away as much blood as possible. A chunk of Killion's neck was missing—like a bite out of a peach. Blood gushed from the wound, instantly replacing what Glo had wiped away. She applied pressure again. The gauze wouldn't be enough to stop the bleeding, and she didn't think she could stitch it. The reality of the situation overwhelmed her. How was she the most qualified person in camp to do this? Had things gotten that bad? And would each day become worse until no one remained to fight back?

"What do you need?" Tristan asked, snapping Glo out of her self-induced trance.

"He'll probably need a transfusion, but first we have to get this to stop bleeding."

"We could cauterize it," Tristan suggested, then he shrugged. "I don't know, I saw it in a movie once."

Glo thought about the option for a moment. She had been studying medical manuals to pass the time, and she remembered a chapter on emergency cauterization.

"That could actually work," she said. "I need something made of metal, large enough to cover the bite."

Tristan pulled a wide hunting blade from his belt and held it between them. "Will this work?"

She sized it up. "It should."

Tristan started a fire. As Glo heated the metal blade over the open flame with her free hand, Killion began to stir—a good sign, though she hoped he wouldn't wake just yet.

"You'll need to hold him down," Glo said. "Here, keep pressure on the wound while I do this."

"Yeah, no problem."

Quinn rushed into the tent, followed by Axel.

"I tried to stop her," he said. "She wouldn't listen to me."

"We're the same blood type," Quinn said, her face glistening beneath a fresh coat of tears. "He needs me."

"Quinn, you don't need to see—"

"It's fine," she said. "I can handle it. I just want to help."

"Fine," Glo said. "What I'm about to do is going to hurt him, but it might be the only way to stop the bleeding."

"Do whatever you have to." Quinn ran her fingers through Killion's matted hair. "My poor Nikolai."

"Okay, Quinn. Find something for him to bite on—a towel or belt or something."

"Why does he—"

"Just do it," Glo said. "We're running out of time."

Quinn gingerly removed her own belt and handed it to Glo, who wedged it between Killion's teeth.

"Okay." The blade in Glo's hand glowed orange. "Now you all need to hold him down. Two of you hold his arms, and someone sit on his legs. I don't want him to be able to move at all."

Quinn and Tristan each took one of Killion's arms. Meanwhile, Axel leaned the bulk of his chest onto Killion's shins. It looked painful, but it didn't wake him.

"Hold on tight. If he starts flailing, he could hurt himself. Ready?" They all muttered their agreement. "I'm cauterizing the wound on three. All right, here we go." She took a deep breath. "One."

Tristan removed the soaked rag from Killion's neck. More blood pooled around the wound as soon as he stopped applying pressure.

"Two."

She removed the blade from the flame while doing her best to clean the area.

"Three."

She held the side of the blade against the bite wound, which immediately sizzled. Killion's eyes shot open, wild and terrified.

"Hold him," Glo yelled.

Thrashing and screaming, Killion yanked his arm free from Quinn's grip, nearly knocking the knife out of Glo's hand. She held it there as long as possible, but Killion's writhing quickly ended her efforts. She didn't want to burn him anywhere she didn't need to. The others held him down until his heavy, struggled breathing became less desperate. He passed out again, tears still pouring from his eyes. Glo checked her work. The cauterization looked nasty, and it would leave an ugly scar, but the bleeding had stopped.

"I think we did it."

•|•

With the direct blood transfusion between Quinn and Killion underway, Glo began to clean herself up. Adrenaline still coursed through her body. Beneath all the blood, she found a burn on her hand that she couldn't fully feel.

Scrubbing herself with a wet rag just moved the grime around. She needed a proper bath and some fresh clothes.

Tristan and Axel sat in a corner, bandaging each other's wounds. Neither of them had suffered anything serious. After doing her best to get clean, Glo walked over to them.

"Can one of you take me to the river?" she said, hating that she needed an escort. "I need to clean up."

"You want to go outside?" Axel asked. "After that?"

"Am I not allowed to?"

"Well, not technically."

"I just saved the Commander's life," Glo said. "I think I've earned a little bit of freedom."

"There's a communal tub inside the walls," Axel said. "Safer."

"There's no way I'm using that. It's disgusting."

"I second that," Quinn said from across the tent. The girl had a tendency to eavesdrop.

Tristan and Axel glanced at each other. Would either of them break the rules if the other wasn't watching?

"Listen, guys, I'm going with or without you." She picked up her things and headed toward the door. "But if I get attacked out there, that's on you."

Glo didn't know where the assertiveness had come from, but it reminded her of her brother. A pang of sadness stabbed at her heart as she exited the tent.

"Wait up," Tristan said. He jogged up beside her. "I'll take you."

"What a gentleman," Glo said, unable to keep the sarcasm out of her voice. She doubted there was a single man or boy on Earth who wouldn't want to watch her back while she bathed—or any of the women's backs for that matter. "Just keep your eyes to yourself, okay?"

"Yeah, that won't be a problem." Tristan laughed. "I'm extremely gay."

•¦•

The guard at the gate gave Glo and Tristan a funny look as they exited camp, but he didn't say anything.

"I outrank him," Tristan explained.

Glo followed him toward the river, watching the plasma rifle on his back while he watched the forest. He seemed to be on high alert.

"So," Glo said, "what's it like being the only gay man in camp?"

"You mean the only gay man on Earth?"

"I didn't think of it that way, but sure."

"First of all, I'm the only *openly* gay man here. I have my suspicions, but let's just say the dating pool is very limited. In other words, it sucks."

A small laugh escaped Glo's mouth. "Are you at least going to do your duty to repopulate the Earth?"

"Not if I can avoid it," he said. "Like I said, I'm extremely gay."

Glo had almost forgotten what it felt like to laugh. She even felt a bit guilty about the temporary break from her grief, as if she owed her full attention to that negative emotion.

"What were you doing when you got ambushed?" she asked.

"We were on our way back from a scouting mission."

"Looking for more survivors?"

"Negative."

"Then what?"

Tristan paused. "It's classified."

Glo sighed. "Men and their secrets."

He didn't respond to that. He kept walking.

"Does it have something to do with Reagan's plan to get out of the valley?"

Tristan's pace faltered. "We shouldn't be talking about this."

"I know about the Life Vault. I know the comm systems were destroyed. I know things are getting desperate."

"Okay, but—"

"I'm not some stupid girl."

Tristan stopped and turned around. "Wait, what did you say?"

"I said I'm not some—"

"No, before that. About the comm systems?"

Glo's eyes narrowed. "Reagan told me we lost them in the crash."

"Oh, I thought you said they were destroyed."

"What's the difference? It's still impossible to send a message home."

Tristan shook his head then blew away some hair that had fallen in front of his mouth. "Those comm units are virtually indestructible. We might have lost the systems, but I doubt they were damaged beyond repair."

"Wait," Glo said, "how do you know that?"

"You're not the only one out of your element." He indicated the rifle on his back. "I was supposed to come here as a tech, not a fighter. Desperate times, I guess."

"Why would Reagan lie to me?"

"Maybe the Admiral misspoke, or he didn't know," Tristan suggested. "If the comm systems are anywhere, they'll be near the crash site. No one has been over there in a few days, but we saw it from the hills. The whole area is burnt to a crisp."

Glo grabbed Tristan's arm. "If I can find them, can you help me send a message back to Omega?"

"That's easy enough." He paused. "Wait, you can't possibly be thinking about going there yourself?"

Glo stared at him, pleading with her eyes.

"No way," he said. "It's too dangerous."

"But—"

"You can't do it. You don't know what it's like out there. Burnt trees weren't all we saw at the crash site."

"I have to try." Glo fell to her knees. "My brother. He didn't survive the landing. Neither did his best friend. And so many others have died." Her breathing quickened. "I just need to talk to my mom. She needs to know. The mothers and fathers of the others that died, they need to know."

Tristan sighed and crouched down in front of Glo. "I understand," he said. "Believe me, I've lost people too. But I think there's another way. A better way."

Glo sniffled. "Really?"

"I'm only telling you this to keep you from going on a suicide mission."

"What is it?"

"You were right. The scouting mission today, it was to chart a course out of this valley. It should take us right through the crash site. Maybe we can search for the comm systems while we're there?"

"Okay," Glo said. "And when will that be?"

"The Admiral wants us to leave as soon as possible. He says it's our only hope."

"How soon, Tristan?"

Tristan's face hardened. He clenched his jaw. "We could be out of here in the next forty-eight hours."

27

TONE DOWN THE TESTOSTERONE

The Suvi only let Liam, Wiki, and Zara starve for about twelve hours before Fang delivered their first meal—a clay pot filled with water and a salted fish for each of them. Standing alone in the field outside, he tossed the food between the cell bars, straight into the dirt, the same way he fed his former pet giant. After that, Fang brought their meals irregularly, just enough to keep Liam and his friends alive and take the edge off their hunger, but nothing more. Liam spent the intervening hours either thinking about food or plotting his escape.

It didn't take long to realize that breaking out by force was not an option. Liam wanted to plead his case, to talk his way out of it, but Skai never came to visit. If Fang understood anything Liam said, he didn't show it. Despite Liam's constant curses and aggressive body language, the old man remained stoic every time he returned to the jailhouse, and so did his men.

"Are we going to die in here?" Zara asked one morning.

Liam lazily turned his head toward her. Already her face looked thinner than usual, and her hair hung in greasy clumps around it. Wiki sat beside her, fiddling with a fishbone to pass the time. Neither he nor Liam responded to her question.

"I don't want to die," she said. "I thought I did when we first got here, to this planet, I mean. I wanted to end it. Being stuck in that pod with Nova. It messed me up. I couldn't stop seeing her face, and I just wanted it to stop. But now—"

Zara started to cry, which drew clean stripes through the splotches of dirt on her face. Wiki placed a hand on the back of her neck and squeezed.

"We're not going to die here."

She sniffled loudly. "How do you know that?"

"I don't," Wiki said, "but I believe it. I've studied the Suvi enough to know that they aren't evil. Harsh maybe, but they won't starve us to death."

"I just want to go home, Wiki. I miss Omega. I miss my family. We should have never left."

For the first time in his life, Liam agreed with that sentiment. He didn't miss the city itself, only the way he felt there. Bored, restless, trapped, but at least safe. The Earth Sim had been challenging, but actual life on Earth was proving to be far more complicated than he had ever imagined. Maybe Reagan had been right about Liam missing the mark, about not being cut out for the mission.

"They should have airlocked me," Liam said. "I'm the reason you're both stuck in here. None of this would have happened if I just stayed behind like I was supposed to."

Liam slouched forward. He touched his forehead against his knees to hide the tears beginning to gather. The others stayed quiet for a long time. Then Liam heard movement, felt a warm arm around his neck, a comforting touch that only made him cry more.

"Liam," Zara said, her voice soft. She started scratching his back. "I don't care what the others might think of you. I'm glad you stowed away. You saved my life."

"And mine," Wiki added. "Twice. If not for you, I would have been cougar food on day one. Not to mention what happened on the boulder."

Zara squeezed Liam tighter. "And I thought I would suffocate in that ejector pod, but you pulled me out."

The praise felt undeserved, but Liam listened anyway. He sensed Wiki coming closer.

"Why do you think I followed you up that mountain?" he asked.

"I don't know," Liam said. "You always go where I go."

"No," Wiki said. "Well, yes, that's true. But I only follow you because I believe in you."

"You're probably the bravest person I've ever met," Zara added. "Even though you can be a jerk sometimes."

Liam laughed at that. Then he looked up, wiped the wetness from his eyes. "You can stop trying to make me feel better now. I get it."

"We're just speaking the truth, my friend." Wiki patted his friend on the back. "You need to know that you're not alone. We'll get through this."

•|•

Later that day, the sound of dry grass crunching in the field outside made Liam perk up. It had only been a few hours since their last meal, so this visit had to be about something else. He stood by the bars and waited until Fang came into view. The old man stopped a few meters away from the jailhouse and regarded Liam. He wore the same muted grimace as before, the same furs and antler hood, but something about him looked different. It took Liam a moment to realize what it was. Instead of his usual wooden staff, he held something else in his hand, something from another world entirely.

It can't be, Liam thought.

But it was. Fang's knobby fingers tapped against the metallic barrel of a plasma rifle.

Liam's mouth dropped open. "Where did you get that?"

The answer presented itself in the form of more arrivals, four Suvi villagers escorting two hooded prisoners. Both of them wore the black suits of the armed officers, which fit tightly on the bulky frame of one and hung loosely over the feminine curves of the other.

"What's going on?" Wiki asked from his corner, where he sat re-wrapping his bite wound.

A muffled cry was the only response. It sounded like the prisoners had been gagged beneath their hoods. The procession moved toward the side of the building with the stone slab door—a door that would soon open.

"Get ready to run," Liam said.

"Are you crazy? They have spears."

"Okay, new plan. I'll rush out, grab that plasma rifle from Fang, then—"

The slab began to slide. Liam bounced up and down on his heels.

"Don't do it," Wiki said. "It's a terrible idea. And don't tell me I'm overthinking, you're just not thinking at all."

"This could be our only chance."

"If you get out and shoot up a bunch of villagers, what do you think they'll do to us? That rifle has a limited charge. It could be depleted for all we know." The door was nearly open now. "Trust me, Liam. It's too risky."

Disappointed, Liam groaned. As always, Wiki was right.

"Fine," he said.

The villagers shoved their prisoners inside, forced the pair to their knees, and cut their restraints. The male prisoner tried to fight back, but a spear butt to the temple stopped him. A guttural moan came from beneath his hood. When the hoods came off, Liam took a good look at the bruised and battered Omegan prisoners.

Tai Beryl spat blood—and a tooth or two—into the dirt as the stone slab door slid shut behind him. Raelyn knelt beside Tai, her hair a tangle of fire and underbrush. She looked far less beat up than he did. Both of them stood in shocked silence for a moment, then Tai stepped forward.

"Of all the places on Earth," he said, "you would end up in a jail cell, Liam. I guess I'm not surprised."

Liam glowered. "I would punch you for that, but the Suvi already messed up your face enough for one day."

"I'm sorry, the what?" Raelyn said. "The Suvi?"

Tai and Liam glared at each other, a palpable tension building between them.

Raelyn stood and came between them. "Could you two put aside your little feud for a minute and talk to me?"

"She's right," Wiki said. "This isn't the time or place."

"Tone down the testosterone," Raelyn added.

Liam walked to the opposite side of the cell to put as much distance as possible between himself and Tai. "The Suvi are the people who captured you," he said.

"They've lived here above the valley for ages," Wiki said. "They're seriously tough. My hypothesis is that they descended from a population of immune survivors. Still, even they don't remember their own history beyond a few centuries."

Raelyn ran her bionic hand through her hair and squeezed it. "I can't believe this."

"It shocked us too," Wiki said.

"How did you end up here?"

"We were camping at the crash site," Liam said. "The Suvi came in the night and brought us up here."

"How?" Raelyn asked. "The place was crawling with subs when we passed by. We almost didn't make it."

"Well, that confirms it," Wiki said, which made Raelyn and Tai glance at each other in confusion. "The crash site was empty when we went there."

"You've been locked up this whole time?"

"Well, no." Wiki glanced at Liam. "We were their guests for about a week, then they threw us in here a few days ago because— Look, it doesn't matter why. What about you guys? What happened?"

"Is Glo alive?" Liam added, his insides twisting as he prepared for the bad news.

"She is," Raelyn said. "But she's super depressed because she thinks you're dead. We lost a lot of people. Almost half. Is anyone else here?"

"Just the three of us," Liam said. "What happened with you guys?"

"Tell us everything," Wiki said.

The group automatically formed a circle, some sitting, the rest too amped up to do so. Tai spoke first, his bulky arms folded in front of his chest.

"It all started when I was sent on a scouting mission with another officer."

"Looking for what, exactly?"

"Reagan sent us to find a way out of the valley."

"Why?"

"I don't know," Tai said. "I just follow the orders, I don't make them. Anyway, we found what looks like a safe way out. I mean, it's a long shot, but it might work—unless more subs show up." He cracked his neck and winced. "It's like they came out of nowhere."

"The sound of the crash attracted them," Wiki said. "Or so I've been told. Go on."

"The other guy didn't make it back to camp, but when I got back to give my report"—Tai's hands balled into fists—"I found out that Reagan was trying to get Raelyn into his bed. Grimy bastard."

"Such an asshole," Raelyn added, her eyes blazing. She flexed her metallic fingers one by one. "I'd like to tear that box right out of his throat."

Because of Reagan's behavior on the ETS Resurgence, this news didn't surprise Liam—nor did Raelyn's desire for violence. He would gladly back her up on that.

"Then what?" Liam asked.

"What do you think?" Tai said. "We packed our bags and headed out. We didn't get very far before those freaks threw bags over our heads and dragged us here." Tai spat out more blood. "So, what happens now? Are they going to eat us or something?"

"Probably," Liam said. "They prefer the taste of big, meaty man-children, so I'm sure you'll be first."

Raelyn rolled her eyes. "Cut it out, you two."

Liam could tell that being locked up with Tai could quickly become cruel and unusual punishment—for both of them. He dreaded the days, the weeks, the months to come. Who knew how long they'd be imprisoned together?

"Wait a second." Wiki stepped forward, his hand on his chin. "Let's rewind real quick. Why was Reagan looking for a way out?"

"I told you I don't know," Tai said.

A long, silent moment passed.

"It's obvious, isn't it?" Zara said. "Reagan's planning an exodus from the valley."

Wiki nodded, his face getting paler by the second. "And there's no way he's doing it alone."

Liam paused, the severity of the situation sinking in. "When they leave," he said, "how will we ever find them again?"

28

SEPTIC

"Stand up. All of you."

Skai's voice filled Liam with a strange mix of emotions, a miasma of excitement and fear, joy and pain. He rose from his seat on the dirt floor and faced her. Standing in the field outside, her posture rigid, she had a gang of villagers behind her. Others moved toward the door. Liam tuned out their faces and focused on hers, attempting to read her expression. She didn't look angry, just impatient.

"I said, stand up." The slab door grumbled open. Pebbles and grains of sand screeched under its weight. "Hands behind backs."

"Skai, listen." Liam had spent a lot of time contemplating what he might say to Skai, how he might plead his case for freedom, but the words died in his throat, piling up until he couldn't push past the blockage. He swallowed hard, unsure of how to go on.

"Wise of you to stop speaking, Lion Slayer." She glanced at his hands, which had turned palm-up in supplication. "Hands. Now."

Liam silently obeyed. Soon, leather cords bit into his wrists. He didn't bother complaining about the tightness, because nothing hurt like seeing Skai through the bars of the cell she had put him in. Someone prodded him toward the door, and only then did Liam wonder where they might be going. Would he and his friends be put to work? To death? He never knew with these people. They were so unpredictable, so terrifyingly different.

Direct sunlight stabbed at his eyes and intensified the headache he had been suffering from—a chronic, dehydrated tightness that no amount of stretching or massaging had been able to alleviate. He almost wished the villagers would cover his eyes with a hood, just to ease the pain.

Tai walked beside him, his biceps flexing against his restraints. His gaze darted from villager to villager, weapon to weapon—as if he might spring forward at any moment to fight. In the sunlight, the bruises and cuts on his face looked worse. He glanced at Liam.

"What is this?" he whispered. "Where do you think they're—"

The villager leading Tai delivered an elbow to his ribs.

They marched on.

•|•

Villagers young and old stared as the procession passed, and Liam wondered if all of them hated him for freeing Jarok—or if they even knew about it. The adults watched with squinted eyes while young children hid behind them.

The Suvi spoke in hushed voices. Some wore pity on their faces, others indifference. In more ways than one, the experience felt like an impending execution. Had the giant returned? Had he killed someone?

Despite what Liam said earlier about wishing Reagan had airlocked him, he wasn't ready to die. He wouldn't resist it yet, but like Tai, he prepared to make a stand. Whether the others joined in or not, neither of them would go down without a fight. This much Liam knew.

As they walked, he calculated his chances of success and weighed the few options he had. There were five prisoners including him, all unarmed, only three of whom had any experience with hand-to-hand combat. He counted six burly male villagers armed with spears and knives—plus Skai, who had the plasma rifle slung over her shoulder.

Liam made cautious eye contact with Tai. He looked at the rifle, then back at Tai, willing him to understand.

A slight nod.

Acquiring the gun was their only chance of tipping the odds in their favor. Liam wiggled against his restraints to test whether he might be able to slip his hands free. The villager leading him didn't seem to notice. After a few minutes, he managed to slide one hand partially free, but it got stuck at his thumb joint.

When the group veered away from the cliffs, Liam calmed a little. At least they wouldn't be thrown from the waterfall. He had time to figure something out. Water trickled in the distance. Soon, the trees thinned out, and the group came to a dramatic outcrop beside a stream. Skai yelled something, and the villagers lined the prisoners up beside the water.

"We will untie you now," Skai said.

This is my chance, Liam thought. His muscles tensed for a fight. He held his breath.

"Clean yourselves in the water," Skai said. "We do not owe you this mercy. Be grateful."

Liam exhaled loudly, then one of the villagers untied his hands. Sensing spears aimed his way, he shook out his wrists. There would be no fight. Liam walked toward the waterside, and the others followed.

"Not you," Skai commanded. Liam stopped and turned around, expecting punishment in place of mercy, but Skai wasn't looking at him. She was looking at Tai. "Not yet."

"Why not?" Tai asked. He braced himself for a smack to the head that never came.

Skai reached over her shoulder and grabbed the plasma rifle from her back. "You will teach me how to use this. Come."

•|•

Liam stood waist-deep in the frigid river water and washed himself absentmindedly. While the filth from his body flowed downstream, his focus remained upstream, where Skai stood on the riverbank beside Tai. With Tai's wrists still bound, he had to teach Skai verbally. She was too smart to trust Tai with the gun. Liam couldn't hear them, but he watched as Tai explained how to turn off the safety, how to charge the weapon, and how to release a bolt of plasma. Then Skai raised the butt of the plasma rifle to her bare shoulder—right beside her collarbone scar—and aimed it at a distant tree.

"You like her, don't you?" Raelyn stood beside Liam, her hair soaking wet but still littered with things from the forest. She raised an eyebrow. "And don't bother lying about it. I can see right through you."

Liam let out a long sigh. "Why do you think that?"

"You never looked at me like that. Well, maybe at first."

"That's not true, I—"

He stopped himself from saying anything else. What Raelyn said was true, and he knew it.

"I don't blame you," Raelyn said. "She's pretty. In a wild, and frankly scary, kind of way. But pretty."

More than pretty, Liam thought.

"Are you getting jealous?" he said.

"I didn't say she was prettier than me." Raelyn smirked and flexed her bionic fingers. "And Tai knows what would happen if his eyes wandered too far."

"And you think Skai's the scary one?"

Raelyn wrung the water out of her hair. "I didn't say scarier than me, either. The way you're looking at her, I'd say she's more than a crush."

Fully unprepared to talk to his ex-girlfriend about his other ex-girlfriend, Liam sighed. "It doesn't matter now. She won't even talk to me."

"And why is that?"

"Because she asked me to be careful, and I did the opposite."

Raelyn nodded. "Sounds familiar."

"You didn't see how miserable Jarok looked. I had no choice."

"Yes, you did."

"Then I made the wrong one." Agitated, Liam threw more water onto his body. "I broke the rules, and now she hates me."

"I don't know about that." Raelyn glanced over his shoulder. "She keeps looking at you when you're not looking. Have you considered apologizing?"

"Of course."

"And have you actually done it?"

"I tried, Rae. I just haven't had the chance to tell her I'm sorry."

"No, Liam." Raelyn washed dried mud from her bionic arm as

she spoke. "You can't just tell her you're sorry. You have to prove that you understand why what you did was wrong."

"Maybe I was rude before I left, but I don't think I did the wrong thing after."

"That's the problem." Raelyn twisted some water out of her hair. "You might not feel bad about it, but apologies aren't about how you feel. You have to think about how your actions made her feel. Get it?"

Liam stared into the water. "I think she feels like I betrayed her. Like she expected more from me, and I let her down."

"Understanding her feelings is a good start. Now you just have to tell her it won't happen again. And you have to mean it. You have to prove that you've changed."

Liam looked up from the water and into the eyes of his ex-girlfriend—kind eyes, full of concern for him. "Why are you helping me?"

"Why wouldn't I?"

"I guess I thought you hated me too." He recalled what happened down on Deck Eight of the ETS Resurgence. "Weren't you going to vote to airlock me before Reagan showed up?"

"I don't hate you, Liam. You just never spent time with me. When I asked you to be with me, you did the opposite. I get it. You were chasing your dreams, doing what *you* wanted, but that made you a terrible boyfriend. There was no *us*."

Liam recalled all the times he had blown her off to chase records in the Earth Sim or hang out with Wiki.

"But you don't have to be like that now," Raelyn added. "Who you were doesn't have to control who you are. Every day you get to choose who you want to be."

Liam stared at his feet through the rippling water, then he looked up. "Thanks, Rae."

"Don't mention it," she said.

Back upstream, a hole appeared in the tree that Skai had been aiming at, billowing smoke. Her lips were curved into a proud smile, which quickly faded when she made eye contact with Liam.

"And for the record"—Raelyn gripped Liam's shoulder—"I was going to vote to keep you safe."

•|•

After such a short and unfulfilling tease of freedom, Liam dreaded going back to the cell. He joined Wiki in the back of the group, meandering to make his time in the open air last as long as possible. Still, he maintained a pace fast enough to avoid the spears at his back.

Beside him, Wiki dragged his feet in the dust. His hair stuck to his neck and forehead. Thinner and paler than usual, he looked borderline malnourished. Liam hadn't noticed Wiki's state in the dimness of their cell, but the daylight illuminated the extent of his physical deterioration.

"You feeling okay?" Liam whispered. "You look bad."

"I think I'm running a fever."

"That's not good."

"It might be," Wiki said. "Having a fever means my body's fighting."

"Fighting what?"

A spear tip poked Liam's back, just hard enough to get his attention. Instead of retaliating—because he wanted nothing more than to punch somebody—Liam turned his attention to the people walking in front of him.

Zara, who had to take two steps for each of Tai's, was doing her best to keep up with the group. However, it looked like her short legs would get her a poke from one of the villagers soon enough. Raelyn walked in front of Zara. Her hands were tied behind her at the wrist, and Liam couldn't tell if the villager escorting her was staring at her lengthy hair, her bionic arm, or something else in that general area. Then there was Tai, who had two escorts of his own.

How strange, Liam thought, that not long ago he and Wiki had watched their avatars being eaten in the Earth Sim—and how fortuitous that the five of them were now reunited in a reality much more dangerous than those simulated streetscapes. Shuffling his feet, he longed for simpler days—when danger was a game and death was just an illusion.

•|•

Later, the five Omegan prisoners sulked in their cell, engaging in meaningless tasks to fill the time. Zara sat behind Raelyn, untangling the puzzle of her hair strand by strand. Tai paced from corner to corner while Wiki scratched doodles into the dirt with a sharp rock. Numbly, Liam sat against the wall and watched the others—too tired to move, too hungry to sleep.

"Heard you got bit," Tai said. "I've seen some guys back in camp get bit. You're lucky to be alive."

When Liam's eyelids cracked open, he saw Wiki holding up his arm to display the bandage.

"I did," Wiki said.

"You're not going to show us?" Tai said.

Wiki folded his arms. "You'll just have to take my word for it."

"I got a pretty bad scar, myself." Tai lifted his shirt and displayed a pair of crooked scabs across his bruised abdomen. "Those subs have some wicked fingernails. Come on, let's see yours."

Liam noticed Wiki's hands were shaking. "It's still healing. I should keep it wrapped."

"Whatever, man."

Tai sauntered off to sit with Raelyn on the other side of the cell.

"Show me," Liam whispered.

"It's fine, really."

"Let me see it." Liam reached over and grabbed Wiki's wrist.

"Liam, no, I"—Wiki exhaled loudly through pursed lips—"Just give me a minute, okay? I'm actually a little scared to look at it."

Liam let him go. "All right."

Hands shaking, Wiki began to remove the ragged strip of cloth from his upper arm, making a faint peeling sound as he unwrapped it. Liam smelled the wound before he could see it, a putrid sweetness not unlike decaying shrimp. It nearly made Liam lose what little food he had in his stomach.

When Wiki revealed the bite wound, Liam recoiled. Yellowish pus leaked from a circle of tooth-shaped indentations. The surrounding skin and inflamed flesh were bruised black in places, purple in others.

Wiki gulped. "The infection is worse than I thought."

"Why didn't you tell anyone about this?"

Wiki wiped the sweat from his brow. "I thought it might heal on its own."

Zara wandered over and joined the conversation. "We should have asked the Suvi for help. They have to help you, right?"

"They don't have to do anything, and I doubt they have what I need."

"They must have something that can help," Liam said. "Skai told me they make medicine from plants."

Zara crouched between Liam and Wiki. "Plants won't do anything," she said, shaking her head as she analyzed the wound. Then she looked at Liam, her expression shifting from solemn to grim. "He needs antibiotics. If this goes septic, he could die."

29

FOR THE FUTURE OF HUMANITY

The evening of the ambush that left Killion bedridden, Reagan called a camp meeting. Everyone but the gate guards and the injured were expected to attend. When Glo arrived around sunset, a bonfire was already reaching toward the sky in the central square. She found Quinn, who stood on a tree stump overlooking the gathering place.

"How's he doing?" Quinn asked.

"Weren't you just with him?"

Quinn flashed a tiny smile and shrugged. "Just making sure. Things can change quickly."

"Don't worry," Glo said. "He's stable."

When Reagan approached the bonfire, the murmur of the crowd faded. His grizzled hair and gray beard had grown scruffier since departing Omega, but his dark uniform still looked clean and crisp; clearly, he had others assigned to the real work. The pink and blue hues of the sky gleamed on his lung vent. Upon stopping in front of the fire, he cleared his throat, prompting the men to stand at attention.

"My friends, my crew." Reagan raised one arm and pointed at the moon in the distance, peeking over the mountainous horizon. "Look how far we've come."

Since loud sounds attracted the subs, everyone knew better than to cheer or applaud. Still, some murmured their agreement.

Reagan smirked and took a couple of steps forward, where he tramped one foot onto a log.

"You should be proud. We have accomplished what many believed would never happen. We have done the impossible. We're all standing here together for the same reason. When things got hard, we refused to cave." Someone placed more wood into the fire, which made it flare up behind Reagan. "We are the sole survivors of the Resurgence Mission. As such, the future lies in our hands and our hands alone. Unfortunately, we've lost some good people along the way, brave men and women who knew the risks of embarking on such a dangerous journey, but who gladly heeded the call anyway."

Not all of us chose to be here, Glo thought.

"For the future of humanity," Reagan said.

"For the future of humanity," the armed officers repeated in unison.

"Despair not, my friends." Reagan coughed loudly into his shoulder then took a moment to collect himself. "None of our fellow crew members died in vain. Every sacrifice made has brought us closer to our goal. Now, as survivors, it is our duty to honor the dead by moving forward, by completing this mission— by promising to never give up, no matter what may come. Do you promise to do that? For the future of humanity."

"For the future of humanity."

More voices repeated the mantra this time. Glo stared at the flames.

"The responsibilities of the dead have become our responsibilities," Reagan said. "Each of us now carries a bigger burden than before, but we carry these burdens proudly because they allow those we've lost to live on through us. We will honor them by seeing this thing through to the end. With that in mind, let us engage in a moment of silence to remember them."

Glo closed her eyes, and the crowd hushed. Listening to the crackle of the bonfire, she searched her mind for memories of Liam. They came in pulses and flashes—a smile here, a laugh there, a lifetime of small moments. Some memories appeared in vivid detail, like the first time her baby brother wrapped his tiny fingers around hers, the day she walked Liam home from his first day of school, his confusion when their mother explained that Dad wouldn't be coming home again. Most memories were fuzzy and distorted, beautiful yet subtle, like the faded graffiti lining the halls of Glo's long lost home. The harder she focused, the dimmer these memories became.

"Thank you," Reagan said. "May those we've lost live on through our actions. Now, I'm sure you're all wondering why…"

Glo ignored Reagan's speech and kept her eyes shut. She didn't wipe the tears from her cheeks, because she wasn't done remembering those she had lost. Basking in the painful memories, she turned her thoughts to Wiki—sweet, innocent Wiki, whom she had nothing but love for. He was the only boy who never had and never would hurt her. She missed his quirks, the way he would get so caught up sharing interesting information that he lost track of time. In those moments, she didn't see a skinny, awkward boy. She saw a confident young man with so much passion and potential—all of it wasted so early in his life.

"Hey," Quinn whispered. "What's wrong?"

Glo swallowed her sadness. "I'm okay," she said.

A tidal wave of memories crashed into her mind, memories of her mother always claiming to be okay—no matter how sick she felt from the radiation, from the cancer, and from the additional radiation used against the cancer. Standing there, Glo mourned her mother as if she were already dead. What was the difference, anyway? Dead? Gone? They both meant unreachable. Until Glo had a comm unit in her hand, she would not allow herself to get her hopes up.

"As you all know, we were not supposed to end up here," Reagan continued. "Beautiful though it is, this valley was never part of the plan. We may be able to survive here for some time, but not indefinitely. Not with half the manpower we once had, in such wild and treacherous conditions. After losing the most important cargo of all—tens of thousands of immune human embryos in the biorepository—we now lack the resources to complete our mission. Even if we could survive here, it's no place to raise the next generation."

Hanging on every word, the crowd went completely silent. Fading sunlight and flickering firelight reflected off their eyes— eyes that silently spoke of disappointment and failure.

"But," Reagan said, "there is a way to recover what we've lost—a path forward. Two hundred kilometers to the west lies a massive bunker containing everything we need to reboot the human race: food, medicine, tech, genetic material, and more—all kept frozen for us. The Life Vault, an oasis left behind by our forebears, will be our new home."

Glo expected someone in the crowd to speak up, to call the Life Vault a myth or a fool's dream, but no one did.

"Getting there will be far from easy," Reagan said, "but we have no other choice. We don't know what we'll find on the way. The roadways are likely long gone, but if they're not too overgrown, we should be able to cover the distance in under two weeks. Lucky for us, Earth was well-mapped before we left. Even without the roads, we'll be able to find our way. We can do this. We are the modern pioneers, the explorers and settlers of this new world."

Listening to Reagan's plan, Glo's mind orbited a single question: How many more people will we lose on the way?

"Arrangements are underway for our departure. The scouts have charted a course out of the valley. The hunting party has gathered as much food as possible. Engineering has built a pair of carts, so we don't have to carry everything. Everyone who hasn't already been assigned a task, take tomorrow to rest up and pack whatever you can carry on your back. We'll be leaving at sunrise the next morning. For the future of humanity."

30

ERASE THE STARS

"I need you to pee on it," Wiki said.

Liam jerked his head sideways to look at his friend. He had been dozing off, dreaming about food.

"Wait, what? You want me to pee on it?"

Wiki nodded firmly. "That's what I said."

Liam's eyebrows drew closer together. "Why would you want me to pee on it?"

"It needs to be cleaned out." Wiki unwrapped his bite wound. "Come on, let's just get it over with."

Liam stood, glanced over at the other prisoners, and shrugged. He stretched his spine and turned to face Wiki head-on.

"I think the infection has moved to your brain or something. Are you feeling all right?"

"I'm actually feeling worse by the hour. And I'll get worse faster if we don't clean this out. Please don't make me ask Tai to do this."

Liam's head tilted to the side. "Can't we just clean it out with water the next time they bring us some?"

"The water here isn't sterile, but urine is. Plus, a stream of liquid will help to flush out the wound." Wiki stretched his arm out farther. "Listen, I know it sounds weird, but I've thought a lot about this. It's the best option given our current situation. Are you going to help me or not?"

Mulling over Wiki's logic, Liam pursed his lips. "Why can't you just pee on it yourself?"

"Never mind." Wiki's head turned from side to side as he began wrapping his wound again. "I guess you can just let me die. Some friend you are. You know, I'd pee on you if you asked me to."

Liam chuckled and only stopped when he saw Wiki's reddening face. "I'm sorry. I'll help you. I will pee"—another laughing fit kept Liam from talking, and tears came from his eyes—"Sorry, I just can't believe that this is what we're doing now. How is peeing on you our only option?"

Wiki shrugged. "Stranger things have happened."

"All right," Liam said. "But if we're going to do this, I need a little privacy."

He walked toward the far side of the room, away from the others, and beckoned Wiki to follow. The situation wasn't funny, but Liam couldn't contain his laughter. In truth, he felt a little sick in the head for experiencing joy while Wiki suffered. Still, his body craved the endorphins. It just wanted to laugh, so it laughed—before, during, and long after Liam dropped his pants in the corner of the jailhouse to pee on his friend's wound.

Time acted differently in captivity. It contracted and relaxed randomly, like a spasming muscle or glitchy android. The chaotic movements of time came in fits and starts. Sometimes it stretched on and on and on—a series of empty moments as barren as vast lunar basins, bleeding one into the other. Monochromatic. Empty. Other moments flashed by like light gleaming on a moving mirror—hardly perceptible, entirely transient, gone as quickly as they came.

Liam's only benchmark for measuring time on Earth was the motion of the sun. Seconds or hours could feel like minutes, but he could always count on the sunrise and sunset to help him count the days. Throughout his incarceration, Liam had been scratching tally marks on the wall using Wiki's sharp rock. He marked one line for each day and a small hieroglyph beneath each to remind him of what happened on those days. Every morning, he added a tally before sitting and staring at the wall, remembering. Every night, he added more detail.

The mark for day one had a crude representation of a parachute scratched below it to signify the day the ETS Resurgence made its explosive arrival on Earth. Liam also knew this as the day he killed the cougar to protect Wiki.

Day two featured a few squiggly lines, an abstract representation of the river, the girl they saved from its depths, and the young woman they were too late to save. Grimly, Liam wondered how fast Nova's body might be decomposing in the ejector pod.

The hieroglyph for day three, the day he and the others got kidnapped and taken to the village, was a stick figure with antlers. Liam didn't draw the constant scowl on Fang's face, but he imagined it every time he looked at the figure.

He didn't have it in him to mark any symbols for days four through seven—the carefree days he spent with Skai before everything crashed and burned. He wished he could go back to those moments, the long conversations they had about their divergent upbringings, the things she taught him, and the quiet embraces that spoke of instinctual human connections—instincts impervious to erasure, even by hundreds of years and hundreds of thousands of kilometers.

Marked by a drawing of a fish, day eight was the day Liam faced his mortality by falling into the giant's pit, the day he fought with Skai, and the day he reaped his imprisonment by freeing Jarok. While he still felt his actions were justified, he regretted them now.

A trio of mountains marked day nine, the day Liam and Wiki spent away from the village, when they climbed the Eagle, established communications with Smythii, and got attacked in the forest on the way back.

Day ten had a crude prison cell to represent their first full day in captivity.

Day twelve, a rifle to mark Tai and Raelyn's arrival—and the last time Liam saw Skai.

Day thirteen—the day Liam urinated on Wiki's arm—was denoted by a single water droplet.

Standing in front of his makeshift calendar, Liam scratched another tally into the stone wall.

Day fourteen.

He stared at the empty space below this new mark. What hieroglyph would he draw later that night? What monumental event would happen to commemorate a second week spent on planet Earth?

Liam looked down at the filthy, tattered undergarments of his pressure suit. He wondered how bad he looked. Judging by the appearance of the others, he couldn't look good. None of them had bathed in—he checked his calendar—at least forty-eight hours. With no fire, they had no smoke to stave off insects, so itchy bug bites covered their exposed skin. Tai had gone so far as to smear mud on himself to keep the bugs off—effective, but kind of gross. The mud covered up his bruises, which had changed colors. Most were now blue and purple, the rest a yellowish green.

The girls looked a little better, mostly because they bothered to clean themselves every once in a while. The way they groomed each other's hair reminded Liam of videos he had once seen of chimpanzees. Still, despite their best efforts, both girls were showing signs of deterioration. Zara, who had chewed her fingernails down to nubs, often screamed in her sleep—not frightened yelps, but hair-raising shrieks that left her breathless and crying. Raelyn seemed mentally intact, but her bionic arm was beginning to malfunction. It moved slower than usual and twitched randomly. According to Raelyn, the prosthetic just needed some basic maintenance, but they had no tools besides a few finger-sized stones.

Liam could smell himself. Or was it Wiki's wound? Or the clay pot in the corner filled with a day's worth of human waste? No matter the cause, a foul odor hung in the air at all times, an inescapable cloud of human smells.

Liam walked to the vertical bars of the cell and pushed his head between two of them. It didn't fit all the way through, but being closer to the fresh air helped dilute the stench. He couldn't see much outside since the jailhouse faced an empty field, but any view was better than the dank interior. He let out a heavy sigh, which had become his default form of expression over the last few days.

"Do you have a breathing problem or something?" Raelyn asked.

Liam hadn't noticed her standing by his side. The girl moved like a cougar. With his gaze trained on the empty field, he sighed again.

"Not funny," he said.

"When's your girl going to stop by again?"

"She's not my girl."

Now it was Raelyn who sighed. "You know what I mean. Have you been thinking about your apology?"

"Actually, I've been thinking about how she owes me an apology for locking us in here."

"No. You need to own up to your crimes and get us out of here before I go crazy."

"Please go away," he said. "I'm trying to—"

"Wow," Raelyn said. "I thought Earth might have changed you, but you're still the same old Liam. Why can't you take responsibility for this?"

Liam withdrew his head from the bars and faced Raelyn. "I can't control when Skai comes to visit, and even if she showed up right now, I couldn't make her listen to me."

Raelyn came closer. "Wiki's not doing well," she whispered. "He's acting like he's okay, but his infection is getting worse."

"I can't do anything about—"

"He's going to die." She grabbed him with her bionic hand, which pinched the skin on his arm. "You have to do something."

Liam pushed her away, harder than he meant to. She stumbled backward and nearly fell to the ground. Before Liam could apologize, Tai arrived in front of him.

"Look, I didn't mean to push her. It was an—"

A surprise jab to the cheekbone jolted Liam's head to the side. The pain came like a lightning strike, sharp and immediate. It instantly filled Liam with adrenaline and woke him from his depressed fog. He leaned forward, kicked off the wall to give himself some momentum, then crashed into Tai's chest with his shoulder. They tumbled down together until Tai's back hit the dirt floor with a thump.

Straddling Tai's legs, Liam got one hit in, a satisfying punch to the jaw. Grunting, Tai rolled out from under Liam, who took the opportunity to push himself onto his knees and back away. The cell filled with a frenzy of yells, but Liam ignored them. With the cheap shots done, both fighters rose to their feet and squared up.

"You think you're so tough." Tai spat blood and raised his fists. "Let's go."

Tai swung at Liam, who dodged the punch and simultaneously kneed Tai in the thigh. "I don't want to fight you."

"No, you don't want to lose."

Backing up, Liam glanced at a nasty bruise on Tai's neck. "I don't want to hurt you," he said.

That was a lie. Liam wanted nothing more than to release the anger that had been building inside him for days, and few targets would be more satisfying than Tai's face.

Before Liam could attack, Tai rushed him again, this time going for a tackle. Instead of resisting the motion, Liam went with it and used Tai's momentum to throw him toward the wall. Tai's torso hit the packed earth with a loud slap. With Tai dazed, Liam grabbed him by the back of the neck, dug a thumb into the bruise, and pushed him face-first against the wall. Yelping and squirming, Tai started throwing elbows in an attempt to free himself. None of the elbows hit Liam's torso—Tai's muscular build made him less than flexible—though they came close.

"Stop resisting," Liam said through clenched teeth, satisfied that he had the upper hand, but not surprised. "It's over, Tai. You—"

The back of Tai's head slammed into Liam's eye. His vision grayed out for a second as he fell onto his back. Then Tai was on him, holding each of his limbs down with bulky hands and knees. Liam tried to slither free, but Tai had him pinned. His smirk appeared as a streak of shiny white across his blackened mess of a face.

"This is over when I knock you out."

Tai freed Liam's left arm and delivered a heavy blow to his temple. Stars exploded in Liam's peripheral vision. Another fist to his face doubled the number of lights he saw. They orbited his head like satellites. Or was it his head spinning?

"Stop, Tai, you're killing him!"

Raelyn's words came to Liam's consciousness as if she spoke through a wall of water. A wave of pain cascaded from his head to his torso. He tried to protect his face with his free arm, but he found he didn't have the strength to move his body.

"Tai, stop!"

Liam's eyes attempted to track the galaxy of moving lights but couldn't lock on. Everything started fading to black, then one more punch erased the stars from Liam's sky.

31

MISSING PERSON

Back in the infirmary tent, Glo began the arduous task of organizing the mess of medical supplies strewn about the space. She sorted the bandages by size, consolidated the meds for lighter travel, and collected a pile of dirty rags and linens to wash in the morning.

"How did it go?"

The unexpected voice nearly made Glo drop an open bottle of antibiotics to the dirt floor. She twisted the lid on and turned to see Commander Killion sitting up in his cot, his blood-soaked hair a disheveled mess above his bruised and swollen face. He would look worse before he got better.

"Sorry," Glo said. "Did I wake you? I'm just trying to get a head start on—"

"It's fine." Killion smiled. At least that part of his face wasn't ruined. "I was already awake."

"How's your pain?" Glo held up a bottle of painkillers. "I'm about to pack these up for the road."

"I can't say I've had worse injuries than this, but I think I'm doing all right. Either way, I don't really like drugs. I do want to know how Reagan's announcement went, though."

Glo shrugged and took a few steps closer to Killion. "I'm not really sure what you mean by that."

"I mean, how did everyone take the news? About us leaving? Did anyone seem hesitant? Did anyone resist?"

"Nobody resisted." Glo paused. "Would it matter if they had?"

Killion clenched his jaw, closed his eyes, and took in a slow breath through his nose. "I suppose not."

Glo sat down on the cot next to Killion's. Up close, she could smell the burnt hair and skin surrounding his cauterization, so she started breathing through her mouth. "What do you think about all of this?"

"It doesn't matter what I think," Killion said.

"So, you don't want to go?"

"I didn't say that," Killion said. "Yes, I have my doubts, but we can't stay here."

She glanced at the gauze covering his neck wound. "You doubt we'll make it there alive?"

"I don't think all of us will make it, but there's a chance most of us will. That might be enough." Killion scratched the stubble on his chin. "I'm just trying to understand Reagan's motives behind rushing the exodus. It seems too soon. If the Life Vault is still intact after all this time, a few more weeks to prepare for the journey couldn't hurt."

Glo was torn between leaving and staying. On the one hand, she felt eager to leave the valley behind, if only to increase her chances of getting in touch with Omega—with her mother. On the other hand, the journey ahead terrified her. Every kilometer would be a battle, and so much could go wrong.

"Once we're on the road," Glo said, "will the women finally be armed?"

Killion frowned. "I don't know. That's up to Reagan."

Glo leaned forward and rested her forearms on her thighs. "Do you think we should be?"

Killion regarded her with a dark and severe expression. "I want whatever is best for all of us. The more guns in hands, the better."

"Really?"

"You don't believe me?"

Glo stood up. "I'm just wondering what changed."

"I've always wanted what's best for my people."

"But you don't think Reagan does?"

Usually, Glo would have been afraid of questioning such a powerful man, but he looked helpless enough sitting there on the cot, bruised and beaten. Plus, she had saved his life. If nothing else, he owed her an explanation. Arms folded, she waited for a response.

"I"—he exhaled quickly through his nose—"I disagree with how he's been treating you. Not just you, but you know what I mean."

Glo let out a bitter laugh. "Messing around with Quinn seems pretty Reagan-like to me."

The color drained from Killion's face. "You don't seriously think I— You don't think I'm like that, do you? That I'm like him? I would never hurt Quinn."

"You're already hurting her. You're twice her age. There's nothing you can do but hurt her."

"That's not true," Killion said. "I'm not like Reagan, not at all. I haven't even touched Quinn."

"Bullshit," Glo said.

"I swear," Killion said. "When Reagan brought her up to my cabin, I was disgusted."

"You mean the night you told her how much you cared about her?"

Killion groaned. "Clearly, she has a crush on me, but I promise the feeling isn't mutual. I did tell her that I care about her, and it's true. She's a bright and kind young lady, but she must have misunderstood. We're nothing but friends."

"Teenage girls and authority figures shouldn't be friends."

"Nothing happened, Glo. I swear."

Glo considered Killion's words for a moment. Quinn did tell her that they stayed up talking that night—nothing else.

"If that's true, you need to talk to her," Glo said. "Whether you're doing it intentionally or not, it's wrong to lead her on like this."

"I agree."

"But you need to let her down easy. She's young and fragile, and she thinks she loves you."

Killion nodded. "I'll think about how to word it tonight and talk to her first thing in the morning."

"Don't bother."

Quinn's voice came from the threshold of the tent.

When Glo looked over, she saw rivers of tears cascading down the girl's cheeks. Quinn shook her head and turned her back on Killion.

He tried to stand. "Wait, Quinn, I—"

The tent flaps whooshed shut.

•|•

Glo gave Quinn fifteen minutes to cool off before leaving the infirmary tent to find her. She wanted to apologize for talking about her behind her back, but mostly she wanted to get her to come back so she and Killion could hash things out.

Outside the tent, nighttime had descended upon the camp. Most of the survivors were already sleeping under the stars, but a few were still awake, gathered around dying fires, talking in hushed voices. Glo walked as quietly as possible to avoid waking anyone. Near the edge of camp, she found Tristan, Axel, and a couple of other guys drying meat over a bed of glowing embers—provisions for the road.

As Glo approached, Axel removed his lips from a bottle and smirked. "Look who decided to join us for once."

Tristan dipped his head and scooted to his left. "Want to sit, Glo?"

Axel burped, then tried to hand Glo the bottle. "From the Admiral's private stash. He said we won't have room to bring it all with us."

Glo could smell the liquor on Axel's breath. "Thanks," she said, "but I'm not here to socialize."

Axel's brows lowered, then he shrugged and took another sip. His eyes looked glazed.

"What's going on?" Tristan asked.

"I'm looking for Quinn."

"That little blonde girl?" Axel asked.

Tristan pointed toward the north wall. "She went that way."

"Thanks."

"Is something wrong?" Tristan asked.

"Just some drama. Girl stuff."

Glo took off before the guys could ask any more questions.

Glo looked everywhere for Quinn. She walked along the inside perimeter of the fence twice, checked every row of sleepers, and even peeked inside Reagan's tent. Still, she had no luck. Inside the walls, there weren't too many places for a girl to hide. As Glo approached the infirmary tent to tell Killion, a terrifying thought came to her: Maybe Quinn's not inside the walls.

In a sudden panic, she jogged to the camp's only entrance, a makeshift gate guarded day and night. The boy standing watch looked no older than sixteen. Glo couldn't remember his name because they never spoke, especially since she had been keeping to herself. He yawned as Glo approached.

"You can't go out there," he said.

"Did Quinn go outside?"

"What?"

"My friend Quinn. I can't find her anywhere. I need—"

"Okay, slow down. My shift started a couple of hours ago, and no one has gone out since then."

"Were you awake the whole time?"

"Yes." The boy yawned again. "Did you check—"

"I've looked everywhere." Glo attempted to look through the cracks between logs, but she only saw darkness. "Open the gate."

"I can't. It's against—"

"Move." Glo stepped past him and began pushing against the wood.

"You have to stop."

"You don't understand." Glo leaned against the gate, but it wouldn't budge. "If Quinn's out there, she's in danger. I have to—"

"What's going on over here?"

Glo glanced over her shoulder. Tristan stood there with Axel and a few others.

"She's trying to get out," the young guard said.

"Obviously."

"I think Quinn left camp," Glo said, still leaning all of her weight against the gate. "We need to go look for—"

"Glo, stop." Tristan grabbed her shoulder. "You can't go running into the forest on your own. You're going to get yourself—"

"I'm sick of being told what I can and can't do." Glo yanked her shoulder out of Tristan's grip. "And don't touch me."

"I'm sorry." Tristan backed away. "Listen, Glo, I want to help you. We'll go look for her. Won't we, guys?"

The other men hesitated and looked at each other for reassurance, except for Axel, who nodded enthusiastically—if not drunkenly.

"Let's do this," Axel said, louder than necessary.

"Fine," Glo said. She ceased her assault on the gate.

"Open it up," Tristan said. "That's an order."

The young guard began fiddling with the latches. As the gate swung open, Tristan and his friends drew plasma rifles from their backs and activated them.

"Hold on, boys." Stepping out of the dark, smoky region of camp, Reagan appeared to materialize out of nowhere. Everyone but Tristan lowered their weapons and stood at attention. "Close the gate, son." He scowled at Tristan. "I make the orders around here, is that clear?"

"Yes, sir." Gritting his teeth, Tristan disarmed his weapon and slung it over his shoulder. "We have another missing person. I was just trying to—"

"Who?"

"Quinn," Glo said. "She was upset, so she ran off. I've looked everywhere in camp. She has to be out there."

"How unfortunate," Reagan said, chewing on the words. "I'll send a search party in the morning."

"But—"

"I can't risk my men's lives to look for a runaway. It's safer out there in the daylight."

Glo seethed at Reagan's words. "That's exactly why we need to—"

"Or would you rather have me send no search party at all?"

"No, I—"

"Gloria," Reagan said. "You don't need to worry. I'm sure she'll scurry back here the second she gets scared." He glanced at Tristan's friends—the two who'd hesitated to leave the safety of camp. "Keep an eye on Gloria tonight. Make sure she doesn't do anything stupid."

They both bowed their heads.

"Yes, sir," they said in unison. "For the future of humanity."

32

AS MY BROTHER

The pain came first, a sharp, throbbing ache that seemed to have no origin. It simply existed, everywhere, all at once. Nausea hit him next, accompanied by the taste of iron. Soon a jumble of sounds ricocheted in his confused mind, indiscernible voices smothered by a high-pitched, ringing, buzzing racket.

One eye cracked open for a split second, letting in a knife of sunlight that instantly intensified the pain. When Liam blinked his eye open again, the room spun around a blurry collection of faces. He had to close it to keep himself from throwing up.

"He's awake."

"Liam, can you hear me?"

Liam tried to speak, but his mind felt broken, as if his brain couldn't communicate with his mouth. Instead, he nodded, or at least he thought he nodded. He couldn't feel anything but the pain.

"Do you know where you are?"

Omega, he thought, in the Earth Sim. A series of images came to his mind: opening a door to the bluest sky he had ever seen, diving into frigid water to save a life, running from ghouls and giants. Did these things happen? He had no idea. Using all of his strength, he opened his mouth and forced his vocal cords to vibrate.

"Where?" he whispered.

"What did he say?"

"Where—am I?"

Memories of his fight with Tai came back all at once, along with a massive hit of fear. Instinctively, he tried to move his arms up to protect his face from another punch.

"Liam." He felt a warm hand on his forearm. "You're okay now."

"How long?" he choked.

"You were only out for a few minutes."

He cracked his eyelids open again, noticing that one eye opened wider than the other, and saw Zara's face fading in and out of focus.

"I'm tired," Liam said, shutting out the painful light.

"We shouldn't let him sleep," Wiki said. "He might have a concussion."

Zara stroked his hair. "Liam, you have to stay awake."

When Liam opened his eyes again, his nausea doubled. Pain coursed through his body. He rolled onto his side and vomited bile into the dirt.

•|•

It took hours for the dizziness to subside. Liam's discomfort didn't lessen, but he got somewhat accustomed to the constant throbbing ache. The pain became static, background noise, just one more layer piled onto his suffering—another flying turd in the howling shitstorm that his life had become.

With Zara and Raelyn watching over Liam and Wiki, the cell resembled an infirmary—an understaffed, poorly stocked infirmary with no beds, no doctors, and no medicine, but one where the healthy did their best to care for the sick and injured with what they had. Raelyn had banished Tai to the opposite side of the cell.

Even considering the beating, Liam was doing better than Wiki, who had gotten too weak to stand without help. His wound looked necrotic, and his filthy forehead shone with fever-induced sweat. By Wiki's own estimate, if he didn't get antibiotics in the next day, he likely wouldn't live.

"Guys," Wiki said, his voice low. "Do you mind if I have a moment with Liam? Alone?"

Something squirmed in Liam's chest. Whatever Wiki was about to tell him couldn't be good.

"Take your time," Zara said.

Raelyn smiled, then both girls got up and left. A long, silent moment passed. Liam leaned against the wall beside Wiki, unsure whether he should speak first.

"I need you to do something for me."

Liam stared at the dirt. "I'm not peeing on you again."

Wiki didn't laugh. "It's serious," he said.

"I'm not going to put you out of your misery, either."

"No, that's not it," Wiki said. "This infection will kill me soon enough."

Liam leaned forward and put his forehead in his hands. He wanted to comfort Wiki, but he couldn't look at him. "I'm not going to let you die, man."

"It's not up to you."

"But—"

"Listen, Liam. I don't know how long I have left, so I need to get this off my chest. There's a real chance I won't wake up tomorrow."

Hot tears dripped into Liam's lap. "Don't say that."

"I've been thinking a lot about my life—accomplishments I'm proud of, friends I've made, things like that. But no matter how many good memories I summon, they're all shadowed by my regrets. I should've written that book. I should've spent less time worrying and more time living. I should've been a better friend."

"You're a great friend." Liam turned to face Wiki and saw that he was crying too. "I should've been better."

"You still have the chance to be better."

Do I? Liam pondered the question, but he didn't say anything.

"I've been able to let go of most of these regrets because at least I got to come to Earth. And here, I've seen some incredible things." Wiki shook his head, smiling sadly. "We've seen some beautiful things."

"We have."

"But there are some mistakes I can't rectify—because we're here, because there's not enough time, because I'm dying."

The finality of Wiki's words stabbed at Liam's heart like a Suvi spear.

"No, Wiki, you're—"

"It's okay. Everyone dies."

"This is all my fault," Liam said. "I should have never brought you up that mountain."

"I chose to go. I chose to follow you. This"—Wiki pointed at his injured arm—"is not on you."

"I'm sorry," Liam said. "I'm so sorry."

"This isn't your fault, but I forgive you. For everything." Wiki nodded firmly. "And I mean it."

Liam sniffled and shook his head. "Thank you."

"All my life, I thought I never had a family. It was hard seeing the other kids going home to their moms and dads. I've been angry about it for a long time. I hated the fact that I was an orphan. It didn't seem fair."

"I know, but—"

"But I was wrong." Wiki's lips bunched to one side. "I do have a family. I've always had one. You're not like a brother to me, Liam. You *are* my brother."

Liam gripped Wiki's hand and pulled him into a hug. "And you're mine."

They cried together for a while, unashamed.

"As my brother," Wiki said, "you need to do something for me."

"Anything."

"I need you to rectify my biggest regret of all." Wiki took in a breath of air. "When you get out of here, when you find the others—because I know you will—please tell Glo what I was always too scared to. Tell her how much I care about her. Tell her that I love her."

33

BIG, STRONG, MANLY

Reagan's thugs watched Glo sleep, or pretend to sleep. Knowing they were there, she found it impossible to rest. One stood near the tent's threshold, scratching at the two-week-old ginger stubble coating his square jaw. His rifle leaned against the wall, but he had a pistol attached to his belt. The other guard lay on a cot, the rise and fall of his fat belly indicating a deep sleep. It looked like someone had been sneaking extra rations—and not just on Earth.

Glo couldn't remember either guard's name, and she didn't try to. Red Beard and Piggy would suffice. Egged on by Reagan and each other, most of the men in camp—Killion, Tristan, and Axel excluded—had blurred into one giant mass of testosterone and power trips. Their unyielding control over Glo was becoming exhausting, and Glo saw no end to it. The men made her decisions for her. They chose to remove her birth control implant. They dragged her to Earth. They told her where she could go and what she could do. Now they had decided that Quinn's life wasn't worth risking a few of their own. "For the future of humanity," they said to justify every action or inaction.

Cowards, Glo thought. Big, strong, manly cowards.

The handle of her plasma pistol felt cool beneath her pillow. It was the one tool she had to change her future. She desperately wanted to use it but couldn't decide how. Maybe she could threaten the guards, make them let her out, go searching for Quinn on her own. Or she could skip the negotiations entirely with two quick bursts of plasma—Red Beard first, followed by Piggy. Then again, she could always wait until morning and use it to threaten Reagan into action.

Having the gun gave her options, and she liked that.

Lying there in the dark, going over every possible scenario, Glo teased the trigger beneath her pillow. Whatever the best course of action was, she needed to make a decision sooner rather than later.

In twenty-four hours, the exodus would begin.

34

INTO DEATH

With newfound purpose, Liam began chipping away at one of the thick logs the Suvi used as cell bars. His only tool was the tiny rock he used to scratch tally marks into the packed earth walls, so progress came slowly. Still, with a few hours of work, he managed to carve out a horizontal groove about two centimeters deep. He didn't know what he would do once the depth surpassed his tool's length, but he felt good about his progress. At least he was doing something.

Liam thought about breaking the clay pot they used as a toilet. A ceramic shard might work better than a rock, but the Suvi would notice the pot's absence. Maybe he could sneak in a better tool the next time they took him to the river? The only problem: He had no idea when that would be. Despite the limitations, he worked tirelessly with what he had, determined to break free at all costs— because he didn't want to deliver Wiki's message to Glo. He wanted Wiki to tell her himself.

"Stop," Zara said. "There's someone coming."

Sweating profusely, Liam ceased his frenzied carving and pocketed his rock, which was hot from the friction. The last thing he needed was for the Suvi to discover evidence of his escape attempts, so he mixed the accumulated sawdust into the dirt with his feet then retreated to the back wall. He folded his arms and tried to look casual.

Fang appeared first, followed by half a dozen burly villagers toting spears, curved blades, and, much to Liam's surprise, another prisoner. She didn't have her hands tied, but a hood covered her face. For a split second, Liam selfishly hoped the Suvi had captured his sister. It would make things easier knowing that she was safe, that Wiki would be able to mend his last regret. But the girl walking among the villagers didn't have the same build as Glo. She looked younger, a bit shorter.

Fang stared into Liam's eyes as he passed, an unreadable expression on his face. As the stone slab slid open, Liam contemplated running through the opening. The sight of the weapons and the pure physical strength of the villagers wielding them held him back.

"Fang," Liam said, gesturing toward Wiki, urging the old man to understand. "Can't you see he needs help? We need to—"

A trio of spearheads—centimeters from Liam's face—silenced him. He backed up, defeated, and saw Fang glance at Wiki. Clearly, if Fang understood, he didn't care.

Instead of shoving the girl through the threshold like they had done to Tai, the villagers gently nudged her forward before unveiling her face. It took Liam's brain a few seconds to register the girl's identity, long enough for the heavy door to begin sliding shut.

"Quinn?" he said.

The last time Liam had seen Quinn, Reagan had been bringing her up to the Command Deck. She looked frightened then, but now she looked terrified.

"How is this possible?" Lips trembling, Quinn stared into Liam's eyes. "Reagan said you died in the crash."

"Do I look dead to you?" Liam said. With his black eye and other injuries, he probably did.

"What is this place?" Quinn said, her voice a nearly breathless whimper. "How are there people?"

"I know it's a lot to process, but you're going to be okay." Raelyn held out her arms. "Come here."

Quinn glanced at Liam then quickly averted her eyes, as if she were walking past an open casket.

"Come here," Raelyn said again as she pulled Quinn into a hug. "Are you okay? Did they hurt you?"

"No," Quinn said dreamily. "I mean, yes, I'm okay. They didn't hurt me. Well, a little, I guess. I'm so confused."

"I know." Raelyn released Quinn then checked her body for injuries.

"Why did they bring us here?" Quinn asked.

"I don't know," Raelyn said, which made Tai scoff from his place in the corner. "Not the time, Tai. Can't you see she's in shock? You should sit down."

"No," Quinn said. "This isn't shock. I'm fine. I'm just— I'm sad about something else."

"What happened?" Wiki asked.

Quinn jumped at the sound of Wiki's voice, like she hadn't noticed him there on the floor.

"It's nothing." Quinn frowned at Wiki. "What's wrong with you?"

Wiki glanced down at his bandage. "I got bit."

"May I?" Quinn asked. She squatted and turned a palm up. "I helped Glo with first aid in camp."

"She's okay?" Wiki said, his voice eager for the first time in days.

"She was when I left," Quinn said. She grabbed Wiki's arm to take a look.

"Don't bother." Wiki sighed. "It's really infected."

"You need antibiotics," Quinn said. "Amoxicillin, or maybe penicillin. Glo told me which one is better for infected wounds, but I can't remember. We've got all kinds of antibiotics at camp. Did you sterilize it?"

Liam and Wiki made brief eye contact. "To the best of our ability," Wiki said. "How's Glo doing?"

"Not great. She's been grieving both of your deaths. Reagan told her you both burned up when we landed."

"What?" Liam said.

"What a snake," Raelyn said.

"I also heard what he tried to do to you," Quinn said.

Raelyn flexed her malfunctioning prosthetic hand. "Touching me would have been the last thing he ever did."

"At least you'll never have to see him again. The whole camp is leaving."

"Yeah, we know. Did Reagan say anything about where they're going?"

Quinn's blue eyes rolled upward, searching for a memory. "Someplace called the Life Vault."

Everyone in the cell turned to Wiki.

"I've heard about it," he said, "but I don't know where it is. When are they leaving, Quinn?"

"First thing in the morning."

Liam's guts churned. He glanced at the notch in the log, which represented hours of labor, and the orange glow outside that marked the end of another day.

Darkness settled upon the jailhouse, and Liam's mood darkened with the environment. His swollen eye was still throbbing, his head ached, and every cell in his body felt extremely heavy. He had no comforts to help him ease the pain—no pills or pillows, not even the luxury of lunar gravity to take the weight off his shoulders. Yet, for someone who had spent much of his time striving for success in the Earth Sim, nothing hurt more than knowing he had failed in real life.

Lying there in the dark, unable to sleep, he stared through a gap between two cell bars at a patch of cloudless sky above the distant mountains. Marveling at the blanket of blackness dotted by specks of light, stars blurred by gathering tears, he felt small enough to disappear, as if the wind could carry him away into oblivion. He almost wished it would. He didn't want to be there anymore—to exist anymore.

Now, like Wiki had, he ruminated on a lifetime of regrets. It started with a torrent of trivial regrets from his childhood, each one biting like an insect, insignificant on its own but capable of adding up to a swarm. He swatted many of them away, like the time he wet his pants in class as a child, the awkwardness of his first real kiss—he still didn't know if he used too much tongue or not enough—and other minor embarrassments that seemed life-shattering at the time. Some regrets stung a bit worse, not things that happened to him, but things he had done to others. He wished that he hadn't bullied some of the kids in school, that he hadn't spoken so much without thinking.

Next, his thoughts turned to the things he never did or should have done better. He should have given Raelyn the time and attention she wanted. He should have been kinder to Zara and recognized her talents sooner. He should have spent less time in the Earth Sim and more time with his mom. The regret of not saying goodbye to her—a thought he had been avoiding like the Terminal Plague since his arrival on Earth—poured over him like buckets of river water. When he stowed away, he left her there alone, forcing her to lose both of her children on the same day.

Why was I so selfish? Why?

The moonlight mocked Liam, reflecting off a place he could never return to. He hoped that Smythii had the sense to tell his mother about his whereabouts. If Liam never got to speak to her again, at least she would know he wasn't in hiding, or worse, on the wrong side of an airlock. Would the news of his survival comfort her? Or would his existence on Earth be a permanent reminder that he had chosen this place over her? Staring at the moon, he fueled his apology and tried to project it up and out of the atmosphere.

I'm sorry, Mom. Please, please forgive me.

But his mother wasn't the only family member affected by his mistakes. He could still recall in vivid detail the last time he saw his sister, floating there on the ETS Resurgence, dragged away by the hands of a monster—hands he had placed her in. Whatever happened to her that night was his fault. And instead of fighting Reagan, instead of correcting his mistake, he just let the creep take her. Lying there, thinking about his saint of a sister, a young woman who would do anything for anyone at any time, Liam berated himself for his cowardice. He felt weak, not in body but in character.

Then there was Skai. Liam still didn't feel bad about freeing Jarok, but he felt terrible about disappointing her. He should have tried to convince Fang to free the giant instead of doing it himself. He should have been more careful.

"I fought for you when no one else would," Skai had said. "I convinced Fang to spare your life, to let you become one of us. I told you to be careful. And this is how you repay me?"

Skai wasn't wrong. She deserved much better than Liam could ever give her. He felt like a fool for thinking she could ever care about him as much as he cared about her.

Liam sighed. He wished he could enter a wormhole, leap backward through time, fix his mistakes. Everything would have been better if he hadn't felt so entitled, if he had just stayed in Omega like he was supposed to. The Resurgence Mission, the journey to Earth, none of it was meant for him like his father had once said. The ETS Resurgence was never meant to be his ride home for one simple reason: Earth was not his home. He doubted his father would have been proud of the man he had become. No, not a man, he thought—a boy pretending to be a man. Men didn't treat people the way Liam had treated people. Men didn't drag their friends into captivity, into death.

No matter what Wiki said, Liam still bore the guilt of the deadly bite. He didn't know how he would go on with the weight of causing his best friend's death on his shoulders. Now Wiki would never get to tell Glo how he felt, and Glo would leave the valley to die at the hands of Earth's monsters—or to survive under the control of an Omegan one.

Unable to stand the negative feelings any longer, Liam rolled over and faced the interior of the cell.

"Is anyone awake?" he whispered.

He heard the clearing of a throat. "I am," Wiki said, his voice even weaker than before.

"Me too," Quinn said. "How do you guys even sleep here?"

"We don't," Raelyn and Zara said simultaneously.

Liam couldn't hear any snoring, which meant Tai was most likely awake too. He didn't know what to say, but he needed to apologize to someone—to unload whatever guilt he could. Stalling, he slowly sipped in a long breath.

"I've been thinking about a lot of things tonight," he said. "About how we ended up here. About how I got us all locked up. I know it's all my fault. I know I—"

A loud thumping tore Liam's attention away from his apology. Then another. And another.

"What is that?" Quinn asked.

Liam rolled back over to face the bars of the cell. The thumps sounded close. He couldn't see much from his vantage point, so he stood up. In the moonlit field ahead, he saw nothing but the occasional patch of tall grass swaying in the wind. He shook his head and prepared to lie back down, but then something scurried into the field, a four-legged animal with a whooshing tail.

"King?" Liam said.

Watching the creature's clumsy gait, Liam had no doubt that it was indeed King. Still, this didn't explain the strange sound. King didn't have enough mass to produce such a thump, not even if he jumped from a tree, and there were no trees in the vicinity.

Liam made a kissing sound. "Here, King."

He noticed Quinn standing beside him. "Wow, he's adorable," she said. "Come on, little guy."

King glanced over and meowed. The cub sat at the edge of Liam's field of vision, licking his front left paw. Then, as if out of nowhere, a massive bare foot stomped down beside King.

Liam recoiled. What he saw couldn't possibly be real.

Quinn squealed and nearly fell backward.

Then Jarok the giant stepped into the scene.

Liam's first emotion was an instinctual fear ignited solely by the fact that giants lived on Earth—that he was in the presence of one. Hope came to mind next. The return of Jarok meant he and the others might be freed, assuming someone in the village could catch him. But hope vanished when Liam remembered Skai's warning: "If Jarok kills anyone, you will be put to death." The giant could easily snap someone in half.

But he didn't kill me, Liam thought. And King didn't seem to fear the giant. The cub rubbed up against Jarok's tree trunk of an ankle.

"Wow," Raelyn said. "He's as big as you said. He doesn't look that scary, though."

Liam and the others gaped at Jarok, who squatted down like a child to pet King's spine with one finger. The cub rolled over and swatted at Jarok's hand, claws extended, but the giant didn't seem to mind. He had thick skin that tiny claws couldn't possibly bother. Jarok made a sound that resembled a closed-mouth laugh, but much deeper.

Liam shook his head. "Are they…playing?"

"Incredible," Wiki whispered. "Absolutely incredible."

Liam wondered how long it would take for the villagers to wake. Had they heard the stomping? Would they attempt to capture the gentle giant? Or would they simply kill him on sight?

Without thinking much about it, Liam spoke Jarok's name.

The giant glanced at the jailhouse. His oversized eyes registered Liam's face for a split second, then his attention quickly returned to the cub. At the sound of Liam's voice, though, King rolled onto his paws, bounded over to the cell, and stepped gracefully between the bars. Quinn reached down to pet him. Running her fingers through the cub's fur, she giggled and cooed—a joyful song. For a moment, seeing her smile and hearing that sound, Liam nearly forgot about all the negative emotions he had been harboring earlier.

But then another thump came from the field, and Quinn's smile faded. Jarok headed toward them, closing the distance to the cell in half a dozen steps. He bent down to look inside. Everyone backed up as the giant tried to force his oversized hand between the bars. Clearly, he wasn't done playing with King.

When Jarok realized he couldn't fit his hand through the gap, he removed it and tried pulling the bars apart. The logs creaked but didn't budge.

Liam heard some frightened weeping, from Quinn or Zara, but he remained focused on the giant. Soon Jarok gave up on the prying method, slumped down to his knees, and began leaning his shoulder against a few bars. The wood warped and groaned, then Jarok backed off a bit. Putting some energy into the motion, he slammed the side of his body against the wall of bars. Dust fell from the ceiling, but the logs held. Spit sprayed from the giant's mouth as he grunted.

"Somebody give him the damn cat!" Tai yelled.

"No," Raelyn said. "If he breaks in, maybe we can get out."

The same thought came to Liam's mind as Raelyn spoke. This was their way out, their only way out.

Tai scoffed. "Or maybe he'll smash our heads together and eat our brains."

Seeing Tai scared granted Liam a hit of satisfaction. "He's not going to hurt us," Liam said. "Jarok's harmless. He's like a little kid."

"Not that little," Wiki said.

Another shoulder slam shook tiny chunks of brick from the place where the logs met the ceiling. For a moment, Liam thought that Jarok might break through. The giant backed up, preparing for another blow. Liam tensed.

But Jarok's hammer of a shoulder didn't strike again. He backed away, his face twisted into a lethal grimace. Apparently, he had lost interest in his furry friend. Jarok turned as if to leave.

"No," Liam said. "Come back!"

Jarok took two long steps away, stopped, and turned around. He looked directly at Liam and stared for a moment, then his face softened. Liam recalled the expression. It was the same one he saw in the pit, right before Jarok picked him up, and the same expression the giant wore when he climbed up the makeshift ladder.

In that moment, like other moments, Jarok looked kind. He looked merciful. He looked human.

Jarok shot forward like a rocket, lifted one leg in the air, and delivered a bare-footed kick to a single wooden bar—the one that stood the farthest from Liam and the others—the one that Liam had been sawing a groove into earlier that day.

The log snapped cleanly in half with a satisfying crack, which brought to mind something Skai had once said…

One stick breaks.

Many sticks hold strong.

35

UNDERSTANDING

A haze of dust rose around Liam and the others. They stared at the new opening, a space just wide enough for them to squeeze through.

Instead of reaching in to grab King, Jarok stood still for a moment then backed up. He sat down, his weight thumping to the dirt about five meters away. His muscles twitched and bulged, but he no longer looked angry or impatient—just tired.

Liam glanced at the others then back at Jarok. "I'll go first," he said, moving forward.

A small hand grabbed his upper arm before he could go. "Be careful," Zara said.

He offered her a slight nod. "I will."

Liam stepped over the broken log, turned his body sideways, and pushed himself into the threshold. He paused there for a few seconds, preparing for the worst, then smiled at the giant and stepped out of captivity.

After so many days with limited sights, Liam felt a bit overwhelmed by the sheer size of the outdoors, similar to how he felt stepping out of the ejector pod on day one. Even with the sky barely illuminated by the first inklings of dawn, he could still see the beauty and the wonder of his surroundings—mountainous silhouettes on a dark blue backdrop, early morning fires glimmering across the cliffside village, and wide-open space in all directions.

Liam took a few careful paces toward Jarok. "Thank you," he said. "I guess I owe you one."

Liam didn't know why he attempted speaking to the giant. Except for his own name, Jarok clearly didn't register any of Liam's words. Still, with his head tilted and his expression soft, he seemed to understand some of the sentiment. Liam took a few more steps forward, which earned no reaction from the giant. Why didn't Jarok harbor any resentment toward the species that enslaved him? Perhaps he hated the crime, but not the criminal.

"I think you guys are good," Liam said. "Come on out."

Raelyn squeezed through the opening first, followed by Tai.

"Ugh, he smells," Tai said, keeping his distance from Jarok.

"And we don't smell any better." Raelyn laughed nervously. "Hello, giant."

Jarok grunted in response.

Cradling King in her arms, Quinn stepped up beside Liam, who stood a head and a half taller than her. "Now what?" she said.

"Now," Zara said, "we need to get out of here before everyone wakes up."

"I second that," Wiki said weakly. He leaned on Zara's shoulder for support. The approaching dawn accentuated the deathlike pallor of his face. "Let's go."

"All right," Liam said. He searched the area for signs of movement. Luckily, the cell was located on the outskirts of the village, where few villagers visited and fewer lived. "I think the way down is that way." He pointed toward the cliffs overlooking the switchbacks. "If we stick to the tree line, we should be able to stay out of sight."

"Good plan," Raelyn said. "Let's jet."

As they hurried toward the trees, a strange emotion came over Liam. He didn't feel how he expected he would feel. For some reason, freedom didn't taste as sweet as he remembered. Something wasn't right about their departure, something was missing, but he couldn't identify why it felt so wrong to leave. He glanced over his shoulder, saw Jarok still sitting in the dirt, as if he were waiting to take Liam's place in captivity—an even trade. Liam stopped and stared at the giant.

"What are you doing?" Raelyn asked. "We have to go now. It

looks like people are already waking up."

Liam didn't respond.

"Do you want to save Wiki's life or not?"

"I do," Liam said. He stared at the broken log lying on the cell floor. "Just give me a minute."

"Are you worried about the guards or something? We have the element of surprise. No weapons, but still. We can take care of them."

"No, it's just—"

"What's the holdup?" Tai dropped into the conversation like a surprise turd. "Let's get the hell out of here."

Liam's gaze swept across the village, from the dark outskirts to the populated center, where the smoke of morning fires slithered into the sky. Standing there, he recalled what Wiki had said during their descent from the Eagle: "The Suvi's speck of light is fading fast."

Yes, these people had punished Liam, but that didn't mean he wanted them to die off. He wanted them to live, to thrive, not only because Skai lived among them but because the Suvi were like him—human. But how would they explore and find others to thrive with? Skai said that no one who left the valley ever came back. And now the place was crawling with a horde of the creatures that killed those wanderers.

"We can't leave yet," Liam said.

"Why not?" Tai asked.

"We can't abandon them."

"Who?"

"These people. The Suvi."

"These people?" Tai laughed. "These people kidnapped us. These people beat the living shit out of me. They locked us up, starved us, and in case you forgot, they hate you. These people are hardly people at all. They're savages. They're—"

"You're wrong," Liam said. "They need us, and I think we might need them."

"Bullshit." Tai grabbed Raelyn's arm. "Come on, babe. We're free now. Liam can die here if he wants to."

"Let go of me," Raelyn said. "I want to hear what he has to say."

The rest of the group was paying attention now—even Jarok, who had stopped picking foliage out of his toes to watch Liam talk.

"I just— I have an idea, all right?" Liam stood his ground. "I need to go back and talk to Skai. It shouldn't take long."

"That's suicide," Wiki said. "Best case, imprisonment. Worst case, death."

"I know it's risky." Liam wanted to leave more than anything, but it didn't feel right. "Just trust me, okay?"

"Do you want us to go with you?" Quinn asked. Once again, she impressed Liam with her bravery.

"No," he said, "but I do need King." Liam took the cub from Quinn's arms. "It's too risky for all of us to go. I can sneak through the village better on my own."

"I don't like this," Zara said.

"Personally," Tai said. "I don't care what you do."

Liam didn't expect him to.

"Listen, guys. I already feel terrible for getting you into this mess." He looked from Zara to Raelyn to Tai. "I completely understand if you want to leave now, but I'm hoping you'll give me one more chance. I can make this right." He stepped forward and grabbed Wiki's shoulder. "And I know how badly you need those antibiotics, but do you think you can hang in there a little longer?"

Wiki smiled, as if he already knew what Liam was planning. "I've always had a strong immune system. At this point, I'm more worried about Skai throwing you off a cliff."

Liam shook his head. "Hide over there, at the edge of the forest." He indicated a spot along the tree line. "If I'm not back in an hour, go down to the valley and find the others without me. Before it's too late."

Liam took a roundabout path through the village. Each step through the shady alleys and narrow streets intensified his nerves. The only benefit of the adrenaline rush was that it slightly numbed his aches and pains. With his empty stomach grumbling and his hands sweating, he made quick work of the outskirts but had to slow down as he approached the populated center of the village.

A few unintelligible conversations reverberated off the exterior walls of dwellings, making it hard to discern where the sounds came from. Once the sun fully rose, there would be many more people out and about, and that would happen soon.

Whenever Liam heard voices, he altered his route. He peeked around each corner before advancing, knowing well that if anyone saw him, he would be thrown into another cell—or worse. Still, this didn't worry him as much as the thought of confronting Skai.

As Liam passed the central gathering space, the smell of cooking meat made his stomach spiral. Though he tried, he couldn't remember his last meal. The salted fish had come more irregularly and less often as the days passed.

Liam came around the final corner to Skai's dwelling, a place he had visited only once before, and prepared himself for her reaction. Upon waking to an unexpected and unwelcome visitor, would she scream, run, fight? Would his entire plan end before it could begin? Liam didn't know, but he had to try something because she was the only person in the village who understood him—not only because their mouths spoke the same language, but because their hearts did.

He glanced around a corner at the final stretch of his journey.

All clear.

Before the situation could change, he hurried to the entryway. There, he hesitated until the sound of approaching villagers forced him to act. He took a breath and stepped inside.

His pupils quickly adjusted to the dim light inside the dwelling, where embers glowed in the corner, the remnants of last night's fire. As he had expected, Skai lay sleeping on her side beneath stitched furs, her chest gently rising and falling. The girl was more or less nocturnal; she probably hadn't been sleeping long. Liam would have to wake her, but first, he took a second to appreciate the lack of anger on her face. She looked so calm, so happy, so beautiful, that he didn't want to ruin her mood yet.

The plasma rifle stood in the corner behind her, leaning against the wall. Liam considered hiding it so she couldn't use it against him. Briefly, he entertained the thought of taking it and sneaking back to the others. With a weapon like that, they would have a better chance of making it down to the valley. He shook the thought away. This wasn't what he came for. He wasn't here to steal the gun back or force her hand, and he didn't want to appear threatening. No, if she wanted to point the gun at him, he would let her.

"Skai," he whispered.

She stirred but didn't wake.

"Skai," he said a bit more loudly.

Skai's eyes slowly blinked open. She stared dreamily at Liam—or the space between herself and Liam—for a second before her expression shifted to recognition. She said something in her language, loud enough to draw attention to his intrusion. The last thing Liam needed was a band of riled-up villagers to come barging in.

"Skai, calm down, I need you to—"

"What are you doing here?" she said. She didn't look frightened—few things scared her, it seemed—but she did appear startled. Liam didn't blame her. "How did you escape, Lion Slayer?" Her tone changed from confused to angry. "No one has ever escaped."

"I can explain." He held up his hands. "I'm just here to talk."

Skai glowered then glanced at the weapon leaning against her wall. "Why would I listen to you?"

"I know you're angry."

"What are you doing here?"

"It's Jarok," Liam said. "He came back. He"—Liam shook his head, still in disbelief—"he freed us from the cell."

Skai stood, her brown eyes growing wide. "Jarok is here? In the village?"

"No," Liam said. "Well, kind of."

Skai shouldered her furs and grabbed the gun from its resting place. "Take me to him."

"Skai, you don't understand. Jarok doesn't want to hurt us. He wants to—"

She aimed the plasma rifle at the center of Liam's chest, fingered the trigger. "Now, Lion Slayer."

"Fine," Liam said, his palms still exposed to show that he meant no harm. "But don't attack him, not until you see what I'm talking about."

"No promises." Skai inclined her head toward the threshold. "Go."

Flustered, Liam stumbled out of the dwelling, the barrel of the rifle brushing against his spine. "You watched Jarok lift me out of that pit. You know he's—"

"Silence."

"Skai, I—"

The barrel of the rifle dug painfully into his back.

"You never listen," Skai said. "You never learn."

Liam's lips sealed like an airlock. He didn't want to prove her right, so he stayed quiet while she escorted him straight through the village center. As they passed, the Suvi stared. Some of them offered to help Skai with the escapee, but she refused.

To Liam, many of the villagers looked tired. No, beyond tired. They looked exhausted. But this wasn't the kind of exhaustion that came from waking up early. This was the exhaustion of the overworked, the malnourished, the desperate. Liam knew the look all too well; he had seen it often enough in Omega.

At that moment, Liam remembered something else that Wiki had told him about the Suvi: "Now they have all those subs to contend with—invading the valley, trampling their fields, eating up all the wild game."

A young boy ran past, about the same age as Kal, the orphan boy Liam used to feed with stolen rations. If Kal looked skinny, this child looked skeletal. His ribs protruded out of his torso like the Eagle and her sister peaks. Liam had to look away. How had things gotten so bad so quickly? Gravely, he now understood why the salted fish had stopped coming regularly.

"Do you see what your people have brought upon us?" Skai said, as if she could read Liam's mind.

Liam sighed, miserable with guilt. Now he fully knew the repercussions of his people's arrival in the valley. His imprisonment—and the imprisonment of his friends—was about much more than freeing Jarok.

"We can fix it," Liam said.

Skai didn't respond. As they exited the village proper, the back wall of the jailhouse, the empty field, and the tree line beyond came into view. For a moment, Liam worried that Jarok had fled, that the sound of the waking village had scared him away.

"This is a trick?" Skai asked. "Another lie?"

"He was just here. He was—"

"There," Skai said.

As Jarok's head appeared above the cell's flat roof, Liam felt the barrel of Skai's gun leave his back. Then she was walking beside him, aiming at the giant instead.

"Skai, don't."

"Giants killed many ancestors," Skai said.

"Not this one," Liam said. "Just come around the building and see what I mean."

Skai tilted her head. "First, you."

Liam led her along one wall until Jarok's full body came into view. The giant looked down at them curiously, first at their faces then at the rifle in Skai's grip. There was no way he could know what the gun was capable of, but he took a step back anyway.

"Lower it," Liam said.

She aimed at Jarok's head.

"Skai, please."

The gun stayed steady in Skai's hands, and her intense gaze never left the giant's face.

"Look." Liam pointed at Jarok's enormous hands, one of which held King while the other stroked the cub's back.

"Impossible," Skai said. "Giants, they are, they are—"

"Monsters?" Liam asked.

Skai lowered her aim to Jarok's chest. "Yes."

"Does he look like a monster to you?" Liam indicated the broken cell bar. "He's kind. He's fair. I think he helped me because I helped him. I think he learned from us."

"It makes no sense," Skai said.

Liam let out a long breath, summoning up the words he had been waiting to say. "I don't think we can judge any single creature by the crimes of his species. Maybe all subs are violent—I don't know—but this giant isn't."

Skai stood there, lips bunched to the side as she considered Liam's statement. The barrel of her gun slowly fell to the dirt.

"I messed up," Liam said. "But what my people— What your people are dealing with goes beyond one person. Your rules aren't stupid. I was stupid."

Skai's gaze fell to the ground. "Yes, you were."

"I don't expect you to forgive me for letting you down. I don't expect you to forgive my people for hurting yours." Liam touched her arm gently, cautiously, worried that she might slap him for touching her. She didn't. "I didn't understand before, what you were trying to teach me, but I do now."

Skai looked up from the ground. "Do you?"

"You and I, we can save this place. My people might be few, but they have more of these." He put a hand on the plasma rifle between them. "You have a lot of soldiers, but it takes more than spears and arrows to survive in this world. Right now, our people are scattered. Yours are hiding, and mine are leaving the valley for good. We need to bring them together."

Skai stood there for a moment, her expression blank, impossible to read. Beneath Liam's calm surface, his nerves boiled. He wanted to speak more, to reiterate his point so he could convince her to help, but he just waited. Then, after a moment that felt like an eternity, Skai nodded.

"How?" she asked.

"I need you to gather everyone in the village center. As many as possible."

"I can call a gathering. I cannot promise the people will listen to you."

"I have to try."

36

STRONGER TOGETHER

Liam stood on a flat rooftop overlooking the crowd, a congregation of villagers numbering in the hundreds—a good number of people, but far fewer than Liam thought the village held when he saw it the first time. From his elevated vantage point, he could see how much the Suvi's population had dwindled since their peak, before famines and diseases decimated them.

Skai squatted on the rooftop beside him, her lips pressed against the mouthpiece of a horn carved from bone. She inhaled deeply then blew. Liam expected a low, bellowing sound, but the tone was high-pitched and hardly audible. Still, the crowd went silent. Skai spoke a few sentences in her language, no louder than necessary, and turned to Liam.

"Ready, Lion Slayer?"

Liam gulped and stepped closer to the edge. He glanced at his friends sitting on the ground in the front row. He and Skai had gone to the forest to get them before Skai called the gathering. Tai didn't want to return to the village, but Raelyn strong-armed him into it—literally.

"Hello," Liam shouted, though he didn't need to. The villagers wouldn't understand him until Skai began translating. "I'm sure you're all wondering why I'm up here, why I'm not in my cell, why Skai blew the horn."

Skai nudged him. "Get to the point," she said. "You will bore them."

"Right." Liam cleared his throat. "My name is Liam Stone. I know what you think of me and my friends. You blame us for attracting the ghouls, for making your home less safe."

Skai translated this first bit while Liam collected his thoughts. He had been nervous earlier while mentally preparing for the speech, but confident enough to feel comfortable. Now his mind was as empty as the lunar horizon. He felt unsteady, like he could tumble over the edge without warning. Sweat dripped from his palms.

"You're not wrong," he said. "It is our fault."

Skai finished her translation, and an undertone of agreement came from the crowd.

"My people came from the moon," Liam said, gesturing toward the sky. "It wasn't our choice to end up here, but here we are. I know that our arrival has made life harder for you, and I know it was already hard to begin with. Life on the moon was hard for us too. That's why we came to Earth. Eighty of us, minus some who died in the crash. I know you've lost people too."

Liam paused to give Skai time to translate. While she spoke, he watched the crowd, trying to gauge their reaction. Some nodded. Most just stared.

"Your people," Liam said, "and my people. We seem so different. You fight with blades and spears. We fight with weapons that probably seem like magic to you. Your people stay strong, even in old age." He found Fang in the crowd, nodded. "Where I'm from, most of us die young from living too close to the sun. You hunt and fish and farm. You cook elegant, delicious meals. My people are raised on flavorless diets just to stay alive. We speak different languages. We have different histories. We even look different."

Liam glanced at the pale faces of his friends standing out in the crowd.

"We're different in so many ways, but we're also the same. We all value peace." He glanced at Skai. "We all appreciate beauty. We love the same. We bleed the same. We just want the best for those we care about. We may fight with different weapons, but we're all fighting for the same thing—to protect our own. Yes, my people came from the sky, but before that, we came from Earth."

A murmur swept through the crowd as Skai translated.

"Besides a few of my friends sitting with you, everyone I came to Earth with is leaving this valley. Today. I know you want them gone, but you know better than anyone what dangers lie beyond the safety of their camp. If they try to leave, they'll die because they don't have enough fighters. And if we don't stop them from going on this suicide mission— It might not be today, it might not be until years from now, but I saw what you're dealing with when I hiked to the top of the Eagle. You can't face this alone. You need our knowledge. You need our weapons."

After translating Liam's words, Skai raised the rifle above her head with one arm and fired a bolt of plasma into the sky. The scent of ozone hit Liam's nostrils as the crowd collectively gasped.

"Your people have taught me so much in my short time here," he said, "but the most important lesson was the hardest one to learn. I wanted to leave, to go back to my people, but I shouldn't have been thinking like that. I shouldn't have made a distinction between my people and your people. I realize now that we should focus on sharing our resources and knowledge. United, we can fight to reclaim your home—and we can win. Our people will be stronger together than we could ever be alone."

Liam watched Wiki nodding along to the speech. He hoped he was making his friend proud.

"So," Liam said, his mouth now completely dry. "I'm asking for your help. Will you help us? But more importantly, will you let us help you?"

The crowd went completely silent while Skai translated, and it stayed silent for a long time after she ceased speaking. Fang stared Liam down, his face emotionless beneath his hood. Many of the Suvi villagers were watching him, waiting for their leader's reaction. Liam worried that one would never come, that Fang would turn and walk away, that the villagers would follow him. Liam drew in a shallow breath and prepared for the final, disappointing verdict.

Fang took a long look at Skai, then at the faces of a few nearby villagers. Perhaps his counselors? The wrinkles beside the old man's eyes doubled in depth as he opened his mouth and spoke a few words.

Nodding solemnly, the crowd's reaction was unreadable.

Liam turned to Skai. "What did he say?"

Skai's lips curved into a broad, victorious smile.

"Sharpen your blades," she said. "We march immediately."

"It worked?" Liam asked in disbelief, elation rising in his chest. "We did it?"

Peering over the crowd, Skai gripped his shoulder. "You did it."

37

NUMBERS FOR THE REVOLUTION

Everyone in Camp Resurgence woke before dawn and gathered near the gates. They stood in the dim light, surrounding a pair of carts packed tightly with supplies. Many wore backpacks, lighter than they would have been without the aid of the carts, but still heavy because most of them were filled with bags of purified water—a precaution that Reagan had ordered.

On the outskirts of the group, Glo felt extra burdened. It wasn't only the luggage weighing her down. The deaths of her brother and Wiki, the disappearance of Quinn—it all felt like bags of sand strapped to her ankles, like rocks in her stomach.

"Are you all right?"

Glo's shoulders tensed at the sound of a man's voice, but they relaxed a few notches when she realized who stood beside her. Commander Killion watched the crowd through a pair of black eyes, his bloody and torn clothing replaced with a crisp uniform, fresh out of a vacuum-sealed pouch. His injuries looked worse in the daylight, but at least he was on his feet.

"Better than you," she said.

Killion winced from laughing, still focused on the men and women preparing to leave the valley. Glo liked that he wasn't watching her.

"That sounds like something"—Killion exhaled sharply— "Never mind."

"It sounds like something Quinn would say?" Glo asked.

Unable to twist his injured neck, Killion turned his entire torso to look at Glo. "She could still be out there, you know."

"Is anyone even looking?"

"We've had fewer attacks lately. We think the subs are migrating." He nodded, as if his body needed convincing of his words. "It's safer out there now."

"Look at your neck."

He glanced downward. "Well, that's impossible."

"You know what I mean. Look what the subs did to you. And you're a soldier. Quinn's just a—"

"A brilliant young woman who knows what dangers are out there. She could be hiding in a tree just outside camp for all we know."

"You're unbelievable."

Glo turned to leave and immediately realized she had nowhere to go. The tents had all been torn down and packed, and no one would let her outside the gates. Not yet.

"Glo, wait," Killion said. She felt his hand on her arm, not an attempt to stop her, but something gentler. "I have something for you."

Glo indicated a full pack sitting in the dust beside her. "I don't have any room left."

"I think you have room for this," Killion said, his voice dropping to a whisper. "You see that ration pouch leaning against the tree stump over there?"

She did. "Extra algae paste?"

"I had to disguise it for you," Killion said. "It's an electroshock incapacitator."

"A what?"

"A stun gun," Killion said. "Fully charged. It has a range of about three meters and should fit in your pocket."

Shocked but unimpressed, Glo remained silent for a moment.

"I wanted a gun," she said. *A second gun*, she thought. "Thank you, but why are you giving this to me now?"

"Protection," Killion said. "I don't like how Reagan had his guys watching you sleep the other night. If anyone gets too close, you can—"

"Aren't these men under your command?" Glo asked. "Why don't you just order them to leave me alone?" She glanced at the other women in the crowd. "To leave all of us alone?"

"I think we both know who's really making the calls here."

"Then let's change that. Let's do something."

"It may come to that, but now is not the right time." Killion watched the crowd, bonfires reflecting in his eyes. "Revolutions are complicated," he said, "and they take time. With enough people—with the right people, the good people—they come to a tipping point, but we're not there yet. The Admiral still has his loyalists, and they've already indoctrinated some of the younger men. They would hurt people for him. They would kill for him. But we want this to end with as little bloodshed as possible. I'm giving this to you because I trust you."

"If you really trusted me, you'd give me a plasma rifle."

"You can't hide a rifle, and we have to stay in the shadows for now. Listen, Glo, I'll get you an arsenal when the time comes, but—"

"You're worried I'll hurt someone?" Glo's homicidal ruminations from the other night came to mind. "That I'll kill someone?"

"I just know you're angry," Killion said, "and understandably so."

"Believe it or not, Commander, some women do have control over their emotions."

"Glo, that's not what I— Do you want the stun gun or not? I'm aiming for a non-violent revolution here, and I hope you won't even have to use it."

She did want it, but she had a hard time trusting Killion. What was in it for him? Was he sincerely planning something, or was he just telling her what she wanted to hear?

"I'll take it," Glo said. "Does it work on subs?"

"It'll stun anything with muscles."

Glo began her own assessment of the crowd, wondering if Killion had been counting numbers for the revolution as he watched. Maybe she could trust him. Maybe she had to.

"There's something you should know," Glo said, her decision final.

"Yeah?"

288 · LIFE ON PLANET EARTH

"Tristan and his friend Axel, they're the right people, the good people."

He nodded. "They seem good."

Glo's gaze fell on some of the women in the crowd, sisters in her suffering: Drea, whom the Resurgence Mission had separated from her husband; Aurora, the gorgeous woman who was the constant catcall target of drunken officers; and others whose whispered stories Glo had listened to around late-night embers. These women were doing the dirty work, the hard work, the work that no one else would.

"They can be trusted," Glo said, doing some counting of her own, "and there are more."

38

WEAPON AND SHIELD

Fang and Skai led the march out of the Suvi village, followed by Liam, most of his friends, and a militia of nearly one hundred villagers—some as old as Fang, others as young as Quinn. The group carried a somber energy down the mountain, but excitement steamed beneath the surface.

By the time they reached the switchbacks, the sun had fully risen over the distant peaks, painting the valley in a warm glow. Storm clouds rolled in the distance, dark gray and ominous. The beautiful day wouldn't last long.

Liam walked proudly, in awe that his plan worked, that the Suvi listened to him. In addition to his furs and the worn-out undergarments from his pressure suit, he wore leather armor over his chest and brandished one of the Suvi's curved blades, which he had spent all morning handling. Despite his origins, he now felt like one of the Suvi. His friends were similarly outfitted, except Wiki, who rode in a sling hung from Jarok's shoulders. The giant walked among the group, led by Quinn and King. Jarok was responding to the commands that Fang had worked so hard to instill. Liam wondered if they would encounter more giants in the valley—and whether Jarok would help them fight.

"Are you afraid, Lion Slayer?"

Liam turned to Skai, who marched beside him. "Should I be?"

"Great dangers lie ahead." Skai frowned. "There will be blood."

Liam turned the blade in his hand, watched the sunlight gleam on its jagged edge. "Not ours."

Skai's smile shone brilliantly in the light. "You still have much hope. This is good, but don't let it steal your caution."

"I won't," Liam said.

"Bravery is a weapon." Skai rounded the sharp turn of a switchback. "But fear is a shield. You need both to survive."

Liam nodded. "When did you get so wise?" he said. Instinctively, he braced himself for the butt of a spear to hit the back of his head, retribution for talking back.

"Careful what you say." Skai feigned anger then smiled. "If you are not enjoying your freedom, we can lock you up after this."

It felt good to be around Skai again—to talk to her, to see her up close, to entertain her jokes with real laughter.

"I missed you," Liam said. "I missed you a lot."

Skai looked forward quickly, her face now vacant of its former joy. Liam wondered if he had gone too far, if he had mistaken her kindness for flirtation. All at once, he felt foolish and embarrassed. There was no way she had forgiven him for everything this quickly, no chance she still felt the same after what happened.

Still looking forward, Skai brought a single finger to her lips. "I missed you as well," she whispered, "but look."

Liam followed her gaze to the bottom of the switchbacks, where a pack of subs was beginning to climb—a dozen or so devolved humans cutting corners, scrambling up the cliffs between switchbacks.

"If we survive the day"—Skai smirked and pulled a pair of daggers from her belt—"perhaps we can go for another swim."

Liam's heart leaped like a cougar. He grinned and raised his weapon to chest level, his body sizzling with adrenaline. He already had so much to fight for—Wiki, Glo, the entire population of the valley, perhaps of humankind—but now he had Skai to fight for as well. If bravery is a weapon, he thought, and fear is a shield, then love must be what makes the fight worth it.

•|•

Liam's charge toward the pack brought to mind all the early

mornings and late nights he spent in the Earth Sim. He thought he had been tired then. Now that he truly knew exhaustion, he mentally scoffed at his former naiveté. His body had never felt so heavy, so grounded—but with that heaviness came strength. Racing toward the pack, he felt like a boulder rolling down the hillside, all momentum and speed and crushing weight.

This didn't mean he wasn't afraid. His fear just manifested itself differently now. In the Earth Sim, it had been dulled by the knowledge that he couldn't really die in the simulation. Those sensations were the product of a simple fight or flight response, a rush of chemicals brought on by the sounds and images laid before him, assets designed to instill fear. Now the fear was primal, stalking. It came like a friend wearing a terrifying mask—familiar in a way, yet entirely gut-wrenching. The sight of the subs up close caused a buzzing beneath his skin as the distance closed between him and the pack.

When Liam raised his weapon to strike, time shifted like a slowing simulation. He noticed every tiny detail. Saliva fell like molasses from the mouths of the subhumans. The closest one had a missing ear, a couple of mangled strips of flesh dangling around its infected cave of an ear canal. The one behind it walked with a limp on the twisted stump that had once been its right foot. One was completely hairless, another so filthy it looked nearly invisible against the earth and stone behind it.

Liam's mind worked so quickly that he managed to count the number of angry, ravaged faces peering back at him.

Thirteen.

The blade in his hand entered the nearest sub's ear canal. He heard a sucking noise as he withdrew the weapon from its skull—then a thud as its corpse fell to the dirt.

Twelve.

He slashed the limping one across the throat. Fireworks of blood shot into the sky.

Eleven.

Skai pounced on the bald one and plunged a dagger into each lung. Simultaneously, Liam carved a large chunk of mud-covered flesh from the dirtiest sub's belly, painting the earth with gore.

Nine.

A waterfall of arrows came from the higher switchbacks and decimated the pack.

One.

The last sub stood farther down the mountain, staring up at the mess of bodies. It had an inflamed scar from chin to forehead, a perfectly straight line. A wet, guttural noise came from its throat before it turned to run away.

Liam sheathed his blade and began the chase.

•|•

Despite being locked in a cell for days and suffering the beating of a lifetime, Liam felt stronger than ever. His long runs through the village had clearly paid off. Sprinting down the switchbacks, he managed to keep the fleeing sub in sight at all times.

"Wait!" Skai shouted from far behind him.

Liam didn't wait. He continued chasing the sub, determined to take it down. With his gaze locked onto the back of the sub's head, he envisioned cracking its skull, imagined that this was the same sub that killed the little girl who went missing. Blade drawn and dripping blood, he quickened his pace.

Soon, as the path down to the valley passed a waterfall, the switchbacks gave way to narrow stone steps. Though he had been blinded by a hood at the time, Liam remembered trudging up these steps the night the Suvi took him. He had no idea how precarious the journey had been, how one misplaced step would have sent him tumbling to his death that night—a bone-crunching roll down the cliff-face followed by an explosive splat at the bottom. The thought made him cringe.

The sub slowed once it reached the steps, appearing wary of the slick, mossy slabs of granite beneath its bare, battered feet. Liam didn't take the same precautions. With the advantage of shoes and sure feet, he started closing the gap between him and his target. The cool mist from the waterfall invigorated his senses as he got closer and closer to the sub. He didn't have the luxury of a Halo to calculate the distance, but he guessed it was about five meters ahead—then four meters ahead—then three.

Liam got so close he could see the filthy hair matted to the back of its neck, could smell the putrid stench of whatever organic matter was rotting beneath its fingernails and between its teeth. It glanced over its shoulder then sped up. Liam sped up more.

I got you now, he thought.

As Liam erased the final meters between him and the sub, it spun around to face him and came to an abrupt stop—so unexpected that Liam couldn't slow down, even if he had time to think about it.

Midair, he locked the handle of his weapon in his fist, blade facing the earth. He raised it above his head, prepared to strike. The tip was aligned perfectly to come down on top of the sub's head, and it had the full force of Liam's downhill momentum behind it—a lightning-fast death. Easy. Clean.

But the sub ducked down and to the side in time to avoid the blade. Liam's elbow collided with its face, crushing its nose, as he tumbled over the crouched beast. His body rolled across a pair of stone slabs before sliding over the edge.

Completely disoriented, he clung to the cliff with a single hand. He dropped his blade into the ravine below and grabbed on with his other hand, but before he could pull himself up to safety, the sub arrived in front of him. Panicking, Liam looked up. Blood poured from the sub's ruined nose. It looked like Liam's elbow had ruptured the center of its massive scar. Bloodshot eyes peered down at him, encrusted in filth—but the sub didn't look enraged at all. Far from it.

It took a calm step forward, directly onto Liam's hand. The overgrown toenails digging into the back of Liam's knuckles hurt worse than the crushing weight. This creature wasn't a giant like Jarok, but it stood taller than a normal man, and its tattered skin covered veiny muscles that even Tai would envy. Liam's forearms began to quake.

This is the end, he thought, too afraid to be angry at himself.

Drops of blood hit his face and hands. The sub could have easily pushed him over the edge, but it just stood there, looking down, as if it enjoyed watching Liam suffer. The fingers of Liam's free hand clung firmly to a sheet of moss, but even that was beginning to peel off the wet stone. He dared to look down, to see if there was anything below to catch his fall—a ledge, a tree branch, anything at all.

He found nothing but empty space.

Then the sub crouched. Its spine bent down farther than humanly possible until its head sat between its shins—less than a foot from Liam's face. A wet cough came from its mouth, throwing blood and saliva into the air, where it mixed with the mist.

Another foot came down on top of Liam's other hand, locking him into place. He realized he couldn't fall into the ravine if he wanted to, not until this sub was finished playing with him. Even the worst simulations had never come close to this terrifying.

Grunting, Liam flexed his biceps and pulled himself closer to the sub. He tried to yank one hand free to grab an ankle—if he was going to fall, he wanted to take the sub with him—but it wouldn't budge. Cold against the stone, his hands were going numb.

"No," he cried. "No!"

Twisting his arm at a sharp angle, he managed to get an elbow onto the ledge. His breath came in terrified, labored gasps. Sweat poured from his temples.

"Please, no," he begged.

Icy hands gripped the back of his neck, thumbs pressed roughly against his cheeks. Fingernails broke skin as the sub pulled him up by the head. His neck cracked like an automatic weapon, and the gravity he had grown so accustomed to felt even more substantial now. With his face level with the sub's, he rested as much weight as he could on his elbows.

Decay wafted from the sub's mouth. Hot breath condensed in the cold air between them. Liam recoiled as the mouth opened wider, revealing a mess of sharp, blackened teeth. Panic blossomed like poisonous flowers in Liam's gut. This thing didn't want to watch him suffer before throwing him over the edge. It only wanted to wear him out before devouring him, face-first.

The sub snarled and clacked its teeth, turned its head to get a better biting angle.

Liam writhed, desperate to free himself, but none of his efforts helped. The sub's grip was unbreakable. He sealed his eyes shut, felt the hot breath pouring over him, into his mouth and nostrils.

Then, as he prepared to die, he heard a strange sizzling sound, and the sub let him go. All at once, it released its grip on his neck, and the weight of its feet came off his hands. Liam scrambled to stay on the ledge. One elbow dug into a crevice in the stone.

Once he stabilized himself, he looked forward at the sub, confused about why it had released him and terrified that it would change its mind. But it was lying on its back now, entirely still. Liam couldn't believe it. The sub was dead, and he was alive. Steam rose from a hole where the sub's eye had been.

Before Liam had time to process and celebrate his survival, Skai arrived—one hand extended to help him up, the other clasped around her plasma rifle.

"Have you already forgotten what I said about fear?"

39

BIRD SOUNDS

Descending the last of the stone steps, Liam massaged the back of his neck with one hand. At Skai's insistence, he now walked among the group rather than running ahead. He dragged his feet several meters behind Quinn and Jarok. Snoring softly, Wiki slept in the sling on the giant's back. Those who marched closest to the giant eyed him cautiously. The rest kept their distance.

Growing bored of the silent journey, Liam jogged until he caught up to Quinn.

"Hey," he said. "You doing okay?"

"Better than you by the looks of it." She cradled King in her arms like a baby. "You get yourself in a lot of trouble, don't you?"

Liam laughed. "You could say that."

Quinn walked on silently, eyes squinting to filter the light reflecting off the overcast.

"So," Liam said, "I never got to say thanks."

"For what?"

"For having my back on the ETS. It was brave of you to stand up to Reagan. You didn't even know me."

Quinn shrugged. "I couldn't not do it."

"But why?"

Gravel crunched beneath their feet, especially Jarok's, as they stepped onto flat terrain. The forest canopy loomed ahead, framed by gray mist and nothing else.

"I saw your sister defending you, and Wiki defending you, and

I just had to say something. I had to join in." She drew in a long breath. "And I wasn't standing up for you, really. I was standing up for us. Because I knew that we all needed each other. Does that make sense?"

Liam grinned. "It does now."

"It's kind of like your speech. I think we're stronger together. All of us." Scratching King's head, Quinn cooed. "And I'm not always brave, you know? Only when I have to be."

The giant ducked beneath a branch as they passed the tree line. The shade caused a sudden chill to creep up Liam's spine.

"What about right now?" he asked. "Do you feel brave?"

A wave of silence began at the front of the group, ending the buzz of idle conversation. The villagers ahead put fingers to their closed lips until the giant's footsteps became the loudest noise. Everyone slowed down, spoke in whispers.

"So, how is this going to work?" Quinn said.

"How is what going to work?"

"We sneak through the forest until we find them, and then what?"

"You know the plan," Liam said, his gaze penetrating the forest as deeply as the growing fog would allow.

"Yeah, but I also know Reagan."

Leaves swayed in the forest.

"What do you mean?" Liam asked.

A fallen branch cracked beneath Jarok's foot, drawing concerned looks from the Suvi.

"He wouldn't let any of the girls have guns," Quinn said. "What makes you think he'll give them up?"

"Because it's the only way," Liam said. "I just have to make him understand."

"And if he doesn't?"

"He will. Once he sees how many lives are actually at stake, he'll have no choice."

"Because he's always done the right thing," Quinn said.

"If he doesn't, I'll make him."

"It's not just him you have to worry about," Quinn said. "He has followers."

Another broken branch, louder this time, and Liam's hand found one of the small daggers hidden in his furs. King hissed and squirmed in Quinn's arms.

"Wait," Liam said. He put an arm out in front of her.

When Quinn stopped, Jarok stopped, and so did many of the villagers ahead and behind. Silence reigned for a moment. Then Liam heard it, a rustling in the foliage beyond the fog. He drew his weapon, looked around for his friends. Skai stood with Fang at the front of the group. Tai and Raelyn weren't far behind her.

"What is that?" Quinn whispered.

"Stay close."

Liam dropped the furs from his shoulders. The chill of the forest awakened his senses. Why hadn't they left Quinn and King behind? This was no place for young animals and inexperienced fighters.

The rustling came back in spurts, the cause of it invisible and elusive. Liam searched fruitlessly through the fog for signs of movement. Except for the slowly shifting sheets of gray and white, he saw nothing but stillness.

Then, all at once, a trio of leaves fell from the nearest tree and spiraled down to the mulch below. For a moment, Liam felt foolish—drawing a dagger to fight the wind—but then something followed the leaves.

The sub swung down in one smooth motion then hung there upside down, fingerlike toes gripping the branches above. Quinn opened her mouth to scream, but Liam put a hand over it just in time. He froze, unsure of what to do. He could charge toward the sub with his dagger, but what if there were others?

Eyes clouded in white, the sub twisted its neck until it faced Liam. Less than three meters away, it hung there, sniffing the air, completely blind. If it screeched, who knew how many more would follow? Gripping his weapon, Liam prepared to charge. He would have to do this quickly, efficiently—silently.

The sub opened its mouth wide, stretched its fingers toward the ground—some broken, others bruised—then an arrow bloomed out of its ear. The corpse crumpled into the foliage beside the path with a crack and a thump. In awe, Liam turned around and saw Zara's grin as she nocked another arrow.

•|•

At Fang's command, the Suvi spread past the boundaries of the path and arranged themselves into a defensive formation. Wielders of the curved blades marched on the outskirts to protect spearmen and archers on the inside. Clearly, the soldiers had been trained well. Liam felt like he had underestimated them. Perhaps they didn't need guns, after all.

As the troops spread out, Liam and his friends joined Skai and Fang at the front of the group. Within an hour, they made it to the river without incident. They only encountered duos and trios of wandering subs that the Suvi quickly dispatched with their blades. Where were the vast herds that Liam had seen from the mountaintop?

The group followed the river until Fang came to a stop. He turned and faced Liam and the others, wolf teeth rattling on his necklace, and spoke.

"We will rest here," Skai translated. "Eat something. Drink water. Quickly."

The spearmen set up a perimeter around the group while everyone else sat down on the riverbank. The place looked familiar to Liam, but then again, much of the forest blurred to monotony, especially in the fog. He went down to the water's edge, where he began cleaning the blood off his arms.

"Don't you want to leave it?" Tai squatted beside him. "Makes you look more badass than you are."

"You want some?" Liam extended a red hand. "I don't see any on you."

Tai's teeth clenched. "That's because I'm not an idiot."

"Really?" Raelyn stood above them, her hair in a tight braid. "You two are still fighting?"

"Old habits," Liam said. Finished with his left arm, he started scrubbing his right.

"Well, quit it," Raelyn said.

"I can't help how annoying he is," Tai said.

"Tai." Raelyn folded her arms. "Let me lay this out for you. It's pretty simple, really. You're currently my boyfriend. Liam used to be my boyfriend. That's it. I care about you both, but I'm seriously considering dating one of those men"—she pointed at a group of topless Suvi downstream—"if you two continue to act like little boys."

Liam almost laughed but stopped himself. He knew better than to test Rae's patience.

"Now grow up," Raelyn said. "We've got more important things to worry about."

"You're right," Liam said. He shook the water from his hands and turned to Tai. "I'm sorry for— What am I sorry for exactly?"

Tai's mountainous shoulders rose and fell.

"No, really, why am I apologizing? You tried to get me airlocked, you beat the shit out of me in the jailhouse, and— Oh yeah, you stole my girlfriend before all of that."

"First of all, I'm not property," Raelyn said. "But it's good that you two are talking. Continue."

"I," Tai said. "I don't know why I did those things. And honestly, I didn't think you even cared about Raelyn."

"I did." Liam glanced up to see that Raelyn had left. "I do."

"You have a funny way of showing it," Tai said. "You know how many times she came crying to me after you ditched her?"

"I was training," Liam said. "You understand that."

"Yeah." Tai spat. "Priorities. And I didn't steal your girlfriend. You lost her all by yourself."

Even with Liam's head throbbing, the words still stung. Not because they were false. Because they were true. He sighed, shook more water from his numb fingers.

"You're right," he said. "I'm sorry I've been hard on you both. It was an awkward situation, and I didn't know how to react."

He held out his right hand and made eye contact with Tai—something he realized he had hardly ever done. It was like staring into the giant's eyes and seeing something less than monstrous for the first time.

"We don't have to be friends," Liam said, "but I don't need more enemies than I already have."

Tai didn't grip Liam's hand, but he nodded, his face softening to some form of understanding. It was a start.

•|•

"Lion Slayer." Skai crouched beside Liam on the riverbank. "My scouts bring back news of footprints up the river."

"Good," Liam said. "We can track them."

"The prints are fresh, but rain is coming—and worse."

"What do you—"

"Herds in all directions. We must go now."

Bone-weary, Liam stood and nearly fainted when the blood rushed from his head. Washing the gore from his body had destroyed his appetite, so he hadn't eaten anything during the break. Hunger clawed at his stomach lining. Fatigue weighed down his eyelids.

"Let's go," he said.

Thick and cool, the breeze pressed against his face as he exited the comfort of the huddling masses. He and Skai found Quinn and Jarok sitting on a fallen tree, its broken roots flayed toward the sky. For a moment, Liam wondered if the giant had knocked the tree down just for them to sit on.

"How is he?" Liam asked, indicating Wiki's resting place on Jarok's back.

"I got him to drink some water," Quinn said, "but he's really groggy. Whatever they gave him seems to be helping with the pain. It's definitely keeping him asleep."

"Strong medicines," Skai said. "He will sleep for hours more."

"That's probably a good thing," Liam said. "Come on."

The fallen trunk creaked as Jarok and Quinn rose to stand. They followed Liam and Skai until they found Fang giving orders to the crowd, his voice hushed but still severe. As the Suvi prepared their formation, Zara, Tai, and Raelyn joined Liam and the others.

"Good news, then?" Zara asked.

"We know where they're headed," Liam said. "We just have to pick up the pace."

"Fine by me," Tai said, leaning forward against a tree to stretch his calves. "The sooner I have a plasma rifle in my hands, the better. Fighting with sticks is fun, but I want to live through this."

•|•

Liam jogged among the group, shoulder to shoulder with new friends and old. They couldn't travel as quietly this way, but it didn't matter. They were close to reaching their goal, and they needed to hurry. The spearmen lurking in the trees would take care of any stray subs, and the scouts farther out would warn them of any approaching herds. According to Fang, most of the herds had congregated toward one end of the valley—the direction that Glo and the others were heading.

Skai jogged beside Liam, her hair blown back by the breeze. He wanted to reach out, to touch her, but Fang was watching. Surprisingly, even the old man could keep pace with the group. Unlike Liam, he hadn't bothered to wash the blood from his body, which did, in fact, make him look more badass.

"Skai," Liam said between breaths. "How do the scouts know where the herds are?"

"I have not told you about the Watchers?"

Liam shrugged.

"The Watchers live alone on mountaintops and along the valley floor—some in trees, others in caves."

"And they—"

"They keep us safe." Skai spoke calmly, as if their jog along the river stole none of her breath. She wasn't even sweating. "Some of them watch with something called telescopes."

"Wait," Liam said. "How do they have telescopes?"

"They were discovered here. Old artifacts."

Liam hadn't bothered to think about what technology the Suvi might have inherited. Everything they used seemed so primitive—and would have seemed primitive to his ancestors seven hundred years back.

"And how exactly do the Watchers communicate?"

Liam prepared for more startling news, perhaps that the Suvi had rediscovered walkie talkies.

"Bird sounds," Skai said, as if it were obvious. Then she chirped a shrill note, and the surrounding Suvi echoed it to her in unison. "It is our second language from a young age. The ghouls and giants ignore it because they don't hunt birds." She smiled. "Too hard to catch."

Liam tried to whistle the note that Skai had made, but the sound came out too airy. "Are you joking? I've never heard you do that."

"If I joked, you would laugh. Bird sounds are for—how do you say—emergencies?"

"Right," Liam said.

He was about to catch his breath and ask more about the Watchers, but something glistening on the riverbank ahead caught his attention. Some of the Suvi pointed at it, but none of them slowed to take a closer look.

The ejector pod looked smaller than Liam remembered—not like it had shrunk, but like he had outgrown it. It was hard to believe he came to Earth in something so tiny.

As Liam got closer, dread grew in his gut because he knew what this exact pod held inside. His instinct was to keep running, to leave it behind like a hermit crab's old shell, but his feet slowed instead. A few runners passed, but Skai matched his pace.

She nudged his shoulder. "What are you doing?"

"I"—he didn't know what to say—"We have to stop."

"We can't," Skai said. "You know this."

More runners passed. Liam glanced backward and saw that the end of the line was approaching. Zara jogged among the stragglers, unaware that her ejector pod stood just ahead.

"There's someone in there," Liam said. "A body. We can't leave her in there."

"We don't have time to—"

"I'll do it," Liam said. "It won't take long. I can catch up."

Zara arrived at the scene, her cheeks flush. "What's going on?"

Then her eyes found the metallic coffin rocking in the shallows. She looked at it for a moment before staring into the mud. Liam turned to face Skai and put his arm around Zara.

"Her name was Nova," he said. "And I'm not going anywhere until I bury her body."

Skai glanced at the pod then back at Liam's face, her lips tight. Zara began crying into Liam's shoulder. Before the final runners could pass, Skai nodded firmly.

"You will need help," she said.

A three-note birdcall escaped her lips, and the Suvi came to a halt.

40

THE BRIDGE

Glo trudged through the forest, her fist clenched around yet another thing she would have to leave behind. With her free hand, she rubbed her left earlobe, which now felt woefully bare. Since her mother handed her the set of earrings on her thirteenth birthday, she had hardly taken them off. They were a gift from her father, left behind for his only daughter. She knew the weight of a single earring was negligible, but now her head felt lopsided, as if her body knew something was missing.

Since leaving camp, Glo had been looking for a place to put the earring. She wanted to leave it somewhere to commemorate Liam, Wiki, and Quinn—or to lead Quinn back to the group if she was still out there.

Despite her best intentions, Glo didn't know if she could let it go. She considered leaving something else behind, but this was the only thing that distinguished her from the rest of the survivors.

It was special. Not only because of the rarity of the purple crystal, but also because of who gave it to her. Part of her father lived within the stone, his essence reflected in each and every facet. His hands had touched it, and now it would touch Earth. In a way, it was like he had come down in the Earth Transit Shuttle, like he had been with Glo all along. The thought almost made her smile. Almost.

The people we love never really leave us, she thought.

That was what her mother said on that last day. Glo didn't know if she believed it anymore. If they never left me, she thought, then why can't I feel them?

For the first time in her life, Glo felt truly alone. Already, her mother's voice was fading from her memory. Eyes closed to block the weeping, she tried to focus—to remember. What did her mother sound like? And what would she say now?

•|•

Glo and the other women watched from a safe distance as a few men took turns blasting holes through a pine tree by the river with their plasma pistols. Puffs of steam rose where the bolts of plasma collided with the water and mud, adding to the fog.

"Comm check."

Glo and several of the women standing beside her shrank in unison. It had been weeks since she heard anything through her implant. She had nearly forgotten it was there.

"Looks like it worked." Reagan's voice dropped directly into Glo's ear. He sounded jovial, and she hated having him in her head. *"Did you see everyone jump?"*

"I can hear you loud and clear," Killion said. *"Good work, Tristan."*

"It was no problem," Tristan said. *"Just a bit of tinkering."*

"Scouts, please report," Reagan said, as if he had already grown impatient.

Ten seconds later, another voice entered Glo's ear, unrecognizable through the static.

"The crash site is clear," the scout said. *"The storm unearthed more wreckage if you want to scavenge for supplies."*

"Copy that," Reagan said. *"The bridge should be done any minute. Anything else to report?"*

"We've got infrared on several large groups of subs outside the crash site. Proceed with caution. It's a straight shot for now."

Glo shivered, more from the fear than the cold. They had been lucky to only encounter small groups since leaving camp. Now things were getting real.

"We'll hurry," Reagan said. *"I want updates every ten minutes."*

"Yes, sir."

Another bolt of plasma sliced through the tree beside the river.

With a loud crack, the tree splintered at its base and began tipping toward the water. Glo watched it fall, mesmerized by how slowly it seemed to move, until it crashed into the water with a massive splash.

"Glo," Killion said. Surprised to be addressed directly through her implant, Glo shifted uncomfortably. She saw Killion down by the river, his face turned away from the crowd gathered beside the bridge. *"If you respond, I won't hear you. Just scratch your left elbow if you hear me."*

After a moment, she did so.

"I had Tristan set us up with a private channel," he said. *"Only the people we can trust for now."*

Glo almost nodded but stopped herself. When had Killion and the others found time to do this?

"Our prime objective right now is to find a proper comm unit at the crash site and get in touch with Omega."

Almost everyone started heading toward the bridge, but Glo stayed back for a moment, listening to the conversation she could not yet join.

"I think I might have already found one." Glo couldn't be sure, but it sounded like the scout speaking again. *"At least it looks like what you described, Tristan."*

"I guess we'll find out," Tristan said. *"Keep looking, and hide anything else you find."*

"Copy that. I'll hide a swig of this moonfire in my belly right now."

"Axel," Tristan said sternly.

"Don't worry." Axel burped through the radio. *"My tolerance is high."*

41

GO NOW

Nova's burial passed by in a blink. After the Suvi opened the hatch and removed the body, Liam covered Nova's face with one of his furs. He left the rest of the work to the soldiers, who worked with practiced efficiency. How many bodies have they buried, Liam wondered, and how many more will they need to? The soldiers dug a deep hole, no taller or wider than it needed to be, and lowered Nova down gracefully. Zara said a few words and shed a few tears as they filled the hole, then it was over.

"Thank you," she said to Liam when they left the grave behind. "I mean it."

The rain began as a trickle after that, as if the sky were mourning too. Scattered droplets drummed on the leaves and branches above in chaotic rhythms. Distant thunder rumbled in the highlands, hardly audible over the white water to the group's left. Still, the sound boomed more than in the simulations. It vibrated the bones in Liam's chest.

As he jogged, he watched shorelines eroding in real time, pieces of driftwood dislodging from their homes and floating downstream to stick elsewhere. He still couldn't believe it—the raw power of nature to shape the world, to kill one or millions without thought.

How lucky I am to be alive, Liam thought. If the wind had blown differently, it might have been his body left to decompose in an ejector pod instead. He never would have set foot on Earth. He never would have heard the songs of birds, smelled the floral grasslands, or tasted the sweetness of Skai's lips. Even with near-certain death looming in the fog, he felt grateful to have experienced so many things that Nova never got the chance to.

The realization made each moment feel like a gift, especially the present moment. Skai had forgiven him, none of his friends were dead, and they were closer than ever to finding his sister. His body had never felt worse, but it didn't matter. Soon he would unite his people and the Suvi. They would clear the valley of danger, then he could rest.

A flash of lightning and nearby thunder tore Liam from his thoughts about the future.

"The storm approaches," Skai said. A chorus of birdsong came from somewhere beyond Liam's field of vision. "And a herd is coming closer."

They moved faster after that, driven by fear, chased instead of chasing. The first sounds of struggle came a few minutes later, from the forest to Liam's right and the riverbank behind him. Not screams—the Suvi were too disciplined for that—but the grunts of physical effort, the guttural retching of dying subs, the thumps of dead weight falling to the ground.

"Look," Skai said, pointing downstream.

Liam squinted through the fog, where he saw a fallen tree bridged across the river, its needles still green.

"This was not here before," Skai said.

"Did the storm—"

"No," she said. "The moon people did this."

They arrived at the bridge behind Fang, who was squatting to examine the mud. Diluted blood dripping from his skin, the old man uttered a few words.

"Fresh tracks," Skai translated. "We are close."

Fang stood and examined the bridge, then he pointed at a nearby branch jutting out of the fallen tree. There, hanging on the end of one offshoot, a single purple crystal glistened, wrapped in metallic wire.

"That's Glo's earring," Liam said. He placed it in the palm of his hand and took a closer look, then a shrill note came from deep beyond the trees—a warning from the Watchers.

"We must cross," Skai said. "Now."

Liam pocketed the earring as Zara and the others approached the bridge.

"They went this way," Liam said. "Follow them."

At Fang's command, some of the Suvi had already started crossing. They walked across the tree in the spaces between branches, using the branches themselves as handrails. The water beneath the bridge sped past, violent and careless.

"This looks sketchy," Quinn said. "I don't think—"

A scream turned all their heads to the forest. It was not the sudden sound of fear or death, but the bloodcurdling racket of someone being eaten from the bottom up. The blood drained from Quinn's face.

"Go," Liam said. He nudged her toward the bridge. "Now."

"I don't, I mean I can't—"

"You have to," Liam said. "You're brave when you have to be. Remember?"

Quinn looked from face to face, clearly unsure of herself.

"Come on," Raelyn said, standing on the end of the bridge. She reached out to Quinn with her bionic arm. "I'll make sure you don't fall in, and if you do, I'm diving in after you."

"But—"

"And I'll be right behind you," Zara said, coming forward.

Quinn hesitated for a moment. Hands shaking, she grabbed onto Raelyn's hand. King squirmed in her arms. As soon as they began inching across, Jarok took two big steps forward, trying to follow.

"No." Liam stepped in front of the giant. "We need you here."

For a moment, Liam expected Jarok to walk right over him, but he came to a stop. He glanced at the bridge then patted the sling on his shoulder, which held Wiki. More screams came from beyond the fog.

Fang yelled something, and many of the Suvi began to scramble across the bridge. The rest got into a defensive half-circle. Skai stood among the archers, her plasma rifle pointed into the gray.

The giant knelt on the riverbank and slowly lifted the sling off his back. He set Wiki down gently, looked at him, then pointed across the river. After untangling the sling, Liam helped his friend into a sitting position.

"What?" Wiki coughed. "What's happening?"

Wiki's skin shone white, overcast light reflecting off his sweat. He looked on the verge of death, but somehow he was still there. The Suvi's medicine had done wonders to slow his decline.

"We're almost there," Liam said. The thrum of bowstrings breaking air alerted him of more arrivals. "You just have to cross this bridge."

"I— I don't think I can walk."

"Tai will carry you," Liam said.

"I was going to stay and fight," Tai said.

"Go."

Liam couldn't believe the depth of his own voice as he made the command—or that Tai obeyed it. Jarok stood and joined the defensive perimeter. With his friends safely crossing the river, Liam drew his blade and stood among the fighters on the front line.

"Can you hear it?" Skai whispered from behind him.

Liam focused beyond the slosh of the river and the patter of rain on leaves until he heard a more substantial sound, a sound he only remembered from dreams and simulations—dozens of bare feet running.

At the first sign of movement, Skai fired a bolt of plasma that took down two subs. Arrows whizzed through the air around them before burying themselves in eyes and throats.

"There are too many," Liam said. "We should run."

"Not yet," Skai said, indicating the bridge with a head toss.

Behind them, several people were still crossing, and dozens more were queued up. Liam, Skai, Fang, and twenty or so soldiers made up the final line of defense.

"Go if you want," Skai said. "I must stay."

Jarok picked up a fallen log and bolted forward. He cracked it across the skulls of four or five subs who had managed to evade a rain of arrows. One survived and latched onto his thigh, hair dripping mud as it bit and clawed at his skin. Liam rushed forward and sliced its jugular with his blade.

One by one, Fang dismissed soldiers from the line and ordered them to cross to safety. When Skai's turn came, she fought him on it. Liam couldn't understand their words, but he knew that Skai wanted to stay and fight. Liam wanted her to cross as well, but he also knew that her plasma rifle was doing most of the damage. Without it, the battle would quickly turn out of their favor.

A pile of bodies grew in front of them, a barrier that the approaching subs had to stumble over. Out of arrows, the remaining archers ran toward the bridge, which was mostly empty. Jarok began picking up fistfuls of river rock to pelt the subs with while Liam guarded his lower half. Liam had no Halo to track their Kill/Death ratios, but if Skai had most of the kills, Jarok was a close second. The pile grew until it towered over all but the giant's head.

When Skai's plasma rifle ran out of juice, a birdcall from Fang prompted the remaining spearmen to retreat toward the bridge. Skai and Liam backed up with them, but Jarok stood his ground.

"Come on," Liam said.

Skai dropped her depleted plasma rifle to the ground.

"No," Liam said. "Bring it."

Meanwhile, the giant kept throwing rocks. Liam heard bodies falling on the other side of the pile. He ran up and pulled on Jarok's arm.

"We have to go," Liam said.

All at once, twenty or more subs crested the pile of bodies—far more than Liam and Jarok could deal with alone. Some jumped down and landed on all fours, while others stumbled over the top and rolled down.

"Hurry!" Skai yelled from the bridge, drawing the attention of the pack.

Settled on the ground no more than ten meters away, the subs ran.

"Let's go," Liam begged the giant. "Now!"

Jarok turned his massive head and looked down at Liam. With one hand, he touched Liam's shoulder. With the other, he reached down to pick up another log.

"Go now," Jarok said.

Then he turned and charged toward the pack.

42

EARTH'S LAST HUMANS

Footprints. Hundreds of them. That was the first thing Glo noticed as she descended the ridge overlooking the crash site. The prints formed a mosaic in the mud, each one overlapping another, toes splayed and frightfully bare. She saw the divots where toenails had scraped the dirt, the strange indentations where mangled feet met wet earth. Even though the herd had moved on, Glo still felt its presence there.

No one in the group spoke. Some swapped grim glances, but most just stared at the ground. The trails led every which way. Danger surrounded Earth's last humans, yet they still hadn't encountered much of it.

Not yet, anyway.

Reagan's voice dropped into Glo's implant. *"Gather what you can, everyone,"* he said, his voice scratchy and gruff. *"We're moving on in half an hour."*

Everyone spread throughout the clearing, the men with their guns aloft, the women with nothing but their backpacks and hidden weapons. Glo moved about idly for a few minutes, eyes trained on the ground, unsure of what to do.

After a few minutes, Killion's voice came online. *"Come in, Axel."*

"Go for Axel."

"Good to hear you're sober," Killion said. *"Where's the package?"*

A burst of static. *"I know my limits, Commander. It's on the north side of the clearing, right behind that big aluminum sheet."*

Glo didn't know which way was north, but she did see a large piece of metal jutting out of the ground at the tree line ahead.

"Tristan," Killion said. *"I need you to check out the package while I keep an eye on things over here. Make sure it's an actual comm unit. Reagan will notice if I'm missing. He could finish his patrol any minute."*

"Copy that."

Glo passed a pair of women digging a small crate out of the mud. Bursts of plasma in the forest made her skin tingle with fear.

"Nothing to worry about," Reagan said. *"Just a few uglies."* He laughed. *"Look at them sizzle, boys. That one's still squirming. No, don't shoot it. Let it suffer."*

Glo shook her head at their leader's depravity. Up ahead, Tristan meandered toward the tree line. Glo picked up her pace until she caught up to him.

"I wonder what's over there." Glo pointed toward their target destination.

"It's probably just shrapnel," Tristan said, concealing a smile.

"But shouldn't we check? What if there's more food? Or medicine?"

Glo spoke loudly so others would hear, but not enough for her voice to carry far. "You can protect me while I scavenge in the dirt."

Once they broke away from the group, Tristan glanced over his shoulder.

"Good," he said. "We're not being followed."

"Aren't you being a little paranoid?" Glo said. "Reagan told us to look for supplies. It's not like we're disobeying him."

"He doesn't trust us," Tristan said. "I can tell."

"The feeling is mutual," Glo said. "He's just one man, though. He can't be everywhere."

They passed a fuel tank, which was still intact but leaning to the side.

"If Reagan was the only bad apple," Tristan said, "we wouldn't have a problem. But he's poisoned so many of the others."

"How can they follow him? Can't they see what he is?"

"They're afraid of him," Tristan said, "but they're more afraid of facing this world without him. He knows what it takes to survive.

In their mind, he's the one who kept them alive all this time. They feel like they owe him something."

"For the future of humanity?" Glo said.

"Exactly."

"Why can't we just take over? We"—Glo stopped herself—"I mean you and Killion have guns. We can take him by surprise. We can—"

"We can't." Tristan glanced over his shoulder again. "Or at least we shouldn't. Killion wants to consult the council before we do anything."

Glo groaned. "What's the point? They can't do anything. They're not here."

"They can help us make a decision," Tristan said. "Look. Killion is the opposite of Reagan. Reagan left Omega's laws behind the second he boarded the ETS, if not before, but Killion still respects Omegan authority. He wants to give Reagan a fair trial."

"He doesn't deserve one," Glo said. "You know he wouldn't give Killion a fair trial if their roles were reversed."

"Maybe not," Tristan said, "but if we all started making up our own rules, we'd be no better than Reagan. There would be chaos. We need a leader, and I think Killion is our best choice."

"Fine," Glo said. "I guess you're right."

Glo had to admit she was beginning to trust Commander Killion. Still, she didn't entirely agree with his approach. *If I found a bad apple,* she thought, *I wouldn't give it the pleasure of explaining itself in front of a council. I would throw it away before its rot could spread.*

•|•

Glo and Tristan found the comm unit quickly enough. After pulling it from beneath a bush, Tristan turned the device in his hand to inspect it. It was a black box about the size of Reagan's handheld tablet, but much thicker.

"See?" he said. "I told you these things don't break."

"But does it work?"

"I'll have to pair it with my Halo," Tristan said. "It's supposed to be used with an antenna or satellite dish. That way, you can video-chat and send large files, but we should be able to get a message through—assuming the moon is in the sky."

"I saw it earlier," Glo said. "Before we left camp."

Tristan nodded. He pulled his Halo out of his bag then began pressing tiny buttons on the side of the comm unit, which made an array of LEDs light up. The device started beeping.

"Someone's going to hear that," Glo said. "Can't you hide it and work on it later?"

"Who knows if there will be a later?" Tristan said. He pulled his hair back and tied it into a bun so it wouldn't interrupt his work. "This will only take a minute. Just keep watch."

Leaves danced in the forest, awaking Glo's fear response. "We should go," she said. "It's not safe out here."

"I'm almost done." Tristan knelt on one knee, focused on the task like a child playing with a puzzle. "Do you have room for this in your bag?"

"Sure." With her back turned to Tristan, Glo took the plasma pistol out of her bag to make room for the comm unit. She tucked the gun in her waistband against her lower back, safely hidden beneath her jacket, then stole a look at the clearing. "Can you hurry?"

"I'll literally be done in ten—"

Branches snapped behind them, silencing their conversation. Another voice joined in.

"What did you find?"

Glo didn't have to turn around to see who stood there. She could tell by the artificial pace of his breathing, his arrogant tone.

"Anything useful?" Reagan said.

Tristan attempted to hide the comm unit, but he had no way to conceal it. Glo slowly turned around. Reagan leaned against a tree, one hand on the pistol attached to his belt. Two of his men stood with him, their smirks perfectly matching Reagan's attitude. These were the same men who watched Glo sleep the night Quinn went missing: Red Beard and Piggy.

Glo opened her mouth to speak. "It's just—"

"Oh, I know what it is," Reagan said. He stepped forward, pulled the gun from its holster. "What I want to know is why you're hiding it from me."

Tristan set the comm unit down. Subtly, but not so subtly that Glo didn't notice, he tapped a button on the side of his Halo. When he spoke, Glo heard his voice in person and, with a slight delay, through her implant.

"It's not what you think, sir," he said.

"Repeat," Killion said on their private channel.

Tristan spoke again, slowly and clearly this time. "Why don't you *three* put the *guns* down and let me explain?"

Clever, Glo thought. But would it buy them enough time for Killion to arrive?

Glo stepped forward. "This is my fault, Arthur."

She waited for Reagan to respond, but he didn't. He just stared, his chest rising and falling gently with the help of his mechanical lung.

"I only wanted to talk to my mom," Glo said. "I knew Tristan was a tech, so I asked him to help. I begged him, really."

A menacing smile came to Reagan's lips. "I thought he of all people would be able to resist your charm."

Reagan's men laughed.

"Very funny." Tristan rose to his full height. "Anything else you want to say?"

"You better stay back, son," Reagan said.

"I want to know why it's a problem that Glo wants to reach her mom."

"Tristan." Glo grabbed his arm. "Don't."

Reagan stepped forward, flashed his chemically whitened teeth. "Well, look who grew a pair of balls."

Tristan took another step forward, glowering. "You told Glo all the comm units were destroyed."

Reagan shrugged, his pistol raised to keep Tristan from coming closer. "I guess I must have missed this one."

"That's not the point," Tristan said. "These things are virtually indestructible. What happened to the rest of them? Why are you lying to us? To everyone?"

As quick as thought, Reagan raised his pistol until it was level with Tristan's forehead. "I don't need to explain myself to you."

Tristan backed up and nearly tripped over a tree root.

"Stay calm," Killion said on their private channel. *"I'm almost there."*

"Take his gun," Reagan ordered. "Tie him up."

Speechless, Glo didn't know what to do. She considered drawing her own plasma pistol, ending the confrontation in three quick bursts, but Tristan wasn't panicking. He kept his mouth shut as Red Beard disarmed him and tied his wrists together behind a nearby tree. Perhaps Glo just had to trust Killion as much as Tristan did.

"Take his boots," Reagan said. "We'll need those for the road ahead. Belt, too."

"Arthur," Glo said, touching his arm.

"Funny how I'm only Arthur when you need something."

"Please don't do this."

"Don't bother, Gloria. That shit won't work on me anymore."

Having removed Tristan's boots and belt, Red Beard tore the shirt from Tristan's chest and shoved it into his mouth.

"Try to scream if you want," Reagan said. "But the subs will find you faster."

"You can't do this." Glo fell to her knees. "He was just trying to help me. I only wanted to tell my mom about Liam. That's it."

"You can't, Gloria."

Reagan glanced at the gun in his hand. In one quick motion, he aimed and fired a bolt of plasma through the comm unit.

"I can't believe I missed one," he said, as if the thought bored him. He holstered his pistol and put an arm around Glo. "You say a word about this, and we'll leave you behind like your friend here."

"But—"

"You know, I heard that some of these uglies will mate with human women instead of eating them. Or was it *before* eating them? So, you'll stay quiet, won't you, Gloria?"

Numb, Glo let Reagan lead her two steps away from the sizzling comm unit before he came to an abrupt stop.

"You know," Killion said, standing just ahead with his plasma rifle trained on Reagan's face, "she really prefers to be called Glo."

43

NO MOON WOMAN

Liam stood by the river and watched the dying flames at the end of the tree bridge, which burned while Fang counted survivors. Thinking about Jarok's sacrifice, he stared through the smoke and fog. Skai joined him, laced her fingers through his.

"Why do you cry?" she said.

Liam sniffled, his eyes watering from the smoke. "I don't understand. Jarok was— I just don't get it."

"What do you not understand?"

"Why would he do that for us?" Liam shook his head. "Why would he help us? After your ancestors killed his. After Fang threw him in that pit."

"Maybe to him," Skai said, "it wasn't a pit. Maybe to him, it felt like a home."

Liam hadn't considered that. It was a pleasant thought, but it didn't make him feel any better.

"I guess I took that away from him too. What's wrong with us?"

"You did not know," Skai said. With her head on his shoulder, Liam could smell the rain and earth scent of her hair. "You tried to help."

"Look where it got me. It made me a prisoner, and now"—he inhaled sharply, held the smoky air in his lungs until it burned— "Jarok. He's just gone."

Grief swelled in Liam's chest, up to his head, until it found tear ducts. Skai kissed his cheek. Her fingers trailblazed his hair.

"If you did not free Jarok," she said, her voice humming gently against his neck, "he would not be there to defend us. His death was not for nothing. You can still honor it."

Liam wiped his eyes with the back of his hand. "How?"

"By finding your sister. By punishing the man who hurt her."

The fire crackled, shooting sparks into the sky. Liam and Skai stood together for a while, propping each other up.

"Did you hear Jarok speak?" Liam said. "Did you know he could do that?"

"No," Skai said, "but I know legends of talking giants."

What a strange planet to call home, Liam thought, probably for the thousandth time since his arrival.

"If there are others out there," Liam said, feeling out the truth of his words, "I want to find them. Teach them. I want to help them."

Liam felt Skai's smile on his neck. "This will honor Jarok greatly."

Quinn stepped up beside them, her hair dripping from the river's mist. She leaned forward to warm her hands on the embers, watched the fog that blanketed the opposite bank.

"How do you know he's really gone?" she asked.

Liam recalled the sounds of that final fight vividly—the repeated crack of breaking bones, the earth-shaking stomps of giant feet, and the grunts of battle that faded to silence, drowned out by the river. Though the scent of iron still hung in the air and Liam's arms still burned from swinging his blade, he allowed himself the tiniest morsel of hope that Jarok had somehow escaped the massacre. He turned and left the river behind.

The group snaked between the trees, silent and woeful. There were other losses to mourn besides Jarok, nearly a dozen Suvi who had been overwhelmed in the moments leading up to the crossing. Liam shouldered the gravity of their deaths as he trudged through the wet foliage. He and his friends, none of whom had been injured, walked with Fang at the head of the group.

"We are lucky the herd was small," Skai said.

"Small?" Raelyn asked, voicing Liam's thoughts.

"It means not big," Skai said.

"I know what it means," Raelyn said. "I just wouldn't call that herd small."

"The big herds lie ahead." Skai sidestepped to avoid a log. "Don't worry. We will find your people soon. Moon people are no good at covering tracks."

Liam saw what she meant. Away from the muck of the river, boot prints carved a distinct path through the foliage, and discarded nutrient bags littered the trail every so often. The moon people, as Skai called them, had not attempted subtlety, and Liam understood why. They didn't believe subs were intelligent enough to follow tracks, and they were far from worried about humans following them.

"How do you think they'll react?" Liam said.

"What do you mean?" Zara said.

"Look around." Liam indicated the blood-soaked Suvi. "Look at you. Look at me. We're not exactly the definition of approachable. What if they think we're a bunch of subs and start firing?"

"We don't look that bad," Zara said, though she had to suppress her laughter. "We'll go to them first. We can introduce Skai before we bring the others."

The idea sounded good enough to Liam. At least the crew would recognize him, and meeting one of Earth's long-lost survivors would be far easier to process than meeting a large group of armed men.

Liam gripped Skai's elbow. "Are you okay with that plan?"

"I am not afraid of your people," she said.

"Maybe you should be," Quinn said. "Reagan doesn't have a great track record with women."

A fierce smile parted Skai's lips. "I am no moon woman."

44

IMPOSSIBLE, BEAUTIFUL

Pain ignited in Glo's torso as the barrel of Admiral Reagan's plasma pistol dug into her ribs. With his arm still perched on her shoulder, his right hand wandered along her collarbone, but his gaze never left the barrel of the gun aimed between his eyes. He drew air into his mechanical lung then sighed.

"Not you too, Nikolai."

"Weapons on the ground," Killion said. "Now."

Reagan shook his head, wafting the stench of his sweat toward Glo. "I would not advise you to—"

"Now!"

Killion's head stayed still, but his eyes darted back and forth, surveying Reagan and his men.

"Do you really want to risk me pulling the trigger after I'm shot?" A puff of air escaped Reagan's nostrils. "I would hate to burn a hole in her pretty little chest."

Squeezed by panic, Glo felt herself shrinking.

"What do you want?" Killion spoke between clenched teeth. "It doesn't have to be like this."

"You do realize that you're outnumbered? Look around you, Nikolai. What's your next move here?"

"You're not fit to lead these people," Killion said. "Did you hit your head when we landed, or have you always been this mad?"

Reagan smiled and twisted the barrel against Glo's torso. "No great mind has ever existed without a touch of madness. Aristotle."

Sweat glistened on Killion's bruises. "I think you got thawed out a few too many times."

Reagan yawned. "Shoot me if you're going to. We have places to be."

"I don't want to do this," Killion said, "but I don't see another way."

Glo's eyelids fell shut. Would Killion really shoot Reagan and risk getting her killed? They needed to get the upper hand. They needed more people. Where was Axel? Fear buzzed around her, a scattered swarm of worrying thoughts.

"She is pretty," Reagan said, his right hand groping downward while his left threatened. "Perhaps the prettiest girl left on Earth. But if you don't lower your weapon in the next ten seconds, Nikolai, her beauty will be wasted. I don't think anyone wants that tragedy."

"Tell me," Killion said. "How does this behavior serve your cause?"

"Every king needs a queen." Reagan kissed the side of Glo's head. "I suppose I can find another one if you don't put that gun down in ten…"

Suddenly, Glo remembered the stun gun in her front pocket—and the plasma pistol tucked in the back of her waistband. She doubted she could get the gun out without Reagan's men noticing, but maybe she didn't need it. She slid her hand toward her front pocket.

"Nine," Reagan said.

"Stop," Killion said, sweat barreling down his temples.

"Eight. Seven. Six."

Glo's hand entered her pocket. She left it there because she felt Reagan's head leaning against hers and worried that he would see. He stopped counting and inhaled the scent of her hair. The touch of his mechanical lung vent was ice against her ear.

"Such a shame," Reagan said then laughed. "All right, shall we continue? Five. Four."

Glo pulled the stun gun out of her pocket, far too quickly, and almost dropped it. Her clammy fingers fumbled, scrambling to find the trigger.

"Three. Two—"

"Reagan!"

Glo recognized the voice. It didn't belong to Killion or Tristan. It didn't belong to anyone. She had only heard this voice in dreams since arriving on Earth. Like her mother's, it was a voice she had nearly forgotten. Yet, at the same time, it sounded foreign. Altered.

For a moment, she thought that Reagan had already pulled the trigger. Because the voice belonged to someone dead. She opened her eyes to check if she was still alive and saw the world filtered by tears. The details of everything blurred together, but she could make out the shapes of several people standing in front of her—people who weren't there moments before.

"Get your hands off her," the impossible, beautiful voice said.

As the world came into focus, Glo looked up at a bruised and battered young man wearing animal furs. His face looked vaguely like her brother's, but it couldn't be. With a plasma rifle aimed at Reagan, he stood with others like him, some holding long knives and others aiming spears at Reagan's men.

Glo pocketed the stun gun and wiped the tears from her eyes. Finally, clearly, she could see the truth that had been hidden from her. When she spoke, her voice came out as a whisper.

"Liam?" She swallowed tears. "Oh, Liam."

45

NOT ALL MONSTERS

From what Liam could see, the weeks had not been kind to his sister. Glo's skin shone as pale as her platinum hair, which hung in ragged curls beneath overgrown roots. The skin beneath her eyes looked like eclipses. He didn't understand how such a thin neck could support her head. Had she been eating at all? Ignited by rage, he turned his attention to the man with his hands on his sister.

"Wow," Reagan said, beating Liam to the first word. "Look at you."

"Let her go," Liam said, surprised by the fire in his own voice. "We need to talk."

Killion aimed his rifle at one of Reagan's men while Zara shifted her focus to the other, an arrow nocked on her bowstring.

"Let's put the weapons down," Killion said. "And untie Tristan. Be civilized, will you?"

Liam glanced over at the man bound to the tree. Zara's bowstring thrummed, and an arrow pierced a tree trunk right above her target's head. She nocked another before the redheaded man could react.

"Oops," Zara said. "My finger slipped. I don't usually miss."

The redhead placed his weapon on the dirt and started untying Tristan, but the other man kept his rifle aimed at Killion.

"You idiots!" Reagan shouted.

He moved Glo in front of him, wrapped his arm around her

neck, and positioned his pistol beneath her chin. A human shield, Glo stared at Liam but didn't speak. It was like some twisted rendition of the staring game they played as children. She must be in shock, Liam thought.

"Okay, okay," Reagan said, "no need to be so tense. We can talk."

"Let her go," Liam said.

"Do you think I'm stupid, son? If I let her go, you'll shoot me."

"We won't," Killion said.

I'll do worse, Liam thought.

"How can I be sure?"

Reagan coughed violently, but his weapon never left Glo's chin. Liam watched his trigger finger, unsure of what his next move should be. The plasma rifle in Liam's hands held no charge—Skai had depleted it during the crossing—but Reagan didn't know that.

"We should kill you, but we won't," Liam said, though the adrenaline in his veins said something different. He wanted to pounce, to attack, to end it. "There's someone you need to meet."

Reagan's eyebrows tilted downward as Skai came forward from the back of the group. Her furs brushed against Liam's elbow as she passed, and Liam glanced down at her hands. She held neither blade nor spear.

"It would not be wise to hurt Lion Slayer's sister—more than you already have."

Glo's eyes widened when Skai spoke, but Reagan didn't respond the way Liam expected. He didn't seem surprised at all. Instead, he laughed, the sound oozing condescension.

"Lion Slayer, eh?"

"Liam Stone's sister," Skai said, her voice tight and severe.

"I know who *she* is." Reagan glowered. "Who the hell are *you*?"

"If you don't hurt her, you will live," Skai said. "If you hurt her, I will feed you to the ghouls myself."

"The ghouls," Reagan repeated, as if the term amused him.

"The right choice is simple." Skai stepped forward. "Well?"

Reagan spat into the foliage. "How is it that your kind inherited the Earth?"

"In this valley," Skai said, "there is no mercy for men who hurt women."

Liam noticed that Reagan's other guard had lowered his weapon. He stared at Skai, his chin sinking into the flab of his neck.

"There are more like her," Liam said. "More survivors. More human beings. And they need our help."

"Well," Reagan said, "that's unfortunate."

"What?" Liam said. "How can you—"

"He already knew." Killion stormed forward. "Didn't you? You son of a—"

"Stop right there." Reagan dug the barrel of his pistol into Glo's chin until she winced. "The only way she's walking out of here alive is if you let me leave. If any of you move, if any of you speak, I'm pulling the trigger. I don't care if I die with her."

Blood trailed down Glo's neck as Reagan broke her skin with his pistol. Everyone lowered their weapons and took a step back.

"That's better." Reagan loosened his grip around Glo's neck.

"You knew?" Glo choked. "Did you know?"

Reagan took two careful steps backward. "We started picking up radio signals, oh, I don't know, a couple hundred years ago. The centuries blur in cold sleep."

The revelation was like a hammer to Liam's gut. Who else knew that Earth had been habitable since long before the Resurgence Mission?

"No," Glo said. "Did you know my brother was— Did you know Liam was alive?"

Reagan sighed. "Oh, Gloria. I can—"

In one swift motion, Glo pulled something out of her front pocket and shoved it against Reagan's leg. His mouth spewed profanities, and his body convulsed. He dropped his pistol, which danced across the ground, and he fell to his knees. Glo turned and stood above him, electricity crackling in one hand. She reached behind her, drew a pistol from her waistband, and trained it on Reagan's forehead.

"I told you that would come in handy," Killion said. "Tie him up, Tai."

"My pleasure." Tai walked forward, cracked his knuckles. "Do you want me to rough him up first?"

"No." Glo circled Reagan like a predator. "Nobody touch him."

Liam stepped forward and gripped his sister's shoulder. "It's over, Glo. We'll take it from here."

"It's not over," Glo said, both of her weapons held at the end of shaking arms. "He lied to me. He lied to all of us. He"—Glo choked back tears—"He hurt me, Liam. Don't you understand?"

Liam remembered the pain on her face as she left Deck Eight with Reagan, the sacrifice she made to keep him alive.

"It's my fault that happened, Glo. If I never—"

"No," Glo said. "He used you as leverage, but he would have taken what he wanted eventually. It's why I was chosen for the mission, wasn't it?"

Reagan put his hands behind his head and sank toward the ground. "Gloria, I—"

The handle of Glo's pistol cracked against Reagan's skull.

"He'll be punished," Liam said. "I promise."

"First I want answers," Glo said.

"Of course." Reagan wiped the blood from his cheek. "Anything. I'll tell you anything."

"Did you know my brother was alive?"

"No," Reagan said, his tone vacant of its usual condescension. "Not really."

"You said his ejector pod burned up."

"Yes, but I—"

Another blast from the stun gun sent Reagan rolling onto his back. Limbs shaking, he whimpered like a wounded animal.

"Please," he said. "Please stop. I'm sorry, I'm—"

Glo kicked him in the ribs. "And Quinn? You left her out there to die."

"I'm sorry. I didn't mean to." Reagan trembled beneath Glo's wrath. "What are you—"

"Quinn's fine," Liam said. "She's with us. We need to get out of the woods."

Liam reached out to pull Glo toward safety, but she evaded him. He thought the news about Quinn's survival might calm her, but it only angered her more.

"Please," Reagan said. "Just take me with you to the Life Vault. I'll do anything. I won't—"

Foamy spit flew from Reagan's mouth as another charge from the stun gun shook him.

"Liar," Glo said.

Liam said, "You're going to kill him, Glo."

"Good!"

"Doesn't he deserve worse than death?"

"If I let him live," Glo said, "he might hurt someone else."

Reagan mumbled something that Liam couldn't make out.

"What was that?" Glo squatted and pushed the plasma pistol against Reagan's ribs. "More lies?"

Liam leaned forward to listen.

"I. I. I'm." Reagan spoke in whispers, his face showing its true age. "I'm already dying. The Life"—he coughed up blood—"The Life Vault. I need to go there. It's the cryo— The cryo-cough. It's killing me. Have mercy, please."

Glo stood. For a moment, Liam thought she might spare the Admiral's life, that she would turn and walk away.

"This." She glanced down at her weapons. "This is mercy."

Glo threw her stun gun aside, gripped her pistol in both hands, and aimed it at Reagan's heart.

"Glo," Liam said. "Just think about what you're doing. His men could retaliate. We can't fight each other. We need to—"

"He's not a good person, Liam. Can't you see? He's a monster. What happened on the shuttle was just the beginning. I mourned your death because of him. And Wiki— Oh, is he all right?"

"He's sick," Liam said. "He needs you."

"I'll help him," Glo said. "I will. As soon as this is over."

Reagan squirmed on the ground, terror etched into his face. He tried to prop himself up on his elbows, to scoot away, but each attempt left him breathless. Glo stared him down, unwavering, while Reagan's men stood silently, their eyes averted.

"It's okay," Killion said after a few tense moments. "After what he did to you, I wouldn't blame you."

Tristan stepped forward. "But you said—"

"I know what I said." Killion frowned. "But things have changed."

"I think he deserves it," Raelyn said, her hands balled into fists.

Liam glanced back at his friends. Tai was nodding along to Raelyn's words, his arms crossed in front of his chest. Skai's blade twirled in her hand, tasting the air like a snake's tongue. With an arrow nocked, Zara also looked ready for revenge.

Glo circled Reagan again, walking on her toes. She seemed energized by the others.

"Is there anything you want to say, Arthur?" Glo switched to a one-handed grip. "Anything true?"

"Please." Reagan's voice came out as a hoarse whisper. "Please."

"Please, what?"

Hand shaking, Reagan reached for his front right pocket. Glo watched him carefully. He turned his pocket inside out, and a few small items fell to the dirt: an empty nutrient pouch, a pill bottle, and something green and made of stone. An elephant toy? Reagan ignored the other items and squeezed the elephant in his fist.

"Bury her with me," he whispered. "Please."

Glo scoffed. "So not everything you said was bullshit?"

"I'm sorry, I—"

"Stop," Glo said, and Reagan had no choice but to obey. Her aim wavered between his head and his heart. "This world will be better without monsters like you."

"Wait," Liam said, though he didn't know why.

Reagan didn't deserve to live. The man had been dishonest and lecherous, egotistical and cruel. Liam wanted him to die, but there was a problem: He didn't want to want it.

"If this is what everyone wants to do," Liam said. "If this is what's best for the group, then pull the trigger."

"I have to, Liam."

"I get it," Liam said. "Not all monsters can be tamed. I just can't watch you put this one down."

Glo nodded. "Then go."

Liam walked past his friends into the clearing, utterly exhausted and sickened by the day's violence. Beams of sunlight pierced the clouds above, illuminating the remaining survivors in a somber light. There were far too few of them, but all of them were working hard, oblivious to the revenge unfolding beyond the tree line.

With the wind rustling the leaves, Liam could barely hear the plasma as it singed the air behind him.

46

SIX WEEKS LATER

Liam woke up gently, the sunlight coming through the window warm on his face. With his eyes closed, he clung to the freshness of his dreams—visions of the future and what it might bring. He dreamed in two languages now, a good sign of his learning according to those who knew better. Understanding the words of the Suvi, he now saw everything through a new lens.

Fighting the urge to get up and do something, Liam rolled over and put his arm around Skai. He pulled the bed furs higher to cover his shoulders and soaked in her heat, the scent of her hair, clean and curled from last night's dip beneath the moonlight and the waterfall.

Sounds of the village came from outside, sounds made sweeter by their implications. Liam heard the clank of metal on metal, the thud of wood thrown into a firepit, the conversations of people and birds alike—conversations he now understood better than ever.

It all meant one thing: Humankind was alive and well.

As this thought began to coax Liam back to sleep, Skai stirred and stretched.

"The day has come," she said.

"Yes," he said in Suvi. "I'm going to miss this bed."

Skai faced him and smiled. "Isn't the bed partner more important than the bed itself?"

Liam pressed his forehead against hers, kissed both corners of her mouth, her cheek, her neck. He took his time, savoring these carefree moments while he could.

"I'm glad you're coming with us," he said.

Skai propped her head up in her hand, leaning on one elbow. Beneath the covers, she traced Liam's scars.

"I will go with you always," she said.

"And I with you," he said.

"Just promise me one thing," she said.

"Anything."

"Will we come back here someday?"

"I hope so," Liam said. "I want to."

Skai's lower lip trembled, ever so slightly. "I know we might die."

Liam nodded. "We might."

Skai said something in Suvi that Liam didn't fully understand.

"What does that mean?"

"It is better to die for something honorable than to live with regrets."

Liam let her words sink in until he fully understood them. He watched her expression, looking for doubt, for fear, but he saw only the same strength and courage he had always seen.

"But I wonder," Skai said after a silent moment passed. "Would it not also be honorable to stay?"

•|•

Unsure of what to take and what to leave behind, Glo stood in her hut, surveying a collection of personal objects. Some had come with her from Omega, others the Suvi had gifted her. The journey ahead would be arduous, so she wanted to pack as lightly as possible.

First, Glo picked up her knife and removed it from its sheath. She scratched the edge of the blade against her fingertip. It was stained but almost as sharp as it had been the day she used it to create a makeshift rope. She still recalled her first steps on solid earth after climbing down from the ejector pod, how heavy she felt—and how terrified. She sheathed the knife and placed it in her pack's side pocket.

Next, Glo grabbed her earrings from the stump beside her bed.

Afraid to lose them, she left them there every time she bathed in the river. She put them on instead of packing them. These small pieces of her home felt like a part of her body now. Without them, she felt incomplete.

Slowly, methodically, Glo rolled and packed a few articles of clothing, including a vacuum-sealed pair of leggings, a few shirts, and a fur poncho Skai had made for her. Glo smiled as she packed the poncho, remembering the day Skai started calling her "sister."

One of the last items was her plasma pistol, which still held a nearly full charge. She had only used it once, and she hoped she would never have to again. Still, she knew she might not have a choice. Who knew what dangers she would encounter throughout the journey to come? After checking the safety, she tucked the gun into a leather holster fashioned by one of the Suvi craftsmen.

Finally, she picked up her homemade makeup kit, which held nothing but the basics—foundation, mascara, and blush. What a stupid thing to bring to Earth, she thought. She hadn't used a single cosmetic product since leaving Omega, and she didn't intend to. She set the bag aside, making a mental note to give it to Quinn, but then picked it back up. One zip later, she held her compact in her hand. She cracked it open and looked at herself in the circular mirror.

What she saw surprised her. Even in the dim light, the color of her suntanned skin glowed brighter than any foundation she had ever worn. Her eyes still sparkled without the contrast she had grown accustomed to, and her cheeks no longer appeared so hollow, so hungry.

Glo turned the mirror until she could see her hair. It looked faded and tired. In contrast to her brown roots, the platinum seemed too artificial, an irrelevant remnant of the past. Like Glo herself, her hair had been through so much, but unlike Glo, it hadn't changed. Feeling from the roots to the split ends, she traced the timeline, remembering each painful moment.

"Forget this," she whispered.

Before she could change her mind, she set the mirror down and unsheathed her knife. Then she grabbed a fistful of her hair, took a deep breath, and began cutting.

•|•

Liam accompanied Skai as she walked through the village to say her goodbyes. They stopped at almost all of the inhabited dwellings and communal areas to see who they could see. With every farewell, the guilt in Liam's chest grew. How could he ask Skai to leave her home behind, to embark on such a long and treacherous trip?

"Are you sure about this?" he asked her, and not for the first time.

"Yes," she said again. "If I did not want to go, I would not go."

Eventually, the scent of cooking vegetables drew them into the village center, where they sat down to enjoy breakfast. As Liam was about to dig into a helping of deer jerky, he noticed Quinn in the distance, watching a group of children playing with King. Blonde hair aside, she looked like she belonged there.

"I'll be right back," Liam said and handed the jerky to Skai.

He stood and walked over to Quinn. The children were taking turns dragging a stuffed rabbit through the dirt. They laughed every time King pounced on it.

"Having fun?" he asked them in Suvi.

Too busy playing, the children ignored his question.

"Today's the big day, huh?" Quinn said.

"It's time." Liam moved some gravel around with his feet. "You know, I'm sorry about—"

"It's fine," she said. "I get it."

"If it was safe to take you, we would."

"It's not so bad here," she said. "It's kind of growing on me, actually."

"We'll be back," Liam said.

"Not the tail," Quinn said sternly to one of the kids. She had picked up the Suvi language faster than anyone. "Sorry. It's like they want to get bitten."

Liam laughed. "You're good with them."

"Someone has to watch them while their parents are out hunting. Before I got here, they just let them run around like animals. It wasn't safe."

"I know," Liam said, remembering the Suvi girl who never came home after going out to get water.

"So." Quinn let her gaze wander from the children to Liam. "I'm guessing you're here to get King."

"Actually," Liam said, "I was wondering if you could take care of him while I'm gone. Until I come back."

"He'll be fully grown before that happens."

Liam squatted and scratched King's head. The cub had nearly doubled in size since the day he wandered into Liam's campsite.

"I can't think of a better person to raise him."

Quinn sighed. "That's a lot of responsibility."

"I know," Liam said. "That's why I'm asking you to do it."

"Okay," she said. "But you have to promise me something."

"What's that?"

Quinn turned and faced him head-on. "Don't let anything happen to Glo out there. She's been through enough."

"I promise," Liam said.

"Good."

When Liam went back to Skai, Fang was sitting beside her, a platter of fire-roasted vegetables in his lap. He no longer wore his hood of antlers.

"How's retirement, old man?" Liam asked.

Fang swallowed a mouthful of sweet potato. "The work never ends. It only changes."

"I guess so," Liam said.

"You have chosen a difficult path, not just for yourself, but for Skai as well." Fang put his arm around Skai. "Do you believe it is the correct path?"

Liam paused before speaking, a habit recently instilled by his interactions with the Suvi. He thought about the path ahead and the various ways it might fork. There was no guarantee of success, no promise of survival. So much could go wrong, but if everything went right, the course of human history would change entirely.

"Yes," Liam said. "I do."

"Then I believe it as well." Fang clapped a hand against Liam's back. "And you will protect her?"

Liam laughed, glanced at Skai. "I think she'll be the one protecting me."

"You will protect each other." Fang used his walking stick to help himself stand. "Now, I must go and feed our guest."

"Wait," Liam said. "I'll do it."

The old man smiled and handed him a smoked fish.

"There is something else, young man. Good news."

"What is it?"

"The Watchers found fresh footprints in the forest below." Fang offered Liam a gap-toothed grin. "Jarok-sized footprints."

•|•

Even with Glo's pack bursting at the zippers, Earth's gravity felt softer as she left her hut and meandered through the village. She rubbed her short hair for the tenth time, feeling for uneven spots. It would take some getting used to, but she already loved how light she felt—how free.

"Nice haircut." Wiki jogged up and started walking beside her. "You look tough."

Glo couldn't help but smile. "That's what I was going for. Thanks."

"I almost forgot your natural color," he said. "You haven't had brown hair since when? Your fourteenth birthday?"

"How do you even remember that?"

Wiki looked at his feet. "I'm chronically observant."

"That's not a bad thing," Glo said.

They passed some Suvi children drawing pictures in the dirt with sticks. The kids ignored them. It had been weeks since anyone in the village gawked at their new neighbors.

"Anyway," Wiki said, "Killion has a surprise for you at the tower. He sent me to get you."

"What is it?" Glo said.

"Not sure," Wiki said, and Glo knew he was telling the truth. He never lied to her, not even to stop himself from spoiling a surprise. "But we have time for a detour. Walk with me for a minute?"

"Sure," Glo said. "Where do you want to go?"

"It doesn't matter," Wiki said. "I just want to talk."

"You know we're going to be walking together for a long time, right?"

"Yeah," Wiki said, "but that's different. Come on."

He led her toward the outskirts of the village until they reached the community garden. Here, a grid of newly erected planters formed paths between lush plants. Though they were still young, the genetically modified seeds salvaged from the crash site were thriving.

"Amazing," Glo said. "I haven't been here since the planting."

"A little collaboration can go a long way. After the harvest, we should never go hungry again."

At first, Glo and the other survivors had thought of the population as two groups, but now there was no distinction between "us" and "them." Everyone ate from the same garden.

Glo sat down on the edge of a planter. "So, what did you want to talk about?"

Wiki sat across from her, his face turning pink.

"What is it?" Glo leaned forward. "You can trust me with anything, you know?"

"I know," he said. "It's just— Well, I don't know how to word it."

"Just try," Glo said.

"Okay." Wiki took a long, slow breath, then moved his gaze from the dirt path to Glo's face. "There's something I've wanted to tell you for a while now. I should have said this six weeks ago, but we've been so busy with everything, and it never felt like the right time, but now we're leaving and—"

"Spit it out, Richard."

"I love you, Glo." Wiki nodded, his eyes on her and only her. "I always have. You're the most incredible person I've ever met."

Glo nodded softly. She always knew that Wiki had a crush on her—these things were obvious—but she never suspected he loved her. Besides the fact that his words made her feel special, she didn't know how she felt.

"Wiki, I—"

"You don't have to say it back. I just needed you to know."

The lack of pressure was refreshing. "I care about you, too. But what do you want? What do you expect?"

"Nothing." Wiki's smile washed over her like a calming breeze. "Seeing you alive and happy is all I need."

Glo still felt the splinters of her trauma, duller now but still there. "I don't know if I'm happy."

"Then I'll do my best to fix that."

Glo stared into his eyes, searching for a reason to doubt him. She found none.

"Can we take it slow?" she said.

"We don't need to take it anywhere, Glo."

A silent moment passed. Then she reached out, laced her fingers through his. "How about we start here?"

It was strange to Liam how much smaller the Suvi jailhouse looked from the outside. He approached the back wall of the one-room building slowly, then stopped ten meters away. Did he really want to do this? It took him a few minutes, but eventually, he swallowed his hesitation and advanced to the front of the building.

Judging by the thickness of the new logs, the Suvi had done a good job of giant-proofing the cell. Liam walked along and peered through the cracks. It took a minute for his eyes to adjust to the shadows inside the cell.

Lying there on his back in the dim light, Admiral Reagan looked like a dead man. But his chest still rose and fell, his breath still came in artificial rhythms. Barefoot and shirtless, he stared at the ceiling from his cot, his hands resting on a bandage covering his crotch. To Liam, he looked like a giant baby wearing a diaper. His bare skin shone pale and clean. Clearly, the Suvi had taken to heart the Omegans' advice about sanitation.

Liam cleared his throat to make his presence known. Reagan flinched, but his gaze never left the ceiling.

"What now?" he said, his voice quiet yet harsh. "What is it?"

"I brought your breakfast," Liam said.

Reagan rolled onto his side and sat up.

"Oh," he said. "It's you."

"You mean the guy who saved your life?" Liam pinched the fish between two fingers and dangled it between the bars.

Reagan sighed like a child getting his toy taken away. "Fish? Again?"

"You shouldn't complain," Liam said. "I never got three meals a day when I was locked up. I didn't even have a bed."

"Is that supposed to make me feel better?"

"Does it hurt?" Liam inclined his head. "Down there?"

Reagan didn't answer the question verbally, but his jaw clenched.

"If she aimed a little higher"—Liam winced and breathed through his teeth—"Consider yourself lucky."

Reagan glowered. "Because getting mutilated is lucky. Why don't you just go away?"

"I'll be leaving soon enough."

"Good riddance."

Liam squatted to get on Reagan's level. "So, you're finally done begging to come with us?"

"Did you come here to torture me, son? Because I've already had the worst of it."

"That's not why I'm here." Liam leaned in closer. "Do you remember our first conversation?"

"Not really," Reagan said.

"Well, I remember it vividly. You told me you don't make mistakes. Do you still believe that?"

"I believe you're a pain in my ass."

"So, you wouldn't have done anything differently?"

Avoiding eye contact, Reagan fiddled with his elephant statuette. "I would have airlocked you."

"You're showing a lot of *testicular fortitude* for someone with no balls." Liam glanced at Reagan's bandage. "Hurting Glo was your biggest mistake of all. Your wife would be ashamed."

Reagan stared at the statuette in his hands, and his face seemed to age another ten years. "Do you think she'll ever forgive me?"

Liam didn't know if Reagan meant Glo or his wife, but the answer was the same either way. "No," he said, "I don't."

Reagan's sigh sounded like it physically hurt him. "She should have killed me."

Liam shook his head. "You got what you deserved."

Mutilation, imprisonment, and the knowledge that he

dishonored his long-dead wife—Reagan's punishment was worse than death, but was it worse than the crime he committed? Liam didn't know, but he also wasn't the victim. Glo decided Reagan's fate.

"I have another question," Liam said. "Why didn't you tell everyone there were still people living on Earth?"

"If everyone knew, no one would have made it here. Imagine three thousand people all wanting out at the same time. It would have been chaos."

Liam considered Reagan's words. "So, you do care about humankind?"

"We made it, didn't we?"

"And some of us still have our humanity intact." Liam tossed the fish onto Reagan's cot. Then he unzipped his pack, pulled out a tablet, and held it between the cell bars. "Take this."

Despite his earlier complaints, Reagan immediately began eating.

"I have my own," he said through a mouthful of fish.

"It's not to keep," Liam said. "I want you to write something down for me. Take it."

Reagan set his food down on the cot and crept forward like prey from a burrow. He grabbed the tablet with greasy fingers, the ends of his fingernails crescent moons of filth.

"Write down what you need," Liam said. "From the Life Vault."

"So you can destroy it? Come back and taunt me with it?"

"Tempting, but no. If you're still alive when I get back—and if you happen to rediscover your humanity—you can have your cure."

"*If* you get back," Reagan said. "I highly doubt you, or anyone else for that matter, will make it there. Not without me."

"You better hope you're wrong. Because no one else is going to help you."

"It's over two hundred kilometers away."

"I logged over six hundred in the Earth Sim—without dying once."

"That's a game."

Liam smirked. "Isn't everything? But that's beside the point. It doesn't matter how hard I trained."

"And why's that?"

"Because of the people coming with me. They're the best of the best." Liam stood. "I'm leaving in five minutes. With or without that tablet."

"Why are you helping me?"

Liam shrugged. "You can't serve your life sentence if you're dead."

Reagan shook his head and backed up slowly, his face darkening as he retreated from the light. With the permanent scowl and pallid skin, the hunched back and bloodshot eyes, he looked like a monster returning to its cave. Still, even if it took a lifetime, Liam believed this monster could be tamed.

Reagan sat and started typing.

The control tower didn't look like much from afar, just a glistening shaft of metal reaching for a sky it could never touch—at least not physically. It stood on the roof of a Suvi dwelling, the same one, Glo had been told, that Liam delivered a speech from six weeks earlier.

The closer she got, the more ramshackle the tower appeared. It was built of scraps gathered from the crash site—sheets of aluminum cut and formed into beams, wires harvested from life support systems, and various instruments engineered by Tristan, Wiki, and others with brains that worked differently from Glo's. On top of the tower, a small satellite dish was attached to the end of a robotic arm, which tracked the moon's movement. Below this sat a swirling anemometer measuring wind speed and direction. The wooden cups of the anemometer had been carved by a Suvi craftsman. Glo approached the building, hand in hand with Wiki.

Inside, she discovered a flurry of activity. Electric lights hung from the ceiling, illuminating a series of workspaces: a table with a half-constructed android on top, a pair of monitors mounted to the wall, and other machinery that Glo didn't understand. Killion stood in front of the monitors, the first of which displayed a stream of code beside a live video of his face. The other monitor showed nothing. Before Glo could greet him, Tristan walked over from one of the machines and spoke to Killion.

"The second printer is now operational, Admiral. Bioplastic substrate is in production."

"Great," Killion said. "How long until we can start producing solar tiles?"

"Soon," Tristan said. "Engineering says we should have enough before we run out of fuel. Today's gas run should do it."

"Thank you, Commander."

Looking at the video feed like a mirror, both men noticed Glo at the same time.

Killion turned and smiled. "Just in time," he said. "Moonrise is in a couple of minutes."

"How are you?" Tristan said. He glanced at Glo and Wiki's clasped hands and smirked.

Glo felt hot, but she didn't let go of Wiki's hand. "I've been meaning to ask you the same."

Tristan grinned. "Let's just say the Suvi are very…open."

"It's time," Killion said, all business.

Everyone in the room gathered in a semi-circle around the monitors. Killion cleared his throat and tapped an icon to begin transmitting.

"This is Colony One to Omega," he said, his voice clear and loud. "Requesting a video uplink."

Several seconds passed with no response. Then Smythii's voice came through speakers mounted below the screens.

"Let's try this again," Smythii said. *"I'm sending you the codes now."*

A moment later, the text displayed on the screen changed. Tristan swiped up from the lower region of the monitor to summon a keyboard, and began tapping away. Wiki woke his peripherals and started typing out his own notes for the history books.

"I can see you on my end," Smythii said. *"Let me just— There we go."*

The second monitor lit up. A grainy image of Smythii's broad shoulders and balding head appeared. Everyone in the room cheered. The picture changed every half second or so as Smythii moved around.

"It's buffering," Tristan said.

Smythii's delayed response came through. *"It must have worked."*

All at once, the video became crisp and clear.

"Is she ready?" Killion said.

"She is," Smythii said.

Killion turned and faced the group. "Clear the room, please."

Everyone began filing out. Confused, Glo followed.

"Not you, Glo." Killion walked past her and paused in the threshold. "There's someone who wants to see you."

"Who?" Glo said.

Killion indicated the monitor behind her with a quick nod. She turned around, saw Smythii leaving the frame. He came back a moment later, pushing a woman in a wheelchair. Glo took a step toward the monitor. Transmitted from hundreds of thousands of kilometers away, her mother's smile still filled her with peace.

"Hey there, starshine."

•|•

"Sorry, I'm late," Liam said, rushing through the door into the control tower. "Reagan types like you blasted his thumbs off instead of his you-know-what."

Glo turned and faced him, her head framed by a glowing monitor behind her.

"What happened to your hair?" Liam asked. "Did someone prank you?"

"I cut it myself, you ass."

"It looks…interesting."

"You're a jerk, you know that?"

"Language, young lady." The voice came from speakers on the wall. *"Just because you're an Earthling now doesn't mean you have to curse."*

"Sorry, Mom," Glo said.

"Come closer, Liam. I can hardly see you."

Liam froze. This was not what he had in mind when Killion mentioned a surprise. Though he had rehearsed his apology over and over in his head, shame held him in place. He lingered in the shadows, hesitating.

"It's okay," Glo whispered. "Come on."

She grabbed Liam's hand, pulled him toward the monitor until its glow illuminated his face. For ten seconds, he looked at his mother's smile until the delay passed, and she saw him.

"Hello, my son."

Liam knew what he had to say, the words that would earn him forgiveness, and now he had a chance to speak them. He disappeared from his mom's life with no explanation, and that was his fault. Someday soon, she would die alone, a fact that weighed heavily on Liam. Though he would never forgive himself for being so selfish, he hoped she would. The time had come to apologize, and the time would come to offer a final farewell, but first, he wanted to say something better than goodbye. Liam squeezed his sister's hand and smiled, sending his love through the airwaves.

"Hello, Mom."

47

TOGETHER

By the time Liam and his traveling companions reached the valley floor, the sun burned in the middle of the sky. It had been over a month since he had made a trip down. That was when he and the others finished clearing the valley, grueling work that took weeks. The sight of pits filled with bodies, the stench of burning corpses—these things would never leave his mind.

At the bottom of the switchbacks, the tree line was a welcome relief. Beneath the shade, with the breeze brushing his skin, Liam could almost forget that summer still had a month left. What wonders would he witness before the season changed? What dangers would he face? How many more bodies would he have to burn?

Unwilling to let the future bother him, Liam focused on the present moment. Nature's music soothed his mind, a symphony composed of birdsong, leaves rustling in the wind, the distant roar of waterfalls ripe with snowmelt. His gaze never left the forest, but not because he was looking for danger. Rotting wood, moving water, blooming flowers—even after two months on Earth, none of these things had ceased to fascinate him. He hoped that would never change.

Liam hiked with new friends and old, some who would join him on his journey and others who would return to the village that night toting fuel from the crash site. By late afternoon they reached the burned-out clearing, where they stopped to rest, to say goodbye.

Nothing remained in the clearing but the fuel tank, the same one Liam camped beside the night the Suvi kidnapped him, Wiki, and Zara. He and the others gathered near it.

"Start filling the gas cans," Killion said to some of his men. "We'll have to head out soon if we want to get back before dark."

As the cans filled, everyone sat down to have one last meal together. Liam would have sat with Skai, but he wanted to give her some space to enjoy what time she had left with Fang. Instead, he joined Raelyn and Tai.

"Hey." Liam sat down in front of them. "I guess this is it."

"It is," Raelyn said.

"You know," Liam said, "if you changed your mind, I'm sure we have enough supplies."

Tai swallowed a mouthful of meat. "What? Are you going to miss us or something?"

Liam punched Tai's arm lightly. "I never said that. I'm just surprised you guys want to stay."

"It's not that we want to," Raelyn said. "We have to."

"Come on," Liam said. "Killion has plenty of help here."

"It's not that," Raelyn said.

"Then what?"

Raelyn and Tai looked at each other.

"Should we tell him?" Tai said.

"I don't know if he can take it."

"Yeah, probably not," Tai said.

Liam groaned. "I regret asking."

"Okay," Raelyn said. "Liam, I"—she put her mechanical hand on Liam's shoulder and her real hand on her belly—"I'm pregnant."

"What?"

"I've only known for a week. That's why we changed our minds. It's going to be safer for the baby here."

"That"—Liam laughed, overcome with some strange, bubbly emotion—"That's awesome."

Raelyn smiled. "Really?"

"Yeah," Liam said. "Yeah, no, I'm happy for you guys."

He patted Tai on the back and pulled Raelyn into a tight hug. "Does anyone else know?"

"You're the first person we've told," she said.

Liam could hardly believe the news. Unless anyone else was pregnant, Raelyn's child would be the first Earthborn Omegan. The Resurgence had already begun.

"If it's a boy," Liam said, "you guys should name him after me."

Raelyn chuckled. "That's a little weird."

"Yeah," Tai said. "I don't know about that."

"If it wasn't for me, you two wouldn't be together. You kind of owe me."

"We'll think about it," Raelyn said. "Don't get your hopes up, though."

Killion whistled, signaling that it was time to head back to the village.

"Goodbye, then?" Liam said.

"We'll see you when you get back."

Liam nodded, unsure of when, if ever, that day would come. There were too many variables at play, too much that could go wrong. As the two groups separated, Liam witnessed similar farewells: Wiki shaking Admiral Killion's hand, Quinn and Glo crying in each other's arms, and Fang removing his canine necklace to put it around Skai's neck. Liam hugged and said goodbye to everyone he could, whether he knew them well or not. It didn't matter who was staying or going, who was Suvi or Omegan. For a moment, they were all just human.

•|•

That night, Liam, Skai, Glo, Wiki, and Zara camped at the mouth of the valley, along with a dozen other humans who had agreed to accompany them to the Life Vault—and a newly constructed android that had no choice in the matter. In charge of the first watch, Liam stayed up late while the others slept. Warming his hands over the fire, he watched the moon until it started setting behind the Eagle and its sister peaks.

Thousands still lived up there. Old men and women who'd labored to build the ETS Resurgence long before Liam was born. Hundreds of people, like his mother, who were dying of radiation poisoning and cancer. Children peering through silica domes at a planet they might someday get the chance to walk upon. Once everyone up there knew the truth, would Omega dissolve into chaos like Reagan said? The question troubled him deeply.

"Is it my turn yet?"

It took a moment for Liam to recognize Glo in the moonlight. With her short hair, at first glance, she no longer looked like his sister. She stood on the opposite side of the firepit, her shoulders wrapped in furs.

"Can't sleep?" Liam said.

Glo came around the fire and sat on the log beside him. "I tried."

Liam put his arm around her. "What's wrong?"

She exhaled loudly. "I can't turn my brain off. I keep thinking about everything that could happen. We have no idea what the world is like out there."

"I know," Liam said. "You could have stayed."

"I thought about it." Glo rested her head on his shoulder. "I just know I would have worried about you every day."

"Just like Mom." Liam's gaze returned to the sky, where half of the moon now hid behind the mountains. "I'm happy we got to see her."

"Me too," Glo said. "I never wanted to leave her. I was sick about it. But if I stayed, she would have left me alone eventually. At least here, we have each other."

Liam marveled at his sister. Her warmth and compassion seemed to envelop not just the whole camp, but all of humanity. As he looked around at the sleeping group, he saw not only the people but what they held inside them: Wiki's intelligence and loyalty, Skai's love and bravery, Zara's friendship and impeccable aim. Even from afar, he still felt the presence of those who stayed behind in Colony One, brave men and women who would be in touch to help however they could. As the moon—that permanent Watcher in the sky—disappeared behind the horizon, Liam considered himself the luckiest man on Earth for one simple reason: He had people to care for and people to care for him. Whatever dangers he would face beyond the valley, he would not have to face them alone.

THE END

THΛNK YOU!

In an age when attention spans are short and content is consumed in bite-sized pieces, making it to this page is an accomplishment worthy of praise. Thank you for spending a few hours of your life reading *Life on Planet Earth*. I hope you enjoyed it!

Q: Will there be a sequel?
A: Yes, and probably more than one. Be the first to know about my new books by joining my mailing list. You'll also get an exclusive short story for free! Just go to www.AuthorAndyGorman.com/lope to sign up.

Q: Can I tell you how much I liked the book?
A: Of course! I would prefer you did it with Amazon and/or Goodreads reviews. I read every single one of them, I promise. Writers—especially independent authors like myself—rely on readers like you leaving kind reviews. It's the best way to help other people discover our books.

Q: How can I keep up with your writing?
A: I'm glad you asked. Pick your poison...

• **Facebook: @AuthorAndyGorman (my reader community)**
• **Twitter: @_AndyGorman (original jokes and random thoughts)**
• **Instagram: @_AndyGorman (mostly photos of me at the pool or lake)**
• **My Website: www.AuthorAndyGorman.com (blog posts and free stories)**
• **Email: Andy@AuthorAndyGorman.com (if you want to chat)**

ACKNOWLEDGMENTS

The first person I want to thank is my fiancée, Lawren Linehan. I should be calling you my wife right now, but the COVID-19 pandemic ruined our plans (as I'm sure you're aware). That doesn't matter, though, because "wife" is just a title, and who you are is so much more. You're my best friend, my biggest supporter, and my partner in everything. Thank you for encouraging me when I feel talentless, for loving me when I can't seem to love myself, and for keeping the cats off my keyboard when I'm trying to work. My love for you is infinite.

To my friends and family near and far, thank you for inspiring me. There are pieces of you in everything I create—at least the pieces I could get my hands on. Whether we've spoken recently or it's been a while, I want you to know that I love and appreciate you. My writing wouldn't be what it is today without your support (and the DNA samples I've collected).

Let's talk about editing! It takes a team to polish a pig…or is it to put lipstick on a turd? Whatever the saying is, the manuscript in your hands—or perhaps tentacles—would be fundamentally flawed without the help of a few talented individuals:

To Bonnie Kopf, my 9th grade English teacher, thank you for your invaluable feedback on my third draft—and for calling me an "amazing story architect" with "*New York Times* Best Seller potential." Compliments are my life force, so I'm really looking forward to your Amazon review.

To Cade Hagen for trading manuscripts with me over the summer. Having line edits and comments from a talented writer like you was extremely helpful—even if I suffered from creative writing workshop flashbacks. I look forward to sharing your bold and imaginative stories in the future. *www.cadehagen.com*

To my editor, Michael Waitz, the only person on this list who—excuse me—whom I haven't met in person. Thank you for your quick turnaround time, your attention to detail, and most of all your encouragement. If I'm ever in Boone, North Carolina, I'll hit you up (so probably never). *www.sticksandstonesediting.net*

Finally, I'd like to thank my Early Reader Book Club for giving *Life on Planet Earth* one final pass before publication. If no one buys this book that I spent years on, at least I'll know that several people were willing to read it for free.

Andy Gorman
April 2021